PRAISE FOR

"Jackson creates two fascinating worlds that coalesce seamlessly into an un-put-downable fantasy narrative and seem likely to lead to an exciting sequel."
Publishers Weekly, starred review of *Time's Children*

"If you love books that mix tropes of sci-fi and fantasy with abandon, make time for this one."
B&N Sci-Fi & Fantasy Blog

"Intricate plotting, innovative world building, and characters who grab your heart and refuse to let go."
Faith Hunter, New York Times Bestselling author of the Jane Yellowrock and Soulwood series

"Jackson has a deft touch with characterisation. The two young protagonists are very relatable and recognisably young adults. Even their main antagonist, the assassin, feels like a well-rounded professional… Time's Children *is a compelling novel, enjoyable and fun. I'll be looking out for the sequel."*
Locus Magazine

*"*Time's Children *is a tour-de-force, setting a fascinating tale of magic and intrigue amidst aworld filled with dark corners and creatures who are not to be trusted."*
Reviews and Robots

*"*Time's Children *is both an epic and personal fantasy novel that is awonderful series starter and introduction to a very original fantasy milieu. I'm slotting this on mybest of the year list…"*
SFFWorld

D B JACKSON

TIME'S DEMON

BOOK II OF THE ISLEVALE CYCLE

**ANGRY
ROBOT**

ANGRY ROBOT
An imprint of Watkins Media Ltd

Unit 11, Shepperton House
89 Shepperton Road
London N1 3DF
UK

angryrobotbooks.com
twitter.com/angryrobotbooks

An Angry Robot paperback original,
2019

Cover by Jan Weßbecher
Map by Argh! Nottingham
Set in Meridien

This novel is entirely a work of
fiction. Names, characters, places,
and incidents are the products of
the author's imagination or are used
fictitiously. Any resemblance to
actual events, locales, organizations
or persons, living or dead, is entirely
coincidental.

ISBN 978 0 85766 793 9
Ebook ISBN 978 0 85766 794 6

Printed and bound in the United
Kingdom by TJ International.

9 8 7 6 5 4 3 2 1

For Bill and Joan Berner.
This is a story about family.
Thank you for making me part of yours.

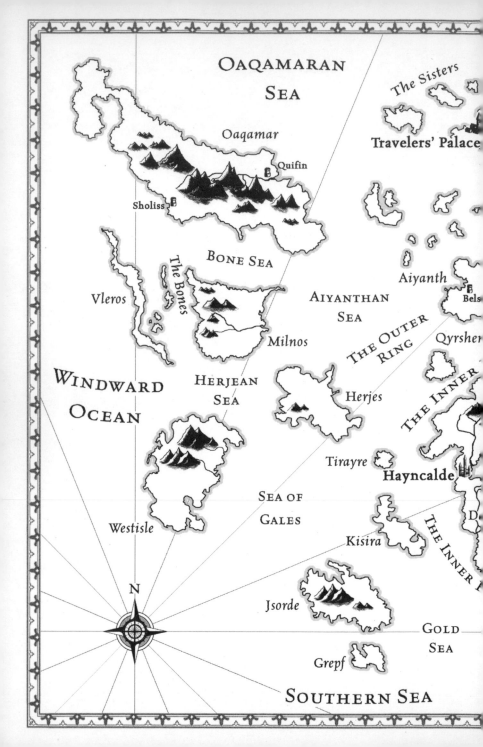

WHAT HAS COME BEFORE:
A SUMMARY OF TIME'S CHILDREN

Tobias Doljan, a Walker, born with the ability to journey
back through time, is summoned from the Travelers' Palace in
Windhome, where he has lived since he was a boy, to the court of
Sovereign Mearlan IV on the island of Daerjen.

The chancellor of the palace arranges passage for him to the
royal city of Hayncalde aboard a merchant ship captained by Seris
Larr. The night before he sails, his friend Mara, who is a Spanner,
capable of crossing great distances in mere moments, speaks of
wanting to follow him to Daerjen and then kisses him passionately
before fleeing to the girls' dormitory.

Droë, a Tirribin, has been watching. She tells Tobias that she
finds the girl distasteful. Tirribin, or time demons, appear as
children, but are lethal predators who feed on human years and
live for centuries. Because Walkers' years are tainted by journeys
through time, time demons do not prey on them. Droë and Tobias
have developed an awkward friendship. But when Droë threatens
to feed on Mara's years, Tobias forbids her to do so, despite being
powerless to stop her. They argue, and part on poor terms.

Tobias's interactions with Mara and Droë are observed by a
Belvora, a winged demon that has been sent to kill Tobias. The
following morning, as a palace master escorts Tobias to the waiting
ship, the Belvora attacks. Another master intervenes and saves
Tobias's life. The master who was to accompany him is killed.

Grieving, fearing for his life, Tobias sails for Daerjen. During
the voyage, Captain Larr offers him employment on her ship. She
has long wanted a Walker in her crew, and she promises to secure

for him a chronofor, the golden, watch-like device Walkers use to facilitate their magick. Tobias politely refuses.

Quinnel Orzili, and his beloved wife, Lenna, are Travelers, he a Spanner, she a Walker. They are also assassins employed by Pemin, the autarch of Oaqamar. Orzili Spans to Pemin's court to inform him that the Belvora has failed to kill the young Walker. Pemin orders Orzili to kill the boy when he reaches Daerjen. Failing that, Lenna is to Walk back through time and kill him in the past. Whatever the cost, he wants the boy dead.

Tobias reaches Daerjen, which is at war with Oaqamar, as well as with Westisle privateers, and is taken to meet the sovereign. During their initial conversation, Tobias confirms for Mearlan the essential truth of Walking: for every day he journeys through time, he ages that amount. The sovereign reveals in turn that Daerjen's wars go poorly.

That night, Tobias is feted at a banquet. He meets Mearlan's beautiful daughter, Sofya, who is about his age. He also meets Mearlan's charming Minister of State, Gillian Ainfor. After the banquet, Tobias retires, only to be awakened by warning bells tolling in the castle courtyard. Assassins have infiltrated the castle and are hunting for Tobias. He Walks back in time to warn others. The assassins are killed, though not before revealing that they are Spanners, once trained in Windhome. Someone doesn't wish for Mearlan to use his new Walker.

The next day, the sovereign admits that he wants Tobias to Walk back fourteen years to warn a younger version of himself against beginning Daerjen's ill-fated wars. This time, Tobias's passage through the between nearly proves fatal. Still, he reaches that distant past, now appearing to be a man of nearly thirty years, and delivers his warning to the younger Mearlan.

Pemin is incensed by the failure of the second attempt on Tobias's life. He orders Orzili to send Lenna back to kill the boy. Orzili is reluctant. When he and Lenna learn how far back she must Walk, that reluctance turns to grief. Having no choice in the matter, she Walks back after the boy. Upon arriving in the past, she finds the younger Orzili and enlists his aid in tracking down Mearlan's Walker.

During Tobias's first evening in the past, he encounters several intruders in a castle courtyard. They carry golden devices that resemble Bound sextants like those used by Spanners. Before Tobias or nearby guards can question them, they vanish.

Tobias sups with the sovereign and his family, including Princess Sofya, who is an infant in this time. During the meal, assassins attack the castle, killing all of Mearlan's family and ministers except Tobias and Sofya. Tobias fights his way free and spirits the princess away from the castle. During the fight, his chronofor is broken. He cannot Walk to another time until he replaces or repairs it. He realizes that the assassins Traveled like Spanners, but did so clothed and bearing weapons, which shouldn't be possible.

He and Sofya are alone in the streets of Hayncalde. The castle has been taken by soldiers of Sheraigh, Hayncalde's bitter rival. And Tobias is helpless to do more than hide himself and the child.

Back at the Travelers' Palace in Windhome, Mara wakes sensing that something with the world is not right. And, indeed, the palace is a bleaker place, patrolled now by dour soldiers of Oaqamar and Belvora demons. A different set of wars rage throughout Islevale. Spanners and Crossers are now the most valued Travelers; using what are called "tri- devices," modified sextants and apertures, Spanners and Crossers can now Travel in groups, clothed and armed.

Mara takes these changes for granted, because for her, in this future, they are the norm. But that night, when confronted by the Tirribin, Droë, she begins to understand that her perception of disruption is rooted in her nascent time sense. She is a Spanner, but she also possesses abilities common to Walkers. Droë confirms that the world has changed, and says these changes are tied to Tobias. Mara, in this new "misfuture," has no memory of Tobias. Droë tells her that she and the boy were friends and more.

Mara shares what she has learned from the Tirribin with Wansi Tovorl, the palace Binder. Wansi gives Mara a chronofor and has her Walk back in time a single bell. Mara is able to do this, despite the harsh effects of the between. She begins to practice Walking, honing her skills as she contemplates going back in time to find Tobias. She is intimidated by the prospect of such a lengthy Walk, but after their Oaqamaran masters viciously punish a friend for a minor offense, she resolves to make the journey.

Droë has feelings for Tobias as well. Romances between Tirribin and humans are rare, but she doesn't care. Though jealous of Mara, she believes the girl can help her find Tobias and correct the misfuture, which is like a poison to her.

The morning after Mearlan's assassination, Tobias and Sofya are nearly discovered by Sheraigh soldiers conducting house-to-house searches. The pair are taken in by an older couple, Jivv and Elinor, who remain loyal to House Hayncalde. They shelter the fugitives and treat Tobias's injuries. The Sheraighs have placed a bounty on them, and that night Tobias is forced to chase and kill a young man who has discovered where they are. After killing the lad, he encounters Teelo and Maeli, brother and sister Tirribin, who sense that he is a Walker and befriend him.

Knowing that they cannot remain hidden for long, Tobias ventures to the city's Temple of Sipar, hoping servants of the God will help him and the princess. Orzili captures him there, takes him to the castle dungeon, and tortures him, in the hopes of learning Sofya's whereabouts.

Elinor goes to the temple, intending to find Tobias or enlist the aid of the God's servants. Using a system of ancient tunnels beneath the city, agents of the sanctuary free Tobias, return him to the temple, and heal his wounds. The high priestess arranges passage for Tobias and Sofya aboard a temple ship, despite a Sheraigh blockade of Hayncalde's wharves. An agent of the temple escorts them to the pier, but assassins murder the woman and attack Tobias and Sofya. With help from Teelo and Maeli, Tobias kills their assailants, though not before the ship sails without them. The Tirribin take Tobias and Sofya to the Notch, a shadow city located along the shoreline. Tobias and Sofya find shelter in a boarding house, under assumed names.

Back in Windhome, Mara prepares to journey back in time and across the sea to Daerjen. Droë helps her, but remains jealous of Mara, and envies her the chance to find Tobias. With Wansi's aid, Mara Walks back in time in increments. The between is brutal, and she barely makes it through. Once in the past, she seeks out Droë, who confirms that she is in the correct time, and that the misfuture has begun, though only barely. Mara then undertakes the long Span to Daerjen.

After speaking with Mara in this past, Droë is intrigued by the idea that she might love this Tobias, whom she has yet to meet. She seeks out Tresz, a Shonla, or mist demon, who carries her away from Windhome toward Daerjen. Droë tells Tresz that she searches for the Walker, but does not reveal that she wishes to change her very nature, to take grown-up form and make herself a rival to Mara for Tobias's affection.

Mara reaches Daerjen and seeks shelter in the same Sanctuary that gave aid to Tobias. The priestess marks her as another Traveler and tells her of Tobias's disappearance and the murder of the temple woman who accompanied him. The priestess does not know Tobias's fate, but she sends Mara to find someone who might.

This turns out to be Gillian Ainfor, who survived the assassination of Mearlan. She takes Mara to a shelter in the Notch, arriving there as the Binder Bexler Filt, her husband in this time, slips a tri-Sextant into hiding. Mara recognizes the device, prompting Gillian to knock her unconscious. When Mara wakes, bound in the back of the shelter, she realizes that Gillian and Filt have betrayed the sovereign and hope to use her as bait to lure Tobias and the princess.

While exploring the Notch, Tobias encounters Seers who warn him of impending danger. Teelo and Maeli do the same. The Tirribin summon an Arrokad demon for him. The Arrokad, Ujie, is distractingly beautiful and dangerous. She agrees to help Tobias in the future, for a price: an undetermined boon.

The next day, Tobias is approached by Gillian. Relieved and delighted to find her alive, he follows her to her shelter, where she and Filt turn weapons on him and demand to be taken to the princess. Tobias refuses. With help from Mara, he overpowers and disarms his would-be captors. Gillian escapes; they tie-up Filt. Tobias and Mara hurry to the boarding house, gather Sofya, and flee. But Gillian has managed to alert Orzili and his Sheraigh allies to Tobias's whereabouts. Soldiers converge on the Notch.

With help from the Seers, Tobias and Mara escape the Notch and hurry to an expanse of shore where they hope to gain passage on a ship leaving Daerjen. As they flee, however, they are found by Orzili and his trained assassins. In the ensuing battle, Mara and Tobias fight off their attackers. Orzili is forced to run, though not before shooting Tobias and nearly killing Sofya.

Tobias survives, and on the strand he finds, to his amazement, a younger Seris Larr, the captain who transported him from Windhome to Daerjen. She agrees to carry Tobias, Mara, and Sofya from Daerjen. As book I ends, they sail from the isle, knowing that Orzili and Sheraigh forces are hunting for them.

CHAPTER 1

12th day of Sipar's Ascent, Year 615

His memories of the first day were blurred by tears, distorted by fatigue, darkened by fear and homesickness and the surety that he would never belong.

He was tall for his age, gangly, awkward, and yet everything he saw – the gates through which he passed, the refectory in which he first encountered others of his kind, the keep in which he would sleep for years to come – made him feel small, insignificant. He was also old, at least for a fingerling, as new novitiates were called. His father, dispassionate to the last, assured him that this would make his transition easier. One final lie.

That first night, after the evening meal, which Cresten barely touched, an older boy confronted him in the middle courtyard. The boy was two hands taller, and broader as well. A dozen other novitiates stood with him, leering, predatory eyes glinting with torchfire.

"New boy. Big baby. You get lost on the way here? You wander in circles for five years?"

Cresten toed the grass. "We didn't know–"

"What's that? I can't hear you."

He looked up. "We didn't know I was a Spanner," he said in a raised voice. "Not until recently."

"You shouting at me? That what you're doing?"

"You said you couldn't hear–"

The boy shoved him with both hands. Cresten stumbled back a step, and fell onto his bottom. The others laughed. The boy stared, daring him to get up. He did.

"You need to learn manners, fingerling."

He knew better than to run or cry for help. Either would only delay the inevitable.

The only way past is through, his father often said. Wisdom he offered in place of affection. Cresten had always hated his aphorisms. But he heard this one in his father's voice, and knew it for truth.

"Maybe. There anyone here smart enough to teach them to me?"

That was all it took. The boy lashed out with a closed fist, his blow catching Cresten square in the face. Cresten staggered, fell again, tasting blood, feeling it flow from his nose. His eyes stung and he willed himself not to cry.

The boy loomed over him, goaded by the cheers of his friends. He kicked Cresten in the side. Cresten gasped, retched. This time he couldn't keep tears from falling.

"What's all this?"

A man strode toward them, bald pate shining in the torchlight, a single, thin plait of dark hair swinging with every step. He shouldered his way through the circle of novitiates, and planted himself in front of Cresten and the older boy.

"I asked a question, Mister Tache," the man said. A burr shaded his words. "What are you up to?" Before the boy could answer, the man – one of the palace masters, no doubt – turned to Cresten. "You're new," he said. "And not having a grand time of it, are you?"

He extended a hand. Cresten gripped it and allowed the man to pull him up.

"What's your name?"

"Cresten Padkar, sir."

"You arrive today?"

"Yes, sir. A bell or two past midday."

"I see. How'd you come to be bloodied so?"

Tache eyed him, wary and tense.

The next several years of Cresten's life would be determined by how he answered. He could make himself an outcast. Or he could make himself a perpetual victim. In the end, he chose a third path. His father would have chided him for giving in to his emotions, his temper, his need for vengeance. But four days ago his father had walked him to the dock in Qesle and put him on a merchant ship with a change of clothes, a few pieces of silver, and a token from the village warden that marked him as a candidate for entry to the palace.

"If you are found wanting, you will find work making *gaaz*," his father had said. "It will not be a bad life either way. And someday perhaps, if the Two see fit, they will send you back to us." That was all.

His father could rot for all he cared.

"I've missed a lot," Cresten said, "coming so late to the palace. Mister Tache was teaching me some combat moves. I guess I'm a slow learner."

The master narrowed his eyes, slanted a look at Tache. "A slow learner," he repeated.

"Yes, sir."

A faint smile touched his lips. "Very well. It's time the rest of you were off to the keeps. It's late to be… training. Welcome, Mister Padkar. I'm the weapons master, Grenley Albon. I suppose I'll see you in the morning and we can get to work speeding up your reflexes, if not your capacity for learning."

Cresten's cheeks flushed hot. "Yes, sir."

Albon nodded to the others and walked off, leaving Cresten with Tache and his friends.

Tache watched the master walk away before facing Cresten, grudging respect in his expression.

"That was—"

Cresten had already coiled himself to strike, and didn't let him say more. He threw the punch as hard as he could, his fist cracking Tache in the jaw. The boy went down in a heap.

Others gaped at him. Tache scrambled to his feet and raised his fists, murder in his eyes. Blood seeped from a cut at the corner of his mouth.

"You're a corpse!"

"That's enough."

Tache faltered and glanced in the direction from which the voice had come.

Another novitiate stepped into the circle: a girl, older than Tache, plain-looking. She had straight bronze hair and a wide mouth. She was no taller than Tache, but she was solid, like an Aiyanthan warship, and there was a wildness in her pale eyes that reminded Cresten of the feral cats that prowled Qesle's waterfront.

Tache had gone still, but his fisted hand remained poised. He eyed the girl, appearing unnerved by her arrival.

"Did you see what he did to me?" he asked. "I should kill him."

"I saw," the girl said. "Saw what you did to him, too. It's over. You're even."

"That's not—"

"It's over," she said again, enunciating the words. "He didn't spill to Albon. Ask me, and I'd say you owe him."

The obvious response hung in the air, waiting to be given voice. No one had asked her. Cresten took it as a measure of how much Tache feared the girl – how much they all did – that the words remained unspoken. The girl smirked.

"Get going," she said. "All of you. Children shouldn't be out of bed so late."

Tache and the others stared at her. None of them argued, but neither did they flee. The girl returned Tache's gaze and raised an eyebrow, no more.

"Fine," he said, sounding disgusted. "We're done here." He regarded the girl again, flicked a look in Cresten's direction, and stalked away. His friends followed, whispering among themselves. Several glanced back at the girl, but as many spared a peek at Cresten as well. One way or another, they'd be talking about him.

He meant to thank the girl once they were alone, but before he could, she said, "You need a special escort? Someone to tuck you in?"

Cresten rounded on her. She had already started away.

He hurried after her. "Wait! Who are you?"

She didn't slow. "Someone who's too busy to wetnurse slack-witted fingerlings."

The words stung, slowing him.

"At least tell me your name," he said, resuming his pursuit.

She whirled. Cresten startled to a halt.

"Why would you hit him? You'd won already. You didn't dob him out to Albon. They were ready to accept you. And then you ruined it all. You haven't the brains of a stick."

She walked on.

"If I hadn't hit him," he called after her, "someone else would have figured out they could stomp on me any time they wanted, and they wouldn't even get in trouble."

The girl halted again, her back to him.

"It wasn't enough to get away," he went on. "I had to make a point."

She wheeled, considered him with her head canted, and crossed back to where he waited.

"That's not the dumbest thing I've ever heard." She eyed him a moment longer. "Wink."

Cresten frowned, but tried to blink his right eye.

The girl laughed. "You really are a fool, aren't you? That wasn't a command. It's my name. Wink. Short for Wenikai."

Cresten blushed, but smiled. "I'm not sure how I was supposed to know that."

She shrugged, the smile still on her lips. When she grinned, she was pretty. He was smart enough not to say so.

"Is Wenikai your family name or your given name?"

"It's hard to tell, isn't it?"

After a brief silence, he realized this was the only answer she intended to give. She turned to head back to the middle keeps, gesturing for him to follow.

"What's yours?"

"Cresten Padkar."

They walked in silence for a few strides.

"You know where the boy's keep is, right?"

He pointed.

"Good. You're not to follow me around like a puppy. I don't need friends and I'm not interested in mindless followers, like those idiots with Tache. I helped you, and you're grateful. You admire me, think I might be the answer to all the doubts and fears that have been niggling since you crossed through the gates. I'm not. I'm the best Spanner in the palace, and also the best at combat – fists, blades, and pistols. You, on the other hand, are lint. You're dust. You're the stuff I scrape off my boot before stepping inside. Got it?"

Harsh as the words were, Wink's tone remained mild.

"I understand."

"Say it back to me. 'I'm lint.'"

"No."

She halted, and grabbed his shoulder, stopping him, too.

"You're skin and bones, and about the height of a shit-beetle. I could crush you with my toe." She leaned in, looming over him. "Plus, I saved you from a beating. And you're telling me no?"

Cresten still ached from his fight with Tache, and he was certain Wink could do worse. He didn't care. His mother and father had given him precious little in his few years, but they had instilled in him a sense of pride. Not with praise, the Two knew, nor with kindness. Like Herjean pox, their own had been infectious. He couldn't help but contract it as well.

"You're too busy to be my friend," he said. "I get that. But I'm not lint. If you want to hit me for saying so, go ahead. That won't change my mind."

Wink straightened, appraised him anew. "You come from money?"

Cresten dropped his gaze.

"Right, I thought so."

"We weren't rich," he said. "Just…"

"Just not poor, like the rest of us."

"Don't tell anyone. Please."

"You keep acting like a rich man's son, I won't have to. They'll beat you to a bloody mess so fast, you won't be able to leave this palace soon enough."

He scowled to hide his fear. Pride again. "What am I supposed to do? Call myself lint and let everyone pound on me?"

"If that's what it takes."

Tears welled. He swiped at his eyes with a vicious hand.

"Why are you here, anyway?" she asked, acting like she hadn't noticed. He almost thanked her. "Your parents shouldn't need the gold."

There are other kinds of poverty. "There are a lot of us," he said, keeping the other thought to himself. "I have five brothers and a sister, all older. I was... They didn't need me." *They didn't want me.* "And they couldn't afford to keep me. Even with their money."

"Well, then you're not that different from the rest of us, are you?"

They shared wan smiles.

"Just... don't be so damn sure of yourself all the time."

"You won't tell?"

"And let them know I took time out of my busy evening to talk to you? 'Course not." She cushioned this with another grin. "Go on. Tache bothers you again, tell him I'm watching. Not for you, but as payback. He'll understand."

Payback for what, he wanted to know. He thought better of asking. He lifted his hand in a small gesture, something between acknowledgment and a wave, and started toward the boy's dormitory.

"Hey, shit-beetle."

He gave an inward groan, knowing that name would stick. Still, he faced her again.

"That was a good punch. Few more like that, and it might not matter who your father is."

CHAPTER 2

13th day of Sipar's Ascent, Year 615

Palace stewards had set his bed just inside the door of the chamber shared by the younger boys. It was covered by the thinnest blanket, the dingiest linens, the flattest pillow. He assumed the other boys had picked over his bedding like vultures. He didn't care.

None of the boys said a word to him, and he made no effort to speak with them. He undressed, slipped into bed, and curled into a tight ball, his face to the wall.

He shed his tears silently, holding himself still against sobs that should have wracked his body. Eventually he fell into a dreamless slumber that carried him to morning.

Cresten woke to the pealing of bells in the tower overhead. The boys rose, straightened their bedding, donned dark trousers and pale tunics, and hustled from the dormitory to the refectory. Cresten followed their every example. His side hurt from Tache's kick, but he kept that to himself.

He spotted the older boy in the courtyard, sporting a dark bruise on his swollen jaw. Cresten probably looked worse. The skin on his cheek was tender and tight. Still, he took some satisfaction in the wound he had dealt. Tache made a show of ignoring him, which pleased him that much more. Remembering Wink's warning, he masked his enjoyment.

Their breakfast was ample, if simple. After, his group of novitiates began their lessons with history. Cresten sat in the back of the room, absorbing every word. The class was studying Oaqamaran history, and Cresten had missed all that came before the Resurgence, the subject of this day's lecture. He was fascinated nevertheless. Other boys and girls asked questions, phrasing them with a precocious eloquence that seemed common here. Cresten had questions as well, but held his tongue. He suspected Wink would approve.

Protocol, finance, and science proved no less stimulating than history. Only when he reached Master Albon's training grounds, though, did he truly begin to understand the gift his parents had given him. Inadvertently or not, they had sent him to the place where he most belonged.

Albon had them work with wooden blades. He paired Cresten with a boy named Vahn Marcoji. Vahn was only nine, like Cresten, but he had been in the palace for several years, training with the others. It showed. He was better than Cresten at everything. He was faster, his footwork more precise, his strokes stronger.

They didn't speak much as they sparred. Beyond exchanging names and a smattering of details they had little to say. Vahn was from Onyi, the oldest of three boys, born of parents who made gaaz, like everyone else in their village. That was the extent of what they shared. Albon hovered nearby, assessing Cresten's skills, occasionally offering words of advice.

"Keep your knees bent; as soon as you lock them, you've lost."

"You're lunging. Center your weight over your feet. Always fight from a solid foundation."

"Less wrist; more arm. When you graduate to steel, you'll need the power."

With each interruption, Vahn waited for the master to make his point, and then resumed his attacks. He betrayed no impatience with Cresten's mistakes.

Too soon, the bell tolled, bringing an end to their training. Cresten could have gone on for another bell. Following the others, he set his sword on the rack, his tunic damp with sweat despite the cold wind. He hoped the master would say something about his work, perhaps praise his progress. When he racked his weapon, though, Albon didn't nod or offer a word of encouragement.

Vahn did. "That was good for your first time," he said, falling in step beside him. He was shorter than Cresten, better proportioned. His skin was the color of strong tea, his features soft and delicate.

"So I wasn't that bad?" he said.

"Oh, you were awful. But considering you'd never sparred before, it could have been worse."

Cresten deflated. "Oh. All right."

"You'll be fine. We can practice in our free time. That's the only good part of fighting with wood instead of steel. We don't need permission to train."

"Thanks."

They walked some distance without speaking. Cresten gathered they were headed back to the refectory. Good thing: he was famished.

"You're the one who bloodied Jaer, aren't you?"

"Jaer?"

"Tache."

"Oh. Yes, that was me. Is he a friend?"

Vahn laughed, high-pitched and abrupt. "Not at all. No, I was going to thank you." He studied Cresten's bruise. "He give you that?"

"And more."

"Good thing you hit him, then."

Cresten grinned, winced at the soreness in his jaw.

"Heard Wink took an interest in you. All in your first day?"

"I didn't ask for any of it."

"I wouldn't think so. Still, that could have been worse, too. People are talking about the fingerling who bloodied Tache, and with Wink telling everyone she doesn't want you touched, you don't have to worry about him coming back at you."

Cresten stopped. "She's telling people that?"

"You didn't know?" Vahn asked, halting as well.

"I swear I didn't."

The boy whistled through a gap in his teeth. "Well, that makes things difficult. You don't want Tache thinking he can take his revenge whenever he wants, any more than you want Wink thinking you're ungrateful. Either would be really bad."

"Why is everybody afraid of her?" Cresten asked.

They resumed walking. Already he could smell food. Stew? Roasted meat? Whatever, it made his stomach rumble.

"Well, she's mad, isn't she? She'll say anything, do anything, fight anyone. She's not afraid, ever, even when she should be. Most say she'll get herself killed before long. Until then, you don't want to cross her."

"Have you seen her fight?"

"Me?" Vahn said, eyes widening. "No. I mean, only on the training grounds. She's very good. Probably the best we've got. I've never seen her in a real fight."

"Have any of your friends?"

"Not that I remember. I'm sure someone has, but…"

Cresten nodded, trying to suppress a grin.

It didn't work.

"What's funny?"

"Nothing." At a skeptical look from his new friend, he said, "She's managed to make a reputation for herself, and yet none of you has ever seen her do anything that you could actually call unhinged. Whatever else she might be, she's smart."

Vahn sent another glance his way. "I have a feeling she's not the only one."

As Cresten finished his midday meal, he was approached by a woman wearing a satin robe of blue and gold. She introduced herself as a herald of the palace, and told him he was to follow her to the chambers of the chancellor. The children around him oohed and ahhed at this, as if Cresten had been summoned to a dungeon. Vahn assured him that the chancellor spoke to all new novitiates. He followed the woman from the refectory, feeling small and vulnerable under the scrutiny of so many.

They crossed the middle courtyard to the north keep, and ascended two stairways to a corridor, which ended at a ponderous oaken door. After a brief wait, Cresten was admitted to the chamber.

Portraits of somber men and women adorned the walls. The

stone floor was covered by a plush rug woven in shades of brown and gold and blue, and a cage filled with cooing messenger pigeons rested by the shuttered window.

The herald exited, leaving Cresten alone with a slight man who sat at a cluttered desk. Thick white hair framed a tapered face that was the same color as Cresten's. The man's eyes were green, as was his silk robe.

"Mister Padkar, I believe," he said, in a voice higher and softer than Cresten had expected. "I am Banss Samorij, chancellor of Windhome Palace."

"It's an honor to meet you, Lord Chancellor."

"You are settling in to your new home?" the chancellor asked.

"Yes, thank you."

The man looked him over, the smile crumbling. "Is that a bruise?"

Cresten dabbed at his wound with careful fingers. "Yes, I was… I mean, there was… an accident. Clumsy of me."

"Indeed," the chancellor said, frowning.

"It won't happen again."

"I would hope not. Next time, duck." Amusement lifted the corners of his mouth, and his eyes sparkled with lamplight.

Cresten couldn't help but smile in return. "Yes, Lord Chancellor."

The chancellor reached for a piece of parchment and scanned it. "Your father believes you might be a Spanner. Do you have any idea why he thinks so?"

"No, sir."

"Have you ever used a sextant?"

He shook his head, certain his father would consider his every denial a betrayal.

"You are old for a new arrival. You understand this?"

"Yes, sir."

"And you understand that we cannot send you back."

He did. His father had made this clear.

"I'll learn what I can while I'm here, Lord Chancellor," he

said, trying to sound brave. "And I'll try to master Spanning, or Crossing, or even Walking. If the power lies within me, I'll find it."

Another smile greeted this. "Well said, Mister Padkar." He laid the parchment atop a pile on his desk. "I thank you for coming. I hope you'll be with us for a good many years."

Cresten stood, recognizing the words as a dismissal. "Thank you, sir. I hope so as well."

He let himself out of the chamber, found the herald awaiting him in the corridor, and followed her to his next lesson.

The days that followed passed in a blur of lessons and training, meals and sleep, conversation and laughter and teasing, some of it playful, some intended as torment. Without realizing it, Cresten had found in Vahn a friend nearly as valuable as Wink. Everyone knew the boy – old and young, boy and girl, Spanner and Crosser and Walker. More, most novitiates liked him, and so many came to like Cresten as well. Perhaps this was what Albon had in mind the morning he first paired them.

It helped that Cresten had made the right enemy. Tache had few friends in the palace, aside from his coterie of sycophants. If Cresten accomplished nothing else in his years in the palace, he would long be remembered for cracking the bore in the mouth.

As it happened, Cresten made a name for himself in other ways, too. He excelled in his studies. Upon his arrival, the masters placed him in lessons with the youngest children, unsure of how much he had learned prior to reaching Windhome. Within a few days, they realized their error, and let him join the novitiates closer to his age, including Vahn. He was least prepared for advanced history lessons, but they moved him anyway, and instructed him to read what he had missed in his spare moments.

Because he was tall for his age, the masters had placed him with novitiates as old as him on the training ground, and here he struggled to catch up with his peers. With Vahn's help, however, he made progress. It would take him some time to rival the best boys and girls in the group, but after the first turn, he no longer embarrassed himself.

On occasion, as he crossed the courtyards with his new friends, he caught sight of Wink. She never acknowledged him, and Cresten didn't push for more. Tache and his allies kept their distance, rather than challenge Wink's decree that Cresten be left alone.

One night, nearly three turns after his arrival in Windhome, Cresten had to return to the Binder's workshop. Of all the disciplines he studied, his work with sextants and apertures troubled him most. He had never been good with his hands – one more reason why his father had been eager to send him off. He was useless as a craftsman's apprentice, and his father was already training his older brothers to be merchants. How many sons would he need to run the family trade?

On this day, Cresten had marred the arc of the sextant he was building. Binder Komat demanded that he salvage the piece if he could, or start a new one in its place. Cresten managed to correct his mistake, but the work took him nearly two bells. By the time he left the Binder's workshop, he was exhausted.

Stars shone overhead, and a gibbous moon cast long shadows on the rimed tiles of the courtyard. Cresten's breath billowed silver in the moonlight. His steps echoed like pistol fire off the palace façade. He buried his hands in his pockets and walked at a brisk pace.

At a noise from within one of the archways he halted and spun, nearly losing his footing on the frosted stone.

Movement caught his eye, a shadow shifting among shadows, the flicker of shining metal. He took a step in that direction.

"Stay there, shit-beetle."

He halted. "Wink?"

She emerged into the moonlight a spirecount later, her steps uneven, an odd bulge under her overshirt. As she neared him, Cresten saw that she bore a bruise near her right eye. He also caught the scent of spirit. Wine or whiskey. It had to be on her breath. He nearly asked if she was drunk, but bit back the question.

"What are you doing out here so late?" she asked, her voice throaty, the words running together.

"Coming back from Binder Komat. I wrecked my sextant today

and needed to fix it."

"Komat's an ass. Always has been, as far as I can tell."

His gaze flitted to the bruise, and he sniffed the air again. Her eyes had a glassy look. Despite the moonlight, he could see her color was high.

"Wink, are you all right?"

Her expression turned guarded. "Sure. Why wouldn't I be?" She said it with more clarity, but this seemed to take great effort.

"No reason, I was only… Never mind."

Guarded gave way to flinty. "I don't need your worry, shit-beetle. I don't answer to you."

"I didn't say you did." He stepped around her, muttered, "I'm sorry," and started on toward the keep.

"Shit-beetle, wait."

Cresten would have preferred to leave her, but he halted. She walked to him.

"I shouldn't have said that." The words slurred again. She leaned in. "Can you keep a secret?"

"Of course," he said, unsure of whether he wanted to hear it.

She bent closer still, hovering over him. The stench of her tainted breath enveloped him.

"I'm the best Spanner here," she whispered. *ImthbestSpann'rhere.* "These walls can't hold me." *Th'sewallscan'thol'me.*

"I- I know that, Wink. Everyone knows you're the best."

Wink shook her head. "You don't know. No one does. There's more to me than this place." She waved a hand, indicating the palace walls. "More than any of you know." *More'nanyo'youknow.*

"I don't understand."

She sobered at this, straightened, backed away.

"It's nothing. I was… I was joking."

Cresten didn't know what to say.

"You're all right, shit-beetle. Cresten." She offered a dazed smile. "Go on. It's late."

He dipped his chin, confused still, and worried. He tried not to let that show. He raised a hand in farewell and hurried on to the dormitory.

Cresten didn't see Wink for several days after that, and when at last he did catch a glimpse of her, on a cold, clear afternoon, as he and the other novitiates shuttled between lessons, she was laughing with friends, looking and acting normal. The bruise was gone. She gave no indication of having noticed him.

Later that same day, Cresten left the refectory after the evening meal, flanked by Vahn and a girl named Lenna, who was a year older. The three of them intended to study protocol together in the Windward Keep. As they crossed the courtyard, a figure detached itself from one of the archways and approached them.

Cresten recognized Wink in the dim glow of distant torches; his companions were deep in conversation and didn't spot her until she spoke.

"Padkar."

Thanking the Two that she hadn't called him shit-beetle, he slowed and cast a look at his friends. They eyed him, then Wink.

"He'll catch up with you," Wink said. "Wherever you're going."

Vahn kept walking, eager to keep his distance. Lenna flipped her hair, a haughty indifference in her expression as she regarded Wink a second time.

"Something you want to say to me, Doen?"

Lenna faltered. "No." She followed Vahn.

Their footsteps receded. Other novitiates exited the refectory and made their way to the dormitories, some singly, most in pairs and clusters.

"I think she likes you," Wink said, staring after Lenna. "She seems jealous."

"I think she likes Vahn. Everyone likes Vahn."

Wink didn't deny it. "Walk with me." She started toward the lower courtyard.

They crossed in silence through the broad archway that led to Albon's training ground.

"Do I remember that I spoke to you the other night?"

His mouth went dry. "Which night?"

"It's all right. I'm not mad at you."

"We talked, but not a lot. I was on my way to the Leeward Keep, and you were… I think you had other things on your mind."

A dry laugh escaped her. "Already a master of diplomacy." She paused, scanned the grounds. He did the same. They were alone.

"Did you tell anyone?" she asked.

"No!"

"Not Marcoji, or Doen, or anyone else? You didn't mention it to any of the masters?"

"I didn't say anything to anyone. You told me it was a secret." He hesitated. "Besides, I'm not sure what I would have told them. I didn't understand any of it."

She blew out a breath. "Thank you."

"What would you have done if I had told someone?"

Wink sidled closer. "I wouldn't have had a choice. I would have had to slit your throat. Then, when you were dead, I would have cut off your head and limbs, wrapped your parts in old cloth, and dumped you in the privies."

Cresten gaped, and Wink stared back at him, a strange tension in her face. After a fivecount, she burst out laughing.

"You believed me!"

He felt his cheeks redden. "No, I didn't."

"Yes, shit-beetle, you did."

He turned away, a grin on his lips. "Yes, I did. That was pretty good."

She mussed his hair. "You're all right. Definitely more than others your age."

"You said something similar to me that night."

Her smile faded. "What else did I say?"

"You don't remember?"

"If I did, would I have asked?" She huffed a breath and pushed a clawed hand through her hair. "No, I don't remember."

"You were drunk, weren't you?" Cresten asked. "And you'd been in a fight."

Wink stood before him for another moment, then pivoted and walked away. "Never mind. Sorry to have taken you away from your friends."

Cresten remained where he was. "You said you had a life beyond these walls," he said, taking care not to raise his voice too much. "You said this place couldn't hold you."

She paused. "I didn't know what I was saying. You were right. I was... I'd drunk too much wine. I was talking nonsense."

"That's what I thought, too. Then you called Komat an ass, so I assumed you were pretty coherent."

She laughed, and walked back to where he waited. "You really aren't what I expected that first night."

He almost asked her to explain, but wasn't sure he wanted to know. Instead, he said, "I wouldn't tell, Wink. I know I'm just a shit-beetle, but you're my friend, and I wouldn't get you in trouble. I'm trying to understand what happened that night."

Cresten didn't think she would answer. She surprised him.

"I have a... a friend in the city. I visit her sometimes. I Span out of here."

He gaped. "You do?" Leaving the palace could get a novitiate expelled. Even one as old as Wink.

"She hides clothes near her place, and I hide clothes here. I've done it enough that I can Span back and forth in my sleep."

"And you get drunk together?"

She gazed past him. "Sometimes. We went to a tavern that night, and we got in a fight with two sailors from Herjes. Asses."

"That's where you got the bruise."

"A lucky punch." She sounded defensive. "We gave them worse."

"I don't doubt it."

She smiled at that. "Look, it's not... I can take care of myself. I promise. And I don't want anyone else to know."

"Then I won't tell," Cresten said. "You have my word."

"Thanks." She waved him forward. "Come on. We should get you back, before Lenna sends out an army to search for you."

His face warmed again. He returned with her to the middle courtyard.

In the turns that followed, Cresten continued to adjust to life in the palace. His sword work and marksmanship improved, he caught up with his cohort's history lessons, and he discovered that he had a facility with languages, which enabled him to learn the rudiments of Oaqamaran, Aiyanthan, and the common tongue of the Ring Isles. For a time, he convinced himself that all was right with the world. He had found a home. Often he surprised himself by feeling grateful to his parents.

He and Wink passed each other in the refectory several days after their conversation in the courtyard. They didn't speak, but she did nod his way. Similar interactions followed: a shared smile here, a brief greeting there. She no longer ignored him, but neither did she seek him out for conversations. In a sense, his relationship with Wink grew as comfortable as the rest of his life. He could hardly have asked for more.

But with the end of his first year in Windhome, news came he had dreaded.

The novitiates and masters had gathered in the refectory for the evening meal, as they did each night. Before the priestess could lead them in a prayer of thanks, a rising murmur of voices at the front of the hall drew Cresten's attention. The chancellor himself had come. He stepped to a dais near the masters' table.

The man gestured for them to sit and be silent.

As whispered conversations died away, he greeted them in a soft voice. "I am pleased to dine among you this night, and to share with you glad tidings. Fesha Wenikai, known to all of you by the far more friendly sobriquet of Wink, will be leaving Trevynisle tomorrow for a posting as king's Spanner in the royal court of Caszuvaar on Milnos. We wish her good fortune, and pray that the Two bless her through all her years."

"Hear us!" came the reply from all those gathered around the tables.

All, that is, except Cresten. He stood dumbfounded. He craned his neck, seeking Wink. She looked back at him, a sad smile on her lips and an apology in her dark eyes.

Cresten turned again, to find the one other person who would appreciate the significance of Wink's news.

Tache was watching him, his smile smug and chilling.

CHAPTER 3

27th Day of Sipar's Waking, Year 616

Wink found him after supper, that same melancholy look on her face.

"You're going to be all right," she said, before he could speak. "You're not the helpless fingerling you were a year ago."

"I'm not strong enough to fight Tache either."

She lifted a shoulder. "You'll be all right," she repeated.

"I hope you're happy in Milnos. I've heard it's beautiful there."

"I've never liked the Shield. Or Oaqamar for that matter. I never thought I'd be summoned to either one. Then again, we don't get to choose so..." She shrugged again.

"Well..." He trailed off, not knowing what to say. "I guess I'll see you sometime."

"I suppose so. Be good, shit-beetle."

"You, too."

They stood together for another moment. Then they turned simultaneously, he toward the Leeward Keep, she toward the Windward.

Cresten barely slept that night, and he spent much of the next few days peering over his shoulder, expecting to see Tache and his friends bearing down on him.

They caught up with him on the fourth evening after Wink's departure. Cresten didn't try to run, knowing any escape he managed would only delay the inevitable.

He held his ground, Vahn and Lenna standing with him.

"Couldn't get her to take you along, eh?" Tache said, planting himself in front of Cresten. "I'm sure you begged her."

"I didn't. And I never asked her to protect me, either. Her telling people I wasn't to be touched – that was her idea."

"You expect us to believe that?"

"Yes."

Tache faltered, though only for the span of a heartbeat. "It doesn't matter. She did it, and that kept me from paying you back for that dirty punch you threw."

Cresten didn't deny it. It had been unsporting. He understood that now. Wink tried to tell him as much at the time.

"All right."

The boy frowned. "All right, what?"

"You want to fight me, to set things right. That's fine."

Tache grinned, and glanced back at his friends. "You think you can beat me?"

"I know I can't. You're right, though: it was a dirty punch. You deserve a chance to get back at me."

"Cresten–"

He raised a hand, silencing Vahn. He didn't take his eyes off Tache. "It's the right thing to do," he said, directing the words at his friend. To Tache he said, "You'll leave them alone, right? This is just you and me."

Tache nodded, solemn. "Nobody touches them. My word."

Cresten backed away a step, removed his overshirt, and handed it to Lenna. Tache removed his as well.

The two of them began to circle. Cresten tried to put to use some of what he had learned from Albon, and from Vahn. That didn't last long. After Tache's first punch connected high on his cheek, he fought merely to survive. A second blow to his nose drew blood and put him on the ground. He pushed himself to his feet and fought on. He even landed a punch.

Tache staggered back, but soon advanced again, buffeting Cresten with kicks and fists. Cresten had learned to defend himself. He blocked as many punches as got through, but Tache threw a lot of punches.

When he fell a second time, Vahn told him to stay down. He didn't.

After the third time, he tried again to stand, only to find that he couldn't. His vision swam. Blood coursed from his nose, his split lip, a cut below his right eye.

He lay still until he spotted a hand hovering before him. He grasped it and allowed Tache to pull him to his feet.

"We're even," the boy said. "That was… I didn't expect that."

"I did. I knew you'd pound me bloody."

Tache blinked, then laughed. "Let's get you cleaned up. Or we'll both be scrubbing privies until Kheraya's Awakening."

They walked back to the boy's dormitory, trailed by Tache's followers and Cresten's friends. They washed the blood from Cresten's face and burned his bloodstained shirt in the hearth. The next day, several masters scrutinized his cuts and bruises, but most said nothing. He told those who did ask that he had been practicing hand combat with a friend, and still had much to learn.

The lone exception was Albon, who lifted an eyebrow at the sight of him and said, "Well, that didn't take long. She's been gone, what? Five days now?"

"Yes, sir."

"Keep practicing, Mister Padkar. You'll get the hang of it."

So he did. Over the course of his second year and into his third, the movements and tactics drilled into him by the weapons master, and reinforced by his sparring sessions with Vahn, imbedded themselves in his mind and muscles. By his twelfth birthday, he had learned to fight not from memory, but from instinct.

His blade work improved as well. With a sword in hand, his long limbs and lean frame proved an advantage. He wasn't as strong as many of the other boys, but he could reach them before they reached him. Once he graduated to steel, he would need more strength. For now, with wooden swords, height was more important than power.

He spent most of his time with Vahn, Lenna, and a few of the other novitiates in their group. To his surprise, his fight with Tache had bound them into an unlikely friendship. Tache often invited

Cresten to join his group, and not merely as a follower. They sat together at meals, practiced sword work together. The older boy asked Cresten for help with Aiyanthan, which Cresten spoke fluently. Tache even gave Cresten a new nickname: Whip.

"You're skinny and you're fast," Tache said, "and you can do more damage than a person might think."

Cresten had to admit that he liked it.

Vahn didn't approve of Cresten's friendship with the older boy. After a qua'turn during which he and Cresten didn't share a single meal, he said as much.

"Just because he doesn't want to pummel you anymore, that doesn't mean you have to be his friend."

"I want to be his friend. He's pretty nice, once you get to know him."

Vahn's eyebrows lifted in skepticism. Cresten didn't pursue the point.

In truth, Tache wasn't nice. He could be charming and funny, and surprisingly clever. But he spoke ill of other novitiates, and nearly all the masters and mistresses. He longed to be summoned to the royal court in Oaqamar, not only because he coveted the autarch's gold, but also because he wished to Span for the most powerful man in Islevale.

"The palace sells us for gold, right?" Tache said one night, as they walked together through the middle courtyard. "They get as much as they can from the courts. So why shouldn't we want the same? Gold and power. That's what the world is about."

Cresten hadn't given much thought to where he would choose to serve, given the opportunity to decide for himself. He still didn't know if he would ever be called to a court. The masters who specialized in Spanning, Crossing, and Walking only began to train novitiates when the children turned twelve.

Cresten's father had told him he would be a Spanner, mostly because the oldest of his father's aunts was one. Despite what Cresten told the chancellor upon his arrival in the palace, notwithstanding things his father had said to anyone who would listen, Cresten had shown no sign of being a Spanner, or any other sort of Traveler. The tests to which he was subjected soon after coming to Windhome had been inconclusive.

He did know that his father profited from sending him to the palace, and the palace would profit if and when they sent him to a court. Didn't this prove Tache's point about gold?

"He wants to go to Oaqamar?" Vahn said, when Cresten related the conversation. "Really?"

"That's what he told me."

Lenna shook her head. "Where he wants to go is…" She made a small motion, brushing away the remark. "Who cares? I mean, the autarch is a pig, but that's not important. What bothers me is that he thinks being a Traveler is his path to wealth. That's just wrong."

She was thirteen now, and well into her training with Master Denmys. To the delight of Chancellor Samorij and the masters and mistresses, the promise of her early tests had been confirmed after her previous birthday: she was that rarest of all Travelers, a Walker. The palace hadn't seen one since the last was summoned to Westisle four years before. Cresten thought her status as a Walker-in-training imbued her opinions with added weight.

He would never have said as much to Tache. Nor did his diminished opinion of the older boy keep him from spending time in Tache's company. His friendship with Tache enhanced his status. It reminded others of their early confrontation, of Wink's protection, and of his bravery in facing Tache after Wink left. He sensed in Vahn's disapproval, the merest hint of envy. And he believed he had risen in Lenna's esteem since his second fight with Tache.

In recent turns it had occurred to him that Lenna was quite pretty. Beautiful, in fact. How had he not seen this before? Her skin was the color of stained cherry wood, her eyes large and dark and liquid. She had silken bronze hair that she often wore tied back from her oval face. She was taller than most novitiates their age, including Vahn, but not quite as tall as Cresten. He thought she liked this about him.

Cresten found excuses to spend time with her, and sensed that she liked this as well. Sometimes they took walks together through the palace grounds – the two of them, without Vahn. He knew Vahn resented this. Probably his friend cared for Lenna as much as he did. But Vahn had lots of friends. Boys and girls gravitated to him. It was harder for Cresten, despite his renown.

Besides, young as he was, he knew that older novitiates sometimes paired off. *Paired.* Two, not three. Cresten didn't want to see his friend hurt, but neither did he want to be hurt himself. The three of them still studied together and ate most of their meals together. But on occasion, Cresten contrived to spend time alone with Lenna. And she allowed it.

On a mild, moonless night late in Sipar's Stirring, the two of them sat in the lower courtyard, staring at a velvet sky, watching for falling stars. They didn't say much. Now and then, one of them pointed up at a silvery streak.

"You're a Walker."

They both jumped at the voice and scrambled to their feet. Cresten's pulse pounded. Lenna stood so close to him that their shoulders brushed.

"Who's there?" Lenna asked, the words tremulous. "Who are you?"

"I can tell you're a Walker. Your years are altered. You've been practicing."

The voice was that of a child, a girl. She stood a short distance from them, a shadowed form barely visible in the darkness. Light hair shifted in the soft wind, and ghostly eyes reflected the faint glow of distant torches. She wore rags; her feet were bare. When the breeze lifted, it carried the sick, sweet stench of rotting meat.

"Where did you come from?" Lenna asked, taking half a step in the girl's direction.

Cresten put out a hand to stop her.

"He fears me. He should."

"Why? Why should we be afraid of you?"

"Not you," the girl said. She pointed a slender finger at Cresten. "Only him."

Again he caught the elusive, putrid scent riding the wind.

"Do you smell that?" he whispered to Lenna.

The young girl's dim features resolved into a scowl. "That's rude."

He shouldn't have been afraid. She was tiny. Yet her tone froze his blood.

Lenna lifted both hands, a gesture intended to calm. "He wasn't saying it's you."

"Yes, he was. And it is."

Lenna let her hands drop, edged closer to Cresten again. "What are you?" she whispered.

"My kind are called Tirribin. We're–"

"Time demons."

Cresten glanced at Lenna, wanting to ask what time demons were.

"That's a human term," the girl said in the same tone she'd used to call him rude.

"I- I'm sorry."

The girl glared. "I was going to say that we're able to sense your years. Yours are... confused, altered. His aren't. And he's young, so they'd be quite lovely to feed on."

"No!" Lenna said. "I have a riddle!"

The girl eased forward, leaning in their direction, her hands clasped together. "A riddle?" she said, longing in her question.

"That's right. Only if you swear you won't hurt either of us, ever."

"Yes, all right." She wrung her hands, eyes wide. "What is it? Please."

"We have your word?"

"Yes!" the demon said, urgency in her tone. "I give you my word: I'll never harm either of you. The riddle! Quickly!"

"All right. It goes like this:

A carpenter, I build without hammer or nail,
A traveler, I journey without wheel or sail;
An artist, my work is the most elegant lair,
A hunter, I rely on the deadliest snare."

The girl drew a gasping breath, her head twitching side to side, her lips moving. Cresten thought he heard her repeat Lenna's rhyme.

He bent his head near to Lenna's and whispered, "Shouldn't we get away from here?"

"You should. You're the one in danger. Tirribin don't prey on Walkers. Our years are different, and they feel a… a kinship with us."

"How do you know this?"

"My mother's a Walker. She told me about them. She also taught me the riddle, just in case. You should go."

"We both should."

"No. If she can't work out the riddle, and I'm not here to give her the answer, our bargain is broken. Then we *both* might be in danger."

"Well, if you're going to stay, I will, too."

Lenna's eyes met his. "That's… that's sweet of you."

Their gazes remained locked, until Cresten realized the demon had ceased her mumbling. He turned, found her studying them.

"You're young to be in love, aren't you?"

He colored to the roots of his hair.

"We're not in love," Lenna said. "Because you're right, we are young."

"*He's* in love. I can tell. I thought love was something that adult humans did, not children."

"We're not—"

"Can you engage in the act of love at your age?"

"That's not—" Lenna shook her head, clearly flustered. "Work out your riddle, before I tell you the answer and ruin it for you!"

The demon eyed them, then lifted a shoulder and went back to her mutterings and the strange movements of her head.

Lenna stared at the ground, refusing to look Cresten's way. She had moved away from him. Not far, but enough to keep him rooted to where he stood. Cresten watched the demon, afraid of what she might do. Every so often, he peeked at Lenna, but she remained as she was, silent and withdrawn.

Eventually, the girl approached them, hands intertwined and twisting.

"What is it?" Her voice was pitched higher than before. "You have to tell me what it is."

"A spider," Lenna said, the word coming out low and flat. "The answer is a spider."

The Tirribin closed her eyes and let out a sigh. "A good riddle. Very good. You must ask me another some day. That was… exquisite."

Lenna didn't answer, nor did Cresten.

The girl frowned. "Something's happened. What's the matter?"

You happened, Cresten wanted to say. *You came and ruined everything.*

Lenna fixed a brittle smile on her lips. "Everything's fine. We have to go now."

The demon's puzzlement deepened. "I'm sorry. I didn't mean to make your love stop."

"We already told you, we aren't in love." Lenna raised a hand in farewell. "Goodnight." She started away.

Cresten followed.

"Droë."

"What?"

"That's my name: Droë."

"Oh. I'm Lenna. This is Cresten."

The demon nodded. "All right. Goodnight, then."

They continued toward the middle courtyard. Lenna strode with purpose, her arms crossed over her chest. Cresten walked beside her, dismal, unsure of what to say. *He's in love. I can tell…* He winced at the truth of this, and at the things Droë said next. He'd done nothing wrong, but that didn't matter. Lenna's embarrassment, and his own, if he was honest with himself, had opened a chasm between them. One he had no idea how to cross.

He followed Lenna to the entrance to the Windward Keep, because he didn't know what else to do.

She paused on the threshold, seemed to force herself to face him.

"Goodnight, Cresten."

"Goodnight. I'll see you tomorrow, right?"

"Of course. We have lessons, and training."

"And I'll see you at breakfast?"

She hesitated. "Yes, I suppose so."

Not the answer he'd wanted, but what could he do?

"All right then. Goodnight." He'd already said that.

He spun away and stalked across the open space to the Leeward Keep. He felt he'd been robbed of something precious.

Cresten lay awake for much of the night, trying to convince himself that their embarrassment would pass, and that everything between them would go back to how it had been.

It didn't. Lenna, Vahn, and he sat together at breakfast, but what little she said she directed at Vahn. Vahn couldn't conceal his pleasure at this development. He wasn't the type to gloat, but he made no attempt to draw Cresten into their conversation. Just as Cresten hadn't scrupled to draw Lenna away from the other boy, now Vahn did all he could to win her back. Cresten couldn't blame him. Rather, he focused all his ire and resentment on the time demon.

Her questions had been foolish, mortifying, even inappropriate. He and Lenna were children, and she was asking them about… about things no child should have to discuss. No wonder Lenna was humiliated; no wonder she could barely bring herself to look at him.

For days he brooded, watching Vahn and Lenna grow closer, feeling ever more superfluous to both of them. It was like falling down a stairway one tread at a time. Each new impact jarred him, and he knew the next would hurt more, but he didn't know how to stop or how to shield himself from the pain. All he could do was fall.

After a qua'turn, Cresten gave up eating with his friends. His presence made Lenna uncomfortable, and being with the two of them made him feel like a third oar on a dory.

At that evening's meal, he sat alone far from Vahn and Lenna's table. The palace chef had prepared roasted fowl with baviseed and greens. It was one of Cresten's favorites, but he picked at the food, hardly eating.

"Why aren't you with that pretty Walker?"

Cresten peered up from his platter. Tache and his friends stood around him, their own platters in hand.

He shrugged.

The others sat, Tache taking the spot beside Cresten. His friends resumed conversations of their own, but not Tache.

"I see her," he said. "She's with your friend, Marcoji."

"I know." He had no interest in discussing this part of his life with the older boy, not that Tache would care.

"I thought she fancied you, not him."

"She did, I think. Once."

Tache smirked. "You foul it up? Say something stupid?"

"Not me, but that's what happened."

"What do you mean, not you? Did someone backbite you? Someone I know?"

This was part of Tache's charm, the thing about him that Vahn and Lenna couldn't have grasped without knowing him as Cresten did. He was mean and full of bluster and motivated by pride, greed, and spite. But once he accepted someone as a friend, as he had Cresten, he was loyal to a fault.

"Tell me who it was, Whip. I'll beat him bloody."

"It's not like that. I don't think you should get involved."

Tache's expression frosted. "You think I couldn't take him?"

"It's not a him. It's not even–" He broke off, shaking his head. "I shouldn't have mentioned it."

"Not even a what?"

"It doesn't matter."

Cresten reached for a piece of bread. Tache seized him by the wrist, grinding the bones in a pincer grip.

"Ow!"

"Not even a what?" he demanded again.

Cresten yanked his hand away. "Not even a person," he said, rubbing his wrist, and not caring that he sounded like a sullen child. "We were talking to a Tirribin."

Tache's ire gave way to calculation, and thinly masked eagerness. "A Tirribin," he said. "You're sure?"

"Lenna was sure. I'd never heard of them before."

"Of course. A time demon would be interested in your Walker friend. Anything having to do with time."

Cresten nodded, pretending he knew, hoping Tache would say more. Perhaps if he learned about Droë and her kind, he might find a way back into Lenna's good graces.

That avid gleam lingered in the boy's eyes. "They're a menace, of course, like all demons. But old as they are, they're more like children than like other Ancients, so how dangerous can they be?"

"Lenna seemed pretty scared. I think they're more dangerous than they look."

"This one was in the palace?" Tache asked, ignoring Cresten's warning.

"On the grounds. Lower courtyard."

"Interesting," the boy said. "I wonder if she comes here a lot. If they're drawn to Walkers, then this would be the place, wouldn't it? Not recently, maybe, but the palace has seen lots of Walkers over the years. And Tirribin live a long time. Centuries. Maybe more. Imagine the stuff she might know."

"I'd rather not," Cresten said. "I'd prefer never to see her again."

Tache laughed and thumped him on the back. "You're thinking about this all wrong, Whip. Never mind the Walker. Sure, she's pretty, but there's others prettier. You'll forget her before long. That time demon, though – her kind know things. They can tell when time is different, and they remember stuff the rest of us don't."

Tache's excitement insinuated itself into Cresten.

"The demon said something like that. She could tell Lenna had been Walking. She said her years were... were changed somehow." He reached for the memory. "'Confused,' she said."

"Yeah, I'll bet she has all sorts of information. Knowledge of this place, the masters and mistresses. She might be able to read our futures."

"I don't know if—"

"The lower courtyard, you said?"

Cresten faltered. Hurt as he was by Lenna's recent treatment, he regretted having revealed so much. It felt like a betrayal.

"Whip?"

He twitched a shoulder. "It was only that one time. I don't think she comes there a lot."

"Well, I suppose we'll find out, won't we?"

A betrayal of her trust, of what they'd shared that evening and before, of their entire friendship, however brief it had been. He should have said nothing. He should have lied.

He reached for the bread again. This time Tache let him eat. Later, as Cresten gathered his platter and utensils to leave, Tache stopped him.

"You let me know if you see her again, you understand?"

"The- the Tirribin, you mean?"

Tache laughed too loudly. "Of course. You think I care if you see your Walker friend again?"

"Right. Sure I will."

He scuttled away, refusing to glance back, despite the laughter that chased him from the table. He didn't look at Lenna and Vahn either. Not since his first night, years ago, had he felt so alone.

Cresten tried to avoid them all – Tache, Lenna, Vahn, the time demon – but the palace, which he thought so huge when he arrived, now proved to be terribly small.

A ha'turn after their first encounter with the Tirribin, as Cresten walked back toward the keep from another late session with the Binder, he heard Tache call to him.

He slowed, unable at first to spot the older boy. Tache materialized out of the darkness, pale eyes shining.

"I've been waiting for you," he said. "She's down there again."

Cresten didn't have to ask who he meant.

"I don't want to go, Tache."

"I don't care. I want to meet the Tirribin. You're going to introduce us."

What could he do? He followed Tache to the lower courtyard, where Lenna and the demon – Droë – stood together in the bone-white gleam of a half-moon.

As they neared the pair, Lenna spun. Seeing who had come, she glowered, flicking a glance at Tache before directing the full weight of her anger on Cresten.

"What are you doing here?"

"I wanted a word with your friend," Tache said, though she hadn't asked the question of him.

"*You* wanted," she fired back. "What business does a mediocre Spanner have with a Tirribin?"

"Careful, Doen," he said, velvet menace in his voice. "You may be a Walker, and the masters' favorite, but I don't tolerate that from anyone."

She glared at Cresten again. "How could you bring him here?"

I didn't bring him. He made me do this. The denials withered before he could give them voice. If she hadn't hated him before, she did now.

"I've always wanted to meet a Tirribin," Tache said, looking past Lenna to the time demon.

Cresten could see her more clearly this night. Moonlight illuminated dark, perfect features – high cheekbones, a delicate nose, full lips – and lent its glow to long, golden hair. Her eyes, as light and haunting as they had been during that first encounter, registered amusement.

"I almost never wish to treat with humans, unless they happen to be Walkers." She shifted her gaze to Lenna. "Did he threaten you a moment ago? I thought I heard a threat in what he said."

"You can read the future, can't you?" Tache asked.

The demon ignored him, her attention still on Lenna, a question in her raised eyebrows.

"Yes, he threatened me, but it's not important."

"Hey!" Tache snapped his fingers. "I asked you a question."

Droë's smile slipped. "He's quite rude. I don't think I like him." She lifted her chin in Cresten's direction. "What about this one? Is he still your friend? Something's changed."

Yes, you changed it.

"He's still my friend," Lenna said.

His eyes met hers. He read an apology in her glance, and also forgiveness. He essayed a smile, but she had already turned away, back to Tache.

"You should leave," she said.

Tache shook his head. "I'm not finished speaking with your friend. I want an answer to my question. Can you read the future?"

"No," Droë said, ice in her tone, her expression, her very stance. "That's not how our powers work. I read time. I can tell when years don't match the person, or when time has been altered. You want a Seer, not a Tirribin."

"I think you're lying. Tirribin are supposed to be powerful. What you're talking about…" He shook his head. "It's nothing. It's nonsense." A breeze stirred the air, and Tache wrinkled his nose. "What is that stink?" He frowned at Droë. "Is that you?"

"He's very, very rude," the Tirribin said.

She continued to glower, and she opened her mouth, revealing small, dagger-sharp teeth. At the sight of them, Cresten backed away.

"You're right, Droë," Lenna said. "He is. I'm leaving. You and I can speak another time."

She tried to walk past Tache, but he grabbed her arm, spinning her around. She gave a small cry and struggled to break free.

"You're not leaving until I'm done talking to the demon."

Cresten took a step toward Tache.

"Release her," Droë said.

Tache grinned. "Not yet. Tell me what else you can do."

"Release her or pay in years." A rasp roughened the threat.

Lenna ceased her struggles, her eyes going wide. "Droë, no!"

Tache let go of her and raised his hands for the Tirribin to see. "No need to get angry," he said. "She's fine."

Lenna stumbled away from him.

"You," Droë said to Lenna, her voice grating still. "And that one." She indicated Cresten with another nod. "That was our arrangement."

"Yes, but—"

Lenna had time for no more. In a blur of golden, moon-touched hair, wraithlike eyes, and breadknife teeth, the Tirribin launched herself at Tache.

He managed a truncated scream, fell under the fury of her assault. Fists flailing, feet lashing out, he tried to fight her off, but she held fast to him, her mouth at his throat, a nimbus of sliding colored light surrounding them both.

Lenna screamed, but didn't move. Cresten thought he should try to pull Droë off the boy, but he was too horrified to make the attempt, too frightened of what the Tirribin might do to him.

He heard voices and footsteps. Others approached from the upper courtyards. Novitiates and at least one master. As they drew near, Droë lifted her head from Tache's still form. She eyed Lenna and then Cresten before dashing away. After a few strides, she blurred to unearthly speed. Cresten lost sight of her.

He crept closer to Tache's body. The boy stared at the stars with lifeless eyes, his cheeks sunken, his skin desiccated, as if he had died days ago. Cresten sensed Lenna beside him. She drew a sharp breath and screamed again. He reached for her, intending to comfort. She shrank from his touch.

CHAPTER 4

Kheraya's Emergence, Year 634

Orzili emerged from the gap in the middle ward of Hayncalde Castle, naked as a newborn, blood pouring from the knife wound in his thigh and the bullet wound to his back. The injury to his leg was the more painful of the two. He didn't know yet if the hole in his back would prove deadly.

He had landed on his knees, his skin abraded by the Spanning wind. The precise golden edges of his sextant bit into his cramped fingers and tears leaked from his eyes. This, too, he blamed on the wind.

Forcing himself to his feet, he stumbled toward the nearest tower, scanning the torchlit plaza for guards. He considered going to Lenna's chamber, but dismissed the notion. The Lenna of his own time would know better than to mock him. She would tend to his wounds, whispering words of sympathy. This older Lenna, the one brought back to him through the years by the exigencies of war and assassination, was less predictable. He wanted her, was drawn to her wisdom, her biting wit, her honed beauty, but he was wary of her.

He limped to his own quarters. Along the way he passed two Sheraigh guards, who appeared amused by his state of undress. Their mirth diminished when they noticed his wounds, and evaporated entirely when he identified himself and threatened to have them taken to the dungeon and stretched beyond recognition. By the time he ordered them to have a healer sent to his chamber, they were desperate to oblige.

Upon entering his quarters, he downed a generous cup of

Miejan red, grabbed a blanket off his bed, and sat near the hearth. He covered himself without allowing the blanket to touch his thigh, and without leaning back.

He was well into his second cup of wine when someone knocked at his door.

"Come!"

The door swung open, revealing a woman with steel gray hair, and, behind her, a younger man bearing cloth, herbs, oils, and tinctures. They entered. The man set his burdens on a table near the hearth, and left.

"You're the healer?" Orzili asked.

"I am now," she said, crossing to him. She eyed the knife wound, peered at his back, and knelt by his outstretched leg. "This looks terrible."

He glanced at it, that was all. He had never been squeamish, but this... It *did* look terrible. He would give every gold round in his purse to have that bloody Walker back in the dungeon. Tobias wouldn't escape him again.

"Spare me the observations and heal it."

She glanced up at him, her expression mild, an eyebrow quirked. She unstoppered one of her bottles and poured a small amount of liquid onto a cloth. The smell of spirit reached him.

"This is going to sting. Or would you prefer I kept that to myself as well?"

His mouth twitched. She had mettle. He admired that. "No, I appreciate the warning."

She wiped away the drying blood, circling closer and closer to the wound itself. When at last the damp cloth touched his gash, it felt as though she had thrust a hot needle under his skin. He sucked a breath between his teeth.

The healer didn't pause. He gripped the arms of his chair, weathering the pain of each brush of that cloth. Finally she stopped and examined the wound more closely.

Saying nothing, she retrieved a second cloth, doused that one, and shifted her attention to the bullet wound.

He had to smile. "Very well, healer. I surrender. I would hear your observations."

"I wouldn't want to presume, my lord."

He half-turned his head, allowing her to see the lift of his lips. "Please."

"Very well." Her cloth touched the injury itself, drawing from him another hissed breath. "You were fortunate with this wound. I take it this was done with a firearm."

"Yes. A pistol, from distance."

"Still, the God was kind."

"And the other? As terrible as you thought?"

"A blade wound, yes?" At his nod, she went on. "It slashed through muscle, and nearly to the bone. I can heal it, but you'll need to tread gently for a time."

"I can't."

"No, I didn't expect you would. But as your healer I have an obligation to make the effort. Now, if you damage the leg permanently, it will be your fault and not mine."

He laughed. "Did you poison the old healer? Is that how you came by this position?"

She didn't answer. Bending over the wound, she laid her hands upon it. A misty glow enveloped her, as silver as a winter moon. Cold penetrated his flesh around the injury. For a tencount and more, it clawed at him like a forest beast. He clenched his teeth and squeezed his eyes shut, cursing Tobias Doljan under his breath. In time, the cold abated enough that agony gave way to relief. Not long after, the glow around the woman diminished and vanished entirely. She straightened to scrutinize her work. A bold scar remained where the gash had been.

"That will fade with time," she said. "How does it feel?"

He shifted his leg, winced in anticipation of pain that didn't come. The woman knew her trade. "Better. Thank you."

"Don't be fooled. You're not healed yet." She stood, stretched her back, and addressed the second wound. "I meant what I said about rest." She probed his back with deft fingers. "The old healer left," she said, answering his previous question. "It seems he was a Hayncalde man. A loyal subject of the old regime."

"The Sheraighs let him go?"

"They had no choice. He fled in the middle of the night."

Again he laughed. "And so they found you. A Sheraigh sympathizer?"

"A skilled healer who knows to keep her mouth shut."

"Yet you tell me this, despite my ties to the Sheraighs. Perhaps you know less than you think."

"Forgive me, my lord," she said, sounding less than contrite. "I didn't think you were from Sheraigh. I didn't mean—"

He stopped her with a raised hand. "Don't bother. I *don't* come from Sheraigh."

After a brief silence, she said, "I need to extract the bullet. I don't believe it's very deep, but it would be better if you slept while I did this." She positioned herself in front of him again. "I can prepare you a sleep draught." She glanced at his empty cup. "It won't be as pleasant as the Miejan red, but neither will it give you a hangover. It will also work more quickly."

"All right."

She moved to the table that held her herbs and bottles.

Another knock echoed in the chamber.

"Enter."

Lenna breezed in. She paused at the sight of the healer before finding him in his chair. Her eyes flicked over his body and she flushed attractively, looked away. He smiled at her discomfort.

Her bronze hair was streaked with silver. Her Walk back to this time had left tiny lines around her lips and dark, liquid eyes. His own Lenna, the one who waited for him in Kantaad, was as young as he, and more beautiful than any woman he had ever known.

This older Lenna, though, had insinuated herself into his emotions. She was whip smart, wise almost beyond imagining. Age had roughened her beauty, but also deepened it. He wanted her more than he had wanted anyone, her allure heightened by her refusal to join him in his bed.

The healer went about her task with discreet efficiency, no doubt sensing that he and Lenna waited for her to leave. Within a few spirecounts, she had her draught ready. She placed it on the table beside his wine cup.

"Drink it all, my lord, and lie down. It should keep you asleep through the surgery." She cast a glance at Lenna. "Summon me when you're ready."

"Thank you, healer."

She nodded to Lenna and let herself out of the chamber. Only when she was gone and the door closed, did Lenna face him again.

"I heard you were shot."

"And stabbed."

"I'm sorry. Are you all right?"

"I'm well enough, thank you."

"And the Walker?"

He glowered at the empty hearth. "He escaped. Two of my men were killed and the third was captured. We lost the tri-sextants."

Lenna's eyes widened, but she had the grace not to comment.

"We'll get him back."

"I've no doubt," she said, subdued.

"You can't leave yet, Lenna. I need you in this time."

"Why? We've already determined that the boy doesn't have a chronofor. If he did, he'd have gone back by now to warn Mearlan of the attempt on his life. You don't need me to follow him through the years. And anything else you require, the younger me can provide."

"She knows nothing about this. You know everything. That's reason enough for you to remain."

She knelt beside him, the gossamer scent of honeysuckle surrounding her. He breathed her in.

"Let me go, love. Please. You'll be happier with the me that belongs in this time."

"That's not—"

"I won't love you. I've told you as much. Keeping me here in the vain hope that I will is… It's cruel, to all of us. Both of you, both of me."

"Then leave."

She blinked. "You would let me?"

"How would I stop you?"

"That's not what I mean."

"I know," he said, pressing his advantage. "You've told me repeatedly that you wish to return to your time, to the older me who you left there. And you've also said that you won't go without my permission. Only recently has it occurred to me that this is an evasion on your part, a way to remain here while claiming that I've kept you from Walking back."

She scowled, stood, walked to the hearth. "That makes no sense."

"I disagree. I think you're afraid that the older me you claim to love so much might reject you. Fourteen more years? More silver in your hair, more lines on your face? What if he won't love you as he once did? That's what holds you here. Fear of his indifference, and the understanding deep within you that you need my love." A faint smile tugged at his lips. "I may be the only me you have left."

Lenna crossed her arms over her chest, refusing to meet his gaze but unwilling to turn her back on him. "I don't remember you being this cruel."

"Neither do I. Perhaps it's because of you?"

"You should summon her – the other me. Have her join you here. I'll give you a qua'turn to do so. After that, I'm going back, no matter what."

He held his tongue. She stood before him for two breaths, then strode to the door.

"Lenna," he said, stopping her.

She sighed, regarded him over her shoulder.

"Where might he get another chronofor?"

She lifted a shoulder. "Any major city. Hayncalde, Sheraigh, Belsan, Rooktown." She shrugged again. "They're rare – more so by far than apertures and sextants – and they're dear as well. He would need a good deal of gold. Still, if he seeks one, and I'm sure he does, he'll find it before long."

"Thank you," he said. "Please tell the healer I'm ready for her."
She left him.

He stood, limped to his bed, and drank the healer's tonic.
Before sleep could take him, he realized what day it was – what
day it would be when he woke. Kheraya's Emergence. The Turn
of the Year. On every isle between the oceans, this was a day of
celebration, of drink and feasting and passion. On this, the day
of the Goddess, lovemaking was initiated by the woman. He and
Lenna – the younger Lenna; *his* Lenna – had always laughed about
this. As if she needed the excuse of the equinox. In Fanquir, in
the flat they shared, she would be thinking of him, missing him,
desiring him.

Guilt knifed through him. Maybe the older Lenna was right,
and he was being cruel to all of them. He just didn't know how to
stop.

Over the next several days, Lenna avoided him, and he refrained
from visiting her chamber. The healer checked on him each
morning, and on the fifth day of the new year pronounced him fit
to resume some activities.

"You're still healing," she told him. "Don't do anything foolish."

He wanted to ignore her warnings and go after Tobias straight
away, but he couldn't. He had no idea where the Walker had
gone, and no tri-sextants with which to pursue the lad. For now,
wherever he Spanned he would arrive naked, alone, and unarmed.

And he knew his first Span would have to be to Qaifin, and the
court of Pemin, autarch of Oaqamar. He couldn't imagine a worse
place to go without a weapon or the protection of his men.

After the healer left him, he did go to Lenna, out of necessity.

At her response to his knock, he entered her chamber, his gait
stiff and awkward.

She glanced up from the volume she was reading, and then set
it aside. "You're on your feet," she said, her tone brittle.

"Finally, yes. I'm sorry to disturb you, but I'm going to Qaifin
and I thought you should know. In case… Well, Pemin isn't going

to be happy with me."

"He needs you. He won't kill his finest assassin out of pique."

He found this oddly reassuring. They endured a strained silence.

"Anyway," he said. "I wanted to let you know."

"Thank you. Come here when you're back. I'll want to know...

how it went." *That you're alive.*

So much for reassurance.

From her chamber, he climbed to the castle ramparts and ordered the soldiers there away from him. Once he was alone, he stripped off his clothes and piled them neatly in a crenellation. He calibrated his sextant and aimed it.

It had been some time since he last Spanned any distance in this way. He had escaped the strand a few nights before, but that demanded only a quick jump to the castle, and his mind had been on his wounds rather than the Span itself. Over the previous turns, he had grown accustomed to the ease of Travel by tri-sextant, to remaining dressed, to carrying his weapons and arriving in the company of soldiers or his trained men. Before fleeing the strand that night, he had forgotten how jarring and isolating this primitive form of Spanning could be.

He thumbed the release and was jerked into the gap, his head snapping back, the sextant nearly torn from his grip. Wind abused his skin, seeming to carry shards of glass. Light and sound and smell assaulted him. His leg and back ached, the wounds chafed by that savage gale. He feared his scars would open again. Within moments he was desperate for the Span to end, though he knew he had hundreds of leagues to go.

The gap pounded at him, his senses under siege from every direction. He had Spanned great distances using a simple sextant, but rarely this far, and never so soon after sustaining such wounds. The ordeal stretched on. He could no longer say if he was upright, or even fully conscious. He felt he had slipped into a sort of trance, somewhere between wakefulness and oblivion.

When the gap dropped him onto an expanse of cobblestone, he toppled, rolled, and came to rest leaning against the wheel of a cart. Blinking against the blazing sun, he realized he was on the edge of a marketplace. Surrounded by people. Naked, scraped, and bruised. He clutched his sextant in one hand.

A young woman stepped out from the back of the cart, eyed him, and disappeared again. She spoke in low tones, and a fivecount later a man emerged from the same location. He was older, burly and tall. He dropped a blanket next to Orzili.

"Cover yourself up," the man said, the accent of Oaqamar sharpening his words.

At least he had reached the right isle.

The blanket was rough and moth-eaten, and it stank of horse, but Orzili wrapped it around his middle and stood, his legs unsteady.

He turned a slow circle and spotted the autarch's castle. Not as close as he had hoped, but not so far that he couldn't cover the distance.

"Thank you," he said. He nodded to the young woman behind the man. She barely glanced at him; the man frowned, but said nothing.

Oaqamarans, he remembered from past visits, didn't care for Northislers, particularly Travelers. Pemin himself had plenty working for him – Spanners and Crossers. No Walkers that Orzili knew of. Other than Lenna.

Pemin's subjects were a different matter. During previous visits to the autarchy, Orzili had heard others with his coloring called "gaaz demons," "shit-skins," and worse.

"If you'll be here for a time, I can return the blanket," he told the man.

The peddler wrinkled his nose. "Keep it."

Orzili didn't know if the man was disgusted by the blanket itself, or by the thought of reclaiming cloth that had touched a Northisler's skin. He didn't care to find out.

"Good day, then," he said, and walked away, carrying himself with as much dignity as circumstances allowed.

He followed a winding, ascending lane to the castle, drawing stares and more than a few gibes, none of them too barbed, and several that made him laugh.

"Hey! I once rolled dice with the same fella that fleeced you!"

"Did you used to be a horse?"

"A man with a pillow came by before. He went that way."

Guards stopped him at the gate, of course.

"You lost?" one asked, grinning at his companions.

"Before you say more," Orzili said, keeping his voice low, "you should know that my name is Quinnel Orzili. I'm a Spanner–" He held up his sextant, "–and a trusted agent of the autarch. His Excellency will want to know I'm here, and he'll expect to see me forthwith, clothed and shod."

Instantly, their bearing changed.

"Of course, my lord," another said. "We'll inform him of your arrival and find you clothes immediately." He nodded to the others, who scurried away.

Within a quarter bell, they'd found him a chamber and ministerial robes: black satin, trimmed in shades of brown and gold. From there they led him down a short corridor to the autarch's antechamber.

Floors of pink marble, curved walls adorned with works by Oaqamar's greatest artists, and grand wooden doors inlaid with exotic woods to create an image of a barred lion: the isle's sigil.

One of the guards knocked, and at a word from within opened the door and indicated that Orzili should enter.

He was weaponless, as always when in Pemin's presence. On this day, he felt especially vulnerable.

Pemin stood in the center of the chamber wearing plain garb: black breeches, a white satin shirt, and a sash embroidered in gold and brown. Most royals and nobles strove to outdo one another with ostentation: jewels, busts of themselves and their ancestors, crass art and weapons notable for their gaudiness rather than their practicality. Not Pemin. His chamber was simple, sparse, understated. This was a man who did not require finery to accentuate his authority. Indeed, his subtlety, and the confidence it conveyed, had impressed Orzili the first time they met, and remained the quality he most admired in the man. He was to those other leaders what a battle blade was to a gem-encrusted ornamental sword.

He was tall, lean, as elegant and graceful as a falcon. Pale gray eyes stared out from beneath a shock of straight brown hair, untouched by the smile on his lips.

Orzili bowed. "Your Excellency."

"Be welcome, Orzili," he said, extending a hand.

Orzili took it, pressed his brow to the back of it.

Pemin moved to one of several dun chairs near the hearth. He waved at another. "Join me, please."

Orzili followed him, waited to sit until the autarch had settled into his seat.

"I didn't expect you."

"No, Your Excellency. Please forgive the intrusion."

Pemin considered the robe Orzili wore. "One of mine, I see. You Spanned here?"

"Yes."

"By yourself. No tri-sextants."

It was offered as a statement. No doubt, guards had described for him the exact nature of Orzili's arrival.

This was the dark counterpoint to Pemin's royal bearing. He toyed with those who served him – ministers, Travelers, assassins – no doubt intent on reminding all, at every opportunity, that his was the keenest mind at any gathering.

"That is correct, Your Excellency."

"Out with it, then. Obviously you've failed me. What's happened?"

More direct than usual, that. Orzili tried to keep his pulse steady.

"The Walker has escaped."

The autarch waited, gaze unwavering.

"I fear he has Mearlan's child with him."

"A baby, and a boy cloaked in the body of a man – these two

proved too much for you?"

"They had help."

"An excuse?" Pemin demanded, voice rising.

"No, Your Excellency. This was my fault, and mine alone. I miscalculated."

"What of the tri-sextants?"

Orzili resisted the urge to look away. "One was destroyed, the other two were taken."

"Time and gold, wasted."

Orzili bit back his first response. "I apologize, Your Excellency. I fully intend to find the Walker and the princess."

"Is the woman still with you? The one from the Walker's true time?"

He wanted to lie, to tell Pemin that she had already Walked back to her future. He knew where the question might lead. He didn't dare, though, not even about this. There was no better measure of how much he feared the autarch.

"She is," he said.

"Why haven't you sent her back?"

"To what end, Your Excellency?"

Pemin glared. "To alter an unsatisfactory outcome!"

"She wasn't there, Your Excellency. She had nothing to do with the events of that night. Sending her back would not change the outcome."

It seemed he was willing to lie to the man after all. Because there were things Lenna could do. She could warn him, and thus compel him to bring more men to the strand. Had he Spanned with ten Sheraigh soldiers in addition to the men he had lost, he would likely have prevailed.

He had resisted doing this, unwilling to spend still more of her days. Eventually she would return to her own time – additional years together lost to both of them. She accused him of being cruel to his future self, and to the Lenna he loved in this time. The truth was, he sought ways to protect all of them. The damage done already was almost incalculable. He wouldn't compound it by sending her farther into the past.

He had reconciled himself to tracking down the Walker and Mearlan's child, knowing it might take him turns, or a year, or more. As long as it took, that was how long he might keep the older Lenna here in this time. She would spend those turns with him, away from his older self. But every day she spent with him was one day fewer she had to Walk back to her own time.

It was a ledger he never would have shared with Lenna, but one that allowed him to justify keeping her with him for another day, another turn.

His one advantage in speaking to Pemin of such things lay in his own knowledge of Traveling, and the autarch's ignorance of the finer points of being a Walker or a Spanner. With a bit of luck, and his superior understanding of Lenna's talent, he might survive this exchange.

"Why didn't you have her with you?" Pemin asked. He sounded less sure of himself than he had.

"This Lenna is aged, Your Excellency – from her own years and the Walk back. She isn't as young and capable as the Lenna I left in Kantaad. Her mind is nimble, her experience vast, but she wouldn't have been an asset in combat."

Another lie, though not one Pemin was likely to discover. Of course, Lenna would have been furious with him. Both Lennas.

"Couldn't she bring you word of what happened? Wouldn't that allow you to take precautions you ignored this first time?"

Maybe his advantage wasn't as great as he thought.

"Possibly, Your Excellency. If you insist, I will return to Daerjen and have her Walk back so that I can try again. It is a risk, of course. I barely escaped with my life this time. If I'm killed in a second attempt, you'll lose more than tri-sextants. You'll lose all that I know of the matter and any chance we might have to track them down quickly."

Pemin's frown narrowed his eyes, but he didn't argue the point. Orzili forged on.

"If instead, you allow me to dedicate all my resources to pursuit of the boy and the babe, I believe I can track them down before long."

Still looking displeased, Pemin said, "You'll need to have that Binder make you more tri-sextants."

"Yes, Your Excellency. That would be my first priority."

"Very well," Pemin said. "Before you return to Daerjen, though, I want you to dispatch the winged demons."

Orzili tried to conceal his distaste. And failed.

"This is not a negotiation, Orzili. For now at least, I will let you have your way with regard to the woman. I believe sending her back might yield more than you suggest, but there are other considerations, particularly when we're spending her years at such a rate. I might yet need to send her back to her time, and I want her to arrive there with strength enough to be of use to me." He paused, allowing what he'd said to sink in.

Orzili had been playing a more dangerous game than he knew.

"The Belvora are mine to command. As are you, lest you forget. I want them patrolling every sea and isle between the oceans. Do I make myself clear?"

He hated working with any demons, but the Belvora most of all. They were vicious and stupid, an unfortunate combination. Still, given the choice between employing the Belvora and sending Lenna farther back in time, he would always choose the demons.

"Of course, Your Excellency."

"Good. You will Span to the Sana and give them their orders. If you must, remind them of the protections I've offered their kind, and the cost to them of defying me." The autarch gave a small grimace. "You should stop here again before Spanning to Hayncalde. Report to my guards and let them know you've succeeded in contacting the demons." *And haven't been killed.* The words hung between them, unspoken but palpable. First Lenna and now Pemin. Everyone was so concerned for his safety. It might have been funny, had he not shared their fears. Treating with any Ancients carried risks, but the Belvora could be particularly difficult, especially for Travelers, whose magick the winged ones craved most.

"Yes, Your Excellency. I'll do that as well."

Pemin stood, forcing Orzili to do the same. Their conversation was over.

"I'm sure you understand the perils of failing me again."

"I do, Your Excellency. And so I won't."

"I'm glad to hear it." Pemin held out his hand. Orzili made obeisance and turned to go. Before he reached the autarch's door, Pemin spoke his name.

"You say you almost died?"

He should have known that revelation would capture the man's interest. "I did."

"The boy did this?"

"He's Windhome-trained, Your Excellency. He's also a full-grown man, despite his years."

Pemin's smile shaded toward a smirk. "I meant no offense. I was merely curious."

"Of course, Your Excellency. He managed to stab me, and then to shoot me. The bullet struck nothing vital, or else I might not have survived."

"How fortunate for us all that you did."

He said it with mischief in his eyes, but sincerity in his voice. Orzili wasn't sure how to respond and so chose the safest path.

"You're too kind, Your Excellency."

He let himself out of the chamber and climbed the nearest tower to the castle ramparts. Though he longed for his chamber in Daerjen, Pemin had made his desires clear. First he would Span to the Sana Mountains in central Oaqamar. The distance wasn't great, but he would have to confront the Belvora naked, weaponless. He didn't expect them to offer him a blanket.

CHAPTER 5

5th day of Kheraya's Stirring, year 634

This venture into the gap was nothing compared to the last. A few moment's discomfort and it was over.

He emerged from the wind, light, and din onto a sloped field covered with fragments of sharp, gray rock. The shards bit at his bare feet. His skin pebbled in a cold wind. Jagged, snow-crusted peaks loomed above him, bathed in golden sunlight. Below where he stood, shadows from the summits had already reached expanses of spruce and fir. Here, he saw only grass, low shrubs, and scattered wildflowers. A pair of ravens scudded past, their calls echoing off the surrounding cliffs. Overhead, a lone hawk circled on splayed wings.

The air smelled of snow and lupine, but the faintest hint of rotting meat rode the chill wind. Belvora lurked nearby. If he smelled them, they had already scented his magick. Best then to engage them and leave, before they began to stalk him.

"I would speak with the Winged Ancients," he called. The shadows and mountain air swallowed his words. He felt small and weak. He would have given a stack of gold rounds for clothes. Or better still, armor and a blade. Too late, he wondered if his wounds, and the residue of healer magick, would be to Belvora as blood to sharks.

He scanned the sky, but he also reset his sextant for the return to Qaifin and faced eastward. Belvora could not follow him into the gap. If this went poorly, he would Span himself out of danger.

He checked the sky again. Perhaps the demons weren't as close as he thought, or hadn't heard his summons. He was prepared to call a second time, when a lone flying figure wheeled into view high above the surrounding peaks. His heartbeat quickened.

Two demons soon joined the first. Then another, and two more. Within a spirecount, eight circled over him like buzzards. The first tucked its wings and commenced a swift, spiraling descent toward the basin in which he stood. The rest followed. Orzili set his thumb on the sextant's release, ready for the first sign of trouble.

The vortex of Belvora closed on him, as pale as ghosts, their translucent wings aglow with the blue of the mountain sky. The fetor of rot followed them down. As they neared the ground they pulled out of their glide, shifting the angle of their wings to catch the wind. They landed as lightly as birds and folded their wings close to their backs. Rock crunched beneath huge, clawed feet.

Orzili watched with alarm as they arrayed themselves in a circle around him. Their stench was overpowering. He tried not to let his disgust show.

They were taller than any human, with long sinuous arms that ended in taloned hands. Manes of hair – some gold, some silver – framed narrow faces. Their ears were long and pointed, their features blunt, their eyes large, amber, alert, like those of wild dogs.

They regarded him in silence, some grave, others with razor teeth bared in grins. Wind stirred their shining hair. Orzili shivered.

A blade, he realized, would have done him no good. Neither would a pistol or musket. He needed his men; he needed tri-sextants. Once again he cursed Tobias and the woman with him, who had been clever enough to shoot a tri-sextant out of the grasp of one of Orzili's assassins.

"We are not accustomed to being summoned by prey," one of the Belvora said, her voice like the shriek of a forest owl.

The others laughed.

"I'm not prey," Orzili said with as much force as he could muster.

"You smell like prey. You certainly look like prey. I see nothing in you that could keep us from making you prey."

"Kill me, and the autarch will send a thousand men to slaughter you, as your kind have been slaughtered elsewhere."

That appeared to give the demons pause.

"You come from the autarch?" the Belvora asked. She was taller than the others, with hair like burnished silver and talons as long as Orzili's little finger.

"I do. He has a task for you and your brethren."

The demon shifted her gaze to the male beside her and then to the others.

"He offers payment?" she asked, her eyes finding his again.

"Your quarry ought to be payment enough: two Walkers, and a human child."

A murmur passed through the demons, words he didn't understand circling him like wolves.

"Where are they, these Walkers?"

"We don't know. You will have to search for them. They could be anywhere between the oceans."

"Such a quest will demand that we leave this place, perhaps for many turns. Two Walkers is scant payment for so much effort."

"And the child," Orzili reminded. "The autarch grants you refuge here, protection from others who wish to see your kind wiped out. This is small recompense for all he has done."

The other Belvora muttered again, the sound more menacing this time.

"Bold words from a puny, naked human," Silver-Hair said, her lip curling.

"I'm merely repeating what the autarch told me to say. I think you'll agree that he and his army have proven themselves capable of backing up bold claims."

Her features resolved into a scowl. "Still, we tire of feeding on goats and elk and bear. Humans are rare up here. And Travelers are rarest of all."

This last she said with too much ardor for his taste.

"Then this hunt will be a boon to you." He kept his voice level, refusing to show fear. "You may feast along the way. The autarch cares only that you find the Walkers and the child."

The Belvora glanced past him again. Her quick, malicious grin froze his heart.

"You have your orders," he said. "The autarch will expect you to follow them."

He didn't wait for a reply, but raised his sextant and pressed the release. The Belvora lunged. Stone shifted and scraped behind him. But the gap sucked him forward before they could touch him. As he entered the storm of light and sound, he thought he heard screams of thwarted hunger.

Orzili emerged from the gap onto the ramparts of Pemin's castle. He reclaimed the robes he had been given and returned to the autarch's chamber, where he told Pemin of his encounter. He omitted mention of those final harrowing moments.

This second audience with the autarch didn't last long. Soon he was atop the castle again, preparing for his long Span back to Daerjen. The sun hung close to the western horizon and the air had cooled so that even here, far from the mountains, the breeze raised bumps on his skin.

He thumbed himself into the gap, submitting once more to the torment. The journey back across the seas stretched interminably. When he reached Hayncalde Castle, his legs gave out and he fell into a stone wall, scraping his cheek and wounded leg. He gasped at the pain.

"Here."

A satin wrap settled around him. Lenna loomed over him in the gloaming. Judging from the light, it must have taken him close to a bell to Span back.

"Thank you," he mumbled.

He tried to stand, but she laid a hand on his arm. "Stay there. You're not ready to walk."

"I've Spanned before, Lenna."

"That far? Twice in a day? After being stabbed and shot?" She softened the questions with a smile. "You may be young, but you're not that young."

His mind cleared slowly. "You've been waiting for me?"

"I knew how weary you'd be." She brushed a strand of hair from his brow.

His heart raced much as it had in the Sana, and yet nothing like that at all. "Why are you being nice to me?"

She stared, then shook her head and laughed. "You really are a fool, aren't you? I'm being nice because I love you. I have for most of my life. Just because I don't wish to be bedded by this particular version of you doesn't mean I love you any less. You should understand that."

He could think of no reply.

"You were gone a long time," she said, breaking a short silence.

"He sent me to the Sana." He spoke without thinking, without any consideration of where the comment would lead.

"Whatever for?"

He hesitated, allowing her to answer her own question.

"Blood and bone," she whispered. "The Belvora. You told him we didn't need the bloody winged bastards?"

"I tried. He didn't give me a choice." One more lie. What else could he say? *It was either that or spend more of your days.* He knew what kind of response that would bring.

She considered him, her forehead bunching. Perhaps she didn't need him to lead her there.

"I'm surprised he didn't order you to send me back with a warning." The words were pointed.

"The idea came up," he said, skirting the truth. "He prefers not to have you Walk any more than necessary. He said, 'I may need to send her to her own time. I want her to arrive with strength enough to be of use to me.' Or something like that."

Lenna scowled. "The two of you should stop coddling me. I know better than both of you what I can and can't do. Let me Walk as I'm supposed to."

"You should sail to Qaifin and tell Pemin yourself. I'm sure he'll enjoy being chastised by one of his assassins."

She looked to the side, lips pressed thin. After a fivecount, she surrendered to a smile.

"Maybe I'll send a message by bird. A ship would be too slow."

Orzili laughed. He braced a hand on the stone and pushed himself up. Lenna stood with him.

"All right?"

His vision spun, but he nodded. "Fine."

She walked him to his quarters, lingering in the hallway as he opened the door and stepped inside.

"My thanks. That was a nicer welcome than I expected."

"Of course."

A pause. Then they both started to speak at once. They stopped, laughed.

"You first," he said.

"We should begin our search for them tomorrow. In earnest. I have no intention of ceding this kill to the Belvora. We started it, you and I. We should be the ones to finish it."

He nodded.

"What were you going to say?"

"That exact thing." The truth.

She started away. "Good. I'll see you at dawn bells."

He snored beside her, and had for much of the night, despite kicks to his ankles and elbows to his side. The man slept like the dead. If the dead could shake the rafters.

Gillian had loved him once. Not so very long ago, when she was still taken with his intellect and reserved sophistication, she had thought that Bexler Filt might make a fine husband. With both of them serving the Daerjeni court, and both of them collecting gold on the side for their work on behalf of Oaqamar's autarch, they would never want for anything.

The autarch, however, had plans of his own, plans he did not share with them. Valuable though they might have been, they were minor nobles. Pemin, on the other hand, was the most powerful man between the oceans, and he had moved against Mearlan IV, who might have been the second most powerful. They were fortunate not to have been crushed in the ensuing conflict.

She longed to be summoned to a court, somewhere. She enjoyed the intrigue, the excitement of being at the center of events. She enjoyed playing at deception. She was good at it.

Yet, for now – and this galled her – Bexler was the more prized of the two of them. Without him, she was just another woman of status in a city still reeling from the assault that killed Mearlan and made Noak sovereign. The Sheraigh Assertion, they called it. She and Bexler had gold, and this small but comfortable flat, because he was one of the few Binders in all of Islevale who knew how to construct tri-devices.

So she put up with his snoring, and his uninspired lovemaking, and his pedantic nonsense.

After she had left Bexler in their shelter in the Notch with Tobias holding a flintlock to his head and a rope around his neck, she feared she had lost him for good. She apologized repeatedly, begging him to understand. She told him how frightened she had been, how certain that they would both die if she remained.

His frosty anger lasted all of a day and a night. She had long been amazed at the ease of seducing a man into forgiveness.

Still, it bothered her that she needed him so much more than she wanted him. She had to find some way to make herself indispensable to the autarch and his men.

She wasn't a Binder. She didn't possess any powers. Except she was clever, and fearless, and men of a certain sort responded well to her attention. Surely Pemin or Noak would have some use for her.

Bexler's breathing stuttered, tipped over into a snort. He stirred, his eyes fluttered open. She pasted a smile on her lips.

"Good morning, love."

He muttered a response, rose, and lurched into the next room, where he relieved himself into a pot. Charming.

A noise from the front of the flat made her sit up. A scratching at the door. Gillian swung out of bed, shrugged on a robe, and hurried into the common room. A folded piece of parchment had been slipped under the door. She turned the key, peered out into the corridor. It was empty, though she heard footsteps on the stairway. She closed and locked the door again, picked up the parchment.

Sextants lost. Three needed. Bring to castle.

"What does it say?"

She turned. Bexler stood in the doorway to their bedroom, his hair disheveled, but his eyes alert.

"They need new sextants. Apparently several have been lost."

"What?"

He crossed the room in a few lumbering strides, tore the scrap of parchment from her hand, and scanned it himself.

"Three? They lost three?" His voice rose. "Do they think I dig these devices out of the ground like turnips?" He closed his fist around the parchment and spun away.

Gillian followed Bexler across the front chamber, which he had claimed as a workroom. He stood at his bench, hands on his hips, staring at a half-completed tri-sextant, the only one he had.

"Three sextants," he said, exhaling the words. "I don't even have the materials. This will take the better part of a turn. At least."

She sensed an opportunity. Bexler was right: losing three sextants in so little time was unusual. Something must have gone wrong for the Sheraighs, or their allies. Perhaps Tobias and his friend had proven themselves a match for agents of the new sovereign. Maybe they needed more than Bound devices.

"How long until you finish this one?"

Bexler didn't look her way. "Not long. I can finish it today. That's not the difficulty. As I said—"

"Materials. Yes, I understand. Finish this one. I'll take it to the castle when you've finished. A promise of more to come. In the meantime we need gold for this one in order to buy what we need for the others."

This did draw his gaze. "Do you think they'll pay?"

"They will if they want the sextants promptly."

A bit of the tension drained from his face. He was actually handsome in a drab way. On those rare occasions when he wasn't mired in despair. "Yes, of course. They need us."

"That's right."

"Perhaps I should talk to them. Explain what it will take to make the devices."

"You have no time to talk to them, darling." She smiled. "As I meet them, you'll be toiling on their behalf, building and Binding the devices they so desperately need."

He considered this. "You're right. That would be better."

"Get to work on this one," she said. "I'll fix us breakfast and then I'll go into the lanes for a time. I want to know what's happening."

"Is that wise? There are still those in the city who would recognize us."

"Trust me." She felt revived, as if roused from a long, uninterrupted slumber. Since fleeing the Notch, they had been confined to this bloody flat. No more. She had purpose again, and it seemed her renewal had infected him as well. He sat, took up his loupe and the tri-sextant. A cloud of glowing Binder magick wreathed him.

Gillian retreated to their chamber, pausing in the doorway when she spotted the pigeons they had taken from the castle. Three of them, cooing softly in a cage near the shuttered window.

A glance back at Bexler confirmed he was fully absorbed in his work.

She tore a narrow strip of parchment and took up a quill. *Word of lost sextants received,* she scrawled. *Will come this evening. Inform guards. Must talk.*

She removed a brown and white dove from the cage, tied her message to the bird's leg, and carried the creature to the window. "Home you go," she whispered, opening the shutters. She tossed the pigeon into the air. It flew off, angling north and west toward the castle, its wingbeats swift and determined. She watched until it vanished over a rooftop. Then she dressed and made her way to the small larder beside their hearth. She sliced bread, slathered it with butter and honey, and brought a piece to Bexler. The other she bit into herself. She also lit a fire and boiled water for tea.

All the while, her thoughts churned. She would start at the wharves, because workers and sailors had access to information that others did not. From there, she would go to the marketplace, where she would walk among peddlers and buyers, listening, chatting, and buying goods they truly did need.

She might learn something from guards at the castle as well, but she didn't dare visit there twice in a single day. As Bexler said, they had been known in the city: the talented young Binder and his wife, Mearlan's minister of protocol. Some had suggested that aside from Mearlan and Keeda themselves, no couple in Hayncalde wielded more influence within the court. Commoners might not recognize her, but even today, with the Hayncaldes swept from power, the closer she drew to the castle, the greater the likelihood that someone would.

Before she left, she would change clothes. She needed to be as plain as possible.

When the tea was ready, she brought Bexler his cup and dressed a second time. Not until she opened the door to leave the flat did he look up from his tri-sextant, magick clinging to him like dew to grass.

"Where are you going?"

"The wharves and the market. I'll find out what's happened."

"Yes, all right." Already he was intent on the device again. He did love his work. Too bad he couldn't be so attentive to all his passions.

She spent the better part of a bell wandering along the waterfront, chatting with sailors, feigning interest in news from other isles, feigning attraction to men and women of all ages and origins. She learned precious little. Most of those she met had as many questions as she did. The most exciting tidings in Islevale still came from Hayncalde, and still revolved around the ease with which Noak had taken the sovereignty for Sheraigh.

"Do you know how he did it?"

"How many men did he bring?"

"Is it true he commanded an army of demons?"

She would have laughed had she not been so frustrated.

The marketplace proved more fertile ground, but only just. Few people here knew any more than she did of what transpired the night Mearlan died.

One older man, a peddler of blades both short and long, did tell her that not long before her own encounter with Tobias, a woman from the sanctuary and three men of a less savory nature died near the wharves. The woman was killed by a crossbow. The men's deaths were more difficult to explain.

"Shriveled up, weren't they?" the man told her. "Like fruit left in the sun for too long."

"How would that have happened?"

"How indeed?" he said, with a keenness that told her he had an idea. He leaned closer, his breath stinking of fish and stale ale. "Demons, if you ask me."

She tried to hide her disappointment. Apparently she failed.

His expression ossified. "You think I'm lying. Or mad."

"No, I–"

"You don't live and trade in the lanes of a port city for as long as I have, without learning a thing or two about time demons. And I'm telling you, that's who did this."

Gillian stared back at him. That she did believe. She had heard of Tirribin, but had been fortunate never to encounter one. They were said to be vicious and canny. They were also drawn to Walkers, not for sustenance, but for companionship. Had Tobias allied himself with one of the creatures? And might the Sheraighs and Pemin's men be interested to know about it?

She bought a small jeweled blade from the man – it was more bauble than weapon, but it sparkled in the morning sun, and he had proven himself useful.

The other peddlers she met had less to offer. A little past midday, she reentered the flat with fresh bread, more honey, the last winter berries they were likely to find this year, and a carafe of Fairisle white.

Bexler wasn't there, but the tri-sextant sat on his workbench. She guessed that he had already finished it, and was making arrangements for additional materials. His single-mindedness had its advantages.

She took up parchment and quill and began to write out what she would say to whomever she met in the palace. She couldn't leave this conversation to chance, and she performed better when she organized her thoughts.

Bexler returned nearly two bells later, arriving in an ill temper. Apparently he would have to wait a ha'turn for the first arcs to reach Hayncalde, and another qua'turn after that for enough of them to complete two tri-sextants. In the interim, Gillian knew, he would be impossible to live with: more incentive to ingratiate herself with people in the castle. If she remained in the flat for all that time, her boredom might well prove fatal for at least one of them.

"Is this one finished?" she asked him, interrupting a tirade about the incompetence of ministers, and the value of tri-sextants.

"Yes, it's ready. I have nothing to do for... for days upon days."

He flounced to a chair near the hearth and dropped himself into it, a boy in a man's body.

"Can't you work on tri-apertures?"

"I suppose, but to what end? They don't need those."

"Not now, perhaps. They might before long."

Bexler nodded. His gaze roamed the chamber, restless. Eventually it settled on her, and his mien shifted in a way she recognized too well.

"You know," he said, smiling, "as long as we've nothing to do—"

"You have nothing to do. I have plenty. I'll be leaving for the castle before long. In the meantime, I'd suggest you get to work on those apertures. If nothing else, we can sell them for food money, until some other noble has need of our services."

He frowned, putting her in mind again of a fifteen year old boy.

"What is that you're writing?"

"Nothing you need be concerned about."

He turned away, sulking. She couldn't have cared less. She penned a few more lines and studied what she had written. Finally, she rose, folded the parchment, and set it on the coals in the hearth. It blackened, smoked, and curled. After a spirecount it burst into flames and shriveled to ash.

She sensed Bexler watching her.

"Maybe I should come with you to the castle."

"That isn't necessary."

"I know that, but it might be a good idea just the same. The sun will be setting before long. Even if you leave right now—"

"Yes, I'm about to go."

"Right. That means you won't be back until after dark."

She laughed. "And you intend to protect me?"

He scowled at her from his chair. "You needn't be cruel."

Gillian sighed, feeling a twinge of regret. Perhaps she had gone too far. She knelt before him and took one of his hands in her own. His hands were his best feature. They were large and strong and yet surprisingly gentle. She laced her fingers through his and kissed the back of his hand.

"You're right, love. Forgive me. I promise to be careful navigating the lanes on my way home. But I believe this is a conversation I should have on my own. You are, for all your gifts, not the most skilled of diplomats, and this might take some tact."

He frowned still, clearly not mollified. "Very well." His eyes met hers and darted away. "Shall I wait to have supper?"

He was asking for more, she knew.

She swallowed her distaste and fixed a smile on her lips. She might still need him, even after her coming audience at the castle. "That could be quite pleasant," she said.

Abruptly, he looked so pleased. It was pathetic really.

Gillian kissed his hand again, released him, and stood.

The flat had cooled with the approach of evening. It would be colder still in the streets. She donned a shawl, retrieved the tri-sextant, and slipped it into a rough cloth sack.

"Fourteen rounds for that, Gillian. More if you can get it. Certainly no less. I spent seven on materials alone, plus the time it took."

She faltered before saying, "All right." It was a lot of gold, more than she imagined the Sheraighs would want to pay.

"Are you sure you don't want me to come with you?"

"I'll be fine." She let herself out of the flat without saying more. The moment she closed the door, she breathed easier. Just being around him darkened her mood.

She wound through the lanes, need of him creeping up on her again. She had laughed at his offer of protection, but as she approached the castle her trepidation deepened. Guards patrolled the streets nearest the fortress in groups of six and eight, all of them carrying swords and muskets. Many of them eyed her with suspicion. Others leered. Bexler wouldn't have intimidated any of them, but at least she wouldn't have been alone.

As she came within sight of the castle's main gate, more soldiers planted themselves in her path and leveled their weapons.

"What are you doing here?" one of them asked. She might have been about Gillian's age, but that was all they had in common. The soldier was squat and powerfully built, with a round, ruddy face, and small, widely spaced eyes. Like the others, she wore a stiff uniform of Sheraigh blue.

"I'm on my way to the castle."

"Clearly. Why?"

"I've an audience."

"With whom?"

The flaw in her plan. "Someone brought a message to my flat today. I replied by dove. The gate guards should know I'm on my way. My name is Gillian Ainfor. I used to be minister of protocol. I'm married to the Binder, Bexler Filt."

"Used to be," the woman repeated. "You worked for Mearlan?"

"Both of us did. We were agents of Sheraigh in the court." She was reasonably certain that their gold had come from Oaqamar, but this didn't seem the time to confuse matters with unnecessary details.

"I see. What's in the sack?"

She hesitated. Tri-sextants were valuable, and soldiers had been known to supplement their poor pay by any means possible. On the other hand, they couldn't allow her into the castle without knowing what she carried.

"Something I was asked to bring. I'll be happy to let the gate guards inspect it."

The commander didn't appear pleased, but she dipped her chin in agreement. "You'll come with us."

She and her soldiers escorted Gillian the rest of the way to the gate. The guards there had indeed been expecting her. They peered into the sack and asked if she was armed. She produced the jeweled blade, drawing smirks. Still, they treated her with courtesy and soon two men led her into the fortress, to the middle ward, and finally to a chamber along a corridor not far from where she and Bexler once lived.

One of the soldiers knocked and, at a word from within, indicated that she should enter. Gillian inhaled, the way she imagined a Walker might before stepping into the between, and entered the chamber.

CHAPTER 6

6th day of Kheraya's Stirring, year 634

A man sat near the hearth, dark skin warmed by the glow of his fire and a host of candles arrayed around the chamber. He remained seated, but Gillian could tell that he was tall and well-proportioned. He wore soldier's garb: black breeches and a rough blue shirt. A sword hung from one side of his belt, a flintlock from the other. His eyes were hazel, his hair bronze and long, framing a square face. He might have been the most beautiful man she had ever seen.

She tore her eyes from him and scanned the rest of the chamber, which was large and generously appointed with chairs and a table, a desk, a broad bed, a wardrobe. Paintings and tapestries adorned the walls. The air was redolent of bay. Gillian couldn't recall whose chamber this had been, but it suited this man well.

"You're the Binder?" he asked, his voice a warm baritone.

She shook her head, gaze settling on him again. "The Binder's wife."

His smile brightened the chamber. "Surely more than that."

Gillian blushed. She blushed! When was the last time any man had warmed her cheeks so?

"I was also minister of protocol under Mearlan, and an agent of the autarchy within his court."

The man sobered. "You work for Pemin?"

"We did. We were his contacts within the sovereignty."

He weighed this. "Then I'm indebted to you." He stood, walked to her and proffered a slender, long-fingered hand. "Quinnel Orzili."

She gripped his hand, which was warm, the palm calloused. "Gillian Ainfor."

With a lift of his chin, he indicated the sack she held. "Is that for me?"

"It is if you're a Spanner, but I'm afraid it's not all you're waiting for." She handed it to him.

He frowned and peered within.

"One tri-sextant is about as useful as a single boot."

"I know. Losing three tri-sextants at one time is somewhat unusual."

His glower chilled her, but he couldn't maintain it for long. "True," he said, his tone more subdued than she had expected. He carried the tri-sextant back to his chair, sat, and gestured for her to join him at the hearth.

Gillian followed and took the chair to his left.

"Your husband is working on the others?"

"He finished this one only a few bells ago, and made arrangements earlier today to purchase materials for the others. But Binding takes time. Securing the necessary metals takes time. And the latter takes gold as well."

His smile returned, bitter. "Of course. How much time? How much gold?"

"He said it would take a turn."

Orzili sat forward. "A turn?"

"He was adamant."

He closed his eyes and rubbed a hand over his brow. "And the gold?"

"Fourteen rounds for this one. I expect the price for the others will be the same."

"Yes, all right."

That was all. No argument. No bargaining. She wondered if Bexler had directed her to ask for too little.

Gillian sensed that in another instant, Orzili would give her the rounds and send her away. She wasn't ready for their conversation to end.

"How did you lose them?"

Anger hardened his features again. Maybe a less pointed approach would have served her better.

She pushed on. "It was Tobias, wasn't it? He nearly killed Bexler and me."

Genuine surprise widened the man's eyes. "When was this?"

"Not long ago. A day or two before the Goddess's Emergence."

He let out a dry chuckle and shook his head. "I ascribed much of what happened to fortune – his good, mine bad. Maybe there was more to it. Maybe there was more to him."

"So it was Tobias."

"Yes. And the woman who was with him."

"A Traveler as well?"

"Probably," he said. "She had the look of one. You encountered her, too?"

"Yes. She's a Walker, and a Spanner. She followed him back through time. I think they're in love."

His glance sharpened at this. "We had more in common than I knew." He spoke under his breath, so that she barely heard. "What else can you tell me about him?" he asked her.

"I know how far back he came. How many years."

"So do I," Orzili said, his voice flat. "What else?"

She hadn't expected that. "Well… I think he might have been working with Tirribin."

"What makes you say that?"

Gillian related what the peddler had told her earlier that day.

"Interesting," he said. "Thank you." He gripped the arms of his chair. Again she thought her dismissal imminent.

"I can help you," she said. Too quick, too eager.

"You have already." He was humoring her.

"I can do much more. I served the autarch in Mearlan's court for more than a year. I'm smart, I'm brave, and I… I want to help." *I don't want to go back to that flat.*

He studied her until Gillian grew uncomfortable. Before he said anything, someone knocked at his door.

"Enter."

The door opened and a woman strode in, only halting when she spotted Gillian. She was older than both of them, but beautiful nevertheless, with coloring like his and long silken hair that cascaded over her shoulders to the small of her back.

Orzili stood. Gillian did as well.

"I'm sorry," the woman said. "I didn't know you had a guest."

"This is Gillian Ainfor," he said. "She was one of Pemin's operatives in Mearlan's court. Minister, this is Lenna Stenci."

"I'm pleased to meet you," Gillian said.

Lenna said nothing, but stared, her dark eyes wide and troubled. "One of Pemin's... How long were you...?" She broke off, shaking her head. "Never mind. Forgive me. It's a pleasure to meet you as well."

Orzili watched the woman, lines in his brow.

"Her husband is the Binder," he said. "It seems we'll have to wait a turn for our tri-sextants."

"I'm afraid it can't be helped," Gillian added.

The woman appeared discomfited, confused. "Yes, of course."

"Lenna—"

"I'll come back later." She pivoted and stepped to the door. "It was nice to meet you."

"And you."

She let herself out of the chamber and closed the door behind her. Orzili gazed after her.

"What would you do?" he asked.

"I'm sorry?"

He faced her. "You wish to work with us. What would you do?"

"What do you need?"

"I don't know," he said. "I need to find Tobias, and the child he spirited away from here. But you're known to him. I assume you're neither a Walker nor a Spanner. You'll be of little help to us in our pursuit of the boy. So I'm asking, what would you do?"

He didn't give her time to think.

"Can you kill?"

"I- I don't know."

He shook his head. "Then you probably can't."

"I'm a spy," she said, knowing it for truth as she spoke the words. "I can win people's trust. I can lie convincingly. And I'm discreet enough to avoid detection and capture."

"Valuable skills, if I didn't already have access to all the information I need."

"Here you do. What about elsewhere?"

"You and your husband would be willing to leave Hayncalde?"

"I'd be willing to leave."

His look heated her cheeks again. "I see."

"He would need to remain anyway. He has tri-sextants to build and deliver."

"Yes, of course." He scrutinized her with frank appraisal – her visage, and then her form. Her embarrassment deepened. "I can see where you might be quite useful," he said.

"I'm so glad," she shot back with asperity.

"You offered your services as a spy, and spoke of winning people's trust. Surely you understand that your beauty would be a valuable tool in that regard."

Of course she did. And yet…

"I understand well enough," she said. "That doesn't mean I'm willing to be treated like a horse at market."

"Very good, minister. You have backbone as well as looks. That bodes well."

She shook her head, feeling unbalanced and overmatched.

"I'm not sure yet where to send you. I have ideas, but need to speak of this with Lenna, and others. I take it I can reach you the same way I did today."

"Yes, but… please keep your messages cryptic. Bexler thinks I'm here only to sell you a tri-sextant and inform you of the delay in delivering the others."

Orzili nodded. If he said, "I see" again, in that same presumptuous tone, she would scream.

He didn't.

He started toward the door, forcing Gillian to follow. "Thank you for coming," he said. "This has been a most illuminating conversation."

She said nothing, taken aback. Didn't he mean to pay her?

He smirked. "Forgive me. Your gold, of course." He crossed to his desk. "I hope you're better at concealing your emotions when your life hangs in the balance."

She swallowed the first retort that came to mind. "I am," she said.

He opened a small pouch, counted fourteen rounds, and held them out to her. She joined him at the desk and he dropped the gold into her open palm.

"When the time comes, regardless of where I send you, I'll provide you with coin."

"Thank you." She slipped the rounds into her purse and returned it to the folds of her gown.

Orzili stepped to the door, opened it, and beckoned to someone in the corridor. A guard halted before him.

"See Minister Ainfor to her home," he said. "You are personally responsible for her well-being."

"Yes, my lord."

She joined Orzili at the doorway.

"Until next we meet, my lord."

"Until then."

The guard led her away from the chamber, and she was content to follow, the gold heavy in her pocket, her spirits lighter than they had been in days.

Lenna stood by her hearth, arms crossed, eyes on the fire. Her heart labored, and had since he introduced her to the minister. The woman's presence here shouldn't have unsettled her so. She was being weak, foolish. She might hold any number of people accountable for the years she had lost. She could blame Pemin, or Mearlan, or the Walker she had followed. She could blame Orzili, and herself most of all. The minister bore responsibility for none of this.

Yet Lenna couldn't help herself.

A single rap on her door made her start. It had to be him. No one else ever disturbed her.

"Yes, come," she said, remaining where she was.

He entered the chamber, closed the door softly. Her glance his way was fleeting.

"Are you all right?" he asked, moving to stand beside her.

"Who is she?"

The baldness of the question made him hesitate. "I told you."

"Gillian Ainfor. Pemin's operative. Yes, I heard all of that."

"And the Binder–"

"I heard that, too. What was she doing here?"

"Why do you care?"

She tried again to ease her breathing, her pulse. Failed. "I shouldn't tell you."

"Shouldn't... What did I–"

"Not because of anything you did. It relates to my time, your future. You shouldn't know."

He waited.

What did it matter, this crumb of information? It wasn't history altering. "Pemin's operative," she said again. "In my future, there was still an operative in Mearlan's court. And the handwriting... The message that told me – us – how far back I would have to go... It was written in a woman's hand."

Orzili let out a breath, and whispered her name. He started to reach for her, but she flinched away. His hands dropped to his sides.

"Even if it was her," he said, firelight in his eyes, "she wouldn't have been responsible. She was a spy, nothing more."

"I know that." She rubbed one arm, unable to get warm. "Forget I mentioned it."

"She wants to spy for us."

Lenna turned. "Do you trust her?"

"I do. Her husband ought not to, but that's not our problem." He smiled; she frowned. He waved off the remark. "It doesn't matter. She strikes me as clever, competent. I think she can help us. I just don't know where to send her."

Away from here. Somewhere I won't see her.

"She's willing to go anywhere?"

"I believe so. I'd like to send her to Pemin's court. It would be useful to have a spy there."

"Why don't you?"

"Because Pemin is too intelligent, and she lacks experience. She'd be dead within a turn, and we wouldn't last much longer."

He lowered himself into the nearest chair, wincing. She should have asked how his wounds were healing, but she'd forgotten. She had never thought of him as someone who could be wounded. Foolishness again. Anyone could be hurt. Anyone could be killed. She thought she had shed all illusions about such things when she Walked back to this time.

"Besides," he went on, "our greatest concern should be finding Tobias and the princess."

"Aiyanth, then," she said. "If we're right about the boy needing a chronofor, that's where he's likely to go. That's where *I* would go."

"I agree. But Tobias knows her. And apparently he knows she betrayed Mearlan."

"That doesn't matter. If she's all you seem to think she is, she can establish herself there and cultivate others to help her."

"Yes, all right."

She felt him watching her, but kept her gaze on the fire. She wished he would go. The silence between them deepened, and Lenna made no effort to fill it. After a spirecount, he stood and smoothed his shirt with an open hand.

"I'll leave you. I'm sorry her presence here upset you."

"You couldn't know it would. I wouldn't have known."

That was all she said. Still she didn't face him. He let himself out of her chamber.

Only then did it occur to her to wonder how employing Gillian Ainfor might change his need for her. Did this mean she could go back to her time sooner? Or would she have to wait? He'd said something earlier about the Binder needing a full turn to deliver new tri-sextants. Would she have to wait for that, too?

Anger welled inside her. Orzili didn't want her to go; he would do everything in his power to keep her here. He spoke of protecting her, of refusing to spend more of her years and preserving what little time they had together in their shared future. Mostly he wished to keep her here because he had convinced himself that he was in love with her.

An irony, because she was deeply in love with the older Orzili. This one she didn't trust. A part of her wished to travel to Fanquir to warn her younger self. Another part knew doing this would create problems that might cause ramifications through the rest of her life.

She slipped a hand into the pocket of her gown, her fingers closing around the cool metal of her chronofor. She pulled it out, held it in her palm. The flicker of her fire illuminated the three circles on its face, the golden stems jutting from its edge.

Lenna was acting on her decision before she knew she had made it. If she initiated the Walk in this chamber she would surely encounter herself, and, assuming the tales of Walkers meeting themselves in the past were to be believed, even a few days' difference might endanger her sanity. Then again, only in this chamber would she find suitable clothing upon her arrival. She thought back to the days before the Emergence. She had passed a good deal of time cloistered here. She had also walked the castle grounds, for bells at a time on occasion. If she could recall the exact day, the exact time, she might Walk to this chamber, dress, and slip away without meeting herself.

Her days here had blurred in her memory. All of them were so similar, she could scarcely separate them. She closed her eyes, and again wrapped her fingers around the chronofor.

She had been more inclined to leave her chamber in the days before Tobias's escape, had in fact enjoyed wandering the castle. After, as she came to realize that Orzili might keep her here indefinitely, she had grown despondent, lethargic. She counted back. Eleven days, then. Perhaps twelve to be safe.

At that time, she also took her meals elsewhere, including her midday meal. In the kitchen or one of the halls. Even in the gardens. If she arrived near to that time, she ought to be all right.

Opening her eyes again, she set the device. Twelve days and seven bells. Not an insignificant interval to Walk, but a trifle compared to what she had endured coming back to this time. She would Walk the twelve days, warn Orzili of the boy's escape, and return to this time. Briefly. With the escape prevented, he would have no reason to keep her here. She could Walk forward to her true time, fourteen years in the future.

She crossed to the door, locked it, and returned to the warmth of her fire, where she unbuttoned her bodice and slipped out of her gown and undergarments. She checked the settings on her chronofor, took a deep breath, and pressed the central stem.

A sudden, violent tug into a world of light, foul smells, vile flavors on her tongue, dissonant assault on her ears. And, of course, no air.

The secret to surviving the between was resisting panic. She fought for calm now. It was a short Walk, she told herself. She would experience nothing like the suffocating ordeal she had endured Walking to this time. A tencount or two and it would be over.

The battering of her senses stretched on. The pressure in her chest built until the breath she had taken spent itself. She squinted against frenzied images, tried to close her mind to the clamor of voice and footstep and rattling carriage.

Unable to stop herself, she released her breath and tried to take another. Panic after all. Had she miscalculated?

In the next instant, she collapsed to her knees on the smooth stone of her floor. She sucked greedily at blessed air, relief bringing tears to her eyes.

She forced herself into motion. Her calculations and memory had served her well. The chamber was empty. For the moment.

Standing, weathering a crashing wave of dizziness, she staggered to the wardrobe. He had arranged for gowns to be made for her. There was an aqua one she wore often and would miss. The blue one was gone; she must have been wearing it. Dark red had never been one of her favorites. The other her wouldn't notice its absence. She dressed hurriedly, chose a pair of cloth shoes that she had yet to wear, and tiptoed to the door.

She listened before easing it open. Seeing the corridor empty, she left the chamber and stole to Orzili's quarters. Her knock brought no response. She let herself in. A risk, but a small one. She hadn't accompanied this Orzili to his chamber since arriving in Hayncalde. Probably he was in the dungeon, trying to extract information from the Walker. He would come back here alone.

She sat near his shuttered window and waited.

A bell passed, and a second. She began to pace. After another half-bell, she wondered if something had happened to further upset their plans. Had her arrival here altered the flow of events in some way she hadn't anticipated? She studied the clothes she had taken, scanned the chamber. She had taken care not to disturb her surroundings – in her quarters or his. Still, her apprehension grew. He had trusted his men to torture the boy. He joined them for short periods, but never would have spent so long in the dungeon himself.

Had she arrived on the wrong day? Had the Walker already escaped?

Doubt gnawed at her. Questions plagued her. And a single thought echoed in her mind: coming back by stealth, without anyone knowing, without *him* knowing, had been a mistake. She was certain of but one thing: if she reset her chronofor accounting for the bells spent here, she could Walk back to the time she'd left a short while ago. She would return to the safety of her locked room, the comforting glow of her fire. She would be trapped still in that past, but at least she would know with surety what had happened that day and the one before.

She crept back to the door, listened, opened it, and surveyed the corridor. No one.

She removed her shoes and scurried back to her chamber, her

footsteps silent, her breaths short and sharp.

She pushed the door open, checked the corridor one last time, and closed the door without so much as a click.

"What are you doing?"

She whirled, her heart vaulting into her throat. Her last clear thought was that she should have fled rather than turn.

Their eyes met. Dark brown and dark brown. Red gown and blue. Bronze hair unbound. Lines in their faces that hadn't been there a turn or two before.

Her thoughts fragmented. Something dropped from her hand. She couldn't recall what it was. She stared. A mirror image that didn't match her movements, her stance. Only fear. In that regard, the reflection was perfect.

She had needed to avoid this encounter. She couldn't remember why. Something about... about time. About the future or the past. About her and the woman before her and also the man – the one the world knew as Orzili.

"Blood and bone," whispered the woman staring back at her. "What in the name of the Two are you doing here?"

CHAPTER 7

18th Day of Kheraya's Waking, Year 634

Droë kept to shadows, following damp cobblestone past derelict shelters and the worn carts of peddlers, which served at night as homes and beds. A storm had moved through Rooktown earlier in the evening, dousing the lanes with warm rain. Lightning still flashed in the eastern sky, illuminating piled clouds from within. Her ears were keen enough to perceive the answering whispers of thunder, but she didn't think the humans around her could.

Any more than they could hear her.

Drunken laughter from behind stopped her, made her turn. She retraced her steps, silent as a hunting cat. Two men, far gone with drink. Had she been hungrier, she might have settled. But the other man she'd been following remained the more attractive prey: young, his years fresher than these two. She turned a second time, listened. Amid low conversations, quiet sobbing, more laughter, another roll of thunder, she heard his steps, quick and light.

She chased after, only to halt again on another sound she knew. Heavy breath, like a pig grunting over food, then a sudden taken breath. Passion, spent now. As fascinating as a riddle, as alluring as prey. More.

She followed the next alleyway, stepping with care. Seeing the couple in the faint glow of candlelight from an open window, she froze.

The woman – hardly more than a girl, really – leaned against the wooden slatting of a shop, adjusting her shift, smoothing her hair. A man, much older, heavy, a rough beard obscuring his face, hiked up his breeches and cinched his belt. The girl held out a hand and he dropped several coins into her palm. He spoke, slurring the words enough that Droë couldn't make them out, and laughed at his own joke. The girl didn't smile, but she pocketed the money.

Droë had seen this before. Passion without love, paid for. A transaction, akin to buying food in a market or a bauble from a traveling merchant. She watched as the man wandered off toward the far end of the byway, wondering which comparison was more apt. Was it survival, like food? Or a luxury, like the bauble? She considered asking the woman, who lingered by the shop wall, dug a hand into her pocket, and tallied the coins she found there.

Droë walked forward, less concerned with stealth now. The woman whirled. A knife glinted in her hand. Droë hadn't seen her draw it.

"Who's there?" She sounded scared.

"I'm not going to hurt you."

Droë stepped into the light. The woman lowered her blade hand.

"You gave me a start." She spoke with the drawling accent of the Ring Isles. Narrowing her eyes, she adjusted her shift again. "Did you see?"

Droë nodded. "Do you enjoy it?"

"Do I what?"

"What you just did. The act of love with that man. Do you enjoy it?"

The woman's laugh was dry as sand. "The act of- tha's not... A girl your age–"

"I'm older than I look."

"I'm not talkin' 'bout this with a child."

"I just want to know if you enjoy it. With a stranger. For coin."

The woman pushed a strand of hair back from her brow. She might have been pretty if her hair had been cleaned and combed, if she'd had decent clothes. Dark, open sores oozed on her cheek and her arms. A bruise darkened her temple. She shook her head.

"Nah, I don't enjoy it. Don't know any girls that do. Get off th' street if you can. If you're old enough to ask th' question, you're old enough for some fat bastard to fuck. Don't do it. Find another way. Steal if you have to. Don't do this."

"Then why do you?"

She lifted a shoulder, stared off to the side. "It's long past too late for me."

"Have you ever loved any of them?"

A smile flickered, here and gone like lightning. "Nah. If I had, I woulda held on with both hands."

She straightened, let the coins fall back into her pocket with the ring of silver and bronze. "But I can eat, can't I? And maybe even have an ale. Tha's somethin'."

"Yes," Droë answered, unsure of what else to say.

"I'm goin' now. Get home or wherever it is you pass the nights. It's late for someone so young to be prowlin' the lanes."

"Goodnight," Droë said. She considered feeding on the woman. She was younger than the man Droë had been following. Her years would have been sweet and plentiful. The woman didn't seem very happy with her life. She might not mind being taken.

After some thought, she chose to leave the woman alone and return to the lane she'd been following. The young man was long gone, of course, but she soon found another.

He wove along the cobbles, stumbling once or twice, but managing to keep his feet. She smelled ale on his breath from ten paces back, and could tell he was several years older than the other man. Still, he would do for now. Knowing Treszlish, the Shonla with whom she journeyed, this wouldn't be their last stop of the night.

She waited until he followed a bend onto a narrower lane and paused before a door. Drawing on her speed, she rushed him, latching onto his shoulders, toppling him to the street. He shouted, twisted, grabbed for her with strong, meaty hands. He might as well have tried to bend iron. As he struggled to push her off, she put her lips and teeth to his neck and drew the years from his blood. He stank of sweat and grime and drink, but his years were ripe enough.

When she had taken them all, she detached herself, intending to creep back onto the main street. People had heard his cry, though. Two of them stood at the corner, squinting into the shadowed lane. Droë pressed herself to the street, as still as stone, body coiled in case they spied her. She could take one of them, and probably scare off the other. She and the Shonla would be gone from this place before daybreak.

They didn't see her, and soon moved on. Droë returned to the waterfront.

Tresz floated over the harbor, a swirling, pale cloud. Droë assumed that a ship lay at the center of his mists. Shonla didn't take life, as Tirribin did, but they fed on fear and screams, sometimes music. Mist demons, the humans called them. The men on that ship would remember this night for a long time. Perhaps, in the future, they would take care to burn more torches.

A bell pealed in the city, from the temple of the Goddess. The appointed time.

Droë lifted her voice in song.

"Away on the sea, past the Axle and Ring,
Where the wind whistles high, and the sailor is king,
I sing for my love, of longing and sorrow,
And pray for a homeward wind on the morrow."

She'd sung the tune often in recent days. Shonla coveted songs, almost as much as Tirribin did riddles, and Tresz seemed to enjoy this one in particular. Droë liked it, too, mostly because it spoke of love in all its verses.

As the last strains of her singing died away, the distant cloud began to drift in her direction, its movement revealing the unfortunate vessel. The fog didn't appear to move quickly, but within moments it had surrounded her, replacing the warmth of Kheraya's storm with its bone-numbing chill.

Droë shivered and crossed her arms. She had been journeying with the Shonla for nearly two turns now, but had yet to grow accustomed to the cold of his mists. As her sight adjusted to the haze, she spotted Tresz, a solid, dark form at its center. Hairless, gray, with glowing eyes that always reminded her of stars peeking through cloud cover.

"I have eaten well," he said, the voice viscous, his thin, formless lips curved in a smile. "They had but one torch – easily obscured – and they were most vocal in expressing their fear. Quite satisfying."

"I'm glad."

"And you? Was your hunt successful?"

"Yes, it was fine."

"Fine," he repeated, drawing out the word. "A human expression that implies contentment without actually meaning it."

She shrugged.

"Do you care to try again? I will wait."

"No, it's all right. I fed."

"Very well."

He waved Droë forward with a squarish hand, stooped low so she could climb onto his back. His skin was cool and smooth, reptilian in its dry, silken feel. She settled in her usual position, clasped her arms around his neck, her legs around his waist.

"Ready?" he rumbled.

"Yes."

As much as she disliked the cold, as slow as had been their progress south from Trevynisle, she couldn't deny that she loved the sensation of flying with him in his cloud of mist. She felt weightless, free. Wind whipped through her hair and chilled her cheeks.

"If I may say so," Tresz said over the rush of air, "I sense in you… restlessness, discontent. Do you tire of our travels?"

She opened her mouth, closed it again, taken aback by the question, unsure of how to answer.

"I will take your silence as confirmation."

"It's not that I'm–"

He raised a hand, stopping her. "I do not take this as an affront. You grow weary of mists and meanderings. In many ways you are young still, impatient. I understand."

Tears blurred her sight.

"You came this way because of me," she said. "I don't want to abandon you so far from... from familiar waters."

The Shonla's growl of laughter tickled her chest.

"I have been pleased to journey beyond the familiar, and I have enjoyed your songs and your company. I am Shonla. I go where the wind takes me, and for centuries, before these past turns, I have done so alone. Do not weep for me, friend."

They drifted, wordless.

After some time, Tresz asked, "Shall I leave you at the next isle?"

"Not yet. Please. Soon, but I'm not ready."

"That is well. Soon. Whenever you wish."

She nodded, though she knew he couldn't see.

"In the meantime, I would enjoy more verses of the song you used to summon me. If I can trouble you so."

"Of course." She held him a little tighter and sang to him. The cloud they shared carried them over the Inward Sea.

They journeyed and hunted together several nights more. Now that she and Tresz had spoken of parting ways, she balked at doing so. The leisurely pace of their approach to Daerjen – a source of frustration not long ago – felt precipitate in the wake of their conversation.

As they neared the isle where, according to the woman who had spoken to her on the promontory overlooking Windhome Inlet, she might find the Walker, Tobias, other emotions surfaced. Excitement at the thought of meeting this human whom she might love. Fear of what that love could mean for her. Uncertainty as to whether she had made a mistake in leaving Trevynisle.

She wasn't accustomed to having her feelings roiled so. Each night, Tresz set her down in the streets of a different port town so that she could hunt while he enveloped another ship in his mists. Her hunts rarely lasted long. Mostly she wandered the lanes, hoping to find other girls like the one she'd spoken to in Rooktown. She had much to learn about human love.

She tried to hide this from the Shonla, and when he asked about her hunting, she always said she'd been successful. She didn't understand her mood well enough to explain it.

Before long – too soon – they crossed the waters from Ensydar to Daerjen. There they followed the coastline, scouting for cities and ships.

"There are many places I might leave you," Tresz said, the first time either of them had spoken in some time. "The human you seek, do you know where he is?"

"No. He's a Walker. I gather he was summoned to a court from the palace back in Windhome."

"Summoned when?"

"A hard question to answer. In a future, one that's already been altered."

A rumble sounded deep in his chest. Not laughter this time – something harder. "Your kind confound me."

"So you've said."

"And yet you continue to do so."

"Isn't that what it means to be confounding?"

This time he did laugh. "Well argued." After a fivecount he asked, "Do you know where the royal seat is found in this future of which you speak?"

"No. I'm sorry."

"It is no matter. Allow me."

They slowed, coming to a halt a few hands above the swells near the mouth of the Gulf of Daerjen. As alien as it still was for her to fly with the Shonla, this sensation was even more strange. They hovered, motionless, suspended only by a cloud of vapor. A gibbous moon lit the Shonla's mists, but Droë could see nothing beyond them. The gurgle of the swells, the far-off slap of waves against land – these gave her some vague sense of where they were, but that was all. She would not miss this feeling of dislocation.

"My kind tell me that power in Daerjen is in flux at this time. A recent attack by the Sheraighs on the Hayncaldes. Surely this will be resolved in your future. I should take you to Sheraigh."

He started forward again, wheeling to the south.

"No," she said.

Once more, he slowed. "You wish to go elsewhere?"

She didn't respond. Something in her memory... What had the woman said? There was a misfuture, changes wrought by the Walker after he went to Daerjen. Which suggested that rather than being in Sheraigh he might be where the old sovereignty had been seated.

"To Hayncalde," she said. "Please."

"The misfuture of which you have spoken."

"That's right."

"Very well. To Hayncalde. Though..." He faltered, and she knew what he would say. "Sheraigh is close, and I would feed before we cover this final expanse."

He left her on a dirt lane fronting the coastline, within sight of Sheraigh's wharves. Droë fed on two sailors, a man and a woman. She took little pleasure in either, but she did feel better afterward. To his credit, Tresz made quick work of his meal. Soon they were soaring above the gulf, cold wind bespeaking the swiftness of their approach to the city. The Shonla did this for her, she knew. He preferred to journey with less haste. She almost told him not to hurry for her sake, but that would have invited questions she didn't care to answer. She clung to him, tasting brine in the air, her cheek resting against his cool back.

"There," he said, some time later.

She raised her head and gazed over his shoulder. He had parted his mists for her and he pointed at a scattering of light ahead of them. Torches. A great many, in a city larger than Sheraigh.

"Where shall I leave you?"

"Near the wharves is fine," she said. "Thank you."

He lowered his arm and the gap in his cloud began to close.

"No, please. I want to see."

"Very well."

The opening broadened again.

The city came into relief: the formidable battlements on the outer walls, the tumble of homes and shops surrounding the castle and the sanctuary, the wharves stretching into coastal waters, and the warehouses behind them. They passed a good number of vessels as they neared the piers. She was sure Tresz would feed again before leaving.

"The lane to the north of the wharves," she said, pointing. "Before the city wall."

He veered in that direction. They passed the wharves and followed the contour of the city wall to a deserted stretch of rutted road. Tresz slowed and floated down to the dirt and grass.

She climbed off his back, stretched cramped muscles in her arms and shoulders. A gentle rain fell, cooled by the Shonla's mist.

"You've been kind to me," she said, looking up into those luminous eyes.

He chuckled. "You grow diffident as our farewell approaches. Are you doubting your decision?"

"No. But I know you didn't want to do this. You didn't want me with you, and you've carried me a long way."

"It has been my pleasure," he said, bearing blunt teeth in a smile. "I will miss your songs."

"Where will you go?"

"Go? Why would I go anywhere?" He waved a hand in the direction of the gulf. "Did you see how many ships we passed? I can feed here for a century."

"And what will you do when word of the hungry Shonla spreads, and every captain orders a dozen torches mounted on deck?"

"I shall journey to Sheraigh and feed there until the sailors and captains of Hayncalde grow lax. They always do, you know. Humans are like that." This last he said more pointedly.

"I know."

His brow creased, and he made a sound halfway between a sigh and a growl. "Very well. I leave you."

He extended a hand, palm facing her. She pressed her fingers to his.

"Hunt well, Tirribin. May you find what it is you seek."

Droë blinked back a tear and had to bite her lip to keep herself from asking him to stay. She had grown used to his company, to not being alone. Which was strange, because she had spent centuries alone.

"And you," she said. "Feed well. May every ship in Islevale run short of torch oil."

She would miss the rumble of his laughter.

Droë lowered her hand and started away. Before she left the cold of his mists, Tresz spoke her name, making her turn back to him.

He walked to her, reemerging from the fog.

"I meant what I said. I will remain in these waters for some time. You know how to summon me. If I am near enough to hear you, I will come."

"Thank you, Tresz."

She walked free of the mist, stepping into warm, damp air, dirt and sand beneath her feet, rain on her brow. Pausing, she watched Tresz glide beyond the wharves and toward a small vessel that bobbed on the gulf's surface. A single torch burned on its deck, mounted near the prow. Not nearly enough to ward off the Shonla.

"Fools," she whispered, and smiled as the vessel was swallowed by Tresz's cloud.

She followed the rutted road toward the gate. Already she sensed the guards there. Young men, all rich with years. Despite having eaten so recently, she felt a pang of hunger but thought better of trying to feed on them. All these men would be armed, and determined to stay together. Getting past them would be simple enough, given her powers. She would feed later, on others.

Within sight of the gate, she slowed, reached for her time sense. She stepped into the between, and out of it again a blink later on the far side of the gate, in the middle of a dark cobbled lane. She took in her surroundings and set out for the castle at Tirribin speed. She reached it in a dozen strides, perhaps a tencount.

Another stone wall blocked her way. A gate, and more guards.

If the Walker – Tobias – was here in Hayncalde he might well be within. Yet she sensed no Walkers. None. She would have, had he been there.

Droë stared at the walls for a long time, casting her time sense through stone and over grass and tile. Nothing. Disappointment warred with relief. Yes, she wanted to find him. Curiosity about this human she might love drew her like the promise of a child's years. Yet she feared that encounter as well. Perhaps it was good that it wouldn't happen so soon. She needed to adjust to this place, to being on her own again. She needed to think about what she wanted from the Walker, and from herself.

She started back down the deserted lane, walking at human speed. After a time, she heard distant footsteps. Many of them, walking together. She soon spotted a cluster of soldiers, all bearing weapons, all dressed in pale blue. Of course. It occurred to her that she'd seen no other humans since the city gate. Garrisoned cities often had their own laws – times after which people couldn't be abroad in the streets. Feeding here at night might prove difficult.

She hid from the soldiers, waited as they passed, and snuck to the lower lanes closer to the gate, where the homes and shops were less polished. There, among the ramshackle buildings and befouled byways, she was more likely to encounter humans after dark. Soldiers wouldn't care as much about what happened in these streets, or who they happened to.

Droë didn't know what exactly she sought, or why she wandered the lanes. A court Walker wouldn't be in this part of the city. He would have been in the castle, and since he wasn't, he could be anywhere. In Daerjen, in Aiyanth, somewhere at sea. For all she knew, he was back in Trevynisle. That thought brought a thin smile. Though agitated, she wasn't immune to the irony.

A scream yanked her from her musings, froze her in mid-stride. It had come from nearby, a few streets to the south and east. She covered the distance at speed and paused at a shadowed corner. Several people, all in tattered clothes, whispered in a cluster at the mouth of a nearby alley. Keeping out of sight, pressed to a crooked wall, she listened.

"...Soldiers might come."

"Does anyone know him?"

"Never seen him before. Not that I'd recognize him in this state."

"I've seen 'im. But as you say, not like this."

"You seen him with anyone? Family? Friends?"

"Nah. Always alone."

"That don't mean nothin'. No claims yet. Not until we're sure there's no one else. Rule of the lanes."

"Rule of the lanes." This last, all of them said in unison.

In time, the humans moved off, heading in different directions, many of them casting furtive glances over their shoulders and down the lanes they passed.

When they had gone, and Droë could no longer hear their voices or footsteps, she edged closer to where they had been. She knew what to expect. Already she saw the rumpled form prone on the street, its contours clear in spite of the darkness.

Nevertheless, as she neared the corpse she stopped, swaying in the shadows, her breath caught in her throat.

The dead man's cheeks were sunken, wrinkled, dried out skin clinging to bone, eyes bulging from their sockets.

A Tirribin had done this. On the thought, she heard a footfall behind her, and then a voice.

"Good evening, cousin."

CHAPTER 8

23rd Day of Kheraya's Waking, Year 634

Droë wheeled, a snarl in her throat, teeth bared, fingers as rigid as a hawk's talons.

"It's not very friendly."

"Not very at all."

Two Tirribin stood a few paces from her, near enough to kill her, far enough apart to prevent her from attacking both at once.

A male and a female, both dark-haired, he with pale blue eyes, she with green. Her hair was longer, but otherwise they could have been twins.

The female began to circle Droë, hands clasped behind her back, her steps as light and sure as a timbercat's.

Droë watched her, but her gaze returned repeatedly to the male. She felt exposed having them on either side of her, having to guard against an attack from left and right, or front and back.

"It's pretty," the female said. "I prefer black hair to yellow, but still..." She looked past Droë to the other. "Don't you think it's pretty?"

"I suppose."

"You're afraid to admit it. You do think so. I can tell."

His eyes raked over Droë. "It looks like other Tirribin. We're all pretty."

"True. Very true." The female continued around, passing the male to begin a second circuit. "I haven't seen it before. I think it must be new here." Her tone was mild, yet mocking.

"Yes. I wonder why it's here."

"So do I. This is our city, after all. We hunt here, feed here. We have for centuries. Why would it come here now?"

"That's for me to know," Droë said.

The female paused. She was opposite her brother once more, flanking her. The two shared a glance.

"Not friendly," the female said again. "Rude even." She resumed her orbit.

"Still," he said, scrutinizing Droë but addressing his sister, "it would be helpful to know its name."

The female wrinkled her nose. "Ew. Why?"

"Just to know. Maybe it will be friendlier if we give it our names."

"Would you please stop calling me 'it,' and speaking about me as if I'm not here? That's more rude than anything I've done."

His brow creased. "She's right."

"I suppose she is." The female joined her brother and together they faced Droë.

"I'm Teelo." The male indicated his sister with an open hand. "This is Maeli."

Droë regarded them both, wary, sullen. But they had done as she asked. Denying them her name would have been rude as well. "I'm Droë."

"If we choose to fight you," Maeli said, "you won't stand much of a chance."

Droë blinked, then realized she was still crouched for battle, her hands clawed. She straightened, let her hands fall to her sides.

"That's better," Maeli said. Again Droë heard mockery in the words.

"Where did you come from?" Teelo asked. She thought his interest sincere.

"Far. Trevynisle."

The two shared another look.

"You sailed?" he asked.

Droë shook her head. "I journeyed with a Shonla."

Their eyes widened at the same time, in precisely the same way.

"What was that like?"

"Cold. And it demanded a lot of singing."

He nodded, smiled. Perhaps he wasn't so bad.

"I still want to know why you've come," Maeli said.

She, on the other hand, Droë didn't trust at all.

"And I'm still not willing to tell you."

"You've come from Trevynisle, you said," she went on, ignoring Droë's remark. "So you probably know Walkers."

Droë tried to keep her expression even. Judging from Maeli's wicked grin, she failed.

"We know a Walker. Don't we, Teelo?"

"Maeli—"

His sister rounded on him. "What? I'm playing. I'm not being mean."

"That's not the point. We shouldn't talk about him."

Displeasure creased Maeli's forehead. "I don't see why not. I never understood why you liked him so. He was rude, too. And he never shared. All the years that—"

"Maeli!"

She stiffened at his tone, eyes widening again in an entirely different way. She glared at him for the span of a breath, then left them at Tirribin speed.

Droë regarded Teelo, unsure of what she ought to say, her mind filled with questions. What Walker had they met? Mara had come here, but Teelo had said "him." Did they know Tobias? And what did they mean about him never sharing?

Teelo's stare didn't leave the spot where his sister had been standing. A frown pinched his features.

"Do I need to leave this city?" she asked, breaking a lengthy silence. "Will the two of you…?"

"Will we kill you?" He shifted his gaze to her. "Probably not. Maeli will want to, especially now. And she's the elder; it's her choice. Still, she probably won't try without me, and I feel no need to."

She knew she couldn't expect more reassurance than that.

"The Walker she spoke of," she said. "Was… was his name Tobias?"

Surprise registered on his face. "Yes, it was. You know him?"

"No. I will, later. I met a friend of his, also from his future."

"His future is lost."

"I know. This other human came back to reclaim it, to repair history."

Teelo shook his head. "Impossible."

"You don't think she can succeed?"

He quirked an eyebrow. "Do you?" He gave her no time to respond. "Have you interacted with any humans since you left Trevynisle? Of course you have. You've fed. Probably dozens of times. So have Maeli and I. We're aware of the misfuture, but that hasn't stopped us from doing what we do. Nor has it stopped anyone else. History is changing constantly, and just because it veers in a new direction doesn't mean it stops, or waits. The future is always changing. That future–" He gestured again with that same fine-boned hand: a vague turn of the wrist that encompassed everything beyond the alley in which they stood. "The one Tobias left. It's gone. It's been gone since he entered the between. He can no more reclaim it than he can reclaim a raindrop from last night's storm. You're Tirribin. You should know this."

Droë could think of nothing to say. Because she did know it, and had since the night she summoned Tresz and decided to leave Windhome. Whatever the woman – Mara – had hoped to accomplish, she was doomed to fail.

Droë didn't care, because she had her own purpose. She didn't want Tobias to return to his time. She didn't want Mara to find him. She searched for the Walker himself, not for any point in time, and certainly not for any thread of human history. Of course, she wasn't about to share with Teelo her reasons for coming to Daerjen. She trusted him more than she did his sister, but that was a low threshold to clear.

"You do know it," he said, narrowing his eyes. "You're no fool. So why are you here? Do you intend to harm the Walker?"

"No!" She said it too quickly and with too much passion. Her cheeks flushed. A human response.

"Interesting," he said, considering her, his head canted. After a brief pause, he went on. "We sent him to the Notch." He pointed southward. "It's a place humans go when they don't want to be found by those with authority. Breaklaws, debtors, people who can't find work. It seemed the safest place for... him."

"Why did he need such a place?"

"I can't–"

"Who was with him? Your sister started to mention someone."

"A mistake. She shouldn't have spoken so."

"And yet she did."

Teelo shook his head, grave and resolute. "It's not my tale to tell. Nor was it hers."

"I'd never harm him," Droë said, knowing her tone betrayed too much.

"I believe you, but it's up to him to decide what you should and shouldn't know."

"Do you always show such loyalty to humans?"

"He's not just a human. He's a Walker. And in this case, I'm not sure you're one to talk."

He softened this with a smile. Droë felt her cheeks redden again.

"Can you at least tell me when you sent him to this Notch you mentioned?"

"It's been nearly two turns now."

"Do you think he's still there?"

His hesitation was answer enough. "We've gone there several times since. We haven't seen him or sensed him."

Her mouth had gone dry. "Gone, or dead?"

Teelo raised a shoulder, an apology in his pale eyes. "He had an arrangement with an Arrokad. Ujie. It's possible that she might tell you more, if you can convince her to help you."

Droë shuddered. "An Arrokad. What sort of arrangement?"

"Neither of them told us much."

"You're still with her?"

They both pivoted. Maeli stood equidistant from them,

completing a perfect triangle, fists on her hips, cold resentment in her expression.

"I was waiting for you," he said. "I knew you'd come back. You always do."

"That's because I'm always bored without you."

"Or hungry," he said.

"Yes, or that."

The girl cast a leery eye over Droë. "You're going to insist that we let her stay, aren't you?"

"Hayncalde is a large city, Maeli," her brother said. "None of us will go hungry."

"That's not the point, is it?"

"What is the point?" Droë asked.

Maeli bared her teeth. "I don't like you. I don't want you here."

"I'm not so fond of you, either. I do like your brother—"

"Yes, I'm sure. He likes you, too. What a surprise. My brother likes everyone."

"Actually, I was going to say that your brother likes you, and so perhaps I should give you another chance."

She saw a sly smile flash across Teelo's face.

"Oh." Maeli appeared genuinely confused.

"I haven't yet hunted in your city," Droë went on. "I won't without your leave. But I wish to remain here, just until I work out where I ought to go next. I ask your sufferance." She finished with the formal words of supplication, her gaze lowered.

The Tirribin looked to her brother again. Droë's submission had caught her by surprise. Droë realized now that she should have started off this way, meek and respectful instead of combative. She was the interloper, not Maeli, and her mere presence here could have been taken as a challenge. *Had* been taken that way, obviously. Her own fault, and foolish. She could have gotten herself killed. It was a lesson she had learned once long ago, nearly to her own doom, and still she had forgotten. She needed to be more careful.

"Do you know how long?" Maeli asked. She sounded more

curious than hostile.

"I don't. A few days perhaps. No longer."

"Where would you go after?"

"I can stay then?"

Maeli dismissed the question with a flip of her hand. "Teelo's right," she said. "There's plenty here. Answer my question."

"I don't know yet. I need to find the Walker first, or at least learn his fate."

Maeli exaggerated a nod. "So you've told her about Ujie," she said to her brother.

"I mentioned her just before you came back."

"I suppose that's good. Saves me the trouble." She heaved a sigh. "Let's do something. I'm bored." She said it to both of them. For now, Maeli had accepted her.

Despite having taken years from the man in the alleyway, Maeli wished to hunt again.

"It's not that I *need* to," she said, in response to her brother, when he pointed to the dead man. "I want to. It's fun." She eyed Droë. "Don't you agree?"

This didn't strike Droë as a good time to side with Teelo. "Of course," she said. "And I am hungry." She wasn't really. Not that this mattered. She did enjoy hunting, and if that was what Maeli wished to do, Droë would join her.

Teelo acquiesced with a shrug, and the three of them left the alley, heading downhill toward the wharves.

"It was bad when the occupation began," Maeli said as they walked. "The Sheraighs blockaded the port and we had no new prey for a turn. Now that the wharves are open again, finding years is easier, even with the curfew."

"Was that before or after the Walker arrived here?"

Maeli regarded her for a few strides before facing her brother.

"It was the same time," he said. "When we met the Walker, the occupation had begun, but he hadn't been here long."

Droë had expected as much, though she hadn't been sure they would answer her question.

"What else have you told her?" Maeli asked him, ice creeping back into her tone.

"Not a lot. She knows he has an arrangement with Ujie. And she knows that he went to the Notch. She already knew his name."

Maeli turned back to her. "Interesting. What do you want with him?"

She didn't think it wise to dissemble. "To find him. To help him change this past back to the way things are supposed to be."

"Such a human notion. The way things are supposed to be? I'm not sure I know what that means."

"This is a misfuture. Already. And it gets worse as—"

"I know what you think it means. I know what the Walker thinks. Others of his kind probably feel as he does. I'm asking, what is all that to us? We feed on years. We perceive them. We know when they're altered or pure. Beyond that, we don't care. At least we shouldn't."

Droë started to answer, stopped herself. She wasn't sure what to say. She felt off balance. If this was a fight, Maeli would have killed her already.

"Interesting," Maeli said again, watching her. To her brother, she said, "You didn't tell her anything more? Not about any of it?"

"I didn't tell her anything I wouldn't have wanted you to tell."

"Did you find that frustrating?" she asked Droë.

"What are you doing, Maeli?" Teelo asked.

She ignored him, waited for Droë's answer.

Droë refused to flinch from the other Tirribin's stare. "You don't want us to be friends. You'll let me stay for now, but when you tire of me, when you're ready to kill me, you want to be certain that Teelo will go along with you."

"She's clever," Maeli said. She still eyed Droë, but once more she addressed her brother. "I'll give you that. And you've always been distracted by the pretty ones. Remember that Tirribin in Streathe? You liked her, too."

"I remember. It was six hundred years ago, but I remember."

She did turn at that. "That wasn't the only time. You're too easily distracted, brother."

"And you're too easily threatened."

"Three Tirribin is too many in one city, even one as large as Hayncalde. Never mind the number of prey. Yes, there are plenty for all. That's not the point."

"What is the point?" Droë asked.

Maeli spun. "Humans get nervous. They'll find their dead, too many of them, and they'll start to hunt for us. This is our home. I won't be forced out because of you."

"So when you said I could stay—"

A cruel smile. "Did I really say that?"

"Maeli—"

She rounded on her brother. "I'm the elder! This is my decision, and you will support me. You don't wish to kill her. That's fine. She need not die. But she will not remain here. If you insist on letting her stay, then I will make you kill her."

Teelo blinked at the outburst.

To Droë, Maeli said, "You may hunt once in this city. Tonight. One life. Take more than I have decreed, or stay longer than I have sanctioned, and your life is forfeit."

Droë looked past her, seeking out Teelo. He stared back, his expression flat, and he said nothing. He didn't have to; he'd already said all that mattered. *She's the elder.*

"All right," she said. "I'll go. I didn't know there were Tirribin here, and I didn't mean to enter the city without your permission."

Neither of them responded. Dispensation was Maeli's to give, and she didn't.

Droë left them and continued on to the waterfront. Once she judged that she was beyond their hearing, she allowed herself to cry. Not for long. She had things to do before she left Hayncalde. But she was lonely, humiliated, scared, hurt. Tears coursed down her face and dripped from her chin.

She didn't bother to hunt. She would feed elsewhere. Upon crossing through the gate, she sped away from the wharves, following the strand southward: the direction Teelo had indicated when he spoke of the Notch.

Once she was clear of the city, she stepped to the edge of the surf and called Ujie by name.

Soon she spotted movement through the distant swells. Moments later a figure emerged from the sea. Naked, beautiful, black hair hanging to her waist, pale skin aglow with moonlight. She walked to where Droë stood, her feet sloshing in the surf. As she drew closer, Droë saw that her eyes were silver, the pupils slitted rather than round.

"Cousin," she said, in a voice like waves sliding over sand. "You summoned me."

"I did," Droë said. "Forgive me."

Ujie halted at water's edge, so that foam and brine lapped at her feet. "There is nothing to forgive. There is a price, however. There is always a price, as you well know."

"I do. What would you have from me?"

The Arrokad lifted an eyebrow. "Your name to start."

"Droë."

"You are here with sanction from the others? The siblings?"

"Not their sanction, but their forbearance. I'll be gone before daybreak."

Ujie sobered. "I see. You have been weeping. They were cruel?"

She faltered.

"Maeli was cruel," Ujie said, answering her own question.

"It was my own fault. I should have been more careful in entering the city."

The Arrokad turned a hand. "Tirribin are odd in that way. More human than my kind would be. They mentioned me to you?"

"They told me you had arrangement with a human I seek. A Walker."

Her expression darkened further. "That was not for them to discuss. With anyone."

"They told me no more than that."

This didn't seem to mollify her. "Why do you seek him?"

"He's part of a larger misfuture. And in another future, I've been told, he and I are friends. I don't wish to lose that friendship."

Droë winced at what she heard in her own words. She might as well have said, *I want to fall in love with him.*

Ujie's eyes narrowed. "I care nothing for the misfuture. Humans will war with each other in one path as much as they will in another. And Walkers are often the agents of change such as this. Nevertheless I find your interest in him intriguing. This is unusual for Tirribin, yes?"

She glanced to the side and nodded.

"Then I ask you again, why do you seek him?"

A tear slipped from Droë's eye. "I don't know. I'm… confused."

"Most interesting."

She bristled, weary of being an object of interest for other Ancients. "What's so interesting? Your kind are known to engage in the act of love with humans. Sometimes you pleasure them and let them go, other times you kill them. Should I find your behavior interesting? Should I judge you?"

The Arrokad raised an eyebrow, silencing Droë.

"Do you wish to love this man, cousin?"

Heat suffused her face. Ujie's eyes widened.

"Well, now I am truly surprised."

"I'm curious," Droë said, her voice barely louder than the advance and retreat of the surf. "I've seen love, the emotion and the act. I… I want to know more." She gestured at herself. "I remain this girl-thing, and I tire of it. I want to be different. I want others to see me as more than a child."

"You thought I would give this to you?"

She shook her head. "No. I wish to know if Tobias is still alive, and if he's here in Daerjen. That's why I summoned you."

"Ah. Well, that is easy enough. He is still alive. I know this, because he owes me a boon, and I him. Arrokad keep ourselves aware of those with whom we have bargains fairly sworn. He has left these waters."

"Can you tell me where he is?"

"I can. I choose not to."

"Why?" Droë's voice cracked on the question.

"I fear you have not considered fully the implications of what you seek, and what might happen if you find him."

"That's not your concern."

Unwise, that last. Ujie drew herself to her full height and glowered down at Droë. "You summoned me, Tirribin. You made it my concern, and you will hear what I have to say."

"Yes, cousin. Forgive me."

Ujie let out a breath. "He may love another, you know," she said, gentling her tone.

"The other Walker, you mean."

"There is another Walker?"

"You don't know of her?"

"I do not. Tell me."

"She is… She perceived the misfuture, vaguely at first, but she recognized it. Once, when all was as it was supposed to be, and Tobias still lived in his own time, they were friends. And more. She felt the change, and she Walked back to this time to find him, and to turn history back to the path they both knew."

"Did she come here?"

"She meant to. That's as much as I know."

"That is information I did not have. Thank you. I consider your debt to me fulfilled."

Droë wanted to counter that the Arrokad had yet to earn what she had given. She knew that Tobias lived, and had sailed from here. Beyond that, she knew no more than she had before summoning Ujie. She could guess what the Arrokad would say if she asked her to grant the other, truer wish of her heart. She kept all of this to herself. Ujie's kind were every bit as capricious as Tirribin, and far more dangerous to one like Droë. Arrokad magick could kill, as could Arrokad teeth and Arrokad hands. So she nodded in acknowledgment, hoping Ujie wouldn't leave her quite yet.

Perhaps Ujie read this in her eyes. "So it is likely that he *does* love another. Would you take him from her? Would you kill for his love?"

She didn't know how to answer.

"I see."

"Can your magick change me?" she asked.

"I do not know. Truly," she added, no doubt sensing Droë's skepticism. "This," she gestured, a graceful turn of her fine, long-fingered hand that indicated all that Droë was, "is more than mere appearance. This is the essence of what Tirribin are. All of you. The longing of which you speak is not all that different from a human wishing she could grow wings and fly, or a Walker wishing she could Span instead. You seek to alter something fundamental. I do not know if it can be done. Arrokad magick is powerful, to be sure. Whether it is that powerful…" Again, a small, uncertain gesture.

"You could try," Droë said. Seeing the Arrokad's features harden, she didn't wait for a response. "You're not willing to do this either."

"I am not. Forgive me."

Arrokad didn't often ask for forgiveness. She was extending a courtesy that most of her kind would never offer.

"Of course, cousin," she said, because she should.

The corners of Ujie's mouth quirked upward, as if she sensed Droë's thoughts.

"I should leave you," she said.

"I'm grateful to you for answering my summons, and for telling me what you have of the Walker's fate."

"You are gracious. I have some notion of what it cost you to reveal what you have. I will not speak of it, ever. You have my word."

"My thanks."

"How long have you lived, cousin?"

Droë's turn to shrug. "A long time. Many centuries."

"I ask because I wonder if you have truly considered what it might mean to change after so long. You have been Tirribin, in the form of this 'girl-thing' as you put it, for your entire existence. Changing that is…" She gestured again, the movement eloquent in its scope. "It is everything. I fear for you. I fear what you seek and what it might mean were you to achieve it. I offer this in friendship. Think on it."

"I will," Droë said.

"Very well. I take my leave."

She waded back into the sea, her hips swaying, moonlight shining in her hair, whitening her back and neck. Even Droë could see how alluring she was, would be to one who could love. She saw the wisdom in contemplating what it might mean to change. She hadn't simply been humoring the Arrokad when she said she would think about it. But watching Ujie dive into the waves, graceful, compelling, desired by men and women both, she knew the time for such reflection had passed. She had already made her choice. She wanted to be like the Arrokad – more, certainly, than she wished to remain as she was.

And the Arrokad had hinted at possibilities. She didn't say that she *couldn't* use her magick to do what Droë wanted. Only that she was uncertain, unwilling to make the attempt.

There were other Arrokad in Islevale, and maybe one of them would be more daring. Droë would commence her search wherever she went next.

CHAPTER 9

Kheraya Ascendant, Year 634

The day of the Goddess's solstice dawned clear and warm in the crystal waters of Trevyn's Sea, along Chayde's western shore. Morning sun gilded the massive, snow-crowned ridges of the isle's coastal mountains, save for the highest peaks, which were obscured by golden tendrils of cloud.

All around the *Sea Dove*, merchant vessels lay at anchor. Dories and skiffs shuttled among the ships or crossed the shallows to the crude wooden piers of Briika. On most days, these smaller boats would be laden with goods for market, maneuvering for position so as to beat their competitors to port.

For this day, however, commerce was forgotten for indolence. The crew of Seris Larr's ship, driven by their captain's strict standards of excellence, were usually an enterprising and efficient bunch. This morning they lounged on the deck, some already on their second or – for a few ambitious souls – third cups of ale. Others swam naked in the waters, laughing and singing, although – because they could not abandon all prudence – on the lookout for green sharks, which frequented these waters.

The captain herself, dark-haired and blade-thin, perched on a barrel at the ship's stern, near the entrance to her quarters, clearly amused by the antics of the sailors under her command, but separate from them even now.

Tobias Doljan stood at the prow, as he often did when his duties allowed. He had yet to have an ale, or dive from the rails into the inviting surf. He laughed with the rest, though, and traded barbs with a few. He wore naught but breeches, as he had for much of the past turn. His skin had been baked by the sun to a deep, warm bay, and his body, no longer new to him despite the fourteen years he had lost Walking back to this time, had hardened, grown lean and nimble as he climbed the ship's ropes and worked its sails.

Sofya Hayncalde, once sovereign princess of Daerjen, tottered nearby, her skin also darkened beyond its usual nut color, faint streaks of gold in her black hair. Nava, as the ship's crew knew her, wore a plain linen shift – a far cry from the finery she would have been wearing if not for the attack on her father's castle that orphaned her – and clutched in one hand a piece of bread, half-eaten, oft-forgotten. Her fingers and lips were slick with butter. Every now and then, she remembered the bread and took another bite. Mostly, she wandered from one crew member to the next, drawing smiles from all, laughing when one or another tousled her hair or grabbed for her nose.

She had learned to walk aboard the ship, and it showed. On the planks of the deck, with the gentle roll of the vessel at anchor, or even the more dramatic rise and fall of the sea, her tiny steps were steady and assured. On those rare occasions when they made port and left the ship for the solidity of dry land, her gait grew ponderous and awkward. Some day, if and when they were forced to abandon this life on the sea, she would need to learn to walk all over again.

"Good morning."

Tobias smiled at Mara's approach.

"Mama!" Sofya said, reaching up, her free hand opening and closing.

Mara stooped and swung the girl up into her arms, eliciting a laugh.

"Good morning, little one. What are you eating?"

"Bwead."

Mara glanced at Tobias. "Bwead," she repeated. "Is it delicious?"

Sofya nodded, took another bite.

Mara carried her to where Tobias stood, eyes meeting his again.

Tobias felt a frisson of tension having Mara so close.

"Blessed day to you," she said.

"And to you."

"This is the first solstice I can remember when I wasn't in the Travelers' Palace."

"Me, too."

Mara peered down at the swimmers, a smile softening her features. She had plaited her bronze hair and donned breeches and a linen shirt, the sleeves of which had been torn off. Like Tobias and Sofya, she had been browned by the sun, her hair touched with gold. Her arms were toned and muscled, her face lean, tapered. Beautiful. He looked away.

"Have you been swimming?"

"No," he said. "Not yet."

"You'll swim with me later?"

"Of course. If the others can watch Nava for a time."

"They can. You'll swim with me later." A statement this time. At another touch of his glance, her smile rekindled.

Tobias's pulse quickened.

They had been like this since first boarding the *Dove* back in Kheraya's Stirring, when the year was young, and the assassins of House Sheraigh still nipped at their heels. Now, at the pivot of the Goddess's journey, as the planting turns gave way to the heat of the growing, they remained in a strange sort of between, their own version of the chasm they crossed as Walkers through time. They were bound to each other: common origins, a friendship he remembered from a future she had never known, the perception – and deception, a matter of survival – that they were husband and wife, father and mother to Nava, who was Sofya. It was enough to make his head spin.

And despite these bonds, they were also children in the bodies of adults. He could have calculated his true age, not counting the time he had lost Walking, and the sum would have marked him as a boy, hardly old enough to shave. Mara was only a year older. But how did one factor the years walked, the wounds endured and the blood spilled, the cost of uncertainty and fear and flight?

How old were they really?

Old enough to be responsible for the life of this beautiful blue-eyed child. Young enough that they had yet to consummate their feigned marriage.

At night, to avoid questions from the others, they retreated to shadows in the hold where they could sleep together in private. Often they had kissed and touched and held each other. As of yet, though, they had not lain together in the truest sense. Mara hinted time and again that she wished to. Tobias was terrified, and never more so than today.

Kheraya Ascendent. A day of celebration and laughter, of good food and Miejan red wine. A night of passion. Always. Both solstices, and the Emergences, God's and Goddess's. In those celebrations named for Kheraya – the Goddess's Day, which marked the start of the year, and also today's solstice – the woman initiated a night of love. He knew Mara wouldn't. He was the resistant one, the frightened one. She would defer to his desires. It fell to Tobias.

"It's just a swim," Mara said, pitching her voice low. "You needn't look quite so panicked."

Her tone was playful, but he detected a tinge of sadness in the bright hazel eyes.

"I'm not panicked."

She lifted an eyebrow.

"All right. I'm panicked, but I'm... I'm not unwilling. To swim." His cheeks heated.

Mara threw back her head and laughed.

Whatever his fears, he did love her. That much he knew.

Sofya laughed as well, tipping her head back in imitation.

"Mister Lijar," the captain called from where she sat. "Join me."

Lijar was Mara's family name. Tobias began using it as an alias for both himself and Sofya even before Mara joined him in this time. His name was known to Mearlan's assassins; they'd had no choice but to leave it behind in Hayncalde.

"Saved by the captain," Mara whispered.

"A temporary reprieve."

"Count on it, Mister Lijar." She kissed him on the lips, lightly, but with promise.

Perhaps he was finally ready.

He smiled and turned away. Sofya called after him, but Mara distracted her with a song. Tobias walked the length of the ship, past the cook, who was setting up a makeshift stove at the front of the quarterdeck.

"Good morning, captain."

"And blessed day to you." She surveyed the ship. "Have you ever spent an Ascendence or Emergence at sea?"

"Only the day we fled Hayncalde on this ship."

"That was… unusual. You're in for a treat today. It's different on a ship." She eyed him sidelong, her grin crooked, wry. "Less prayer, more play. And whatever food the locals offer in trade."

"Trade for what? I thought this was a day without commerce."

"At sea? There's never a day without commerce. But this is different as well. They bring us fish, crab – in these waters, blue conch and barbed lobster, as well. In return, we host them for the evening meal. The deck will be choked with people, rail to rail. I thought you should know."

A chill passed through him, his gaze flicking to Sofya and Mara, who smiled back at him. "My thanks," he said in a whisper.

"If you prefer to remain below, I'll tell the crew that the little one took ill."

Tobias shook his head. "I don't believe that's necessary. There's no reason these people would think we're anything other than what we claim. And it does sound like an entertaining evening."

"That it is," she said.

"Was that all, captain?"

"No." She slid over, making room for him on the barrel. "Sit."

Tobias hesitated, surprised by the informality of the invitation. He set himself beside her, catching Mara's eye again. She gawked slightly at the sight of him sitting with the captain.

"You did well bringing us here," Captain Larr said. "I'm in your debt."

"I'm glad you're pleased, but I believe *we're* still in *your* debt. We'd be dead without you."

She shrugged. "Maybe. I'm more than pleased. Our time in these waters has been profitable, to say the least."

Coming to Chayde had been Tobias's idea. Not only was it far from Daerjen, in a part of Islevale that remained sparsely populated and largely ignored by the great powers, it also stood on the cusp of tremendous wealth. As he learned sailing in his own time, with this same captain, Chayde and the neighboring isle of Flynse would soon be the most cherished destinations of prospectors from every isle between the great oceans. Fourteen years from now, the riches discovered in Chayde's mountains and Flynse's caves would be common knowledge.

In this time, the discoveries were still fresh and known to few. When Captain Larr welcomed the three of them on board, harboring them from Quinnel Orzili and his band of assassins, Tobias suggested they sail north to these waters.

"It will be safe for us," he said at the time, "and lucrative for you and your crew. The first merchant vessels to reach the isles will establish themselves as indispensable trading partners for those who would mine as well as those who will supply the miners."

The captain took his counsel to heart, and he'd been proved right many times over.

"It will only get better, captain," he said now. "These lands will produce riches for years to come."

"I don't doubt it, but my crew grows restless." At his look, she held up a hand. "I know they don't seem unhappy. Really they're not. Their purses are heavy. Even the greatest fools among them can't gamble and drink away every coin they've earned. It's easy to keep sailors happy when times are good."

"Then what? I don't understand."

"I wouldn't expect you to. Call it the intuition of a captain. Men and women go to sea to make their fortunes, but also to find adventure. They've done the former, in large part thanks to you. Now, I sense they're tiring of this place. They're hungry for a new sort of undertaking, something that will challenge them."

"You wish to leave?"

"Aye. And I'm wondering if you have ideas as to where we might go next."

Tobias blew out a breath. He didn't, and what was more, he didn't wish to leave. He, Mara, and Sofya were safe here. His purse had grown heavy as well, but that mattered to him far less than knowing they were hundreds of leagues from where they'd escaped Orzili.

"That's twice I've alarmed you," the captain said. "Forgive me. It wasn't my intention, on this day in particular. I merely wanted you to know what I'm thinking. And the question was sincere."

"Yes, of course. I- I can't think right now of where we ought to go, but I'll consider it. I'll ask Mara what she thinks."

"I'd be grateful. Thank you."

"How soon?" he asked.

"Our departure from these waters, you mean?"

He nodded.

"Within the next qua'turn or so. Kheraya's warmer turns usually bring storms and rough seas." She glanced up into the azure sky. "Not this year, and I want to take advantage of the fair weather by sailing due south, perhaps toward the Knot. If we wait too long, and the storms come, we could be stuck here until the God's Emergence. I don't want that."

"Of course, I understand."

"Very well. Join your family."

"Thank you, captain." He stood, started away.

"Mister Lijar," she said, stopping him. She waggled her fingers, beckoning him closer once more. "Enjoy this day," she said, leaning closer. "Wherever we go, I promise to keep the three of you safe."

"Of course. Again, my thanks."

Tobias returned to Mara and Sofya. The princess held out her arms for him, and he took her from Mara, settling her on his hip. She was getting heavier by the day.

"What was that about?" Mara asked. "It looked serious."

"It was," he said. "I'll tell you later. It's Kheraya Ascendant. We should savor it."

Mara watched Tobias as he played with Sofya. His cryptic hints about the conversation she'd witnessed frightened her, but for now she chose to be distracted. Sunshine, clear water, the beauty of Chayde's mountains and, to the west, fading to the horizon, the emerald rise and fall of the isles of the Labyrinth.

She thought as well about the night to come.

She hadn't known what to expect when first she met Tobias. He had known her in his old life in Windhome Palace, fourteen years in the future, but that future was lost to her. To Mara he was a stranger. Almost.

She had seen – had been shown by the Tirribin, Droë – an image of herself kissing Tobias in that future she would never know. She had Traveled back in time because her abilities as a Walker, latent until then, allowed her to sense a discontinuity between the world as she perceived it, and the world she should have known. She wanted to repair what Droë called a "misfuture." She couldn't deny, though, that the vision of that kiss had lured her back through the years as well.

She arrived in this time enamored with the idea of him. Their turns together aboard this ship, posing as a joined couple, as parents to Sofya, had deepened fascination to love. A transformation as magickal as alchemy. She had followed him onto the *Dove* to save her own life and his, and to protect the sole surviving heir of House Hayncalde. Now, she wouldn't have left him or the princess for anything, not even a chance to return to her own time.

Mara had never imagined herself as a mother. There hadn't been time. Before her Walk to this past, she'd been barely more than a girl, consumed with her studies and her training as a Traveler.

And at first, Sofya had been so attached to Tobias that she barely tolerated Mara's attempts to hold her, or feed her, or change her swaddling.

Familiarity brought affection, and affection deepened to love. The first time Sofya called her "Mama," Mara wept.

They were a family. Tobias was her husband, in all ways but one. She intended to change that this night. If he didn't initiate it, she would. Custom demanded no less.

Tobias spun the princess, held her high over his head, blew loud kisses on her belly until she gave herself the hiccups laughing. He might have been fifteen years old inside, but he looked and acted every bit the father. He was good at it.

The girl began to fuss and he set her down on the deck, allowing her to roam, her steps both awkward and recklessly confident. Other members of the crew called to her by the name they knew – Nava – and she walked among them, delighting in their attention, a true princess in a simple linen shift.

Tobias sidled closer.

"The locals join us for supper this night," he said, speaking softly so only Mara could hear. "The deck will be packed with them. I'm sure it will be a wonderful celebration, but it makes me nervous."

Mara did her best to keep her expression as it had been.

"No one knows us," she said. "We're a long way from Orzili. I think we'll be fine."

"Probably."

"Do we have a choice?"

"The captain said we could hide below. She'd tell the crew that Nava is ill."

Mara glanced his way. He still watched the princess, his face in profile. The strong chin, covered now with a trim beard, the straight, regal nose and full lips. Scars lined his cheeks and jawline, stark reminders of the torture he had endured to keep Sofya alive. They were jagged, raised, ugly, and yet he remained beautiful, at least to her. His hair had grown long, but he wore it loose, so that it rose and fell with the freshening breeze. He was broad in the shoulders and chest, narrow through his waist and hips. The marks on his torso were even worse than those on his face. Mara didn't care. She ached with want of him.

She took a breath and looked away again. "We can do that if you wish. If it will make you feel better."

"No. I mentioned it in case you might think it a good idea. I'd rather not." He took her hand. "I meant what I said. I intend to enjoy this day."

"There's more, isn't there? What did the captain say to you?"

"We'll talk about it later. For now... She wants to leave these waters. She thinks the crew has grown restless here."

"That frightens you."

He lifted a shoulder. "We're about as far from Orzili as we could be. Anywhere we go from here takes us closer to him."

"You must have known we wouldn't remain here forever."

A wry smile curved that perfect mouth. "Yes, but that didn't stop me from hoping."

She stood on her tiptoes and kissed him.

"What was that for?"

"I need a reason?"

He shook his head, intensity in his gaze. "No, you don't."

Mara blew out another breath. "All right," she said, raising her voice so the others could hear. "The rest of you keep an eye on Nava. My husband and I are going swimming."

Without waiting for a response, she untied the drawstring of her breeches and stepped out of them. She pulled her shirt off over her head and dropped it where she stood. She was naked underneath. Several in the crew whistled their appreciation. Tobias's face flushed again, but he grinned, eyes drinking her in. She swung herself over the rail and dove.

Surfacing, she heard laughter from above. She guessed that Tobias had made some remark. He flashed into view, naked as well, arcing over the water and slipping under as smoothly as a dolphin.

As he came up for air, she splashed him. They chased each other through the crystal swells, laughing and splashing. After a time, he stopped, watching her, wet hair swept back from his dark features.

Mara circled him, drawing nearer and nearer until he caught her hand and pulled her to him. She wrapped her arms around his neck, and kissed him, her breasts pressed to his chest. Her heart raced and she felt his keeping pace.

"I'm scared," he whispered, his lips so close to hers she could feel the words as well as hear them.

"Of leaving this place?"

A breathless laugh. "Well, yes, of that. But I meant of tonight. Of... of us."

"So am I, a little."

He pulled back, eyes going wide. "Really?"

"Of course."

"You seem so sure."

She pulled him close, kissed him again. "Can't I be both?" she murmured.

"Do you think we're too young?"

Mara shook her head, her smile slipping. "No. Neither of us is young anymore. Years only tell so much. We're mother and father to Nava. We've killed and nearly been killed ourselves. Look at the scars you bear. Even now we're hunted. We're not children anymore, Tobias. We haven't been in some time."

He kissed her one last time. Then he splashed her, and for that he had to pay.

They pulled themselves from the sea sometime later, climbing the rope ladder back onto the deck. Sofya sat amid a cluster of sailors, men and women, listening as one of the crew, old Yadreg, played his lute and sang. Mara and Tobias slipped into their clothes, and joined the circle. Entranced by the music, the princess barely noticed them until Tobias pulled her into his lap. She leaned back against him, her thumb in her mouth. Eventually she dozed off.

As the sun climbed higher and the air warmed, more dories and skiffs swarmed the waters, joined by sleeker oared vessels. All were filled nearly to tipping with locals, young and old. Many of them, Mara saw, were as dark complexioned as she and Tobias.

Perhaps they didn't need to leave with the *Dove*. They could remain here, search the mountains for gold and silver like so many others, melt into a coastal village where Quinnel Orzili would never think to search for them.

It struck her as a simple solution, and she wondered if Tobias had given the idea thought.

No doubt he would tell her that sooner or later they had to go back to Daerjen, so that Sofya could reclaim her birthright. He might tell her as well that if they chose to live on land, and by some chance Orzili did find them, they would have no means of escape.

They had choices, but none was perfect. Each carried both promise and peril. She wasn't sure how to balance one against the other.

A short time later, the first locals climbed onto the *Dove*'s deck, bearing baskets of live crabs and lobsters, musical instruments of their own, and jugs of what Mara guessed must be a spirit brewed on Chayde or Flynse.

The musicians among them started to play, the rest to dance.

Gwinda, the ship's cook, had set up a crude firebox on the quarterdeck, braced on stones from the coastline and underlaid with a thick layer of sand. She had two pots of water heating over the flames and a pile of shellfish ready to be cooked. She also had a barrel of ale that she had claimed as her own.

"If I'm gonna be cookin', I'm gonna be drinkin'," she said as she filled her tankard for the third or fourth time. This drew laughs from the crew and an approving nod from Captain Larr.

Sofya woke from her nap and demanded to be set free. Tobias obliged, though he followed her everywhere, ready to snatch her back into his arms at the first sign of threat. Mara feared that he acted too protective, conspicuously so, but she kept this to herself and danced with the others.

The day stretched on. She tried some of the clear liquid that flowed from those jugs. Sweet and pungent, like the strongest wine. It burned her throat, but warmed her insides and before she knew it she had finished one cup and started another. Tobias joined her and the other dancers, Sofya now in his arms, her face aglow with the late sun. Her cheeks were flushed and she had a joyous gleam in her eyes. Tobias sipped Mara's drink. Gaped, and then claimed a cup of his own.

Gwinda handed down the first of the cooked lobster and crab, eliciting cheers as well as exhortations to cook faster. And still more people crowded onto the ship, until Mara feared the deck would crack under the weight and the pounding of dancers' feet.

The eastern sky darkened and to the west yellows and pinks blended into indigo. Members of the crew set torches in sconces up and down the deck. The musicians played a slower tune.

Tobias and Mara, with Sofya now in her arms, swayed together, heads bent close, eyes locked.

Yadreg came over and took Sofya from Mara.

"I'll hold the wee one," he said, with a grin and a wink. "You two enjoy your dance."

"Thank you, Yadreg," Mara called after him, as he dipped and looped across the deck with Sofya.

The princess's giggles rang over the music.

Tobias took Mara in his arms. She rested her head on his shoulder. They moved with the rhythm of plucked strings and high flutes, soft drumming and some metal instrument that sounded like nothing Mara had ever heard.

It seemed a dream.

At least until Mara realized she couldn't hear Sofya's laughter anymore. Tobias grasped this at the same time. They released each other, spun, searching the throng. Mara didn't see her.

Then a cry, too familiar, and too far away.

"Sofya!" Tobias shouted, caution gone, terror in the name.

CHAPTER 10

Kheraya Ascendant, Year 634

Panic seized his heart, pressed on his throat until he wondered if he would ever breathe again.

Tobias had heard her voice. He knew he had. But he couldn't see for all the people around him, couldn't be sure of what he'd heard for the din of music and laughter and shouted conversations.

Until he heard it again.

"Sofya!" he bellowed.

"Nava!" Mara shouted beside him.

Idiot! "Nava!" he echoed. The vice squeezing his heart tightened further.

The child's cry had come from amidships. Near the ladders.

Tobias shoved through the crowd, Mara just behind him. Locals paused in their dancing to glare and to chide him in a language he didn't know. He didn't care.

They hadn't gone far when they found Yadreg sitting in a small open space. He bled from a gash on his forehead.

The Two keep her safe.

Several members of the crew stood around the old man, one holding a bloodstained rag, another offering him a cup of ale. Yadreg looked up at Tobias and then Mara.

"I'm so sorry," he said, tears in his eyes. "I didn' see them. One moment I had her. I was singin' to her. The next I was on the deck, an' she was gone."

"Who's gone?" Ermond asked, solid and competent, but alarmingly far gone with drink right now.

"Nava," Tobias said, voice unsteady. "Someone's taken her."

"The wee one?" Ermond growled, more sober by the instant. "Which way?"

Tobias and Mara shouldered past him. The sailor followed, calling for others under Captain Larr's command to follow.

He yelled to a man in the rope lines as well, telling him what had happened. The man shouted back.

Tobias listened for Sofya, still grappling with the horde of people in his way.

"He sees them," Ermond said. "They're near the portside ladder."

"Can he stop them?" Tobias asked, looking back.

"How? Listen to me. Even on water, they won't get far. We're gonna get her back."

He twisted again. The man met his gaze, nodded once. "We're gonna get her back," he repeated.

Ermond called for someone else to alert the captain. They were farther from the musicians now and the throng had thinned. Tobias could make out Sofya's cries. They were faint. She wasn't on the deck anymore. If they hurt her, he'd kill them. He didn't care how many they were or what weapons they carried. He'd kill them.

Tobias and Mara reached the top of the rope ladder a tencount later, in time to see a sleek, narrow boat slide away from the *Dove*'s hull. One man knelt in the bow and another astern. Each paddled with a single oar. A third man sat in the middle of the boat holding a squirming, squalling bundle.

"Give me your pistol," Tobias said, as Ermond joined them.

The sailor shook his head. "No. Not from this distance. You might hit her."

"I can shoot!"

"I don't care! It's too far, and gettin' farther by the moment."

Mara put a hand on his arm. "He's right, Tobias."

He exhaled and pushed his hair back with both hands, his fingers rigid.

"Isn't one of you a Spanner?" Ermond asked.

"I am," Mara said. "It doesn't matter. Even if I had a sextant, Spanning to that boat wouldn't do me much good. I'd arrive without a stitch of clothing, holding nothing but a sextant."

The man frowned.

Tobias started to swing himself over the rail. "I'll swim after them. Maybe I can tip the boat."

"We're going after them, Mister Lijar."

Tobias turned. Captain Larr stood before him with nine more of her crew. Behind her the music continued to play, but a few men and women from the nearby isles had crowded to hear her.

"Drop the pinnace, Mister Wenn. Quickly."

"Yes, captain."

"Six of you are with me," Larr said. "The rest stay here and guard the ladders. No one else leaves until we're back."

Tobias eyed the crowd. "You think these others—"

"No, I don't. I think the men who took her are slavers. But I'm not taking any chances."

The crew lowered the pinnace to the water and in less than a spirecount, they had pushed away from the ship. Still, it seemed to Tobias that all of them were moving through molasses. He held his tongue, knowing they were doing their best, but he begrudged every moment.

The six members of the crew – two women, four men – took up sweeps and rowed. Tobias and Mara braced themselves at the prow, staring after the other boat. Larr took the rudder. The slavers had already put some distance between themselves and the *Dove* and continued to pull away. Soon, though, Larr's sailors found their rhythm. Their speed increased.

"They're heading for those islands," the captain said, pointing to a cluster of tiny isles.

There was no moon this night, but a vestige of daylight still burned in the west, and emerging stars cast some glow of their own. Tobias thought the slavers were steering toward a gap between two hulking boulders.

"I'd prefer if we caught them first. It'll be like a maze in there.

And there may be more of them waiting for us." Larr glanced at Tobias. "Can you really shoot?"

"Yes," he said, eyes fixed on the other boat. "Both of us can."

"Good. There are pistols, balls, powder, and paper in that box." Larr pointed to a chest near the prow. "Be ready to fire."

Tobias and Mara unlatched the chest and loaded weapons. When Tobias stood again and checked their position, he saw that they had gained on the slavers' vessel, though not enough.

"They're still going to reach the isles before we catch them," Mara said.

Larr drew her own weapon. "I know."

"Blood and bone," Tobias muttered. "What will happen to her if they get away?"

The captain cast a fleeting glance his way. "Tobias—"

"Tell me. What will happen?"

She shrugged. "They're slavers. They'll take her to another isle, probably one in the Sisters or the Labyrinth. Somewhere she'll blend in. Somewhere you'll never find her. She'll be sold. Perhaps as a laborer. More likely, given her age, and how lovely she already is, to a house where she can be trained. First as a servant, and then later, when she's older…" She trailed off, her implication clear enough.

They fell silent. The wind had died down. The only sounds Tobias heard were the beat of sweeps cutting through the water, the calm count of the lead oarsman, and Sofya's wails. Twice more, the captain adjusted their course, but she could do nothing to slow down the other vessel.

When the slavers' boat slipped into that gap, vanishing among shadows, Tobias sagged.

"They've not won yet, Mister Lijar."

He counted in silence, gauging their lead. He finished a second tencount as the pinnace was swallowed by that same darkness. Not a lot of time, yet more than enough for their quarry to melt away beyond hope of discovery.

"Oars up," the captain said.

The crew responded with alacrity, lifting their sweeps from the water. In the ensuing stillness, they heard a muffled cry and the soft splash of an oar.

The captain turned them sharply starboard and called for the sailors to row.

The oars carved into brine again, and the pinnace surged forward. They entered a narrow inlet, followed it to a broader stretch of still water. The slaver's boat slid across the expanse, close enough now that Tobias was tempted to sight his pistol.

"We've gained more," Mara said, excitement in her voice.

"Aye. We shouldn't have. Unless…" The captain spat a curse, eyes scanning the inlet again.

After a moment, the pinnace veered to port so abruptly, Tobias nearly overbalanced.

"What is it?" Mara asked.

"Do you still see the third man in that craft?" Larr asked.

Mara peered across the water's surface. "I can't tell."

"I'd wager he's not there." She pointed. "They let him off at that isle."

Of the two isles that formed the gap through which they'd passed, only one had an accessible shoreline. The other was sheer from water's edge to the clifftop two hundred hands above. They gained the sloped landing on the first island moments later. Tobias, Mara, and the captain leaped off the pinnace into the shallows and ran up the strand.

"Track down the others," she told Ermond. "You can fire at them if you're close enough. I don't want them getting away."

"Yes, captain."

He and the rest of the crew rowed away from the isle.

"Tracks," Tobias said, pointing at a single set of footprints in the sand, barely visible in the dying light.

Larr gestured for him to lead them.

The isle wasn't large, but it sloped steeply away from the water to a wooded crown at its center. They climbed in single file, following a path among rocky outcroppings, pistols in hand.

"Is there another way off?" Tobias asked in a whisper. "Could he have a second boat on the other side?"

"He might," Larr said. "I'm not familiar with these inlets."

Not the answer Tobias wanted.

A sound stopped him. He raised a hand, signaling to the others. It had been another muffled cry, but from where exactly? He thought he heard a footfall, ahead and to the left, among the trees.

He walked on, more slowly now, listening, trying to ignore the steps of his companions.

When Sofya cried out again, nearby, no longer muffled, Tobias broke into a run.

The captain called after him, but he didn't slow.

Reaching the peak of the crown, he stopped. A man stood before him in a small clearing, visible but dim in the gloaming. He held Sofya with a lean, muscled arm around her belly. A knife glinted in his other hand, the blade held to her throat. The princess sobbed, her face damp with tears.

"Down!" the man shouted, the word weighted with the accent of Sipar's Labyrinth. "Weapon down!"

"Don't lower your weapon," the captain said, her voice as calm as ever. She stepped past Tobias, her movements slow. Her gaze didn't stray from the slaver. "Don't listen to him."

"Down! Down!"

"He's not going to hurt her," she said. "Because if he does, he's a dead man. He knows that. He wants us to let him go. His freedom for her return."

Mara had stopped beside Tobias.

"Missus Lijar, please keep moving," Larr said. "Keep yourself between Tobias and me. If we spread out, one of us is bound to get a clear shot."

Mara and Tobias shared a glance. She walked on.

"Gold!" the man said.

The captain shook her head. "No gold. The girl."

The man darted his gaze from face to face. "Weapons down!" he said, giving Sofya a shake and shifting his blade.

Tobias sucked a breath through his teeth.

"No," Larr said, without inflection. "We keep our weapons. You put down the girl."

"No! Gold!"

Larr raised her weapon, gestured with her off hand for Tobias and Mara to do the same. "Put down the girl."

The flat crack of a distant weapon echoed among the isles. Two more followed in quick succession. The slaver peered in that direction.

"Your men are dead," Larr said, dragging his wide-eyed stare back to her. "You're the only one left. You shouldn't have come aboard my ship, and you shouldn't have stolen this child. You understand what I'm saying. I know you do. Slavers speak a number of languages."

"Maybe your men dead. Mine had pistols, too."

Another report careened among the rocks and trees.

"We were six to your two. Your men are dead. Put down the girl, and you'll live."

He considered Mara and then Tobias.

Tobias feared for Sofya, and wanted desperately to kill this man, but his pistol hand didn't waver.

"If you kill her, you die," Larr said. "If you try to run, you die. If you try to fight us, you die. Put her down and you live."

Another tencount passed before he moved the knife from Sofya's throat and held it up for them to see. Then he bent, lowering her to the ground, his movements cautious, deliberate, his eyes on Captain Larr. Setting her at his feet, he straightened again. Sofya wailed, her arms raised to Tobias.

"Back away from her," the captain said.

The slaver backed away a single step. She waved him back farther with her pistol. He took a second step and a third.

Larr nodded to Tobias.

He rushed forward to Sofya and lifted her into his arms. She continued to cry, clutching his shoulder and chest.

"It's all right, Nava. You're all right."

"Nava?" the man said. "Sofya."

Tobias and the captain exchanged glances.

"What did you say?" Larr asked the slaver.

"Girl name. Sofya."

"Why do you think that?"

"*He* say," the man answered, pointing at Tobias. "On big boat. He call for her. 'Sofya, Sofya.'" He looked a question to Tobias. "Yes? You say?"

Captain Larr's pistol belched flame, the roar making Tobias jump. Sofya, who had quieted, shrieked again.

The slaver collapsed to the ground, blood gushing from his shattered brow.

Gray smoke hung over the clearing. Tobias regarded the captain and she stared back at him, each waiting for the other to speak.

"That was my fault," he finally said. "I was… I panicked, and I called her name without thinking."

"There's plenty of blame to go around. I've been in these isles before. I know slavers traffic here, yet it never entered my mind as I thought about tonight's celebration. I've never had a child aboard. I should have guessed they might be here today."

"It doesn't matter," Mara said. "He's dead, and she's safe." She walked to Tobias and kissed Sofya's forehead. Sofya reached for her and she took her out of Tobias's arms. "What do we do about the others aboard your ship? They heard her name as well."

Larr weighed this for less than a fivecount. "It doesn't matter. Few will remember, and fewer still will connect the name with the child. If we give them cause to ponder the matter, it becomes something to worry about. If we say nothing, do nothing, I think we'll be all right."

The princess had balled one fist in Mara's shirt and was sucking the other thumb. Her eyelids drooped. Tobias guessed that she'd be asleep by the time the pinnace came for them.

"What should we do with him?" he asked, indicating the slaver's corpse with a lift of his chin.

"Leave him," Mara said, ice in her expression. "That's what he deserves."

They picked their way along the darkening path back to the shore. Tobias led, Larr took the rear. Now that Mara wasn't terrified for Sofya's life and possessed with their pursuit of the slaver, she noticed things she had missed before. She was barefoot, and this path was rough with broken branches, jutting stones, and shattered seashells. Sofya rested in her arms, awake still, but leaning into her, bone weary from her ordeal. It took every bit of Mara's concentration to navigate the slope without falling or dropping the girl.

She still carried her weapon, though she had tried to give it back to the captain.

"Keep it for now," Larr said, reloading her own pistol. "We don't know that the other slavers are dead, or that there aren't more hiding among these isles who might be drawn by the shot I fired."

Well before they reached the bottom of the path, Mara heard the scrape of wood on sand and stone, splashes in the water, and then voices.

"Captain!" A man's voice. "Captain, you there?"

"Fools," Larr muttered under her breath. She stepped past Mara and Tobias. After perhaps ten strides, she said in a voice pitched to carry, but lower than that of her crewman, "Yes, Mister Wenn, we're here."

Mara spotted the sailors, pale forms blocking their way.

"And the wee one?"

"We have her. She's fine."

"The Two be praised," Ermond said.

Those with him murmured thanks as well.

"The two in the boat?" Larr asked.

"Dead. Both had blades, which we took. The boat was empty."

The captain showed no surprise at this. "All right. Let's get back to the ship. Well done, all of you."

She continued toward the shore, but the sailors waited, greeting Tobias and Mara, and peering at Sofya, seeing for themselves that she had come through the evening unscathed. She shied from them, clutching Mara, but she didn't cry.

"Told you we'd get her back," Ermond said to Tobias, his voice roughening.

"Thank you."

The sailor gripped Tobias's shoulder, and they followed Captain Larr.

Their journey back to the *Sea Dove* took less time than Mara expected. Their pursuit of the slavers felt endless, but really they hadn't gone far.

The ship glowed with torchfire, and long before they pulled alongside its hull they heard music, singing, and laughter. Mara smelled boiled shellfish.

"Most of them won't know we were gone," Larr said, so only Tobias and Mara could hear. "None of them will spare a thought for what you called the child."

Upon reaching the ship, Mara handed her pistol back to the captain and passed Sofya up to Tobias, who in turn gave her to a sailor on the *Dove*'s deck. They climbed the rope ladder in turn and were welcomed back by Larr's crew, who awaited them at the rail.

Yadreg, a bandage on his brow, didn't bother to mask his relief.

"Forgive me," he whispered to Mara.

"There's nothing to forgive, and she's fine."

The old man nodded, eyes bright with torchflame and tears.

The dancing, eating, and drinking went on for much of the night. Tobias and Mara remained on the deck, but held themselves apart. They stuffed themselves with crab and lobster. After a bell or two Sofya woke and ate her fill as well. The three of them danced and sang along, making up words to songs they didn't know.

The princess appeared none the worse for all that had happened. But she made no attempt to climb down from their arms, which was fine, since Tobias gave no indication that he would ever again trust anyone other than Mara to hold her.

In time, the locals began to leave the ship. The crew continued to eat and drink, but the festivities quieted. Sofya dozed off again. Mara guessed that she would sleep through the night.

"Come on," Mara said to Tobias. "It's time to go below."

"Are you as exhausted as I am?"

Mara kissed him and breathed, "No," into his ear. She pulled back and smiled. "You didn't think I was going to forget, did you? It's still Kheraya Ascendant. You thought I could be put off by the small matter of a kidnapping?"

His cheeks colored, but he smiled in return. "I didn't think anything. I haven't had a clear thought in a while now."

"Since she was taken?"

"No," he said. "Since our swim."

Mara laughed aloud, drawing glances from those nearest to them, and stirring Sofya for an instant. She took his hand and led him to the hatch leading down to the hold. There they paused and caught the captain's eye. She raised the tankard she held. Mara descended into the hold, pulling Tobias after her.

Other couples were already down here, but Mara didn't care. She led him to the shadowed corner they had long since claimed as their own, and set Sofya on the small pallet members of the crew had built for her. After tucking the princess's blankets around her, Mara faced Tobias and kissed him again, deeply this time, her fingers in his hair.

"Are we going to make a baby?" he whispered.

When she was still in Windhome, one of the other girls, who was far more daring and precocious than she, told her of herbs she drank to keep from getting pregnant. Since coming on the ship, Mara had asked some of the crew where to find those herbs, both because she anticipated this night, and because they needed to keep up appearances.

"No," she said, "we're not."

They kissed again and as they did she untied the drawstring of his breeches. He pulled back and gently lifted her shirt. She raised her arms, allowed him to pull it off her, and shook her hair free. Then she wriggled out of her breeches.

They lay down together on their pallet, kissing, touching. Their first time was over too soon. The girl in Windhome had warned Mara about this, as well. But the times after that were far better.

It was a late night

CHAPTER 11

5th Day of Kheraya's Descent, Year 634

On the fifth morning after the celebration of the Goddess's Ascendance, with a warm wind rising from the west, the *Sea Dove* left the waters of Chayde. They followed a zigzag course, tacking southward, across the open waters of Kheraya's Ocean.

Within half a day of unfurling their sails, they could no longer see land in any direction. For all the many leagues they had covered since joining Captain Larr's crew, Tobias had never felt so removed from his former life. The sky remained clear, but this far out from any isle, the swells grew higher, the waters rougher.

Mara, he knew, had feared that she might prove susceptible to seasickness. By luck, or by design, the captain kept both of them busy with duties on deck; Mara showed no sign of feeling ill. Sofya toddled from one rail to the other, a doll in one hand some kind of food – bread, dried fruit, hard cheese – in the other. She was as sure-footed as any sailor, and as immune to the pitch and roll.

Every so often, Tobias spotted a sea bird skimming above the water's surface, enormous wings held steady, tail twisting with the wind. Pods of dolphins briefly carved through the swells along the ship's hull. Clouds gathered on the western horizon, piling upon one another, a bank of distant gray in an otherwise sapphire sky. When Tobias pointed to them, Captain Larr shrugged off his concern.

"By the time they're here, we'll be elsewhere," she said, standing at the helm, feet braced, stance wide. "Be at ease, Mister Lijar, and count your blessings. This is as comfortable as a voyage across open ocean can be. Enjoy it."

He tried. The sun setting through the curtain of clouds set the western sky ablaze with reds and yellows, pinks and oranges. Stars emerged above them, burning brighter as the embers of the sunset cooled to darkness. The crescent moon chased the sun toward that same horizon. Its reflected glow danced on the peaks and troughs of the Goddess's ocean.

He hadn't wanted to leave Chayde, but never had he experienced anything like this day.

Later, below, he and Mara surrendered again to their passion, as they had each night since the solstice. As discreet as these sailors were about such things, a few of them couldn't help but comment on the sudden ardor of Tobias and Mara's "marriage."

"Been wonderin' what the two of you was waitin' for," Yadreg had said to Tobias the previous morning. "Figured you wasn't ready to risk another wee one. Glad to see you're makin' up for lost time."

Tobias blushed to the top of his head, his scalp prickling as he hurried away.

Yet the deepening of their love and the wonders he found on the open ocean couldn't erase that night of terror in the waters around Chayde. He barely let Sofya out of his sight. He slept with Mara in his arms, but he dreamed of slavers and pistols and that maze of tiny isles. In all his nightmares he chased Sofya's cries, calling for her, desperate to get her back. In all of them, her captors eluded him. He woke often in the darkness, heart tripping with panic, sweat dampening his hair. Some nights Mara woke as well and murmured to him until he drifted back into uneasy slumber. Other nights he lay alone with his fear.

Notwithstanding the captain's assurances, the weather deteriorated steadily. By the third morning after their departure, rain lashed the ship and waves hammered at the hull, sending plumes of water over the rails to soak the crew and slick an already treacherous deck. Captain Larr remained at the wheel, her face pale and streaked with rain, her dark hair plastered to her brow.

Upon seeing Tobias emerge from the hold, she waved him over

with a quick motion before gripping the helm again.

"I owe you an apology," she shouted to make herself heard over the wind and rain. "It came up on us faster than I expected."

"Are we in danger?"

She adjusted the wheel. "No. We've work to do to clear the storm, but the *Dove* has survived worse."

This put his mind at ease.

"We do have a choice to make. We've turned westward. I'm hoping to run straight through the worst of it and so clear the storm sooner. That will take us close to the Outer Ring, and, therefore, closer to Daerjen."

So much for an eased mind. Tobias stared into the rain.

"It's possible that the skies will clear before we reach land. If the storm persists, though, I think we should make port in Fanquir."

It could have been worse. Fanquir was on the eastern shore of Kantaad, which was separated from Daerjen by Fairisle and the Inward Sea.

"If you think the risk is too great, I can steer us south again, but that could mean another day or two of this weather."

"How long would we remain in Fanquir?"

"No more than a day, I should think. We'd wait out the storm, perhaps trade for ale and food, and then continue toward the Knot." She watched the water, steered the ship clear of a huge swell. "I need an answer soon, but not right away."

"It's all right. Make for Kantaad, captain. There's no reason anyone would search for us there. We'll be fine."

"I agree. Still, we'll keep you and your family out of sight." She smirked. "From what I hear, you and your wife shouldn't mind that too much."

He looked away, color rising again, and she laughed.

"Get below, Mister Lijar. My crew and I will steer us through this."

"I came up to help."

She shook her head. "You can't. You're learning still, and doing well, but I can't risk a green sailor in these winds." When he hesitated, she added, "That's an order, sailor."

Reluctantly, Tobias took refuge in the hold.

He hoped they would clear the storm before nightfall. They didn't.

Rain drenched the ship in sheets, and waves battered them. Through it all, the *Dove* continued westward into the teeth of the gale. Tobias, Mara, and Sofya remained below, where the motion of the vessel was more discomforting.

Late in the day, they heard faint cries from above. They ventured onto the deck to investigate and spotted ahead of them, through the deluge, the pale gray outline of a land mass, closer than Tobias had expected, though obscured by rain. Kantaad. Members of the crew assured them they would reach Blackrock Bay before nightfall.

The storm drove them back below. Tobias would have preferred to remain above, in spite of the danger. Anything would have been better than hiding in the hold, his stomach in his mouth.

Sofya fussed at whichever of them held her, not because she felt ill, he thought, but because she wanted to roam as she usually did. But the ship bucked and shuddered, and the hull creaked under the force of high seas and wind. They didn't dare set her down, even below decks.

Mara suffered the most. She hadn't eaten all day, and more than once she stumbled up onto the deck, was sick over the rail, and returned, haggard, sodden, and miserable.

The next several bells crawled by. Having seen Kantaad ahead of them, Tobias couldn't help but anticipate reaching the isle and the relative calm of Blackrock Bay.

Either the wind shifted again, or the currents and swells proved more implacable than the crew anticipated. As the sky darkened, he chanced another foray onto the deck. Kantaad still loomed before them, no closer than before. The storm had worsened.

Captain Larr clung to the helm. Tobias knew better than to approach her. He retreated to shelter, dispirited, nauseated, weary, though he had done little more than sit.

They tried to sleep. Tobias managed to doze off; he wasn't sure Mara did. She had long since emptied her stomach, but she continued to be sick.

At some point, well into the night, he awoke to find the ship's motion less pronounced, the roar of the wind abated, the groan of straining wood silenced.

"It calmed down a short time ago," Mara whispered beside him. "Maybe a quarter bell."

"How are you feeling?"

"A little better. I'm not ready to enlist in Kantaad's navy, but at least I'm not racing to the rail anymore."

He found her hand and brought it to his lips. "I'm glad." He sat up. "I'm going to take a look."

"I'll come."

They donned overshirts, left Sofya snoring softly on her pallet, and climbed to the deck. The *Dove* had entered a large inlet, the gap to the ocean behind them, wooded hills to the north and south, and the muted glow of the city ahead.

Rain still doused the ship, and a strong wind filled the sails. The ship's torches lit whitecaps on the water's surface. Compared to the violent seas through which they had passed, though, Blackrock Bay might as well have been a mountain lake.

Tobias wiped rain from his face, and started toward the hatch. Mara didn't budge.

"I can't go back down. Not yet."

"All right," he said, stepping back to the rail.

The captain joined them.

"Feeling any better?" she asked Mara.

"Yes, thank you. I guess I wouldn't make a very good sailor."

"You've done fine. All of you. A storm like that–" She cast a look over her shoulder, toward Kheraya's Ocean. "I've seen old sea dogs go a little green in such waters." She brushed a lock of wet hair from her forehead. "We'll be at the wharves in another bell or so. You still intend to keep out of sight?"

"One of us should," Tobias said. "As you've said, a ship is no place for a child. She'll draw attention."

"Aye, she might."

"I'll stay below," he said. "With any luck the skies will clear before long."

Larr squinted up into the rain. "They should. No storm can last forever."

Mara appreciated Tobias's offer to stay below with Sofya while she remained on deck. The idea of spending another bell in the hold turned her stomach.

They reached Kantaad later that night and found the docks crowded with ships. It seemed every captain in the bay had sought shelter in port, and few had come farther or arrived later than the *Dove*. The captain was forced to anchor them away from the wharves.

At first, Mara and Tobias thought this a blessing. The ship was safe and they could allow the princess to roam the deck without fearing she might be seen by passersby. Other members of the crew could row to and from the city, securing fresh food and other supplies.

If the storm had passed within the next day, they would have been fine. But dawn brought more dark clouds, harder rain, and a bitter wind. Others ships entered the bay, found the wharves full, and anchored near the *Dove*. As the waters grew more crowded, and vessels took positions within hailing distance, Tobias and Sofya returned to the hold.

The rain and wind raged on. Captain Larr had warned them about the weather they might encounter during Kheraya's warmer turns, but none among the crew could remember a storm lasting so long.

Tobias allowed the princess to wander the hold to her heart's content, but whenever she tried to climb the ladder, he stopped her. This frustrated her no end, until he and Mara both feared that sailors on other ships would hear her squalling. Worse, it drew the attention and suspicion of Captain Larr's crew, who wondered why they confined the child to the hold when the only dangers on deck were wind and rain.

"None of them are fools," the captain told Mara and Tobias after supper on their third night in the bay. They had repaired to her quarters and shut the door. "They know there's a reason you don't want the child seen. I'm afraid they're going to concoct stories that could be far more dangerous than the truth."

"Such as?" Tobias asked, watching Sofya as she tottered around the chamber.

Larr's quarters were cramped, but the princess didn't seem to mind. These surroundings were different, and that was enough.

"That you've stolen her from her real parents. That you're no better than the slavers in Chayde."

"They wouldn't believe that," Mara said.

The captain lifted a shoulder. "I can only reveal so much, and soon my assurances will begin to sound thin."

"You want us to tell them." Tobias offered this as a statement.

"I want you to trust us. All of us."

Tobias started to answer, but swallowed his first response.

Larr's expression flattened. "You don't, do you?"

"I trust you," he said. "And it's not that I distrust the others. You have to understand, captain: we're all that stands between her and the assassins who killed her parents. I don't believe any man or woman on this ship would intentionally do her harm. They wouldn't have to. A careless word spoken in the wrong place could mean her death."

Some of the captain's indignation sluiced away, leaving her looking deflated and fatigued. "I do understand. Truly. But these are good people. Explain to them what you've explained to me, and your secret will be safe. I'm sure of it."

Tobias said nothing.

"If you don't do it," Larr went on, "and the storm persists for another few days, you could be placing her in greater peril. Either one of the stories bandied about on this ship will take root and grow, or you'll have to allow her on deck, which poses its own risks."

"Are there any Oaqamarans aboard?" Tobias asked.

The captain bristled. "Gwinda is from Oaqamar. She left after the autarch's soldiers raided her town and executed so-called 'dissenters,' including her brother. Will you tell her you don't trust her because of where she's from? Do you know how many people I've met who wouldn't trust you because your skin is brown, or because—"

Tobias stopped her with a raised hand. "You're right. Forgive me."

Her expression didn't soften, but she dipped her chin.

"All right," he said, exhaling the words. "When should we tell them?"

The captain stared back at him, eyebrows raised.

"Now?"

"Can you think of a reason not to?"

Tobias sat back. Sofya walked to him and climbed into his lap. "I can't."

Larr stood and strode to the door. "Good. We'll gather below." She left Tobias and Mara to themselves.

"I didn't handle that well," he said.

"She'll forgive you."

"Do you think she's right about what we need to do?"

Mara tried to smile, but wasn't sure she succeeded. "We have to do something, and we have nothing but bad options. This is the least bad."

He blew out a breath. Sofya laughed and copied him, blowing one breath after another. Tobias kissed her nose, eliciting another laugh.

Mara and Tobias stood at the same time, and she took his free hand, led him out of the captain's quarters, and down into the hold.

They joined the captain there, and waited as the rest of the crew descended the ladder.

At last, Captain Larr rapped her knuckles on a wooden post, silencing the sailors.

"Mister and Missus Lijar would like a word. I've assured them that every one of you can be trusted not only to be true, but also to be discreet. Disappoint me, and you'll never sail aboard this ship again. Clear?"

They answered with nods and murmured assent, but already they had directed their stares at Tobias and Mara. She saw curiosity in most faces, but suspicion in a few. The captain was right to have them act tonight.

Tobias still held Sofya, who had put her thumb in her mouth and was eyeing the sailors.

"Many of you have noticed that we've kept Nava below decks for the past several days," he began, his tone leached of emotion. "Some of you are wondering why, and even thinking perhaps we have something to hide." He sighed. "And we do, but not what you think. Please forgive us, but Mara and I have misled you. We're not husband and wife, and Nava isn't our daughter. My name is Tobias Doljan. This is Mara Lijar. And Nava... Nava is the sovereign princess of Daerjen. Mearlan's daughter. I was his court Walker. I saved her the night he and the rest of his family were killed."

Silence. Mara couldn't tell if they were too stunned to reply or didn't believe him.

"How did you get away?" Ermond asked after some time. The big man leaned against a post, his bearing casual, but his gaze intent.

"I had help. I escaped the castle with aid from the former minister of arms. Nava and I were given shelter by an old couple who hate the Sheraighs, and then by the keepers of Sipar's Sanctuary. We found a place to stay in the Notch with help from a pair of Tirribin." He canted his head Mara's way. "Mara found us there, and together we fought off the assassins the night Captain Larr welcomed us aboard the *Dove*."

"So they're still after you."

"After her," Tobias said. He glanced down at the princess and smoothed her hair. "Yes."

Again, the sailors absorbed this wordlessly.

143

Tobias wet his lips. "I don't really have proof. Maybe you've noticed the faint scars on Nava's temple and chin. She got them that night. You can't miss my scars. I got them in the dungeon of Hayncalde Castle, from the chief assassin himself. He wanted to know where I'd hidden the princess, and I refused to tell." He pointed to smaller scars on his temple and ear. "I got these the night Mearlan died."

He went on with his tale, adding details when sailors interrupted him with questions. When at last he finished, the crew said nothing.

"I'm sorry we didn't tell you before," Tobias said, filling the silence. "Both of us are. But we're all the princess has. And we're not nearly enough to keep her safe should the men who are after her find us."

"Why keep her below?" Ermond asked.

Mara sensed that if they could win his trust, the others would follow.

"Captain Larr made it clear our first night aboard that most captains wouldn't allow children on their ships," she said. "We've been afraid that if sailors from other vessels see or hear her, they might wonder who she is. Even something that small could be enough to draw the attention of Mearlan's killers."

One of the women eyed the princess. "So her real name—"

"I think it's easier, safer, if we just call her Nava," Tobias said. "In fact, the best thing any of you can do is treat us all exactly as you already have."

After yet another silence, Ermond straightened. "All right, then. You had me wondering these past few days, but I'm satisfied." He caught the captain's eye and nodded.

"That's all," Larr said. "Off with you now. Night crew is up. The rest of you get some sleep. Here's hoping we can leave this bloody bay tomorrow."

Those who were to work the deck through the night left the hold. The rest stole off to darkened corners, or arranged themselves on pallets and hammocks. The captain joined Tobias, Mara, and Sofya.

"You did well."

"Thank you, captain."

"They won't fail you."

"I believe you."

"Yet you remain frightened."

"Where she's concerned? Always."

The captain grimaced. "I understand. Rest. As I say, I hope to be underway tomorrow."

She moved off. Mara took Tobias's hand again.

"Are you all right?"

"One wrong word," he said so only she could hear. "That's all it would take."

Mara could think of no reply.

The following morning brought no improvement in the weather. Ermond and eight sailors rowed the pinnace to Fanquir to buy food and drink, but beyond that they could only wait.

Tobias said little throughout the day. Mara wondered if he regretted the previous night's confession. Not that they could unspeak the words, or carry the entire ship back through time. That thought set her mind racing.

Perhaps the time had come to take a different approach to combatting their enemies. The greatest weapon she and Tobias possessed was their ability as Walkers. Tobias's chronofor had been destroyed the night of Mearlan's assassination, and hers had been taken from her by the traitors, Gillian Ainfor and Bexler Filt.

They would never have found chronofors in Chayde or Flynse. Bound devices of any sort were rare, none more so than chronofors. Here in the Outer Ring, however, within sailing distance of Islevale's wealthiest and most powerful lands, they might make inquiries through channels known only to a canny merchant like Larr.

She and Tobias carried two Bound apertures that he had taken from Hayncalde. They had some value for trade. They also had the tri-sextants and ministerial robes they had taken from Orzili and his men the night they fought off the assassins and joined the Sea *Dove*'s crew. These items, though, were so rare, so noteworthy, that any attempt they made to trade or sell them, would draw notice. For now, they had to keep them hidden.

Mara didn't speak of this with Tobias, but waited until he took his turn with the princess in the hold. She went above, approached the captain's door, and knocked.

At a summons from within, Mara entered.

Larr sat at her desk, studying a sea chart. "Missus Lijar," she said with genuine surprise. "What can I do for you?"

Mara closed the door, faced her. "We need a chronofor."

The captain indicated the chair beside her desk. Mara sat.

"This is rather abrupt," Larr said. "You've hardly spoken of any device since you joined my crew, and now you need a chronofor."

"We've needed one all along."

"Precisely. Has something happened to make the need more urgent? Do you need to Walk today?"

"Would it matter if we did? Would you be able to secure one for us so soon?"

Larr shook her head. "No. I ask out of curiosity." She picked up a small bronze figure from her desk and toyed with it. "The truth is, I wouldn't know where to find one. Which is not to say that we can't, or won't, but it could take time." She grinned. "An irony, yes?"

Mara couldn't tell if the captain expected an answer. This was her first conversation alone with the woman. Since Walking back in time and losing so many years, she'd had few opportunities to reflect on what it meant to be a sixteen year old girl in the body of a grown woman. Right now, though, facing Larr across the cluttered desk, she felt young and beyond her depth.

"We're Walkers," Mara said, trying to sound reasonable. "We can be of use to you, but only if we have a Bound device."

"I understand." She paused. "I have to ask – and I'd appreciate a candid answer – do you seek a chronofor so that you can serve the *Dove*, or so you can use it for your own purposes?"

That brought Mara up short. She blinked in the candlelight,

unsure of what to say.

"I see."

They eyed each other.

"Don't get me wrong," the captain said, leaning back in her chair. "By taking us to Chayde, you and Tobias have already repaid us and more for sheltering you. You've proven your worth, you've endeared yourselves to the crew. And your… your daughter is much loved."

"But?"

She opened one hand, and with the other set the bronze figure on the desk. "A Bound chronofor is no trifle. For all you've brought to us, it would still be a tremendous expense, particularly if it hastened your departure from the ship."

"We've offered you two Bound apertures. You can trade those–"

"A Bound chronofor is far more dear. You know this."

She did.

"So, you have no intention of finding a device for us?"

"Quite the contrary," Larr said. "I have every intention of doing so. And I'd like to work out an arrangement that would be fair and suitable to the two of you and to me."

"What sort of arrangement?"

"Well, let's begin with the obvious. You're welcome aboard this ship for as long as you care to stay. We'll feed you, we'll pay you a share of all our profits, and we'll keep you safe from the Sheraighs and the autarchy."

Mara tucked her chin, and motioned for the captain to continue.

"I'll begin immediately to try to find a chronofor, and I'll pay for it with resources of my own. It will be yours and Tobias's to use, but, at least initially, I'll expect you to use it in service to the *Dove*. When we all decide, by mutual agreement, that your use of the device has brought me profit equal to one half of the purchase price, I'll take those two apertures as payment for the balance. You'll then be free to leave at a time of your choosing, and the chronofor will be yours to take with you."

Mara hesitated. "Why do it that way? Why not take the apertures now?"

"Two reasons. First, using them to trade for a chronofor could raise questions. I assume Tobias took them from Hayncalde Castle."

She frowned, knowing she should have considered this.

"Second, I don't know when we'll find a Bound device, or what might happen between its acquisition and your fulfillment of this agreement. If you're forced to leave us, or we're separated for some reason, you might need those apertures for a trade of your own. You should hold on to them."

If Mara needed further proof of the captain's goodwill, here it was. This, too, would never have crossed her mind.

"I'll need to speak with Tobias, of course, but this strikes me as an equitable arrangement." She faltered, then said, "We need – I need – a sextant as well."

Larr's eyes widened. Apparently she understood how rare it was for a Traveler to have two talents. "You are full of surprises, Missus Lijar."

"The Two have blessed me."

"Apparently. I'll search for a sextant as well. It can be part of the same arrangement."

"Yes, all right."

The captain reached for the bronze figure again. "Speak with Tobias," she said. "Let me know what he says."

Mara stood, crossed back to the door.

"Does he know you're here?" Larr asked before Mara could leave.

She paused with her fingers on the handle. "No. He's been distracted since the incident with the slavers. He thought he'd lost her, and now he's afraid."

"Of?"

"Everything."

CHAPTER 12

12th Day of Sipar's Waking, Year 618

In the moments after Tache's death and Droë's disappearance, masters and mistresses, novitiates, and guards swarmed from the keeps, no doubt drawn by Lenna's screams and the boy's final cry. As they converged on Cresten, Lenna, and the corpse, word of the calamity spread, distorted by rumor and the first whiff of blame.

"What is this?" Albon demanded, pushing through the throng. "Who was that screaming bef–" He halted at the sight of the boy's desiccated corpse. "Blood and bone." He eyed Lenna, who sobbed still.

Several of her friends tried to comfort her, including Vahn. Cresten stood alone.

"What's happened here, Mister Padkar?"

"It was... It was a Tirribin, master."

"A Tirribin? You're certain?" Before Cresten could answer, he looked down at Tache again. "Of course you are." He rounded on the nearest guards. "I want these grounds searched. If you find the creature, kill it. From a distance. Arrows. If you have to draw your sword, it's too late."

In the dim light of moon-glow and torchfire, Cresten saw the lead guard falter momentarily.

"Yes, sir," he said. He and his comrades fanned out across the lower courtyard and toward the gate.

"Had you seen the demon before?" Albon asked, facing Cresten again.

"Yes."

"So you knew what it was, and you treated with it anyway, disregarding the danger."

Cresten darted a glance at Lenna. Albon followed his gaze, his expression darkening.

"We'll speak of this tomorrow. All of us, Miss Doen."

She nodded, too overwrought to speak.

"Take her to the keep," Albon said to the other girls. "The rest of you, back to your beds. There's nothing to be done here."

"What about the time demon?" one of the girls asked.

The weapons master looked a question Cresten's way. Cresten opened his hands, glanced in the direction Droë had gone.

"It's gone, and in any case, you'll be safer in the keeps. Now off with you."

Lenna's friends led her to the Windward Keep. The other novitiates retreated as well, in pairs and small groups. Albon signaled to two more soldiers, gesturing subtly at the body. The men lifted Tache and carried him toward the middle courtyard and the infirmary. A few of the masters and mistresses lingered, but they spoke among themselves in low, solemn tones. Before long the weapons master and Cresten stood alone.

"Was this revenge, Padkar? Did you finally get Tache back for the beatings he gave you?"

Cresten gaped, unable at first to muster an answer. "N- no!" he said. "It wasn't– That's not what happened! Tache and I were friends. It took time, but we wound up that way. This wasn't–" He'd intended to say it wasn't his fault, but his sense that he was to blame silenced him for an instant. "I didn't mean for any of this to happen."

"What did happen? Can you tell me now? It's just the two of us."

Cresten stared in the direction the guards had taken Tache's corpse. He wanted to tell Albon everything. Of all the masters and mistresses in the palace, no one had treated him better. But when he opened his mouth to speak, a sob escaped him. Before he knew it, he was weeping as he hadn't since leaving his home. Losing

Lenna, watching Tache die, sensing already that blame for the tragedy would fall on him, fearing that he deserved such a fate – it was too much.

Albon sighed and laid a meaty hand on his shoulder. "It's all right, lad," he said. "It's all right."

Meaningless words. It was far, far from all right. Overwhelmed as he was, Cresten understood this. Still, he accepted the man's comfort and, when he had cried himself out, allowed Albon to walk him back to the Leeward Keep. Neither of them spoke, not even to say goodnight.

Cresten climbed the stairs to the chamber he shared with the other boys his age. He heard voices as he approached; he was sure every person in the palace was awake. When he entered the room, conversations ceased. Everyone stared at him. He took a full breath, as if preparing to dive into deep waters, and walked to his bed.

Conversations resumed, now in whispers. After a few spirecounts, Vahn crossed to his bed.

"Are you all right?"

"Yes. Thanks."

"Good." He lingered, and Cresten thought he would ask him about events in the courtyard. After another fivecount, though, he said, "Well, I wanted to make sure." He walked away without waiting for Cresten's reply.

Cresten tugged off his clothes, climbed into bed, and bundled himself in his blankets. The other boys continued to talk, and several times he heard one or another speak his name. He tried to ignore them. It didn't matter what they said, he told himself. The chancellor, and the masters and mistresses, would decide his fate. He wouldn't have to wait long for their judgment.

He slept poorly, chased from dream to dream by the golden-haired Tirribin, and by Tache's withered form. He was awake before dawn.

A palace herald came to the boys' dorm with the first daylight bell.

"Cresten Padkar, Chancellor Samorij has instructed me to escort you to his chamber."

Cresten had already dressed. He stood and followed the herald out of the keep, across the courtyard, and into the chancellor's tower. He felt like a condemned man.

The herald did not bother to knock, but opened the door and waved Cresten inside. The chancellor stood by his desk, his hands behind his back, his expression more severe than Cresten would have thought possible on such an amiable man. Albon stood near the window, with Qemman Denmys, the master of Time Walking, and a dour woman wearing a uniform of purple and black. Cresten thought her the captain of the guard. Two chairs had been set before the desk. The chancellor indicated one of them now. Cresten sat.

"We will wait for Miss Doen," the chancellor said, in a voice like slag.

No one uttered a word. For several moments that felt much longer, the only sounds in the chamber were the coos of messenger doves and the rustle of their feathers.

At the click of the door handle, Cresten started, then twisted to peer back.

Lenna swayed on the threshold, her eyes flitting from one of them to the next. She appeared drawn, her eyes puffy and red.

"Come in, Miss Doen," the chancellor said, his tone more gentle than it had been.

Fear prickled the back of Cresten's neck.

The chancellor pointed to the chair beside Cresten. Lenna stepped to it, sparing Cresten the most cursory of glances, and sat, her eyes fixed on the floor.

"Does either of you have any notion of how long it's been since last a novitiate died on these grounds?"

Cresten had no idea. Lenna shook her head.

"I didn't either," the chancellor said. "Not until I went back through the records last night. This was the first in nearly half a century. The last was a boy who contracted Herjean pox. The palace healer wasn't able to attend to the lad in time. Over the years, Belvora have taken a toll, and once, when the palace was still new, an Arrokad took a girl from the Windward Keep. She was never heard from again, and the chancellor at the time never ascertained the truth of her fate.

"As far as I can tell, until last night, no novitiate had ever been killed by a Tirribin." He paused, his gaze shifting from one of them to the other. "Can one of you explain to me precisely what happened to Mister Tache?"

Neither of them answered.

"I gather that last night was not the first time this particular Tirribin has been in the palace. Is this true?"

Cresten resisted the urge to look at Albon. A part of him was angry with the man for betraying a confidence. A greater part knew Albon would deny that he owed Cresten any allegiance in this matter. Tache was dead. All other considerations paled next to that.

The silence stretched on.

"It is true," Lenna said, in a voice so soft Chancellor Samorij leaned forward to hear her better. "I spoke with her several times."

"Tirribin are dangerous creatures, Miss Doen. Why would you do this?"

She glanced up at him. "They're not dangerous to me. At least Droë isn't."

"Droë is its name?"

"*Her* name," Lenna said, a bit of steel in her tone. "And she would never hurt me. Tirribin are fascinated by time, and they possess knowledge and wisdom that any Walker would find valuable. Our conversations… they've taught me a great deal. And so you know, she wouldn't hurt Cresten, either. The first night we spoke to her–"

The chancellor turned a flinty eye on Cresten. "You saw it – her – too, Mister Padkar?"

"Yes, Lord Chancellor. And I believe Lenna's right. Droë wouldn't hurt either of us. She gave her word that first night."

"That means nothing to anyone except the two of you. Clearly the creature presents a mortal danger to every other person in this palace."

"No, she doesn't!" Lenna said. "She attacked Tache because he offended her, and because he threatened me."

Samorij scowled. "Is the Tirribin your guardian?"

"She's my friend."

"Do you consider her a friend as well, Mister Padkar?"

Cresten took too long to answer.

The chancellor straightened. "I see."

Lenna sent a glare Cresten's way.

He hated the Tirribin. He feared her, and he blamed her for the deterioration of his friendship with Lenna. But he would have said anything to make Lenna care for him again, and, as it happened, he couldn't fault the time demon for attacking Tache. The boy had brought that on himself.

"I don't think Droë would consider me a friend, Lord Chancellor. I'm not a Walker, and so to her I'm just another human. Still, I agree with Lenna: Droë wouldn't have hurt Tache if he hadn't provoked her."

"You don't think," the chancellor repeated, a sneer in his voice. "'She's my friend,' you say. Do you have any idea how naïve you both sound? How foolish? *A boy is dead!* Killed by your friend, Miss Doen. By this demon who you, Mister Padkar, describe as some benign creature who is not to be feared. You have both been breathtakingly reckless."

The chancellor crossed to the window and gripped the sill. He remained there for some time, his back to them, his breathing low and harsh. Neither the masters nor the woman in uniform said a word.

"What will you do with her?" Lenna asked after some time.

The chancellor stirred, roused by her question. "Your thoughts should be for yourself and for Mister Padkar, not for the Tirribin."

"Can't I spare a thought for all of us?"

Bold words. More bold by far than anything Cresten would have dared say. His esteem for Lenna rose ever more.

The chancellor stepped back to his desk.

"If I could have the creature killed, I would, and I assure you that our guards will be more vigilant than they have been." His glance at the woman in purple drew a curt nod. "The fact is, your Tirribin is one of the Ancients. Killing them is…" He opened his hands. "Even if we managed it, there would be a price. Any act that risks war with one of the septs has to be considered with utmost care." A bitter smile flickered across his features. "I expect your 'friend' is safe."

"And us?" Lenna asked.

The chancellor spared Cresten a glance before addressing her. "A more difficult matter. A boy has died, and in time parents will hear of the tragedy. They will worry about their own children. They'll demand to know what happened, and what we've done to prevent a recurrence. Men and women in distant courts will learn of it as well, and my judgment will be questioned." He eyed Lenna. "Yes, that matters," he said, perhaps anticipating her next query. "This palace serves a vital function between the oceans. The royals who summon you and your fellow novitiates to be their Walkers, Spanners, and Crossers must have confidence in me, and in the masters and mistresses who train you. It would be easy to assume that we are an enclave unto ourselves, but we're not. We are part of a vast network whose influence on events throughout Islevale should not be underestimated. The consequences of any damage to our reputation will span kingdoms and seas."

Cresten heard in the chancellor's words portents of his own doom. They might punish Lenna in some way, but there were limits to what they could do to her. She was a Walker. Their only Walker.

He was far less valuable to them. He excelled at his studies, but as a Spanner he was mediocre at best. Only his father's missive to the chancellor held him here – the vague promise of familial history, worth nothing under the circumstances. He wondered if they would send him from the palace empty-handed, or with a few coins on which to live, or with which to return home. He shuddered at the thought. No matter what happened, he would never go back to Qesle.

Cresten decided then that he also would not simply await his fate. If he was expendable, and if the chancellor had made up his mind to send him away, he could at least make himself a hero to Lenna.

"This was my fault, chancellor," he said, meeting the man's glower. "Lenna's conversations with the Tirribin were harmless. She's a Walker. She should be speaking with Droë. Nothing would have happened if I hadn't brought Tache to the lower courtyard."

"You brought him there?"

He resisted the impulse to lower his gaze. "Yes, Lord Chancellor."

"Why?"

Cresten lifted a shoulder. "Tache wanted to meet the Tirribin. He thought he could learn something of value from her."

The man frowned. "You're speaking in circles, Mister Padkar. You say that no harm would have come from Miss Doen's encounters with the Tirribin, but clearly Mister Tache learned of them."

"I told him about Droë, sir. I was–" He chanced a look at Lenna. She regarded him with contempt. "The Tirribin said things to Lenna and me one night that... that ruined our friendship. I was upset. I wasn't thinking, and so I mentioned to Tache that Lenna had spoken with a time demon. After that, he barely talked to me about anything else. He wanted to meet Droë, and he insisted that I take him to see her at the first opportunity. Once Tache made up his mind about something... well, I didn't have a lot of choice. The point is, this was my doing, and his. Lenna did nothing wrong."

"I'm not certain I agree with that, Mister Padkar, but I appreciate your candor."

Cresten glanced at Lenna again. She watched him still, but her expression had softened.

"Miss Doen, do you have anything to add?"

She shifted in her chair. "This wasn't Cresten's fault either. Tache was... no one could control him. No one could tell him what to do. I definitely couldn't, and I shouldn't be surprised that Cresten couldn't either. He insulted Droë; it was like he was trying to provoke her. That's why he died."

She said this in a low voice, eyes on the floor in front of her. When she finished, she regarded him sidelong again. Her mouth twitched in what might have been an attempt at a smile.

"Your defense of each other is heartwarming," the chancellor said, sounding unmoved, "but the fact remains that both of you have acted irresponsibly. We can't simply ignore your behavior, and we can't be seen to condone it."

He nodded to the woman in uniform. She opened the door to the chamber.

"Please wait in the antechamber. We'll speak with you again shortly."

Cresten and Lenna shared a glance, stood in unison, and crossed the chamber to the door. Cresten sensed Albon studying him as he passed, but kept his eyes fixed on Lenna's back. Once they were in the antechamber, the captain of the guard shut the door again. Lenna stepped to a window. Cresten remained where he was, unsure of what else he ought to do.

After some time, Lenna said, "You didn't have to say all that."

"I think I did."

She faced him. "I keep asking myself why you would have brought Tache to where Droë and I were talking. It hadn't occurred to me that he wouldn't have given you any choice. I'm… I'm sorry I blamed you."

He shook his head. "That's not… Listen to me: they're going to punish you. I don't know what they'll do, but it will be bad. Probably embarrassing. They'll want to make an example of you. But you'll be all right. You're a Walker. They can't make you leave."

Her brow creased. "Well, of course not. Neither of us—"

"I won't be here tomorrow. I'm expendable. They have no reason to think I'm anything special. I'm a Spanner, and not a particularly good one. My father once thought I could be good at it, but my father… He doesn't know anything."

"You're speaking nonsense. They won't make you leave. You're smart, and you're getting really good with your sword work."

Not long ago, his heart would have sung to hear her say such things.

"We're all smart. That's one of the reasons we're here. As for my sword work – well, no one paired with me in the lower courtyard has reason to panic."

She smiled, drawing a smile to his lips as well. "Still–"

"I won't go far," he said, speaking over her. "I want you to know that. I won't go home, and I won't have enough coin to go anywhere else. I'll try to find a job in town. I'd be honored if you'd still be my friend."

"Cresten, you're not going anywhere. What you said before about our punishments, that was probably true. It's what they'll do to both of us. And of course I'm still your friend."

He knew better than to argue further, just as he knew better than to share her optimism. She had declared her friendship. That was enough.

They lapsed into another silence, Lenna at the window, Cresten on a low, upholstered bench near the door. After perhaps a quarter bell, the door to the chancellor's chamber opened again revealing Albon, gray-faced and somber.

The last confirmation Cresten needed.

"Miss Doen, would you join us again? Mister Padkar, we will speak with you when we're done with her." That was all. He turned away before either of them could answer.

Lenna fixed a smile on her lovely face. "It will be all right," she said. "For both of us. You'll see."

She started away from him.

"Lenna."

She stopped, waited.

He wasn't sure what he wanted to say, and even if he had been, he wasn't brave enough to speak his heart. "I- I hope you're right. Good luck."

She left him there. Cresten sat once more.

Not long after, the door opened and Lenna reemerged from the chamber, clearly shaken. All the blood had fled her cheeks and her breaths were deliberate, as if she sought to slow her heart.

"Mister Padkar," Albon called, "we'll see you now."

He stood, but all his attention remained fixed on Lenna.

"What happened?"

She halted before him but wouldn't look him in the eye. She seemed in a daze. "They intend to inform my parents of what happened. I'm under a strict curfew – no time in the courtyards after evening meal. I'm confined to the keep. And for two turns, I'll be accompanied by a guard everywhere I go. They say that's for my protection, to keep Droë from hurting me, but I know better. It's like you said: they wish to make an example of me, to humiliate me."

"I'm sorry," he said. "You're stronger than they are, and you're a Walker. There may be no one in the palace with a future brighter than yours. Remember that."

She raised her gaze to his. "Yes. Thank you, I will. I'll see you later."

No, you won't. "The Two keep you safe," he said.

Lenna frowned at this.

"Mister Padkar," Albon called again.

"I have to go. Remember what I said. I won't go far. If you need me, have someone search the village."

The crease in her brow deepened. He didn't wait for her response, but walked into the chancellor's chambers, straight-backed, purposeful. If this was the last she would see of him, she would remember him as brave, resolute, confident.

Albon closed the door as he passed. Cresten reclaimed his chair before Chancellor Samorij.

"Mister Padkar," the man began, "thank you for your patience."

"Of course."

"This is a most difficult situation, as I'm sure you understand. The loss of a novitiate is tragedy enough, but under circumstances such as these…" He gave a solemn shake of his head. "We have, all of us, struggled with our consciences and our judgment. These decisions are... excruciating."

"Really?" Cresten said, amazed by his own audacity, by what he had decided to say and do. "It all seems rather simple to me. Lenna is a Walker. You can't expel her from the palace. She's worth too much to you. She'll bring a good deal of gold when she's finally summoned to a court. In contrast, I'm of little importance." He almost said, *I'm lint.* He thought of Wink, and allowed himself the most fleeting of smiles. "I'm a novitiate with little apparent potential, with Traveling talents that are mundane and poorly developed. Blaming me and removing me from the palace is the simplest solution. Isn't that so?"

"I resent your implication, Mister Padkar," the chancellor said, his tone less forceful than his words. "This has nothing to do with gold, and everything–"

"Please," Cresten said, cutting him off. "I'm not the naif you think I am."

The chancellor bristled, but fell silent.

Cresten twisted in his chair. "I'm right, aren't I?" he asked of Albon and Master Denmys. "It's your intention to send me away."

The Walking master refused to look him in the eye, but after the briefest hesitation, Albon nodded.

Cresten should have been crushed, terrified. Instead, he took satisfaction in having anticipated this. He faced the chancellor again. "I'm willing to go, for Lenna's sake. And I'll keep silent, which I know you would prefer."

Samorij made no effort to mask his surprise. "You will? That is most... unexpected. You're doing a great service to this palace and to all your fellow novitiates."

"Yes, I am. And I expect a few considerations in return."

"Considerations."

"That's right. Some coin, a Bound sextant, and a weapon, preferably a flintlock. A blade would be acceptable."

"That is a presumption, Mister Padkar! This is not a negotiation! This is a matter of discipline, of atonement for causing a tragedy.

If you believe that we are so desperate to keep you from speaking of this to others that we would buy your silence, you're gravely mistaken."

It was bluster, and nothing more. Cresten was certain of it.

"Very well," he said. "Then on second thought, I would rather not leave, and if forced to, I'll shout the reason why from the hilltops. Everyone will know that a Tirribin slipped past your guards and killed a novitiate, and everyone will know as well that two of us were deemed responsible, but only one of us was expelled. Shall we ask Master Albon whose actions he deems more reckless, Lenna's or mine?"

Samorij narrowed his eyes, but shook his head. "That won't be necessary. We are prepared to offer you transportation back to your home village."

"I won't go to Qesle, but whatever you would have paid a captain to take me there you can give to me instead. That leaves the matter of the sextant and the weapon."

"I will not—"

"I believe we can spare a blade, Lord Chancellor," Albon said. "We have plenty of old weapons. I wouldn't feel right sending the lad out into the streets unarmed. There are cutthroats aplenty on this isle, even in Windhome, and we've had Belvora here in my memory. The boy has magick; he'd be in danger from that sort of demon."

Cresten regarded the chancellor and quirked an eyebrow.

Samorij's expression curdled. "Fine."

"Why do you want a sextant?" Denmys asked, his voice a rasp.

Cresten turned. "Because I intend to train myself to be a Spanner."

"You'll never be sent to a court," the chancellor said. "No royal between the oceans would summon an exile from this palace, or, for that matter, a self-trained Traveler."

"Then you have nothing to fear from giving me what I want."

Denmys shook his head. "You can't train yourself. Only the most arrogant of boys would think otherwise."

Cresten opened his hands in what he believed to be a fair imitation of Samorij. "Guilty as charged. I've memorized coordinates, learned all I can about sextants. I know I can train myself. But I need a Bound device."

"Sextants are quite dear," the chancellor said. "All Bound objects are."

"So is my silence. What you're doing here is unjust and cynical. But I care about Lenna and I don't want to see her hurt or humiliated, so I'll go quietly. You get everything you want. You can blame me for Tache's death, and you can get all the gold you've expected for your lone Walker. Under the circumstances you should count yourselves lucky that I'm not demanding more."

The chancellor eyed him, anger in his expression, but also, Cresten thought, grudging respect. "You've come a long way from that first morning so many years ago. I can still see your face, bruised from the beating you'd suffered the night before."

"From Tache, actually."

"Can you get him a sextant without anyone being the wiser?" Samorij asked Denmys. "I hope never to expel another novitiate, but if I do, I don't want to be subject to this sort of extortion again."

"I'll have one here by midday, Lord Chancellor."

"And I'll have a sword for him," Albon said.

"Very well. Captain, if you would accompany Mister Padkar to the Leeward Keep so that he might gather his other possessions—"

Albon raised a hand, stopping him. "I'll take him, Lord Chancellor. That way he can choose a weapon to his liking."

"Yes, fine. All of you are dismissed."

Samorij showed Cresten his back and crossed to his window. Cresten levered himself out of his chair and walked to the door.

"Mister Padkar," the chancellor said, stopping him on the threshold.

Cresten turned.

"Remember your end of this bargain. Only you, Miss Doen, and the masters present for our conversation know what happened in this chamber today. I can keep the others from speaking of our arrangement, but all I have from you is your word."

"That's all you need, sir," Cresten said, pride raising his chin.

"Very well. Come back here when you're ready to leave. I'll have your coin for you."

Cresten left the chamber and allowed Albon to lead him out of the keep. They said nothing as they descended the stairway, but once they were in the middle courtyard, the weapons master eyed him sidelong.

"That was the nerviest thing I've seen in some time."

Cresten tried to suppress a grin, failed.

"You care about her that much?"

"I do. I also care about me. There's nothing for me in Qesle, and if I'm going to make a life for myself here, I need a weapon and a bit of coin."

"And the sextant?"

"I meant what I said. I'm going to be a Spanner. I can't train myself without a sextant."

The master nodded. "I remember you from that first day as well. The chancellor is right: you're not the same lad Tache bloodied that night."

Cresten halted and proffered a hand to the master. "Thank you for all you've done for me. There were times when you were the only person here who I considered a friend. I won't forget you."

Albon gripped his hand. "You'll find your way, lad. You've things to learn yet, but you'll be fine."

They walked on. After a few steps Albon shook his head and chuckled. "Nervy. That's the word, all right."

CHAPTER 13

13th Day of Sipar's Waking, Year 618

The rest of the novitiates were in lessons, so no one saw him pack his meager belongings. He scanned the dormitory, his eyes coming to rest on Vahn's pallet. He pulled out a scrap of parchment and took a quill and ink from a shelf above another bed.

Take care of her. —C

He tucked the parchment under a corner of Vahn's pillow and left the chamber.

Albon awaited him at the base of the stairway.

They went to the armory next. There the weapons master allowed him to choose from an array of swords.

"Take one you like," Albon said.

"I thought you were going to give me something old, useless."

The weapons master winked. "As far as the chancellor will know, that's exactly what I did."

Cresten smiled and considered the selection of weapons. After brief consideration, he reached for a short sword, its blade gleaming with sunlight from the open door.

"A good choice. You're lanky. You've plenty of reach on your own. This will be an easier weapon to master and control." Albon retrieved a worn leather sheath from the corner of the room. "Take this as well."

"My thanks."

A bell tolled in the courtyard.

"It's time for me to be training your friends. Good luck to you, lad. I hope to see you again sometime."

Cresten faltered, tears blurring his vision. It was one thing to speak of leaving the palace. It was another entirely to say farewell to the weapons master. He blinked several times, unwilling to cry in front of Albon.

The master squeezed his shoulder once more and left him there. Cresten started back toward the middle courtyard and the chancellor's chamber. Along the way, he tucked the blade and sheath Albon had given him into his sack. He didn't wish to get the weapons master in trouble.

This time, the chancellor did not invite him to sit. He handed Cresten a small leather pouch that rang with coins.

"Ten treys and ten quads," he said. "I might have given you more, but with the other things you're taking, I feel that we've been more than fair."

A golden sextant on the chancellor's desk drew Cresten's gaze. Sunlight from the window shimmered on its arc, casting ghostly reflections on an adjacent wall.

"Ah, yes." Samorij retrieved the sextant and handed it to him. "Albon gave you a weapon, I trust."

"Yes, Lord Chancellor."

"Good. Then I will wish you well, and bid you leave this place at once."

Cresten thinned a smile. "Yes, sir." He slipped the sextant into his sack, and left the chamber. Once out of the keep, he crossed through the courtyards near where Albon drilled novitiates in sword work. Cresten followed a path along the far side of the open space, striding toward the lower gate, refusing to look at the others.

"Cresten!"

He nearly stumbled at the sound of her voice, but he kept his feet, and didn't slow.

"Cresten, wait!"

He halted, heaved a sigh. Lenna stood in the middle of the courtyard. She gripped a sword in one hand, its tip nearly brushing the ground. A guard stood a few paces behind her, eyeing them both.

"I told you what would happen," he called to her. "I have to leave now. Remember all that I said."

"This isn't fair! To you, I mean."

He shrugged. "No, it's not."

"I'm sorry."

Cresten wasn't sure how to respond. He nodded once, turned from her, and walked to the gate. Lenna didn't call to him again.

The guards must have known to expect him. They made no attempt to stop him.

As he followed the cobbled lane from the palace down toward Windhome, he grew wary. It was midday. Even in the most dangerous parts of the village, he had nothing to fear for several hours. Then again, he had no idea where he would sleep this night, or where he would find food. For the first time in his life, two turns shy of his thirteenth birthday, he was utterly alone.

Cresten paused on the lane to strap on his blade, believing he would be safer if thieves and cutthroats knew he was armed. Then he walked on, feeling both small and conspicuous. He decided his first task should be to secure lodging for the night. He had no desire to sleep in the streets.

The first inn he found, the *Red Mist*, stood not too far from the palace. Cresten eyed the exterior and decided it might be a pleasant place in which to stay. Upon stepping inside he was greeted by scents of warm bread and musty wine. And utter silence. Men and a few women sat at tables. Two serving girls stood in the middle of the great room staring at him, platters held before them.

"What do you want, lad?" asked a burly man by the bar, his tone guarded. He was dark-skinned and bronze-haired, and he spoke with the accent of the Labyrinth.

"A- A room. Please."

"Where's your ma and da?"

Cresten shook his head. "It's just me."

The man stepped out from behind the bar, and approached him. "This ain't no place for children. Or beggars."

"I'm not... I have money."

"It's a trey a night to stay here. The *Mist* is a place for gentlemen and ladies."

A trey a night!

"I'm sorry. I didn't know."

The man nodded once, and indicated the door with a jerk of his chin. Cresten left. As he pulled the door closed behind him, he heard laughter.

Continuing toward the wharves, he passed several inns that appeared from without to be as far beyond his means as the *Mist* had been. As the lanes grew dirtier and smellier, the establishments changed as well. Women stood outside several of them, dressed in gowns both tattered and alluring. He hurried past them. Eventually, he spotted an inn – the *Brazen Hound* – that struck him as run-down enough to be affordable, but reputable enough to be safe. Taking a steadying breath, he pushed through the door into the common room.

"Hey you!" a man called from the bar. "No children in here! Didn't you see the sign?"

Cresten hadn't. He stood stock still for a moment before pivoting on his heel.

"Hold on." A different voice, also a man. He emerged from behind the bar and shuffled toward Cresten, green eyes narrowed, his gaze keen as it raked over him. He was silver-haired, dark-skinned, thin and bent.

"You from the palace?"

Cresten nodded.

"You wash out? No power?"

"No, it wasn't that."

"All right if it was. S'what happened to me."

"You were a novitiate?"

The man grinned, exposing a broad gap where his front teeth should have been. "Long time ago. What's your name?"

Cresten faltered, glanced around. Others watched him. "What's yours?" he said, considering the old man again.

"Ho!" A woman's voice this time, also from the bar. "He's a clever one, Quinn. Best have a care."

For his part, the old man stared down at Cresten, waiting.

"I'm Cresten. I didn't wash out. I was… I was told to leave."

The man raised his eyebrows. "Told to leave. Sounds serious. You need a place for the night? Have passage home in the morning?"

He shook his head. "I'm not going home. I need a place for a while. I have coin."

"It's a quad a night to stay here more than a ha'turn. Two if you eat a meal. You afford that?"

The blood rushed from Cresten's cheeks, leaving them cold. He couldn't afford it for long – less than two turns if he spent his money on nothing else. Then again, it was far better than the price at the *Red Mist*. He didn't know how many places would be cheaper.

"I can afford it for tonight," he said, his voice small.

"For less than a ha'turn it's two a night plus one for the meal."

He scanned the room, taking in the worn floors, the dull, scratched bar, the mismatched tables and chairs, the grimy clientele, with their threadbare clothes. The place stank of sweat, of stale ale and wine and ancient pipe smoke. If he couldn't afford this, what kind of dunghill awaited him?

"I'd better go," he said.

The man gripped his arm, his fingers bony and strong. "Not yet, not yet." He peered over his shoulder. "That small room in the back still free, Lam?"

"What of it?" Lam was the first man, the one who told Cresten to leave. He was younger, broad in the chest, with lank dark hair and a fat gut. His skin was pale, his eyes dark. Cresten guessed that he wasn't from Trevynisle, or anywhere in the north.

"You can have that one for one quad a night," the old man told Cresten.

The younger man stepped out from behind the bar. "Now, see here–"

"My place, my rules."

"*Our* place."

The silver-haired man eyed the other. He was no match for Lam physically, but something in his bearing stopped the younger man. "Fine. Just keep him out of my way."

The old man smiled and held out a hand. "Give me two now," he said. "One for the night, one to show you plan to come back. The rest you can pay as you go."

Cresten looked around again, still conscious of the others scrutinizing him. He pulled the leather pouch from his pocket, plucked two quads from within, and handed them to the man.

"Come along. I'll show you your room."

The man steered Cresten past the bar and down a ramshackle corridor, to a gray wooden door that hung unevenly on its rusted hinges.

Cresten was prepared for the worst, but though the room was cramped, it was clean. An empty wash basin rested on a small, plain chest of drawers, and a blanket covered a pallet of fresh straw.

"It's not much, but I don't suppose you need much, do you?"

"No."

The man started to leave.

"I need a job," Cresten said to the man's back.

The old man faced him again, thoughtful. "That you do. We've got nothin' for you here. Not right now, that is. Can you cut gaaz?"

"If I have to."

"I know someone. Leads a cutting gang. She's hard, but fair. You could do worse. It would be a start, at least." He hiked a shoulder and let it drop. "I can introduce you."

"Yes, thank you." Before the man could turn away again, Cresten said, "You never told me your name. Did that woman call you Quinn?"

"She did. Most do. You can." He shuffled back to Cresten and held out a thin hand. "It's good to meet you, Cresten. My name's Quinnel Orzili."

Quinn walked him down to the Windhome waterfront, and south along the rocky coast to a stretch of shoreline where stone and white sand gave way to a pale, warm brown. There women and children stooped under a bright sun, knee deep in the sea, cutting blocks of mud from the seabed.

Quinn removed his shoes and motioned for Cresten to do the same. Quinn didn't wait, and Cresten slogged after him through cold water. They waded out to a cluster of workers. A diminutive woman stood nearby, arms crossed over her chest, a broad-rimmed straw hat shading her features. She wore a simple shift that hung to her knees, the bottom half of it damp.

"Poelu," Quinn said as they approached her.

She pivoted, eyes narrowed. She spared Quinn a quick glance and looked Cresten up and down. Her bronze hair was streaked broadly with white, but her face was smooth, her bare arms toned and muscular.

"Who's this?" she asked, her accent similar to those of the stewards in the palace.

"His name is Cresten. He needs a job."

She studied him the way she might a horse she intended to buy.

"He's too tall. Bending over to cut gaaz…" she shook her head. "No good for one this big."

"Isn't that something he can decide for himself?"

Poelu scowled. "His hands are big. Hard to pull up blocks with fat fingers."

Cresten peered down at his hands, hoping neither of them would notice. He'd never thought of his fingers as fat.

"He looks strong to me. And I assume he's smart. He comes from the palace."

"Palace people aren't so smart."

"He needs a job, Poelu."

"*You* need him to have a job, so that he can pay you for something."

Quinn grinned. "Yes."

She sighed, her lips twisting sourly. "Why didn't you say so straight off?"

The old man started back toward shore. "You can find your way back to the *Hound*?" he called over his shoulder.

"Yes," Cresten answered, not at all certain he wanted to be alone with this surly woman.

"Good. Supper's at sundown."

When he faced the woman again, she was already glaring at him.

"Cresten, he called you."

"Yes, ma'am."

"Gaaz cutting is hard work. Long, hot, even in the God's Waking. Your back gonna hurt. And you'll need a hat. You pay for that."

"All right."

"You ever cut before?"

Cresten hesitated before shaking his head. She muttered something under her breath that he couldn't hear.

She pulled two tools from a pocket he hadn't seen. One was a long curved blade. It didn't appear particular sharp. The other was straight and tapered, like a dagger, but one edge had a curled lip that he guessed was meant to slip under the cut block and pry it loose.

"Knife," she said, holding up the curved blade. She lifted the other implement. "Handloy." She pointed to a stack of bricks not far from where they stood. As Cresten eyed it, one of the women added several more blocks to the pile. "All should look like that," Poelu said. "You do that?"

"I think so."

She held out the tools to him and gave each a little shake. "Take. Try. Let me see."

Cresten took them from her, bent over to examine the sea floor where he was standing, and knelt, heedless of his breeches. He glanced up at the woman in time to see her nod in approval.

He cut out a brick, trying to match the depth and dimensions of those carved by the others. His lines were reasonably straight. The trouble began when he set down the blade and used the handloy to try to pry up the brick. He struggled to fit the tool into the groove he'd made, and soon had ruined his corners and edge on one side. The woman nearest him had cut and removed two of her own in the time he had taken with this first brick. He tried again from the other side, sloshing around in the low swells to improve his angle.

Poelu made a clicking noise with her tongue.

It took him several more tries, but in time he gouged his brick away from the sea floor and lifted it out of the brine. Misshapen, uneven, it resembled a ball of raw bread dough more than it did a brick.

He hazarded a glance at the gang leader, who stared back at him, her expression flat. She held out her hand, and he gave her the brick. She produced another knife, and after a few seconds of slapping and sculpting had shaped his effort into something resembling a block.

"Again," she said.

His next several efforts were no better than the first, but as he continued to cut and pry, he grew more adept. The last ten or twelve bricks he cut needed only a bit of repair. Still Poelu remained with him throughout the day, instructing him, and berating him for his poor results.

By the time she called for the others to stop, he was exhausted. His knees and back ached. His fingers were raw. Sweat stung the back of his neck, which had been roasted by the sun. The air hadn't been particularly warm this day, and it cooled now as their shadows lengthened. But he knew he would pay for not protecting the skin on his neck.

He staggered to his feet and tried to hand his tools back to Poelu.

"You keep. I'll take out of your pay."

He frowned.

"Not too much," she said. "Don't worry. Tomorrow morning, sunup. You'll be here, yes?"

"Yes."

"Good." She examined his neck and winced. "Get a hat."

He limped back to shore, followed the strand to the wharves, and the city lane to the marketplace. Most of the merchants had left for the night, but he did manage to find a woman who was selling hats similar to those Poelu and her workers wore. He found one that fit and bought it, begrudging the expense.

He thought he would be too weary to eat, but upon entering the inn, he was assailed by the aromas of roasted fowl, fresh bread, and steamed roots. Quinn marked his arrival, waved him to a small table near the back of the common room, and soon had set a platter of food in front of him.

"How was it?"

"I'm not very good," Cresten said around a mouthful of hen.

"No, I don't imagine. You will be soon enough. Or you won't, and she'll cast you off."

He grimaced at this, but Quinn had already started back to the bar. After finishing his meal, and sopping his platter clean with the bread, he stumbled back to his tiny room and fell onto his pallet. His breeches were still damp, but he couldn't bring himself to stand back up and undress. He couldn't remember ever being this tired. Only as he drifted off to sleep did it occur to him to marvel at the fact that he had awakened that very morning in the Travelers' Palace. Already he felt removed from his old life by a hundred leagues and as many turns.

Cresten woke to chatter out in the common room of the inn, and sunlight seeping into his chamber past a shuttered window. He closed his eyes again, then sat bolt upright. Sunlight.

He leapt out of bed, grabbed his shoes, tools, and new hat, and sprinted from the room. Halfway to the common room, he remembered to go back and lock his door. Then he left, hopping to pull on each shoe, and clutching the hat as he dodged and weaved his way through the city lanes and marketplace.

By the time he reached the shoreline and picked his way southward to the gaaz beds, several teams of cutters waded in the shallows.

He headed out through the cold swells, the footing uneven

and slick where teams had already harvested bricks from the mud. Cresten didn't care. He scanned the water for Poelu, squinting against reflected sunlight. Spotting her at last, he strode toward her, splashing loudly, stepping around other gaaz gangs, earning hard stares from their leaders.

"You don't work here," she said, implacable. She held out her hand. "Give me my tools."

"I slept too long. I'm sorry."

"I told you, you be here at sun up." She pointed at the sun. "Sun up three bells already. Give me tools and leave!"

"It won't happen again, Poelu. I swear. Yesterday was… It won't happen again."

"I know it won't! Because you leave now!"

They glared at each other. Poelu gave no indication that she intended to back down. And he refused to give up this job. He had worked too hard the day before; he wanted to be paid.

So he turned his back on her and waded out to where her other cutters worked. There, he dropped to his knees with a splash and began to cut his first brick of the day.

He heard Poelu sloshing after him, but he kept his attention on his work. She halted just behind him, saying not a word. Cresten was certain he had only one chance to get this right. He made his cuts with precision, took hold of the handloy, and slid it in place, the way he had figured out the day before.

With a swift, sweeping motion, and a twist of his wrist, he cut the brick free. He pulled it from the water and held it up, still not looking Poelu's way. It wasn't perfect, but it was his best brick so far, a vast improvement over the first few he'd cut the previous day.

She said nothing, but she walked away from him without telling him again to leave. That was all the confirmation he needed. He set his hat in place and continued to work.

The day dragged. The air was still, the sun's heat unrelenting. After some time he could no longer tell where the dampness from the sea ended and the dampness from sweat began. He couldn't imagine how the other workers survived the hottest turns of the

Goddess. He hadn't brought anything to drink, and none of the other cutters offered to share. He sensed that they resented his mere presence.

By midday, he was famished, but he hadn't brought food either. His muscles ached. Blisters opened on his hands, stinging in the salt water. He worked slowly, but steadily, his bricks piling up beside him. He couldn't yet cut with the speed and skill of the older woman toiling near him, so he didn't try to keep up. He cut what he could, shaped them with care, tried not to worry about the size of his pile next to those of the rest.

Late in the day, Poelu circled back to him. She bent over his blocks and examined them.

"You're slow," she said.

He kept cutting. "I'm new."

"I pay by the brick. You know this, yes?"

"I guessed."

She didn't answer. After a time, he assumed that she had moved on. He chanced a quick peek in her direction. She still stood by him.

"These bricks are good."

Surprised, he couldn't keep from smiling. "Thank you."

"Why you leave palace?"

As quickly as it came, his smile vanished. He went back to cutting. "I did something foolish, and a boy died."

"You kill him?"

"No, but if I'd been smarter, and maybe braver, he'd still be alive."

After another silence, she said, "Getting late. You be here first thing tomorrow, you understand? I let you stay today, but two days consecutive and I'll send you away."

"I'll be here."

"Bring drink tomorrow, and food. I don't want you dropping dead in the sea. Bad for business."

He wanted to tell her that he couldn't afford to keep buying things to bring to the beds. A hat, now a water skin, and food.

Plus his tools. At this rate he would never earn enough to stay at the *Hound*. But these were his problems, not hers.

Cresten slept fitfully that night, waking himself nearly every bell out of fear that he would sleep too late again. When he woke to the soft silver glow of approaching dawn, he rose, dressed, and raced to the gaaz beds. He was there before Poelu.

The next night, he slept better and still managed to rouse himself in time. And in the days that followed, he fell into a rhythm. His body grew ever more accustomed to waking early, and also to the rigors of gaaz cutting. His bricks looked better, and he had more of them at the end of each day. He didn't bother spending money on extra food to bring with him, and rather than buying a skin, he convinced Quinn to give him an old, empty wine flask that he filled each morning with fresh water and stoppered with a clean piece of cloth.

To his surprise, he didn't miss the palace. He'd had few friends, and at the end he cared only about Lenna.

Her he did miss. He thought about her constantly, wondering where she was and who she was with. They had repaired their friendship, and at the time that was enough to convince him he would see her again. Now, only a ha'turn removed from his time as a novitiate, he knew this would never happen. She was a Walker, destined to serve one of Islevale's great powers. He was a gaaz cutter, scrounging for treys and rounds. She was less than a league away, but they inhabited different worlds. Loss of her throbbed dully in his chest, constant, but manageable. She had forgiven him at the end. That would have to be enough.

When Poelu finally paid him for the first time, Cresten was pleasantly surprised. What she gave him was far from a fortune – four treys and eight quads, after what she took out for the blade and handloy – but it was enough to convince him that he could survive in Windhome.

Survival, though, was but one of his goals. Every day he stumbled back to the inn too weary to do more than eat and collapse onto his pallet. His sword and sextant remained hidden in his sack. He hadn't touched either since leaving the palace. How could he train himself to be a swordsman and a Spanner if he couldn't find the time or strength to practice? It also occurred to him that he didn't know where he might work with the sextant. Travelers of every sort plied their skills without a stitch of clothing. Bound sextants, chronofors, and apertures didn't work if travelers wore so much as a ring.

Within the palace, it was commonplace for novitiates to remove their clothing in order to Span, Walk, or Cross. Cresten couldn't imagine doing this here in the village. He needed a place where he could practice in private, and he had no idea where to find one, or even when he might begin his search.

That night, with the coins from Poelu jangling in his purse, he ate his customary meal at the small table near the rear of the *Hound*, and vowed that he would search the next evening for a place to Span.

As he finished his first bowl of fish stew, Quinn approached his table with a second bowl. Cresten hadn't asked for it, but hungry as he was, he wouldn't complain, so long as the man didn't charge him extra.

"You look thin, lad," the barkeep said. "Pinched. You've been workin' hard and eatin' little. Thought you might want a second bowl."

Cresten regarded him.

Quinn smiled. "No charge."

"All right," Cresten said.

Quinn removed the empty bowl and slid this new one in front of him. Rather than walking away, he lingered, watching as Cresten picked up his spoon.

"Mind if I sit?"

Cresten shook his head. Quinn lowered himself into the chair opposite his own.

"How are you getting on with Poelu?"

"Fine. She paid me today. So I can pay you for the rest of the turn."

"That's fine. No rush."

Cresten frowned, took a spoonful of stew.

"You enjoy the work?"

"I don't mind it, and I'm getting better at cutting." As an afterthought, he added, "Thank you for convincing her to hire me." He wasn't certain what the man wanted from him.

"I thought maybe you'd have tired of it by now."

Cresten shrugged a second time.

Quinn leaned forward, forearms braced on the table, eyes locked on Cresten's. "I thought maybe you'd be ready to give it up," he whispered, "and come work for me."

CHAPTER 14

3rd Day of Sipar's Ascent, Year 618

Cresten hadn't expected that.

"You want me to work here, in the *Hound*?"

"No, lad," Quinn said, still keeping his low. "I have other…
ventures that I'm working on. A boy with your talents might prove
valuable. That is, if he's discreet, and clever, and he doesn't ask too
many questions."

Cresten clenched his jaw against his rising curiosity. He was
intrigued, and questions swarmed in his mind. He didn't mind
working for Poelu, but he also knew that with every turn that carried
them closer to the growing season, his work in the beds would grow
less bearable. He wouldn't destroy his chance at whatever work
Quinn had in mind by demanding too much too soon.

When Quinn understood that Cresten had no intention of asking
questions, he sat back and grinned. "Well done, lad."

Cresten took another spoonful and sipped his watered wine.

"What sort of Traveler are you?" Quinn asked.

"Spanner."

The barkeep's eyes narrowed. "Spanner," he repeated. "Would
have preferred it if you was a Walker."

"You and me both."

Quinn stared. After a moment he laughed. "You've got a spine in
you, and a sense of humor. Not too many like that. You any good?"

"At Spanning?" His gaze slid away. "I'm still learning. Or I was. I
need to practice, but I don't know where to do it. I need…" He felt
his face color. "I can't Span where there are a lot of people."

"No, I don't suppose. You have a sextant already?"

Cresten faltered, but then nodded.

"Good. In that case, I might be able to help."

He couldn't help himself. "How?"

Quinn grinned, pushed back from the table, and stood. "Finish your stew. When you're done, find me at the bar."

"Should I get my sextant?"

He glanced back in Lam's direction. "Not yet," he said, voice dropping again. "It would be better if Lam didn't know you had it."

Quinn left before Cresten could ask him more. Cresten bolted down the rest of his stew and bread, downed his wine, and stood.

The barkeep spotted him before he was halfway across the room, and stopped him with a subtle gesture. He pointed toward the corridor leading to his small room. Cresten didn't respond in any way except to veer off in that direction.

Shortly after reaching his room, Quinn joined him there. "Again, lad, well done. I think you'll work out nicely. Grab your device and follow me."

Cresten retrieved the sextant from his sack and joined Quinn as he unlocked and pushed through a small door near Cresten's room. This opened onto a second corridor, one Cresten had never seen before. It was narrow, and cold, and it smelled of urine and rotting wood. Light shone from a doorway at the far end, which opened onto a small enclosed area, roofless and windowless. Shards of glass and dove droppings covered the compacted dirt; the stone walls were badly in need of mortar and paint.

"What is this place?"

"A courtyard we never use. Just the sort of place where you might practice your Spanning."

Cresten eyed the space critically. "It's small."

"That it is. Start in the corridor and finish at the far end of the courtyard. You should be all right."

He was right.

"Don't look so surprised, lad. I told you, I was once a novitiate."

"Can I practice my sword work here, too?"

Quinn handed him the key. "No one uses this place. Lam and I – and now you – we're the only ones who know about it. Lam rarely comes back here. If he troubles you, show him the key, tell him I gave it to you."

"Thank you."

"Don't thank me. If you can Span, you can work for me. This is no favor I'm doing, you catch? This is business, between you and me."

Cresten didn't shy from his stare. "All right."

"In the meantime, you keep working for Poelu. Fewer questions that way. You can keep the coin she gives you. For now, we'll consider your room and meals your pay. Later, when you're workin' for me full time, we'll make other arrangements. Sound fair?"

It did, though the offer also gave Cresten pause. Quinn was being uncommonly generous with him while revealing nothing at all about this work he'd be doing. How could he not be suspicious? Especially since the barkeep had warned him already about asking questions.

"You don't trust me."

"It's not that. I think… Yes, it sounds fair." *Too fair.*

"You'll understand in time. You have my word on that. In the meantime, practice, enjoy your extra coin, and don't speak of this to anyone."

Right. "Yes, sir."

Quinn slanted a look his way, as if searching for signs that Cresten was mocking him. Seeing none, he left.

Cresten didn't allow his doubts to keep him from taking advantage of the privacy the man had found for him. Once Quinn had closed the door on that narrow corridor, he cleared areas of broken glass, removed his clothes, and calibrated his sextant. As Quinn suggested, he started his first Span in the corridor. He aimed with as much care as he could and made certain before thumbing the release that his body was oriented squarely forward.

Still, the moment he activated the device and was pulled into the gap, panic took him. He had never Spanned through such a narrow space. The gap was harrowing enough under the most benign conditions: a violent wind, an assault of light and color, smell and sound. Here the gale was different. It bounced off the confines of the hallway, buffeting him from all sides, threatening to hurl him against one wall or the other.

It probably lasted less than a fivecount. When it was over, he stood at the far end of the courtyard, his face only a hand or two from the stone wall, his skin tender from the abrasion of that gap wind.

He steadied himself with a few breaths, but then returned to the shadows of the corridor to try again. He thought the precision demanded by this particular Span would help him hone his skills. If he didn't kill himself in the process.

That first night, he navigated the gap several times before giving in to weariness. He didn't once hit either wall in the corridor, and he found himself wondering if he even could. As frenzied as the gap seemed, Komat, the palace Binder, had instilled in his novitiates an implicit trust in the precision of their devices.

Cresten learned the limits of that trust the following night. After a long day in the gaaz beds, he ate his dinner, and snuck back to the corridor and courtyard. He Spanned three times without incident, and so might have been careless with his fourth journey. He set his stance, aimed the sextant, and prepared to thumb the release. As he did, he heard a sound behind him, in the corridor on the other side of the door. He peered back. At the same time, his thumb slipped and he activated the sextant.

He was yanked forward, his neck and shoulders wrenched. He flailed, trying in vain to straighten himself, to control his trajectory. He slammed into one wall, careened into the other, bounced back the other way and scraped along that wall for some distance. Upon emerging from the corridor into the courtyard, he fell farther off his line.

The gap released him and he sprawled onto the stone, rolling until he hit the far wall.

He remained there for at least a tencount, breathing, assessing the damage. His shoulders hurt from hitting the walls, and the skin on his left arm had been scraped raw and bloody. He bled from a hundred small cuts – the damned glass. The rest of his body ached from his impact with the stone at the end, but he didn't think he had broken any bones. He examined his sextant, afraid he had marred it beyond use. Aside from a scratch or two, it appeared no worse for the ordeal.

Cresten sat up, wincing at the pain in his back.

"What in the God's name are you doing?"

He craned his neck, gasped at another ache.

Lam stood at the mouth of the corridor.

Cresten crawled to his piled clothes, which he had left near the outer wall, and pulled on his breeches. He tried to keep the sextant hidden, going so far as to hide it under his shirt, which remained on the ground.

"I asked you a question!"

"Quinn said I could use this courtyard to train," he said, climbing to his feet.

"Train for what?"

"Practice," Cresten amended. "As a novitiate I was learning sword work and… and other things. He said I could work on those here, that no one ever used this courtyard for anything."

"And what were you doing just now? You didn't have on a stitch. What's that about?"

Cresten wasn't certain how much he ought to say. He wished Quinn was there.

"Some of what we do in the palace… we have to be naked to do it."

Lam's eyes narrowed. "What was that thing you had? I saw something golden."

Blood and bone. "It's my sextant. I'm a Spanner. I need that to Travel from one place to another. That's what I was practicing."

Lam's gaze dropped to his bloody arm. "Guess you're not all that good at it, are you?"

Cresten bit back the first reply that came to mind, which would only have angered the man further.

As their silence stretched, Lam glanced around the courtyard, his features settling into a scowl.

"I don't want you using this place for anything anymore. You hear me? It's bad enough you're leasing that room for next to nothing."

"You'll have to talk to Quinn about that." These might have been the bravest words Cresten had ever spoken.

Lam took a step in his direction. They remained separated by several paces, but still Cresten had to resist the urge to back away from the man. "I'm talking to you about it."

"And you're telling me the opposite of what Quinn said, so you should talk to him."

Lam sneered. "You palace boys think you're so smart. You wouldn't survive a day out here without Quinn helping you. If he wasn't working one of his schemes again, you'd probably be dead by now."

He wanted to ask what kind of schemes Quinn worked, but he was too stung by the rest of what Lam had said.

"What's this?"

They both turned. Quinn stood behind Lam, arms crossed over his chest. Slight as he was, he looked formidable.

"You tell him he could use this place?" Lam asked.

"I did. You have it in mind to use the courtyard, too?"

Lam's expression shifted from belligerent to sullen. "No. Heard him out here, is all. Wanted to know who it was and why."

"And now you've seen."

"You should've told me he was using it. Should've asked me if I minded."

"He's using it. You mind?"

Lam cast another glare at Cresten. "Fine then." He stalked past Quinn, back down the corridor, and through the door.

"He saw the sextant," Cresten said, once he was confident that Lam couldn't hear.

"He was bound to. Don't fret about it. He talks a lot, but the truth is he's too timid to do much. He won't bother you, and I don't think he'll try to steal it. Still, keep your door locked when you're gone."

Quinn crossed to where he stood, eyeing him critically. "What happened to you? You look a mess."

"It was a bad Span. I'm all right."

The man raised an eyebrow, but said no more. He made to leave.

"Lam said something about you needing me for 'another one of your schemes.' What did he mean?"

Quinn peered over his shoulder. "Didn't we have an agreement about questions?"

Cresten dropped his gaze.

"You'll know soon enough, lad. I promise, no harm's goin' to come to you."

He left the courtyard.

Cresten was too sore to think about Spanning again. He put on his shirt, retrieved the sextant, and returned to his room. That night he began to hide his sextant and sword in the hay of his pallet rather than in his carry sack.

Over the next ha'turn and more, he continued to cut gaaz by day and work on his Spanning in the evenings. Occasionally he brought his sword into the courtyard as well, and in between Spans he performed the drills Albon had taught him. Quinn was right: he'd grown lean since leaving the palace. His work in the beds had strengthened him. He didn't tire as easily as he used to. The sword felt almost weightless in his hands. He worked himself to a sweat almost every night, enjoying the exertion.

Soon the courtyard grew too small. He wanted to Span farther. So one night, after his meal, he placed the blade and sextant in his sack and left the inn. Making sure that no one followed him, he made his way to the shoreline and followed it to the gaaz beds. With the sun setting, and the work day long since over, the strand was deserted.

Cresten halted at the near end of a crescent of beach, set down his sack, and stripped off his clothes. Then he calibrated and aimed his sextant, and activated it. He soared over the sand and then over water. The gap wind bit at his skin and whipped his hair around his face. A rainbow of color danced with him across the shallows. The smells of brine and fish and cooking fires assailed him. But he laughed at the sheer joy of that motion. Freed from the confines of the courtyard, he felt like an eagle. He fell out of the gap on the sand at the other end of the arcing shoreline and gave a whoop of laughter. With the work he had done at the inn, he had made himself into a Spanner. An accomplished one.

His father had been right after all. He surprised himself with the thought, and with the one that followed: His father might have been proud of him, of what he had taught himself to do. He might even have forgiven Cresten for being expelled from the palace.

He aimed again, and thumbed the release on the sextant. Once more, he stepped out of the gap into joyous laughter. Who knew that Traveling could be such fun?

He Spanned a few more times, until the sky began to darken and the first stars emerged in the indigo above him. He leveled and released the sextant once more, and soared back to where he'd placed his sack and clothes.

"You're very loud when you do that."

Cresten whipped around, gasped. Droë stood only a few steps away.

He gaped, unsure of what to say or do. His heart thudded in his chest.

"Are you supposed to be loud? To laugh and cry out that way?"

Still he stared. Her gaze dropped to his privates, and belatedly he grabbed for his clothes to cover himself. Droë sauntered closer.

"Boys look strange down there. A little ugly, actually. And yours is quite small. I suppose that's because you're young still."

"It's not small," he said, finding his voice. "Not for my age. As you said, I'm young. And it's really not polite to look, much less comment that way."

She gaped at him, stricken, eyes wide. "I didn't mean to be rude."

Cresten wondered if all Tirribin were as odd as she. One moment she was menacing, in the next she was coy and disturbingly knowing, and in the one after that, she seemed, as she did now, to be truly a child: innocent, desperate to be liked.

"I know you didn't," he said. "Just... Look away while I get dressed. Please."

She gave another sly grin and tried to see again what he was hiding. Finally, she turned her back. Cresten pulled on his breeches and shirt. When Droë faced him again, he was slipping on his shoes.

"You look older," she said. "Your years haven't changed, but you look like you've Walked."

He wasn't sure what to say. "Thank you."

She started to walk around him, hands held behind her back. "You left the palace because of me, didn't you?"

He faltered. He feared angering her, but couldn't deny that much of what had befallen him in his last days in the palace had happened because of her.

"It's all right," she said, still orbiting. "I promised your friend I wouldn't hurt you, and I won't."

"Yes, I had to leave because you killed Tache. And... and when you talked to Lenna and me about... about being in love, it embarrassed us both. We weren't as close after that."

She nodded, appearing contrite. "I sensed that. I don't understand."

"Children don't– The act of love isn't something we're ready to talk about."

She halted, closer to him than he would have preferred. He caught the faint scent of decay. "Or do?" she asked.

He thought she struggled to grasp his meaning.

"Or do. Definitely."

"And so when I mentioned it, it made you both shy. With each other. That's what I sensed in your friendship."

"Yes, it was something like that."

She resumed her circling. "Thank you. That helps."

"Have you seen Lenna?"

Droë shook her head. "The guards have been vigilant, and there are more of them, all with muskets. It's not yet safe for me to return to the palace."

Cresten sagged a little. He missed Lenna so much, he would even have welcomed tidings from the demon. "Oh. I'm sorry."

"Would you be my friend?"

He hadn't expected that. "I'm… I'm not a Walker."

Her laughter reminded him of the tinkling of broken glass. "I know that." She sobered. "I need a friend. I thought maybe you did, too. Since we both miss her."

Frightened as he was of the creature, he did see in her a connection, however vague, to Lenna. He remembered as well what Tache had said about the knowledge of Tirribin. Tache was a fool, of course; he badly misjudged Droë and her powers. Nevertheless, no one would deny the value of befriending one of the Ancients. And Droë had offered her friendship freely.

"I'd be honored to be your friend," Cresten said.

The Tirribin beamed. "Good. Do you plan to come here again? To Span, I mean."

Cresten's smile slipped. He didn't want her watching him Span, not with her odd interest in seeing him naked. "Well…"

Another coy grin. "I'll only come to the strand when you've finished and dressed again. You have my word."

"Then, yes. I plan to come back quite often."

She clapped her hands. "Splendid."

He slipped the sextant back into his carry sack, and swung the sack over his shoulder. It had grown dark. Stars shone overhead and last hint of daylight clung to the western horizon.

"I should get back to the inn."

"I can walk with you," Droë said. "You'll be safer."

"Are the lanes down here dangerous?"

She answered with a solemn nod. "They can be. The palace is safe, of course. And the lanes near it. But down here…" She shrugged. "Let me walk you back."

Cresten glanced around and tightened his hold on the straps of his carry sack. "Yes, all right."

They walked a distance in silence, following the shoreline back to the wharves and the streets there. After a time, she asked him what he did with his days, and he told her about cutting gaaz. He nearly mentioned working for Quinn, but thought better of it. Soon they reached the inn, and Droë made to leave him by the door.

"If you happen to make it into the palace," Cresten said, stopping her, "and if you see Lenna, tell her that I miss her."

"I will. I think that would make her happy."

She walked away, her strides unhurried. After a few steps, she blurred and vanished into the night.

Droë didn't join him each night he Spanned on the shoreline, but during the next turn, he encountered the demon a dozen times or more. She kept her word, blurring to the strand only after he had finished his practice and pulled on his clothes. Always, though, she arrived within a spirecount or less of him dressing. He guessed that she observed him from some distance, an idea he found discomfiting. He said nothing about it. She kept her word. He didn't dare ask for more, lest he anger her.

They spoke of trifles. She asked him about his family and his home, about Spanning and the gap. He tried to ask her about life as a Tirribin – about her time sense and how she hunted. Always, she evaded his questions and steered their conversations back to him. Often she asked about his feelings for Lenna, and any other girls he had known and liked. These exchanges made him uncomfortable, but she was persistent, and he remained wary of provoking her.

He frequently returned to the inn well past nightfall. On one such evening, Quinn met him near the door.

"Another late night," the barkeep said, planting himself in Cresten's path. "Where have you been going?"

"To the gaaz beds."

Puzzlement furrowed the man's brow.

"The strand is empty most evenings, and it's much bigger than the courtyard. I've been practicing there."

"I see. And?"

Cresten faltered, apprehension building in his chest. Did Quinn know somehow that he had been speaking to Droë? Did he expect

Cresten to confess to this?

"And..."

"How is it going? How far can you Span?"

He tried to conceal his relief. "It's going well. I can go from one end of the beach to the other with no trouble. I'm sure I can go farther if I have to."

"Good. Then we start tomorrow. Don't leave here after your supper. Not until you've spoken to me." He grinned like a man betting on weighted dice. "We're going to make some coin, you and I. You'll see. Now off to bed with you. Tomorrow's a big day."

Cresten burned to know what Quinn had in mind for him. He couldn't deny, though, that the man's excitement was contagious. He went to his room, his mind churning with the promise of impending adventure.

The following day seemed to last an eternity. Cresten toiled in the gaaz beds beneath a gray sky and through a series of downpours. The rain and clouds meant relief from the heat, but made it nearly impossible for him to judge the time of day. He was forced to measure spirecounts and bells by the bricks he cut and piled.

When at last Poelu let him and the others leave, he ran back to the *Hound*, gulped down a bit of supper, and presented himself to Quinn in front of the bar.

The barkeep was deep in conversation with a woman Cresten had never seen before. Quinn paused long enough to cast a dismissive glance his way. "You want somethin'?"

"Uh... I was..."

"The courtyard's open. Why don't you go back there where you won't be in anyone's way?"

Before Cresten could answer, Quinn shifted his attention back to the woman and resumed their conversation. Cresten retreated to his room, unsure of what else to do. After sitting on his pallet for perhaps a quarter bell, he pulled out his sextant, intending to go to the courtyard.

Before he could, the barkeep appeared in his doorway.

"You have a lot to learn, lad. I talked to you about discretion."

Cresten straightened. "Yes, sir. Only, I thought–"

"I know what you thought. But you have to be able to think for yourself. If I'm talkin' to someone, you can't expect me to drop everythin' because you've finished gorgin' yourself. You catch?"

Cresten nodded.

Quinn motioned toward the sextant. "Put that in the sack and bring it with you."

"Where are we–?" At a sharp look from the barkeep, he swallowed the rest of his question.

They returned to the great room. There, Quinn led him behind the bar, through the kitchen and down a dark passage to yet another door. This one opened onto the alley behind the inn. Quinn went out first, and after checking the lane in both directions, urged Cresten on with a wave of his hand.

"Remember I told you I once lived in the palace," Quinn said as they walked. "I would have been a Spanner myself. That's what my ma was. So as a fingerling, I followed the older Spanners. I hung on their every word, and learned all I could from them. Didn't do me any good in the palace. No magick, no glory. Since then…" He glanced back, a rogue's smile on his lips. "You know that a Traveler can't take naught with him when he Spans 'cept his skin and his sextant."

"Of course. That's–"

"Wrong. That's wrong, is what that is. Those Spanners I knew when I was a pup: they taught me a thing or two. There's a few tricks you haven't learned yet."

They walked on, Cresten's curiosity warring with his reluctance to risk questions. Quinn led him down a maze of narrow lanes, halting near the crest of a small rise on the edge of the village. He pointed at the spire of the temple.

"You see that?"

At Cresten's nod, Quinn shifted his hand to the east, until he was pointing at a second, small structure: a house with a steep gabled roof and a narrow chimney that Cresten could barely see.

"You mark that house?"

"Yes, sir."

"Good. I want you to Span there. What you see from here is the back of the house. If you arrive as you should, there'll be a low stone wall, with a gap that aligns with the right corner of the house. There's a shirt, a pair of breeches, and a pair of shoes hidden there."

Cresten blinked.

Quinn smiled again. "Put them there myself after our little talk. Now, you find the clothes, you put them on, and you go 'round to the front of the house. Knock on the door, give them a little something from me. Then you replace the clothes, Span back, and you're done."

"What am I supposed to give them?"

This time, Quinn didn't object to the question. He glanced both ways again and produced four gold rounds from his pocket. "These, lad."

"But–"

Quinn raised a finger, silencing him. "You put them in your mouth. Under your tongue so you won't swallow them in the gap. And you Span, just as you always do. You won't have any trouble. My word."

Cresten eyed the house Quinn had indicated. In the dying light, it looked impossibly far away. He had mastered the corridor and courtyard, and then the strand as well.

This was more than double that latter distance, and he didn't know the terrain.

"Wouldn't it be easier if I just walked?" he asked, still staring at the house.

"Maybe, if you're not very good at Spanning."

Cresten rounded. "I'm good enough," he said, with heat.

"Then let me see."

Cresten continued to glare.

"I want to see how you Span. And I want you to learn that you can carry these rounds with you when you do." He smiled. "Take the gold, lad. Give it a try. I know you can do it. And there's five treys waiting for you here when you're done."

That drew his gaze back to Quinn's. "Five treys?"

Quinn opened his other palm. Triangular silvers winked at him in the gloaming.

Quinn gave the hand holding the rounds a little shake. Cresten plucked the coins from the man's palm. Gold coins had been fairly common in his home when he was young, but Cresten had never taken the time to note their size. They were bigger than he would have imagined. Four of them, in his mouth. He aligned them, and slipped them under his tongue. They felt too large. He gagged, spit them back into his own hand.

"Breathe through your nose."

He tried again, taking deep breaths through his nose, as Quinn suggested. It helped. He held the coins under his tongue for a spirecount, then spit them out.

"All right?"

He nodded.

"Good. I'll be just 'round the corner if you need me." He started away, but halted after a few steps. "And, lad, let my associate see your sextant."

Cresten frowned. "Let him see it?"

"Aye. This once, it'll be all right."

He walked on, and turned the corner. Cresten checked the lane before slipping out of his clothes. Fear and cold air pebbled his skin. He pulled out his sextant, calibrated it, and aimed. When everything else was ready, he set the coins back in his mouth, under his tongue. Breathing hard through his nose, staving off a wave of panic, he aimed his device and thumbed the release.

He jerked forward and was swallowed by the frenzy of the gap.

CHAPTER 15

24th day of Sipar's Descent, Year 618

A cold wind abraded his face and body. Tears leaked from the corners of his eyes. Color and light assailed him. The smells were worse here than they'd been when he Spanned at the coast. The noises were harsher.

And the gap went on and on. He struggled to breathe through his nose, but with the air whipping past, he could barely fill his lungs. He began again to gag, fought to keep his mouth closed. He didn't know what would happen if he opened it and allowed the gold pieces to spill out. Nothing good. He was certain of that. He might never emerge from the gap.

He should have been out already. No Span he'd ever attempted had lasted so long. Had Quinn's gold trapped him forever in this nowhere of light and wind? Had the innkeeper doomed him?

Terror clawed at his throat. Might spitting out the gold save him? Better to make the attempt than to die in this place.

He had gone so far as to lift his tongue and open his mouth when the gap disgorged him onto a stone lane. He stumbled and fell, scraping his knees and hands. The gold rounds spilled from his mouth. The sextant clattered on the cobbles. He reclaimed the rounds and then closed his eyes, his breathing ragged. At last, he scanned the street. Empty.

He fought to his feet, retrieved the sextant, and looked around a second time. The gabled house Quinn had pointed out loomed directly before him. In spite of his struggles, he had Spanned to the exact spot for which he aimed. He managed a smile, even as he shivered in the evening air.

He followed the stone wall that bordered the yard until he was even with the corner of the structure. There he spied a parcel, wrapped in stained, brown canvas, tucked into a small gap at the base of the wall. If he hadn't been searching for it, he wouldn't have spotted it. He tugged it free, unwrapped the canvas, and found a pair of plain breeches, a worn linen shirt, and an old pair of shoes. All were relatively dry.

Cresten dressed. The breeches and shirt fit; the shoes were too big. He pocketed the gold rounds. He felt self-conscious carrying his sextant in plain sight, but Quinn had made his wishes clear. Eyeing the house again, he walked to the lane that fronted the entry.

Men and women walked the street in the failing light, and children played in yards. From all Cresten could see, this was a place for families and homes, not schemes and hidden gold rounds.

He walked to a gap in the stone wall, followed a cobbled path to the entry, and rapped on the oaken door, prepared for any reception he might receive. Or so he believed.

The door opened slowly, revealing a bronze-haired girl who couldn't have been more than four or five years old. She stared up at him with dark solemn eyes, saying nothing.

"Um… I need to speak with your father or mother."

She just stared.

"Who is that, love?"

A woman appeared behind the child. Willowy, dark-eyed like the girl, her hair tied back. Seeing Cresten, she frowned.

"Can I help you?" Her tone conveyed suspicion.

"I- I brought something from Quinn."

The frown hardened. She regarded him, then turned away, pulling the girl with her.

"Da," she called as she walked out of view, "there's someone here to see you." She sounded disgusted.

For a spirecount, the door stood open and Cresten remained on the threshold, waiting, wondering if they expected him to go inside.

At last, a man stepped into view. He was far older than the woman, but with the same dark eyes in a square face, and bronze hair that was salted with white. He was tall, lean, muscular. Cresten thought he must be ten years younger than Quinn.

He cast a critical gaze over Cresten, his eyes lingering briefly on the sextant. "Who are you?" he asked in a smooth tenor.

"I have something for you from Quinn."

"Quinn." He spoke the name as if it were an imprecation. "And what did the old goat send?" He nodded toward the sextant. "That for me?"

Cresten pressed the device closer and shielded it with his free hand. "No. This is mine."

His eyebrows lifted. "Yours? Quinn has a Spanner now?"

"He doesn't… I'm staying at the *Brazen Hound*, is all. And he asked me to do this."

"All right. Well, if not the sextant, then what?"

Cresten dug the rounds out of his pocket and held them out to the man. The gold might have surprised him as much as the sextant had.

"He say anything? You have a message for me?"

"Just the money."

The man glanced at the sextant again. Cresten feared he might try to steal it and thought about backing away.

"I guess you're the message, aren't you?"

"Me? I don't understand."

"That's all right, lad. You tell Quinn you saw me, and that… that we can work together, him and me. You got that?"

"Yes, sir."

The man grinned. "'Sir,'" he repeated. "Palace boy, eh?"

He was tired of everyone remarking on his palace training. Maybe he needed to stop being so polite all the time. "Not anymore," he said, making no effort to keep the asperity from his voice.

The man laughed and closed the door, leaving Cresten alone.

He glanced around to see if anyone had noticed. No one was watching him.

He followed the lanes around to the rear of the house, took off the clothes and stowed them where they had been, and prepared to Span back to where Quinn awaited him.

The journey back proved nearly as harrowing as the first Span. Upon reaching the rise, he managed to keep his feet and hold on to the sextant. His vision swam, and the world around him whirled, but aside from that he was none the worse for his Travels.

Quinn had his back to him. As Cresten pulled on his clothes, the barkeep asked, "Did it go all right?"

"Yes. I gave him the gold. He said that you and he can work together."

"Good lad."

A moment later, Cresten said, "I'm dressed."

Quinn turned and handed Cresten the silver treys.

"He said that I was a message. What did he mean?"

"What did I say about questions?"

"What did he mean, Quinn?"

The man's grin melted, and Cresten thought he had angered him. But Quinn said, "Paegar – that's his name, Paegar Moar – he's sort of a merchant, a man of some import. I bought a few things from him – you just paid for one – but I've wanted our transactions to be more... substantive for a time now. He hasn't thought I had much to offer. Now he knows better. Havin' a Spanner in my employ – well, that changes things."

"So you could have brought him the gold yourself, but you wanted to send me instead, as a way of proving yourself."

"Somethin' like that, yeah." He smiled again, opening his hands. "No harm done, right? You get a bit of silver. He gets some gold that I owe him. And I get to play with the big boys."

Cresten considered this. "That's fair. When do I Span for you again?"

Quinn's smile broadened. "Soon, lad. I promise."

True to his word, Quinn had a new job for him within a few days. The innkeeper told him to take an extra set of clothes with him to the waterfront when he went to the gaaz beds in the morning. He hid the clothes in a safe spot before doing his usual work for the day.

That evening, after supper, he and Quinn returned to the rise overlooking the village.

"You're clear on what I want you to do?" Quinn asked, staring off to the west while Cresten prepared to Span.

Quinn had repeated his instructions several times, until Cresten wanted to shout at him to stop.

"Yes," he said, trying to keep his tone neutral.

And failing.

"No need to be sharp, lad. I'm only makin' sure."

"I'll be fine. You'll see."

"Sure you will. Off with you now. Find me when you're back."

Cresten activated the sextant and surged into the gap. This Span took longer even than the previous ones, and though he had prepared himself, he had to fight off the rising panic of being trapped for so long in that storm of wind and color, sounds and smells. For several spirecounts after his arrival at the strand, he could do little more than breathe and close his eyes against wave after wave of dizziness.

Yet he couldn't help but be pleased. Again, he had Spanned to precisely the spot he intended. He took no small satisfaction in proving the chancellor and Master Denmys wrong.

He reclaimed his clothes and hid his sextant where they had been. This was the part of their plan that bothered him most, but Quinn had insisted.

"The men you'll be dealin' with," he'd said, "they wouldn't scruple to steal a Bound sextant from a priestess, much less a lad your age. It'll be safer wherever you hide it."

"Do I need to use the sextant at all? Can't I just walk?"

"No, lad. Paegar doesn't want you being followed, and neither do I. It's best for all if you Span."

Best for all except me.

The innkeeper also ordered him to take a weapon. Cresten had hidden a borrowed knife with his clothes. Once he was dressed, he followed the shoreline to the wharves, and made his way to a ship that was moored at the end of the southernmost pier: *The Blue Harper.* The air was heavier here, scented with kelp and fish and ship's tar.

Sailors lingered on the ship's deck, which glowed with torches.

"Ahoy, *The Blue Harper!*" he called, as Quinn had taught him.

The ship's crew leered down at him.

"Who are you?" one of the men demanded.

"Quinn sent me."

Most didn't react to this, but the sailor who had spoken said, "Stay there."

He stepped away from the rail and Cresten lost sight of him.

Soon enough, he came back with a second man. They descended a steep plank to the dock and approached him. Both were large, pale-skinned, and bald, save for narrow plaits of red hair that grew from the back of their heads. Cresten assumed they hailed from the isles of the Knot.

The second sailor eyed Cresten and surveyed the wharf. "You alone, boy?"

"Yes." Cresten spoke without inflection, hoping to hide his fear.

"Quinn send money?"

The barkeep had prepared him for this. "You know he didn't. That wasn't the arrangement."

The two men shared a glance. Cresten's heart pounded.

"They won't hurt you," Quinn had said. "I promise they won't. They want this deal as much as I do, and they know what has to be done. But that won't keep them from tryin' to scare you if they think they'll profit from it. Don't let them see you're frightened. That's the secret."

"You know a lot for a little boy," the first man said now.

Cresten merely waited.

"Fine then," the second man said. He pulled from within his

coat a parcel, wrapped in grimy cloth.

He held it out, but when Cresten tried to take it, the man put his other hand over Cresten's, lightning fast, trapping him.

"You listen to me, boy. This is worth more than your life. A lot more. Steal from me, fail to bring me my money, and I swear I'll kill you. I'll cut off your hands and your tongue, and your tiny little prick. And then I'll slit your throat. You catch?"

Cresten trembled, his breathing unsteady and desperate. He couldn't bring himself to speak a word, but he dropped his chin once.

"I'll be waiting right here for the gold. You take more than a bell, and I'll hunt you down. Now get going." He released Cresten's hand and shoved him away.

Cresten reeled, righted himself. He hastened from the ship and the men, breaking into a run before he reached the end of the wharf. The parcel was about the size and shape of a loaf of bread, but considerably heavier, as if it were made of stone or metal or glass. Running with it wasn't easy.

Quinn had told him where to go next, but Cresten soon understood that his instructions had been too vague. He took the first lane the innkeeper described and ran some distance before realizing he had gone the wrong way. He backtracked, running still, gasping, terrified that his time would run out.

Eventually he found the shop Quinn had described. It was the only one on the lane that remained open and lit from within.

He pushed the door open and was greeted by musty air and the glow of oil lamps.

"You must be Quinn's friend."

A white-haired woman sat on a stool behind a wooden counter. She was heavy-set, her face cratered with scars from what must have been a near-fatal case of Herjean pox.

"Yes, ma'am."

"Bring it here. Let me see." Her voice was gravelly, but she offered a smile that exposed yellow teeth.

He crossed to her and handed her the parcel. She started to pull the cloth away, but stopped before the object within was exposed.

"You know what this is?"

Cresten shook his head, hoping she would show him, knowing that Quinn would never tell him, even if he dared to ask.

"Thought not. Best we keep it that way. If Quinn wants you to know, he'll tell you."

She didn't wait for a reply, but rose from the stool and shouldered aside a pair of curtains. She remained behind the curtains for some time. Cresten's apprehension grew. He had taken too long to get here, and the sailor's threat had been vivid, to say the least. The more time the woman wasted, the greater the danger when he returned to the wharf.

She pushed through the curtains.

"All was as it should be. I thank you." She hefted a leather purse. "You don't want my thanks, do you? Neither does Quinn." She opened the purse and emptied its contents onto the counter with the musical clangor of coins.

Cresten couldn't help but gape. He had never seen so many gold rounds in one place.

The woman counted out five and set them aside before dropping the others, at least seven, back in the purse.

She pushed the pile of five toward Cresten. "For Paegar." She gave the purse a small shake and held it out to him. "For the smugglers."

Cresten blinked, drawing a frown from the woman.

"Said too much, have I?"

"No, I… It's all right."

"Our secret then. Yours and mine."

"Yes, ma'am." He took the purse from her and slipped the five rounds into his pocket. "Thank you."

"You're very polite. I appreciate that." She motioned toward the door. "On your way then. It's late, and the men waiting for you aren't known for their patience."

Cresten left her and walked at speed through the empty streets, the jangle of coins with every step as loud as a clarion. He pressed his hand to the leg of his breeches, muffling the sound.

"Isn't it late for you to be walking the lanes?"

Cresten jumped and spun at the voice.

"Droë. You scared me."

She looked as she always did, like the most exquisite of children. Moonlight gleamed in her golden hair, and in her milky eyes. "You weren't at the strand tonight. I waited for you."

"I'm sorry, I was... I'm working."

"I sense your fear."

I'm on my way to treat with smugglers. "I'm all right."

He resumed walking, and she fell in step with him.

"What kind of work are you doing? What's in that purse?"

"I don't think I should tell you. I could get in trouble."

The Tirribin scowled. "You don't trust me."

"No, it's not that. I have to... You're right. I am frightened. The men who are waiting for this gold are... They're dangerous."

"Not for me," she said, speaking with such confidence that he couldn't help but think of Tache lying dead in the moonlight. "I can help you."

"I'm not sure that's a good idea either." He swiped at a mosquito buzzing his ear. The coins in his pocket rang with his next step.

"More gold," she said.

"Yes. For another man." He slowed, instinct bringing renewed trepidation. This was why the sailor threatened him, why he forced Cresten to rush. He would know that Cresten still carried Moar's gold as well. "They're going to steal it from me," he said, to himself as much as to her.

"How do you know?"

"I don't. I'm guessing." He regarded her. *You don't trust me.* The truth was, he did, more than he trusted anyone else. "Do you really want to help me?"

Her eyes widened and she nodded. Cresten produced the five rounds from his pocket.

"I can't carry these when I give the men this purse. Would you hold them for me?"

"Humans are very protective of their gold," she said, her voice low. "I've seen it. You would trust me with this?"

"Yes. You're my friend, right?"

The demon's smile exposed her needle teeth. Cresten didn't allow himself to recoil. She opened her hand and he placed the gold on her palm.

"Just until after I give the men this purse. Then I need it back." She gave a shrug. "I have no use for gold."

Which is why I trust you. "If something happens to me, please see that it gets to Quinn at the *Brazen Hound.*"

"I will."

They continued apace to the wharf. Cresten left her at the head of the pier and walked alone to *The Blue Harper.* He slowed as he neared the ship, expecting the men to ambush him, his eyes straining in the darkness.

"Ahoy, *The Blue Harper!*"

A figure appeared at the rails. With only a single torch burning on the ship's deck, Cresten could barely make out the man's form. His face was shrouded in shadow. He believed this was the second man to whom he'd spoken, the one who had threatened him. He wondered where the first sailor was. *They're smugglers.*

"Palace boy," the man said. He walked to the plank and started down toward the wharf. "'Bout time. We was about to go searching for you. We were already sharpening our blades." He laughed.

Cresten held his tongue.

"You have my gold?" the man asked as he stepped onto the pier.

"Yes, sir."

"Good. Grab him."

Cresten had no time to react. Hands like iron vises clamped onto him, one at his shoulder, one at his neck. He struggled to get free, but the man who held him tightened his grip on Cresten's throat.

"Keep fighting, and I'll kill you," the man said, mouth at his ear, his breath stinking of whiskey and pipe smoke. "Doesn't matter to me. We get paid either way."

He went still.

"That's a good lad. Where's the gold?"

Cresten shook the purse. "Right here."

The second man had reached them by now. He ripped the purse from Cresten's grasp and poured the contents into his hand.

"Is it all there?" his companion asked.

"Hard to see in this light. Hold on." He walked back to the ship and the dim glow of that lone torch. After a tencount, he returned. "That's all of it. Our share, that is."

The man holding Cresten gave him a bone-rattling jerk. "Now then, lad, where is the gold for Moar?"

Scared as he was, Cresten took pride in having anticipated this. It might not save his life, but at least it would help Quinn.

"I haven't got it," he said.

The man shook him again. His vision swam. "You're lying!"

"I'm not. You can search my pockets. I haven't got it."

The second man loomed before him. Something shone in his right hand. An instant later, cold steel pressed against the corner of Cresten's eye.

"You willing to trade an eye for that gold, palace boy?"

He swallowed, keeping utterly still, terrified that the man holding him would shake him again.

"I'll ask one more time: where's the rest of the gold?"

"I swear I don't have it."

The knife flashed. After a moment's delay, pain reached him. Hot and stinging. He cried out. Not his eye, but the flesh beside it. Warm blood flowed over his cheek and jawline.

"This is no game, boy," the first man said, mouth still close. "And next time he'll take something vital."

"I told you to search me! I don't have it!"

"Where is it then?" The second man.

Cresten raised his chin. "Someplace safe."

"Kill him," the first man said. "Thinks he can outsmart us. Little shit. Cut his throat and dump him in the bay. That's what I say."

"I say that you're both very rude."

Droë. Cresten didn't know whether to be relieved or even more frightened.

The second man looked past the first. The first man turned, dragging Cresten with him. The Tirribin stood a few paces away, appearing tiny and innocent.

"Who are you?" the second smuggler demanded.

"Is that blood on your face?" Droë asked, ignoring the man. Cresten heard a rasp in her voice that he recalled from the night Tache died.

"Yes."

"He cut you."

"I'm all right."

"I asked you a question, girlie."

"You're *very* rude," she said, the rasp thickening her words. "I'm his friend. And if you don't release him now, you will both pay a dear price in years."

"A price in years," the first man said. "What does she mean by that?"

At the same time, the second man muttered a curse and said, "Let him go."

"What?"

"Let him go! Now!"

The man holding Cresten pushed him away. Cresten fell to his knees. The Tirribin snarled.

"Droë, don't!"

He thought it might be too late, but though she held herself coiled, like a hunting cat, she didn't attack.

"If either of you ever hurts him again, or threatens him, or says anything that makes him frightened, I will take all your years. You will be nothing but husk. Do you understand?"

"Who are you to—"

"Shut up!" the second man said. To Droë, he said, "We understand. We won't hurt him. We didn't know you had claimed him as a friend. We're… We're sorry."

"Say it to him," she growled.

The man pivoted toward Cresten. "I'm sorry I cut you. It won't happen again."

"Why are you apologizing to him? What's wrong with you? A wisp of a thing talks mean, and all of a sudden–"

He got out no more. Droë sprung at him and clamped onto his neck. He dwarfed her, but still she managed to knock him to the wood, an oily glow of colored light clinging to them both. The man screamed and flailed at her, though with no effect.

Cresten opened his mouth to shout her name again, but he didn't have to. Less than a heartbeat later, she detached herself from the man and stepped away. He lay on his back, his chest rising and falling. Even this far from the ship and its torch, Cresten could see that he had changed. His cheeks were sunken, his face lined with years that hadn't marked him before her attack.

"That was only some of your years," Droë said, her voice husky. "I could take more, and I will if you speak of me or my friend in that way again."

She walked away. Cresten backed away from the men. When he reached the end of the pier, he spun and ran after Droë.

"I should have taken all their years," she said, as he pulled abreast of her.

"It's probably best for me that you didn't. But thank you for helping me. I'm..." He almost said, *I'm in your debt,* but thought that might be a risky thing to say to an Ancient. Instead, he said, "I'm grateful to you."

"You're welcome." She held out Moar's gold and he took it from her. "I could have fed more, and now I need to do so. I shouldn't be with you right now. I believe you're safe from them. Less so from me."

He shuddered. "Yes, thank you. I'll... I'll see you soon."

The Tirribin nodded, but already she was walking away from him. After a few steps, her form blurred and she sped away. Grateful as he was for what she had done, he was glad to have her gone. He sprinted to where he had hidden his sextant, conscious of the blood drying on his cheek and chin. He removed his clothes, hid them, and slipped the coins under his tongue, gagging as he did. Breathing through his nose, he aimed and calibrated the sextant, and Spanned to Moar's house. As instructed, he left the gold in a small purse within the stone wall and Spanned again, this time back to the rise near the tavern. After pulling on his clothes, he scampered to the *Brazen Hound*.

Claya, one of the serving girls, spotted him as soon as he entered the inn. Her eyes went wide and she called for Quinn. The innkeeper emerged from the kitchen, a tankard in his hand. Seeing Cresten, his face fell.

"Blood and bone," Cresten heard him mutter. "What have I done?" To Claya, he said, "Rum, hot water, and a clean cloth. Now."

He walked to Cresten, put an arm around his shoulder, and steered him behind the bar and into a small chamber between the kitchen and the common room. There was a bed, a chest of drawers, a standing desk.

"Is this your room?"

"It is," Quinn said. "Sit." He waved a hand at the bed.

Claya bustled in a moment later with cloths and a flask of rum. "Water's on the fire."

"Good. Bring it in when it's good and hot."

She left them.

"I'm sorry, lad. I shouldn't have sent you. I thought they'd be too afraid of Paegar to steal his gold. But they took it, didn't they?"

Cresten shook his head.

"They didn't?"

"I didn't have the rounds with me."

Quinn frowned. "I don't understand. Who was it who cut you?"

"The men at the ship." *The smugglers.* "They wanted the gold, but I'd left it elsewhere." He thought better of mentioning Droë. "I was afraid they might try to steal it."

"How'd you get away? Men like that, you tell them you don't have what they want, they'll as likely kill you as let you go."

"Then I suppose I was lucky."

The innkeeper studied him through narrowed eyes. "Why do I get the sense that luck had nothin' to do with it?" He unstoppered the flask, took a swig of rum and handed it to Cresten. "Have a drink, lad. You've earned it, and then some."

Cresten took his first sip ever of rum. It burned going down, but it tasted fine, and warmed his gut. He took a second.

"Slow down." Quinn took the flask back, sipped from it again. Then he poured a bit onto one of the cloths. "This is going to hurt," he said.

Cresten turned his head to give the innkeeper access to the wound. At the first touch of the rum, he sucked a sharp breath through clenched teeth. He continued to wince as Quinn cleaned the cut. Soon, Claya brought the hot water, and Quinn traded the rum for that. Before long, the pain had subsided to a dull throb.

"I can put a poultice on it," Quinn said, inspecting his handiwork. "But it doesn't look so bad, and it would probably be best to leave it as it is. While you're at the gaaz beds, splash a little seawater on it. It might sting a bit, but it will keep it clean." He clapped Cresten on the shoulder. "Girls like scars," he said, in a conspiratorial whisper. "They make a lad handsome, don't you think, Claya?"

"I think he was handsome already."

Cresten flushed to the tips of his ears, drawing laughs from both of them.

Claya left them again, and Quinn allowed Cresten one more sip of rum before ordering him to bed.

"I'm sorry for all this, lad," he said, as Cresten started for the door. "I shouldn't have put you at risk. I won't do it again."

"Do you have silver for me?"

"Of course! Almost forgot. I promised five pieces. I probably ought to give you more." He retrieved the treys and handed them to Cresten.

"I won't need more if you keep giving me work."

Quinn didn't hide his surprise. "You still want to work for me after this?"

"You said it yourself: the cut's not so bad."

"There are others I deal with; they're as dangerous as these men."

That gave Cresten pause. He knew Droë couldn't save him every time he was in trouble. Now, though, he had a better sense of what to expect from his work for the innkeeper. He wouldn't be caught unawares again. And he would continue to trust his own instincts, which had served him well this night.

"Then I'll be careful," he said. "But I'm not going to work in the gaaz beds for the rest of my life."

CHAPTER 16

24th day of Sipar's Settling, year 633

Lenna gaped at this second version of herself. The red gown, the cloth shoes the other her had dropped by the door. Clothes she would have taken to avoid detection, things she never wore.

She read confusion and fear in the face of the other Lenna. She had heard tales of Walkers going insane upon meeting themselves in the past. She had met herself once before, but the two of her made sure their eyes never met. Not like this time. Whether this meant both of them were doomed, she didn't know. She didn't feel any different. She certainly wasn't as disoriented as Lenna-in-red appeared to be. Why, though, was she here? Terror clawed at her gut.

She approached the woman. "You need to sit down." She kept her voice low. "Would you like some wine?"

The other Lenna backed away, gaze darting about the chamber.

"You're all right. I'm here. You can trust me." Nonsense words. Empty assurances. She didn't want this Lenna bolting from the chamber.

She approached the other Lenna again, backing her into a corner. She paused to turn the lock and slip the key into her bodice. Then she eased toward herself again.

"I shouldn't be here," said Lenna-in-red.

"No, you shouldn't be. Why did you come?"

"I… I don't remember. I wasn't supposed to…" She stared at Lenna, eyes going wide. "I have to go."

She tried to get to the door, but Lenna kept herself in front of her. "You can't go. It's too late. We've met. The best thing we can do is send you back as soon as possible."

She didn't know if this was true, but she had no other ideas. *What was I thinking?*

Before she sent Lenna-in-red forward to where she belonged, she needed to know what prompted this Walk. The damage had been done; she owed it to herself to be certain her efforts weren't for naught.

"Why did you come back, Lenna?"

The other her mumbled a response. Lenna couldn't make out what she said, but as she gestured, an object in her hand caught the light of a candle, flashing in the dim room.

Her chronofor. Lenna felt the weight of her own within the folds of her gown. Two existing in one time. Peddlers throughout the isles dreamed of such things. She didn't pursue the thought further. That path led to madness. Literally.

"Can I see your chronofor?"

The other Lenna frowned, looked down at her own hand. She might have forgotten she held it. Then she cradled it to her chest, angling away, guarding it as if it were the most valuable item in the world. At that moment, it might have been.

"I won't hurt it, and I won't keep it for long. I need to see it, to know how far you've come."

Lenna-in-red hunched her shoulders and twisted more.

Lenna blew out a breath. "Later then. Are you thirsty? Do you want that wine?" She raised a hand to her bodice, feeling the key beneath the cloth. Confident that the other Lenna was trapped here, she crossed to the table by her hearth and poured out two cups of watered wine. She sipped from hers, held out the other to Lenna-in-red.

The other woman regarded the door, but she walked to where Lenna stood and, after hesitating, took the cup from her. Lenna sipped again. The other Lenna followed her example.

"Better?"

A tentative nod.

Lenna sat, motioned at the chair next to hers. Lenna-in-red eyed it but remained standing.

"Do you remember why you came back?" she asked again.

Lenna-in-red peered at the door. "I need to talk to him."

"About what?"

Her brow creased, her stare lost focus.

"Has something happened? Something he should know about?"

She muttered again. Lenna leaned forward.

"What?"

"Ainfor. Gillian Ainfor." Her gaze snapped up, meeting Lenna's. "The minister. A spy. She sent me back fourteen years."

Lenna sighed, sat back. "Yes, I know about that." She hadn't heard the name before, but what did it matter? "Is there something he should know about this woman?"

"He wants her to spy for us."

"Is there a reason she shouldn't?"

"She's the one who wrote the message. The one that sent me back." She was spouting nonsense. They both were.

"Let me see your chronofor," she said, straightening again. "Please. Just for a fivecount."

Lenna shook her head, clutched it close once more.

"You don't have to give it to me. Just… just hold it up so I can see the face. It's very pretty, isn't it? I only want a closer look."

This last seemed to catch Lenna-in-red by surprise. A small smile lifted the corners of her mouth and slowly she held out the chronofor, face up. Lenna didn't dare reach for it. She merely bent forward to study it.

It had been set for twelve days and seven bells. Whatever had driven her to make this journey back would happen soon. Perhaps it had happened already.

"Thank you," she said.

Lenna-in-red cradled the chronofor again, admiring it herself.

Lenna studied her, her chest tight with emotions that threatened to overwhelm her: grief at the harm she had inflicted on herself; terror at the thought that the damage to her mind might prove permanent, that this dull creature before her might embody her future; rage at herself, and also at Orzili, for putting her in this predicament.

A knock startled them both. After a moment, whoever had come tried the door handle, only to find it locked. Another knock followed.

"Lenna?"

Lenna-in-red took a step toward the door, her eyes wide again. "That's him! I need to speak with him!"

"Lenna, are you all right?"

The other her took a second faltering step toward the door. Lenna considered her, dragged a rigid hand through her own hair. This was on the verge of spiraling beyond her control. She should have sent the other Lenna back to her own time immediately. Now, she had waited too long. One mistake among many. She had mucked this up in more ways than she cared to count.

Orzili was here, worry shading his voice, each knock more urgent than the last. She would never convince Lenna-in-red to Walk back without first letting her see him.

"All right," she said. "I'll let him in, but you have to stay right here. Do you understand?"

The other Lenna nodded, eyes riveted on the door.

"I'm coming," she called, as he pounded the door.

She withdrew the key, unlocked the door, and opened it a crack. "Are you alone?" she asked.

He was frowning already. The question bunched his brow even more.

"Yes."

She glanced past him, and looked both ways along the corridor. "All right."

She moved to the side and allowed him to enter.

"What is this? What are you—"

He halted mid-stride. The shock on his handsome face might have been amusing in some other circumstance. He wasn't an easy man to surprise. Lenna closed the door, locked it again, and stepped around him.

Orzili didn't move. Lenna-in-red looked from one of them to the other, as confused by his reaction as by… well, everything else.

"I came to talk to you," she said after some time. She glanced at Lenna, seeking encouragement.

Orzili eyed them both. "What happened? How is this…" He didn't finish the question. He didn't have to. Blood drained from his cheeks.

"Are you all right?" he asked her.

"I am. She's not. She seems addled, erratic. She can't remember why she came or what she wanted to tell you. And she's…" She winced, unsure of how to finish the thought. "She's not me anymore."

"Why hasn't this affected you?"

She wasn't sure she agreed with the premise of the question. She was frightened nearly beyond words. But she understood what he meant, and she shook her head, shivering at a sudden chill. "I don't know." She considered Lenna-in-red. "Walkers are warned not to meet ourselves in the past. It's part of our training. Instructors, Binders, older Walkers – they all tell us to beware of just this, and we come to take it for granted. Don't meet yourself in the past. It's dangerous. It can drive you mad."

She faced him. "Beyond that, they tell us nothing. I once met a Walker – he was old at the time. I was in Sholiss; I don't know where you were. He swore that he had met himself more than once, and nothing happened."

"Do you believe him?"

Again, she eyed the other Lenna. "I did. Now…" She shrugged. "Maybe it's different for each of us. Maybe for some people it has no effect, and for others it drives both versions of them insane. In my case, in this instance, only she was afflicted."

"Lenna, I'm so sorry."

He took a step in her direction, his first movement since seeing the other Lenna. She dipped her chin, but crossed her arms, and gave him no indication that she wanted him to touch her.

"You mentioned healing," he said. "Might a healer's magick cure her?"

This hadn't occurred to her. "Maybe. That might be worth trying. You'll have to do it, of course. She came back twelve days and several bells." She counted the days in her head. "Which means she'll arrive in the evening on the sixth day of Kheraya's Stirring."

"Why wouldn't we heal her now, before we send her back?"

"The more people she meets, the greater the likelihood that she'll alter our future in ways we can't foresee."

"I understand, but has she told you why she came back? Or has her... her affliction kept her from doing so?"

"I need to speak with you!" Lenna-in-red said, as if she had been awaiting this opening.

Orzili regarded her the way he might a woman with Herjean pox. "So I gather. What is it you came here to tell me?"

She faltered. "I- I came to tell you something. There was a woman... a minister. She was... She sent me back."

He winced, pained by what he saw and heard in the woman.

Lenna thought the other her wanted to say more. She had lost even this fine thread of memory.

"Gillian Ainfor," she prompted.

"Yes! That's the name. She's... it's her writing... She was Mearlan's minister..." She trailed off again.

"Do you have any idea what she's talking about?" Lenna asked him. "Does the name mean anything to you?"

"No. There was a spy in Mearlan's court. Two, actually. I knew little about them. I wasn't told their names." His smile was bitter. "We thought it safer that way."

"Well, as far as I can tell, in the next few days, you'll ask this woman – Ainfor – to spy for us. It may be that you shouldn't."

"It *may* be," he echoed. "All the more reason to seek out the healer now."

She could hardly argue. "Yes, all right."

He started toward the door, stopped and held out his hand.

Lenna gave him the key.

He left the chamber, but soon returned. He didn't lock the door. "I've sent for the healer and posted a guard outside," he said. "No one will come in – or leave – without our consent."

Lenna would have preferred to keep the door bolted, but she said nothing as she took the key from him.

"She's the one who sent me back fourteen years. The minister is."

Lenna and Orzili shared a glance.

"What makes you say that?" he asked Lenna-in-red.

"I just know. I don't like her. I don't want her around. I want to go back to my time. I want..." Her voice caught, her eyes fixed on him. "I want to go back."

Lenna thought she meant back to their own time, fourteen years in the future. Orzili didn't say anything, and wouldn't look at either of them.

Another knock made all of them turn. Orzili was closest. He opened the door with caution, then waved someone in. "Only you," Lenna heard him say. She couldn't make out what followed, but after a tencount, a woman entered. She was small, thin, with hair the color of a storm cloud.

She faltered when she saw both Lennas. Her expression remained as it was, though, and she stepped to the middle of the chamber.

"Which of you requires healing?"

"This one," Orzili said, indicating Lenna-in-red with a lift of his hand.

The other Lenna shied from the healer's approach.

"Is she wounded?"

Orzili deferred to Lenna.

"Hers is an affliction of the mind," she said. "I'm a Walker, and this me has come back in time. I don't know if you're aware of the danger–"

"Insanity," the healer broke in, regarding Lenna-in-red with interest. "A Walker who meets herself in the past risks going mad."

"Precisely."

The healer studied the other woman before pivoting toward Lenna. "I'm sorry. I can't do anything for her."

Lenna sagged.

"Why not?" Orzili asked.

"Healer magick, like Binder magick, works on the physical, my lord." She pinched her own arm. "This… stuff, I can mend. Muscle, bone, the vitals within you. Those I can repair as well. But the mind…" Genuine regret etched her face. "The mind and its afflictions lie beyond my talents. Again, I'm sorry."

"You can try, can't you?"

"I wouldn't know how, my lord. There is no injury, no gash to close, no break to fix. Were I to try, I might well do more harm than has already been done. Perhaps, if you'll forgive me the irony, time can heal what I cannot." This last she said to both of them.

Orzili shook his head. "No, there must—"

"Let it be," Lenna said. "This is my mind we're discussing. My future. If there's the least chance of her doing further damage, I won't risk it."

He thinned his lips until they whitened, but nodded.

"Forgive us, healer," she said. "We troubled you for nothing."

The woman regarded Lenna-in-red a bit longer before crossing back to the door. Lenna followed her and locked the door when she was gone.

Orzili looked stricken. She felt the same.

"Time," he said, huffing a dry laugh. "It was all I could do not to slit her throat when she said that."

"It's not her fault."

He twitched a shoulder.

She approached Lenna-in-red. "It's time for you to go back, Lenna."

"Back to my time?" she asked, her expression brightening.

Lenna had seen herself in reflection since Walking back those fourteen years. She had seen the silver in her hair, the lines on her face, and had accepted these as the price of her gift. Only now, though, seeing this other Lenna, and noting the weariness in her dark eyes, the slight droop of her shoulders, did she realize how old she had grown. It was remarkable that this young, handsome Orzili had been so persistent in pursuing her.

"No," she said. "Back to the time you left more recently. You Walked back twelve days. That's how far you'll Walk forward."

"But I have to tell him! The minister. The spy."

Lenna wanted to weep. "You did tell him. You've done well."

"What if we don't send her back?" Orzili asked.

"What?"

He closed the distance between them, the intensity in his hazel eyes reminding her of the most intimate moments they had shared. Her skin prickled.

"You know now not to Walk back to this time. Whatever happens that makes you think you ought to warn me, you'll know better than to risk this journey. Right? In a sense, you've come back to warn yourself."

She weighed this. "I suppose."

"Then we can avoid this, can't we? We can make it so that it never happens." He faltered, then pushed on. "To do that, we can't allow this Lenna to go back."

Lenna rubbed at her temple. The implications of Walking could be mind-numbing.

"I'm not sure—"

"Listen to me! This other Lenna – her mind is gone. The healer can't help us, and for all we know, she'll never heal on her own. If she Walks twelve days into the future, you'll cease to exist when we reach that day, and she'll be the Lenna who continues. Isn't that right?"

It was crudely put, but accurate enough. "Go on."

"We shouldn't take that risk."

"We can't keep two of us here."

"No, you're right."

Something in the way he said this… Lenna backed away from him, chilled, shaking her head.

"I can't believe you'd consider this."

"To save you? I'd consider anything."

"This might not save me," she said. "This might…" She cast a glance at Lenna-in-red, who watched them, puzzlement creasing her brow. "This might cost me everything," she continued, choosing her words with care. "Do what you're considering, and twelve days from now, I might cease to exist."

"You might? You mean you don't know for certain?"

"I'm sure of nothing. That's the point. If we send her back, she'll take my place and might well continue her life as you see her now. If we… do what you have in mind, it might put an end to both of us. Perhaps, all three of us."

"All three?"

"There's another Lenna, remember? Young? Pretty? Alive and well in Fanquir? Do this and she might… cease as well, when she reaches our age."

"Blood and bone." He eyed the woman, eyes narrowed in concentration. "What if we simply keep her here, in this time – alive?"

"Imprisoned?" Lenna asked, voice rising.

"Of course not. Cared for. Here, in the castle."

She shook her head. "I don't know what will happen in twelve days. She might vanish, or I might. Or we both might continue to live, which would be… odd, to say the least. Every course carries risk and uncertainty. All I know is that sending this Lenna to her time will recombine her existence with mine. Only one of us will go on from the instant of her arrival…"

She saw fear creep into his gaze, but was too lost in her own thoughts to reassure him. Surprise at Lenna-in-red's arrival, and fear that madness would plague her for the rest of her life, had consumed her, muddying her thoughts, obscuring the obvious.

"What is it?" he asked. "Are you all right?"

"I'm an idiot," she said. "There is a way to prevent this. It's a little complicated, and we should probably try it in your quarters rather than mine, to avoid creating this exact problem again."

"Wherever," he said, excitement raising his voice. "Just tell me what to do."

"I'll go back." Seeing his alarm, she added, "Not far. A few bells, to early this morning. I'll warn you about this other Lenna. You'll then send me away for the day, so there'll be no chance of me meeting this Lenna. She'll come back, tell you whatever it is she came to say, and Walk back to her time."

He weighed this. "That should work."

"I have to do this in your chamber, lest I meet myself again."

"Right." He paused, his eyes finding Lenna-in-red once more. "What about this Lenna?"

"For now, she stays here."

Lenna approached Lenna-in-red, who regarded her with manifest suspicion. She and Orzili might have been wiser to discuss their options in private.

"We're going to leave you briefly," she said, trying to keep her tone light. "We want to try something. If it works, you'll feel much better. You'll remember everything you wanted to tell him."

The other Lenna looked past her to Orzili. She didn't appear to trust either of them.

"We can bring you food. Would you like that?"

Lenna-in-red answered with something between a shrug and a nod. She said nothing.

"There will be a guard in the corridor. No one else will come in. No one will bother you. You have my word."

No response.

"Come along," Orzili said. "She'll be fine. In a few moments, this will all be over."

She hated to leave the other woman in this state, but he was right. She and Orzili left the chamber.

"No one enters or leaves," he said to the guard, "except the two of us."

"Yes, my lord."

Lenna followed him to his chamber. Once he had closed the door, she ducked behind a dressing screen, set aside her chronofor, and removed her clothes.

Taking up the chronofor, she asked, "What time were you up this morning?"

"Early, with the dawn bells."

She smiled, though he couldn't see. "Shall I wake you a few bells before then?"

"There's no need," he called back, with a wryness she knew well. "I took my breakfast in here. Dawn should be sufficient, thank you."

She set the device. No turns. No days. Eight bells.

"I'm going now."

"All right. The Two guide you."

Lenna steadied herself with a full breath and pressed the central stem. It clicked.

And nothing happened.

She waited. Sometimes she experienced a delay between pressing the stem and being tugged into the between. As the moments ticked by, she knew something had gone wrong.

"Lenna?"

"I'm still here. It didn't work. I'm going to try again."

She thumbed the stem a second time.

Nothing.

"I don't understand." She checked the settings on the chronofor. She pressed the stem again, and once more.

There she remained. She examined herself. Had she forgotten to remove a piece of jewelry or clothing? No.

She slipped back into her gown, buttoned it in haste, and stepped out from behind the screen.

"It doesn't work," she said, holding up the chronofor.

"Odd. When was the last time you used it?"

"My Walk back from my own time. Other than that—" She stopped herself with a dry laugh.

"What?"

"The other Lenna. *She* Walked today. I thought of this earlier, but didn't reason it through. Two of this chronofor exist in this time."

"Three, actually."

"Yes, that's right. I'd wager all of Pemin's gold that Binder magick allows only one such device to work in any given time. As long as hers is here, mine won't work. And as long as mine is here, that of the young Lenna won't work either."

"So what should we do?"

She opened her hands. "We convince the other Lenna to let us use her chronofor."

"Can you use her device?"

"I assume I can. We ought to try. She's very possessive of it, but if I offer to let her hold mine, perhaps she'll relinquish it."

They returned to Lenna's chamber, which was still guarded by Orzili's man. He stepped aside, allowing them to open the door.

Lenna stepped in, Orzili a pace behind her.

She staggered to a halt, her legs nearly giving out beneath her. "The Two save us," she whispered.

Orzili swore, whirled, and yelled a command to his guard.

Lenna could do little more than stare.

The shutters of her window stood open, allowing cold air into her chamber. Lenna-in-red was gone.

CHAPTER 17

24th day of Sipar's Settling, year 633

It was a long drop, longer than it looked from the window. She landed awkwardly, but managed to stand and hobble toward the castle gate.

She hadn't hesitated to jump. She knew that would have been unusual for some. Not for her. She was a Walker, but also more than that.

Fourteen years. Gillian Ainfor! I have to tell him. Or did I?

She paused to stare back at the tower and the open window. She had told him. She remembered telling him. And then he and the other woman – herself – had spoken of keeping her here, of doing things to her.

Her thoughts scattered like light passing through glass, coalesced, fragmented again. She was confused. But she wasn't stupid. When he spoke of not keeping her here, but also not sending her back, she knew what he intended. They wanted to try something else, they left her alone to make their secret plans. They were afraid of her, of things she said, of the way she behaved. They wanted her to vanish, not just go away, but cease to exist.

The guard by the door wouldn't let her leave. She was sure of that. So, the window.

Her ankle ached. She favored it as she walked. She fought the urge to run, knowing somehow that she didn't have to – instinct, vague memories of who and what she was, confidence in abilities she didn't quite understand.

Guards passed her. They tipped their heads and smiled. She

made a small motion, not quite a wave.

Despite her escape, fear of him – the one they all knew as Orzili – mingled with that inexplicable self-assurance. She had been afraid of him since coming back all those years. (Sent by Gillian Ainfor's handwriting!) He kept her here. He wanted her in his bed, which she didn't want. Yes, he was beautiful. She remembered loving him. An older him. Not in this time.

She faltered again, touched the pocket in her gown that held her chronofor. Maybe she should go there. Back to her time. Fourteen years.

The memory of that Walk, of her torment in the between, propelled her forward again. Not yet. Eventually, perhaps, but she wasn't ready.

She slowed when she spotted the main gate.

They won't stop you, she heard in her mind.

That voice didn't allow for bewilderment or doubt. If only she could embrace it and throw off this addle-minded creature she had become.

She strode on, tried to hide her limp. The guards made no effort to stop her. Two of them smiled.

"Heading to market, m'lady?" a man asked. He held a musket, wore a sword on his belt. The others were armed as well.

There's no need to run. Walk as if you belong here, as if you have every right to leave the castle.

"Y- yes."

"Fine day for it."

"It is," she said.

She was by them. Through the gate. She started to look back, to see if they followed. The voice stopped her.

Just walk.

At the first corner she turned toward the waterfront, the market, as the guards would expect.

Reaching the next corner, she turned again, in a different direction. She wasn't sure where to go, but she knew enough not to follow a path Orzili might anticipate. Soon, he would be hunting her. They all would be. The guards were kind because he made them be. They allowed her to come and go because he told them she could. As soon as he changed his mind and commanded them to find her, they would come after her like wolves.

She had no money, no weapons. Only the chronofor, which she refused to sell and was not yet ready to use.

What if you only Walk the few days you came back?

She halted in the shadows of a small lane flanked on either side by wooden buildings. That was the one thing they didn't want her to do – Orzili and the other her. They spoke of keeping her here, killing her, imprisoning her. All to keep her from going back to the time she had left most recently.

She snaked a hand into her pocket and withdrew her chronofor. Twelve days, seven bells. She could go back. She had been here for several bells, so she wouldn't even have to go this far. It would be easy, a Walk of this length. Not nearly as bad as fourteen years.

Voices startled her. Men and women nearby. She concealed the chronofor in the folds of her gown and walked on. The air was chill on this lane, in shadow. The gown she had taken was sufficient in the castle, but not out here.

It would be dark soon, and she would be truly cold.

"Are you lost?"

She whirled.

A man stood at the mouth of the byway. He was young. Yellow hair, lean frame, pale eyes. He walked toward her, concern on his thin face.

"Are you all right?"

She didn't fit here. That's what he would be thinking.

"What's your name?" he asked, coming still closer.

She took a step back from him. He halted, held up both hands for her to see.

"I'm not going to hurt you. I want to help. I don't think you belong here, do you?"

He didn't fit in either. Not really. He wore dark blue breeches and a shirt of white satin. His waistcoat was trimmed in silver. The knife on his belt rested in a fine leather sheath.

Cold wind gusted through the lane, making her shiver.

"You look cold. Do you need help getting home? Is there someone I should find for you?"

The thought that careened through her mind shocked her. Even if she wanted to answer him, even if she knew what to say, she couldn't have uttered a word.

This is who you are, and this is what circumstance demands. Do what you have to do.

"I've hurt my ankle," she said, her voice low.

She extended her leg and pulled up her gown, more than far enough to reveal her ankle and calf. Her ankle was swollen and discolored; it looked worse than she had expected. She knew, though, that he would be distracted by the rest of her leg.

The man stared. "Well, we should... I'm sure there's a healer nearby."

"I need help walking." She nearly laughed aloud at the irony.

"Yes, I can help you with that."

He came closer until he stood beside her. She had been leaning against the nearer of the two buildings, but now she straightened, winced at the pain in her ankle.

The man started to reach for her, stopped himself.

"How should I–"

She gave him no chance to say more. Balling her right hand into a fist, she struck him in the throat, a short, lethal jab. He staggered back a step, his eyes widening, and grabbed at his neck with both hands. She stepped, pivoted on her uninjured foot, lashed out with the other. The kick caught him in the side. He dropped to his knees, letting out a rasp that would have been a cry if not for her first blow. The impact sent a bolt of agony up her leg.

Gritting her teeth, she positioned herself behind him, grasped his chin with one hand, his shoulder with the other, and gave his neck a vicious twist. The snap of bone echoed in the byway. When she released him, he toppled onto his side and didn't move again.

She gaped at what she had done. No thought. No memory. She

hadn't need of those. She merely acted, guided by knowledge that seemed to emanate from muscle and bone.

A quick scan of the alley confirmed that she was alone, unseen, unheard. Somehow she had known to render him silent first, before the rest. Somehow she had known how to kill, without a weapon, without the man raising a hand to defend himself.

This is who you are. Walker, soldier, assassin.

She trusted the voice, even though it frightened her.

She searched his pockets, found a purse containing two rounds, six treys, and a few quads. She took his blade as well, and a chain watch that she liked. His waistcoat would have warmed her, but the voice warned her against taking it. Better to be cold than conspicuous. With another glance behind her, she stowed the purse and watch within her gown, slipped the blade into her bodice, and left the byway.

She had coin enough for an inn now, but the voice cautioned her again. A woman dressed as she was, alone in the city, would draw attention and questions. Instead, she followed the streets to the marketplace and bought food and a shawl. The latter was heavy, warm, but also in keeping with the rest of her garb.

Wandering in the company of so many other people rekindled her fear, made her think again of Orzili. Surely by now he was scouring the city for her, as were the men he commanded. Still, she lingered in the market, because the voice told her to.

He will expect you to flee, to run until he tracks you down. He thinks you crazed, beyond reason. So remain here, among others. Act as if you belong, and others will accept that you do.

She orbited among the peddlers and buyers as shadows lengthened across the city. She hid where all could see her, strolling, admiring baubles, tasting offered morsels of food, answering greetings with a kind word, or a smile, or a tuck of her chin.

Shadows lengthened. The sun dropped toward the horizon and the sky shaded to indigo. The crowd in the market thinned. She took her leave, because to remain was to make herself obvious.

She followed a lane back toward the castle where the wealthiest denizens of the city lived. People around her would expect her to go there. After only a single block, she turned and turned again, following empty lanes to the waterfront.

By now, she had abandoned all to the voice. It was sure, fearless, guided by instincts she barely fathomed. It had kept her alive, earned her food and warmth. Why would she abandon it now? Without it, she would never escape Orzili.

"Search the castle. Every corner of it. I want her found. Don't harm her, don't make her feel threatened. Treat her as you would this Lenna, but find her."

The guard before him was young, beyond his depth. His gaze flicked to Lenna every few moments, and Orzili half-expected him to point at her and say, "My lord, there she is."

Instead, he sketched a stiff bow, assured Orzili that the woman would be found, and hurried away.

"She can't have gone far," he said.

"Is that what you're telling yourself?"

"She must be close by. The guards won't let her leave the castle."

"Why wouldn't they?" Lenna asked. One might have thought he was the addle-minded one. "They let me leave whenever I want, as you instructed I imagine. You wanted to keep me happy, and thus keep me here."

Too much asperity there.

"This isn't my fault, Lenna."

"No, it's mine. Mine for Walking back in time twelve days from now. Mine for allowing you to keep me here, in this past, when my place is fourteen years in our future."

He had no stomach for this fight. He didn't know when he would, but certainly not before the other Lenna had been found.

"Where do you think she's gone?" he asked.

She crossed to the window and stared out at the ward, arms across her chest. "I don't know."

"Where would you go?"

She eyed him over her shoulder and he wished he hadn't asked.

"You think she's Walked back to your time?" He didn't know if he meant twelve days from now, or fourteen years.

She didn't ask him to clarify. "Maybe. I'll try to Walk again in a short while. If she has…"

If she had, Lenna would go back, and warn them both of this coming catastrophe. If she hadn't, if she continued to exist in this time, mad, lost, alone, this Lenna would remain trapped here, and the young Lenna, the third Lenna, unaware in Fanquir, would be unable to Walk at all.

"Don't assume that if she's Walked forward everything will be all right," she said, after a short, taut silence. "Walking through time is rarely so… clean. If she goes all the way back to the time in which we belong, she could set in motion new historical forces that we can scarcely comprehend."

"You said yourself that you can undo whatever damage she does. You can go back, warn me, prevent her from going mad or Walking forward in time."

"I know what I said, and now I'm telling you that it doesn't always work out so well. Time is…" She opened her hands. "It's messy. It branches, changes. It's subject to currents that we can't always see, much less understand. I can try to prevent this from happening, but every time a Walker goes back to change one thing, she risks altering five others. You can't let her leave this time on her own. Find her, bring her back, allow me to fix what's happened. Then we'll send her back to a specific time. One from which she can't do any further damage."

"Yes, all right."

"The problem is," she went on, "I can't know what this Lenna might do. Her mind is…" She pushed both hands through her hair. "She leapt from this window! There's no predicting where she might go. Maybe she'll behave exactly as I would, but more likely she'll find her own path, one shaped in part by my instincts, and in part by her madness."

This sobered him. Rational Lenna would have been hard

enough to find. She was as accomplished an assassin as he, and as brilliant as anyone he knew. Irrational Lenna... if this Lenna was right, they might never find her.

"So..."

"So have your men look far beyond the castle walls," she said. "Scour the city. Follow lanes into the countryside. Search vessels tied in at the wharves."

Orzili muttered a curse. It was Tobias all over again, except this time his quarry was unencumbered by a child and trained to kill.

"I'll lead the search of the castle," she said. "You go into the streets. If I leave here, I'll cause more confusion."

"Yes, all right." He started toward the door, halted and faced her again. "We will find her, Lenna. And as soon as we do, we'll bring her here, give you her chronofor, and send you back to keep all this from happening. You won't spend the rest of your life crazed. I won't allow it."

She acknowledged this with a stiff nod, her body coiled with trapped emotions. He was sure she would have preferred to join his pursuit. Staying here would leave her feeling helpless, and ever more enraged with him.

He left her, relieved that she hadn't said more.

Despite her certainty that the castle guards had let the mad Lenna leave, Orzili stopped at the main gate to question them.

She was right, of course. They let the other Lenna pass without a second thought. His misgivings deepened. How much more had Lenna been right about?

When two Sheraigh guards told him of the dead man, his fears multiplied. They led him and a group of soldiers to the byway where the body still lay. He knew what to look for: the shattered larynx, the barely formed bruise on the man's side, the broken neck. This had been done without a weapon, to a man in the prime of his life. He had no proof, but this had to be Lenna's work. How many others in this city could kill with such efficiency?

The man's pockets were empty, as was the sheath on his belt. Orzili guessed that this Lenna was now armed and carrying coin, which would further complicate his task.

He straightened.

"Return to the castle," he told a guard. "Tell the captain I need two dozen more soldiers."

"Yes, sir."

He followed the lane to the broader street and headed southward. The soldiers who remained followed, awaiting orders. Orzili didn't know what to tell them. He had never expected to pit himself against Lenna. The idea of it daunted him, something he wouldn't have admitted to anyone, not even her at her sanest. Pride.

"Continue your search," he said, sighing the words. "A standard pattern from here east, to the waterfront. When the additional men arrive, have them scour the streets to the west, just in case."

They would never find her, but if they could herd her in a predictable direction, he might corner her and bring her back.

The soldiers left him and he crossed through the city, searching for that red gown, and for additional corpses. He made a quick pass through the marketplace, but by now it was mostly empty. Lenna would have been easy to spot.

He didn't bother with the wharves. She wouldn't be there. Chances were she had fled the city, but something kept him from ordering men beyond the walls. She would be easy to track in the countryside. Either she would follow one of the few established roads, or she would cut across open land. A crazed Lenna might ignore these risks.

But if the missing Lenna was responsible for the murder, then she was more rational than they had assumed. She might have been mad, but she was also calculating. That begged a simple question: If he was being hunted as she was, where would he go?

His answer was the same one Tobias had found, whether by luck or guile. He continued to the waterfront and followed it away from the city in the direction of the Notch.

He traversed a crescent-shaped strand that was strewn with huge boulders, intent on the cliff face at the end of the cove. The tide advanced, narrowing the gap between stone and breaker at the distant outcropping. If he took too long to reach it, he would be unable to make his way around the bend to the strand beyond.

He pressed on over rock and sand, navigation of the uneven shoreline demanding all of his attention.

Only when he spotted the indentation in the sand directly ahead of him – a perfect imprint of a shod foot, fresh, clearly visible in the failing light – did he think to slow. By then it was too late.

"I thought she would be with you."

The words stopped him, raised the hairs on his neck. Odd that a voice that had warmed him and fired his passion for so long should now chill him so.

He turned. How long had she marked his approach?

She emerged from behind a boulder, a shawl wrapped around her shoulders. The sea breeze swept her hair back. She stood tall and straight, lovely in the cool light of dusk. Even here, under these circumstances, she stole his breath.

Her eyes, though, troubled him. Distant, unfocused. He saw the madness in her.

"She's in the castle," he said. "She feared that having two of you in the lanes would confuse things. One of you might have gotten hurt."

"I came to tell you things."

"I know. You *have* told me. You've done well, Lenna. You can come back with me now."

"I don't… I'm not sure what I told you. My memories are… They're muddy. The only clear thing is the voice."

"What voice?"

She shook her head. "It doesn't matter. You should leave. I won't go back with you, and by yourself you're not strong enough to take me."

Odd that this woman, crazed, out of her time, unmoored from any moment in history, sounded more like the Lenna he loved than the sane one had at any point since arriving in this time. Her self-assurance belied the doubt he read in her gaze, yet he sensed both were genuine.

"It needn't come to that," he said, his hand creeping to the handle of his flintlock.

She grinned. "You're not fooling me. You won't shoot, because you know what might happen to the other me. I heard what the two of you said back in the castle. You want to kill me, but she won't let you, not until she's certain that my death won't bring hers as well."

He kept his hand within easy reach of the pistol, but she was right: he couldn't risk harming her. She had them at an impasse. Her thoughts lurched from insanity to clarity and back again. Yet even addled, she was too clever.

"I have no intention of harming you."

"Then why have you reached for your weapon? Why did you say those things to her?"

He let his hand drop, edged closer. "You don't belong here. You... you shouldn't even exist."

"Two of us, when there should only be one."

"Precisely. And of the two of you—"

"I'm mad."

He nodded, his heart aching for her. He took another slow step in her direction. "That's right. You're doing things that the Lenna I know and love wouldn't do. You killed an innocent man tonight."

She blinked. "No, I didn't."

"You did, Lenna. Perhaps you don't remember. There was a man with yellow hair—"

"On a narrow lane," she said, her voice flat. One hand strayed to her bodice. Was his knife hidden there?

"That's right."

"I didn't... I've killed before."

"You're an assassin. You're paid to kill. Killing innocents though, stealing their purses and their belongings like a common street thief – that's beneath you."

Her face crumpled, and he thought she might cry. She recovered quickly, her eyes finding his. "I did what was necessary to survive. I took what I needed, and I left him dead so he wouldn't tell anyone he had seen me."

Confusion followed by clarity. She was as changeable as sea winds.

"Your mind isn't working right. You remember the warnings: a Walker should never meet herself in the past. That's what you've done. You didn't mean for it to happen, but it has, and we have to find some way to correct the damage."

"With another Walk?"

"Yes! As long as you continue to exist in this time, we can't prevent the two of you from meeting. We can't protect you from this madness. If we send you twelve days into the future – the time from which you came – you and she will become one, and the damage she – you – sustained may be irreversible."

"That's why you want to kill me." The words came out clipped, hard. He thought she might have been trembling.

He winced. "I don't want to kill you. I want you to correct this error so that… so that you can go back to the way you were, so that none of this will have ever happened."

"You mean, so that there would only be one of me. The other one. The sane one."

"That's right," he said, his tone brightening. Another step. He was close enough to touch her now. She didn't seem to notice.

"How is that different from killing me?"

Orzili's smile died on his lips. She grinned again, bitter and knowing.

"The voice said it: I may be crazed, but I'm not a fool. You want me gone. You see me as part of her, a part you want to excise, to cut out and toss away." She shook her head. "I'm not part of her. Maybe I was, but not anymore. I'm me. Whatever that means. I don't want to come back, because I don't want to be removed. I want… I want to go back to my real time. I want to Walk fourteen years, to the time where I belong."

"You can't," he said, with too much urgency. The other Lenna's warnings pealed like ward bells in his mind.

"How do you intend to stop me?"

He didn't want to hurt her, and of course he couldn't kill her. Not yet. But neither could he allow her to Walk forward so many years.

He grabbed for her, his fingers closing around one forearm, grinding bone and flesh. He had no intention of letting go.

She fought to break his grip, grappled with her free hand for something in her bodice. He seized that arm as well. She was nimble and smart and dangerous, but when it came to brute strength he still had the advantage.

Lenna growled, a harsh rumble emanating from her chest, a sound he had never heard from her in all their years together. He thought he was on the verge of overpowering her.

Then she reared back and smashed her brow onto the bridge of his nose. He heard bone break. Pain detonated in his face, his head. Blood flooded his mouth and ran over his chin, dripping onto his clothes and the sand at his feet.

He didn't realize that he had released her arms until her punch landed high on his cheek.

The anguish in his head spiraled. His knees buckled and he fell, landing on his side. He tried to stand, but a kick to the gut made him fold in on himself. He forced his eyes open, tried to lever his hands beneath so that he could push himself up.

Agony exploded at the base of his skull. He dropped back to the sand and knew no more.

She breathed hard, her hands shaking, her gaze fixed on him. When, after a tencount, he didn't move, she tossed the rock away. She would have preferred not to hurt him. Even now she couldn't bring herself to kill him. They were in love. He said so. Her memories confirmed this. Yet she felt nothing for him, except perhaps lingering fear. Maybe the other Lenna still loved him. Or the other, other Lenna. He spoke of three. That stirred a memory as well.

She cared as little for the others as she did for this man prone at her feet. She wanted to survive. She wanted to Walk to her rightful time. She trusted no one other than the voice.

And the voice now told her to return to the city. He'd found her, and in time he would wake and resume his pursuit. She needed a new plan.

The city will be crawling with soldiers.

A ship then, or a path beyond the city walls. Her options were narrowing. She eyed Orzili, thought again of killing him. As he reminded her, she had taken one life this night. A desperate act, but one that struck her as necessary and had proven profitable. If she killed him, it might be days before he was found. If she dragged his body into the sea, it could take longer than that.

Memories of what they had shared stopped her, vague though they were. The other Lennas loved him. That counted for something. She could proclaim her difference, her separateness from them, but she remained more like them than not, more tied to them than she wished to believe. That was what she thought, anyway. The voice was silent on this matter.

She left him there.

CHAPTER 18

24th day of Sipar's Settling, year 633

As she neared the wharves, still following the contour of the shoreline, she spotted a company of soldiers in Sheraigh blue. They carried muskets and stood before the docks. She halted, hidden from their view by the gathering darkness. Other soldiers would be nearby, patrolling the lanes, looking for her.

She scanned this stretch of beach, but just as the gloaming hid her from the soldiers, it also obscured other paths off the strand.

After a fivecount, she started forward again, cautious, surveying the coast, the wharves, those portions of the city she could see.

She had taken perhaps ten steps when she heard a sound to her left, from the city. Halting again, she peered into shadows.

She heard it a second time. A sibilant noise. A person, seeking her attention. She checked the soldiers to make certain they hadn't heard, and took a step in the direction from which the sound had come.

"Yes," came a whisper. "This way."

"I can't see," she answered.

A faint glow appeared before her. She couldn't have said what color it was. It seemed to shift and slide, like oil on water. She eyed the soldiers one last time and angled toward that gentle radiance.

She crossed over soft, dry sand, and then through a narrow copse of trees. Finally, she passed between two old buildings, emerging onto a lane lit only by candle glow from nearby houses.

Two small figures awaited her there. One of them extinguished the oily sheen she had spotted from the strand.

The street was empty save for the three of them.

"Thank you," she said.

They didn't reply, but gazed at her, solemn, appraising. They were children, a girl and a boy. She thought they must be siblings, so similar were their faces and bearing. They had dark hair, pale eyes that looked almost white in the gloom. Their features were delicate, beautiful even, but their clothes were tired and too thin for this time of year.

At a stirring of the wind, she caught the fetor of decay and she glanced around again. The smell dissipated as swiftly as it had come.

"I suppose I should be on my way," she said, after the silence had lengthened uncomfortably.

"I can't tell what it is," the girl said in a voice both childlike and knowing. "Can you?"

The boy shook his head. "Not at all. At least not beyond the obvious."

"Its years are all—"

"Who are you?" she asked. "Why are you talking about me that way?"

"We're having a conversation," the girl told her, as haughty as a court noble. "And you're interrupting. That's rude."

She had to smile. "Isn't it just as rude to talk about someone in their presence, as if they aren't there?"

The two shared a look, worry in their ghostly eyes.

"Yes, it is," the girl said, chastened. "Please forgive us."

"Children shouldn't be out alone in the streets. You should go home."

The girl hid her mouth with a thin hand, her laughter as clear and musical as the splash of a brook. "We're not children. You should know that."

She stared at one and then the other, puzzled now. If not children... Were they creations of her mind, symptoms of her madness? She thought she understood the depths of this Walking-induced insanity. What if she was wrong, and it continued to worsen? What if these two marked the beginning of a slide into hallucination?

"You've confused it," the boy said. "Maybe it doesn't know as much as we hoped."

She scowled. "Stop referring to me as 'it.'"

"What else would we call you?"

"'She,' of course."

He shook his head. "You're not a she, are you? You're not really anything at all."

"I don't–"

"We tasted your years when you were still on the sand," the girl said. "That's why we called for you. We sensed the confusion in you, and we wanted to know exactly what you are. But you don't know yourself."

We tasted...

"You're Tirribin," she said, drawing on a memory from so long ago, it could have been a different life. She took a step back from them. "That's why..." She stopped herself from mentioning the smell. "Why you could taste my years from so great a distance."

The girl glowered, appearing to know what Lenna intended to say.

"That's right," the boy said. "We're Tirribin." To his sister, he said, "Maybe she knows more than we thought."

Suspicion lingered in the girl's glare. "I'm not so sure. You don't need to fear us," she said, a rasp underlying the words. "Your years are muddied. We wouldn't feed on you any more than a human would drink seawater. It would do more harm than good."

"Why? What's wrong with them?" She feared their answer.

"Don't you know?"

Of course she did. Tirribin didn't prey on Walkers because their years were less pure. She remembered a time demon explaining this to her when she was a child in Windhome. Before a boy died and another was sent away. Now she was here, fourteen years out of her time, twelve days out of another, half-mad from having met herself. Whose years could be less pure than hers?

239

"Yes," she said. "I know. But that doesn't make me less than human, and it doesn't excuse you calling me 'it.'"

"You're a creature outside of time," the girl said with relish. "There are too many of you, and your years are beyond repair." She made a small gesture, indicating the lane and the houses. "You bear little resemblance to the humans I sense around me."

"Maeli…"

The girl rounded on the other demon. "Don't tell me I'm being rude. She was going to say something about the way we smell. Humans do that a lot, and I grow tired of it."

"What should I do?" Lenna asked, drawing their attention once more.

The girl laughed again, the sound uglier than before. "Do?"

"Don't you intend to help me? Isn't that why you called to me?"

"We're Tirribin. We're predators, and while your years would be disgusting to us, that doesn't make you more than prey."

The boy frowned but held his tongue.

"And even if that weren't so, there would be no helping you. You are what you are, and can't be changed or redeemed. You didn't exist before today. I can tell. Yet you have all these years. Confused, corrupted, but years nevertheless. We didn't call you here to help. We called to see you. We sensed you, and we wanted to see what sort of being could have such years." The girl raked her up and down with her gaze. "Honestly, I thought you would be more interesting than you are. You seem no different from other humans."

"Then maybe you're wrong about me."

The Tirribin shook her head. "I'm not."

Lenna checked the street, mostly to avoid looking the girl in the eye. Her words stung like sand in a hard wind. She didn't want to believe what the girl had said, but Tirribin understood time as few creatures did. And this one had no reason to lie to her.

The clarity of her own reasoning surprised her.

"My thoughts are clearer around you," she said. "Might that mean something?"

The girl tipped her head. "Clearer in what way?"

"I… I can't really say. They make more sense. I can reason and understand. I haven't been able to do that since I met myself earlier. I've been following the voice."

"The voice?" the boy asked.

She searched for the right word. "Intuition."

He nodded.

"Doesn't that mean you might be wrong?" she asked them. "Isn't it possible that I can get better?"

"You can do nothing about your years," the girl said. "The rest… Perhaps your mind can heal itself. I don't know. They're hunting you, and I don't believe you have much…" She bared needle teeth in a harsh grin. "Much *time*, remaining."

"I can take care of myself. I won't let the soldiers hurt me. I want a life. What was it you called me before? A creature outside of time? Maybe I am. You're right: before today I didn't exist. Or I did, but as someone else." She shook her head, knowing that wasn't right either. "I don't have the words. The point is, every bell that passes makes me more… myself. They want me to go back to being part of the other Lenna, the other me. I don't want that."

"They can't make you go back, can they?" the boy asked.

"They can send back the other Lenna, and she can see to it that none of this happens. That will be the end of me. She'll continue, I'll go back to being her, and I won't be this person anymore."

"You're mad," the girl said. "Wouldn't it be better for all if you went away?"

"Maeli!"

She threw a scowl her brother's way but faced Lenna again.

"That's what they think," Lenna said. "Is it so surprising that I don't agree?"

"I suppose not." Maeli turned to the boy. "I'm bored. I want to feed now."

"Wait! Help me, and I can tell you where you might find someone to feed on. Easy prey."

This caught the girl's interest.

"Who?"

"A man. He's on the strand between here and the Notch. Unconscious, yours for the taking."

"Is he young?"

She did the arithmetic in her head. "He has twenty seven years. Not exactly young, but strong. And he's a Spanner."

Disapproval creased the girl's brow. "Why would that matter? We're not Belvora. We don't feed on magick." She considered Lenna. "Still, you have made payment of a sort. If he's still there."

"You'll help me then?"

"I've told you: there isn't much we can do. I will say, though, that if you continue in a different time from the other you, your mind might heal itself. I wouldn't have thought so, but if being around us – if being near what you would call our 'magick' – makes you feel better, there is a chance."

"A chance," she repeated.

"That's right. About the same as the chance that your strong man will be waiting on the strand."

"Yes, all right."

The Tirribin didn't wait for her to say more. They exchanged glances and blurred away toward the Notch.

Left alone, she eyed the buildings around her and the lanes sloping upward from the waterfront to the castle.

That's where we ought to go. The voice.

She sensed the stirring of an idea. Already, with the Tirribin gone, her thoughts were fracturing again. Only a thread remained, one she could follow from what the demon had said to what her heart desired.

She set out for the castle. Before she had gone far, she heard the scrape of boots on cobble. Soldiers.

Don't be afraid. We have trained for this.

She pressed herself to a shadowed wall as the guards approached. Several of them carried torches, but their glow didn't reach to her hiding place.

When they had passed, she stole after them, using the beat of their footsteps to conceal her own. She had done something like this before, but couldn't recall the circumstances. So she trusted her instincts and the wisdom of the voice.

The soldiers followed a winding path through the city, but she didn't mind. Other companies in Sheraigh blue had no reason to approach this one. As long as she remained hidden from these guards she had nothing to fear.

In time, they circled back toward the castle, and as they neared it, she slipped away and followed one lane after another to the West Gate. Fewer guards patrolled this end of the castle – usually only two at the outer portcullis. Those posted here hadn't seen her leave. They might not know what color gown she wore.

She walked to the gate in plain view, holding up both hands to show she wasn't armed.

"Have you seen her?"

The two guards, a man and a woman, exchanged looks. "Seen who, my lady?" the woman asked.

"The one who looks like me, of course."

"No, we've seen no one. Have…" She glanced at her companion again. "Have you?"

"I'm afraid not. I searched the lanes and inns around the castle. I found nothing."

She had halted to speak with them. Now she walked on, passing between the soldiers and entering the gate. Neither of them stopped her.

Nor did the guards at the inner west gate. Orzili would have been appalled.

She entered the castle proper at her first opportunity and, following memories she couldn't quite trace, navigated the twists and turns of the corridors to her chamber.

She knocked, and at a word from within opened the door and stepped inside.

The other Lenna rose from a chair by the hearth, the fire and candles casting shadows against every wall.

She eyed Lenna, unable to mask her apprehension.

"You're alone."

"Yes."

"No one saw you enter the castle?"

"Guards on the west side," she said. "They think I'm you."

The other Lenna stepped away from her chair to an open expanse of floor. Better ground for a fight, should it come to that.

"And you came…"

"To talk."

The other woman nodded. "I'd like to believe that. Are you carrying a weapon?"

"I am. And you and him – you're the ones who spoke of killing me. I should be distrustful of you, not the other way around."

"Perhaps. Or it's possible that, fearing for your life, you've come to harm me."

She shook her head. "I haven't. You think me mad. And I suppose I am, though not so much as I was." She gave her head another shake, trying to keep her thoughts clear. "I won't hurt you. I give you my word. I want… I want us to find a way forward."

The other Lenna considered her. After a fivecount, she walked in her direction. Lenna tensed, but the other her opened her hands, a gesture of peace. She stepped around Lenna to the door and locked it.

She regarded her again before walking back to the hearth and sitting. She indicated the chair beside her own.

"You must be cold. You should warm yourself."

Lenna edged closer to the fire, but didn't sit.

"Are you hungry? I'd imagine you are."

She nodded.

The other Lenna rose again, unlocked the door, and called for someone. She spoke briefly with a woman in the corridor, taking care to shield Lenna from view. After, she closed the door again and reclaimed her seat.

"She'll bring food shortly. You really ought to sit. You look exhausted."

Lenna hesitated, then lowered herself into the chair. She closed her eyes, savoring the warmth of the blaze.

"Where is Orzili?"

Her eyes flew open. She clutched her hands.

The other Lenna narrowed her gaze. "What did you do to him?"

"He... He followed me, and tried to bring me back. He grabbed me. So I... I hit him. Several times. I left him on the strand. He was... He wasn't awake."

The other Lenna's eyes went wide as well. "You beat him senseless?" At her nod, the other woman laughed aloud. "I've wanted to do that for more than a turn."

"After I left him, I met two Tirribin." She stared down at her hands. "I told them where he was."

All mirth fled the other woman's face. "Blood and bone."

"I didn't know what else to do. He spoke of killing me. You and he spoke of it. And I knew that after I beat him he would be angry. I was scared."

"Do you know if they found him?"

She shook her head. "There's more. I killed a man. I took coin from him and a knife."

The other Lenna blew out a breath, but a knock at the door kept her from saying more.

"Hide behind the dressing screen."

Lenna did as she was told and listened as people entered the chamber. A flurry of activity was followed by the click of the door.

"It's all right."

She crept out from behind the screen. A platter holding cheese and bread, smoked meat and nuts rested on the table beside a carafe of wine.

The other Lenna poured out two cups. She sipped from one and handed Lenna the second. She eyed it warily.

"There's nothing wrong with it. I give you my word. Where is Orzili? I have to send soldiers for him."

"He'll be angry," she said again. *He might be dead.*

"Yes, I imagine so, if he's alive. Where is he?"

She described the place. Again, the other Lenna went to the

door. This time she summoned a guard. They spoke for some time. At last she sat again by the fire, arms crossed, brow creased.

"If they find him, they'll bring him here," she said, her voice low and tight. "We should know his fate soon enough."

"I don't want to see him! I came to speak with you. No one else."

"We don't even know… He won't hurt you. I won't allow it. Sit. Drink your wine."

After a moment she sat.

"You say you killed a man."

"I needed money, and a weapon. He had both."

The other woman shook her head again. "None of this should have happened. It's my fault, and Orzili's. But I don't want him dead, and I'm sure you don't either. This thread of time can't be allowed to continue. You understand that."

"I know you think so. You see me – he does, too – as more of you and that's all. You think we're the same. We're not. I…" She frowned at the flames dancing in the hearth. It had been easier talking to the Tirribin. They gave her clarity. Being with this other Lenna – it was the opposite. Everything seemed hazed, as if her mind had caught fire. "I'm me," she said, knowing the words were inadequate. "I'm not just you anymore. And I'm less that way with every bell."

"All the more reason for me to go back. Give me your chronofor. I can Walk back a few bells, fix everything, and return here. You won't even know I was gone."

"Because *I'll* be gone."

The other woman didn't deny it.

"We are alike," she said after a pointed silence, determined to forge on despite the haze. "So I know what you really want."

The Lenna wearing blue appeared amused by this. "What do I really want?"

"To go back into the future, of course. Not twelve days, but the full fourteen years."

The other woman stared, deadly serious now.

"You want to go back to the Orzili we left there," she continued. "You love him, not this one. If I'd told you what I did, and that the older Orzili's life was at risk, you would have run to the strand yourself, even knowing you could repair history with a Walk. You might have killed me in a fit of rage."

"I love him in any time," the other one said. The hand holding her cup of wine trembled.

"You resent this one. You want to leave him and be with the other. I want that, too, but I want something else even more."

The other Lenna stood and moved closer to the hearth, her back to Lenna. "This isn't... We were speaking of your chronofor. I need to use it, to make all of this right again. Your mind is... Meeting me made you go mad. Which is why you're saying all of these things."

"When I was with the Tirribin it was better. My mind, I mean. It was clearer. They said that it might heal on its own. With time. I won't be mad forever. And I don't want to stop being alive."

"You wouldn't stop living. You would just–"

"Become you? That isn't the same as living, is it? Not really. Not for me."

The other Lenna peered back at her. "No, it's not the same. It's all we have. You Walked here – I Walked here. Whatever the reason for that, we were wrong to do it. And now this with Orzili. So I have to fix it."

"Why do you need–"

"My chronofor doesn't work. There are two of them in this time, and – I'm guessing here – I think it likely–"

"That Binder magick can only work in one device at any time."

The other woman studied her. "That's right. Your mind is clearer, isn't it?"

"I told you. Give me the chance to live, and it will grow clearer still."

The other Lenna crossed to the table that bore the food and took some bread and cheese. Lenna joined her there, famished. For a while they both ate. Several times, they reached for the same sort of cheese simultaneously. The first instance, the other Lenna laughed. After the third or fourth occurrence, she pivoted sharply and walked back to the hearth, clearly unnerved.

"So what do you want?" the other woman asked, breaking another long pause.

"What?"

"You said before that I wanted to return to my Orzili, and you did, too, but there's something you want more."

"To live, of course. I'll give him up if it means you won't take me away from us." She wrinkled her brow at the wording, but went on. "There's a way we can both have what we want. I thought of it when I was with the time demons." She faltered. "I'll try to remember."

"You don't have to," the other Lenna said, her voice hushed. "I think I know. It's... It's brilliant, really. And simple."

Their eyes met across the shadows and flickering light. She remembered their gazes locking earlier in the day, when everything in her mind exploded. This was different, and yet also the same. Recognition, fear, but tinged now with possibility.

"I go forward in time, fourteen years," the other Lenna said. "Back to where I belong. I use your chronofor to get there. You remain here, with my device, which will start to work the instant I leave. And – this is the difficult part – the Orzili in this time never knows."

She nodded, relieved that she didn't have to explain. "We would exchange gowns before you go."

"Yes, of course. In my mind, you're Lenna-in-red. You would have to become Lenna-in-blue." She faced the flames. "There's one problem."

When she didn't answer, the other woman continued.

"The other Lenna. The young one. As long as one of us is here, her chronofor won't work. Eventually, I intended to return to my – our – time. At which point she would be able to Walk. You don't plan to leave this time, and that traps her here. I remember those intervening years. On several occasions, Pemin sent us back to kill.

She can't do any of that if you're here. Nor would she ever come back to this time to help Orzili with the Walker, which means that all of this changes."

Neither of them said anything. She stood by the food. The other Lenna remained by the hearth. When they did finally speak, it was to offer the same words, in unison.

"There is one way."

Pain brought him back to his senses, a stomach-roiling pounding at the base of his skull. He forced his eyes open. The stars above him wheeled. He rolled onto his side, vomited, and flopped to his back again, eyes closed, every breath a hammer blow to his head.

Lenna had done this to him. Not his Lenna. Not either of his Lennas. But still... Anyone else, and he would have vowed revenge. With her, he couldn't.

He didn't know how much time had passed. It hadn't been fully dark when they fought. It was now.

"She spoke true."

He had his pistol out, full-cocked, and aimed before knew what he had done. Two children stood over him, starlight giving him a vague sense of their faces. A sickly odor emanated from them.

"She said he was unconscious. He's not." A boy's voice.

The first words had been spoken by a girl.

"Your pistol is useless against two of us." The girl again. He kept his weapon leveled at her.

"Would you care to test that?" he said, his voice thin.

"You're a fool. All humans are fools."

All humans...

A demon then. Tirribin. Real fear crashed through him. She was right. His pistol was useless. Even if he shot one – difficult considering their speed – he couldn't possibly shoot both.

"A carpenter, I build without hammer or nail,
A traveler, I journey without wheel or sail;
An artist, my work is the most elegant lair,
A hunter, I rely on the deadliest snare."

He blurted it out, giving them no time to attack.

The demons stared at him, stunned by what he had said. Then they were consulting, their heads close together, their hands motioning so quickly they appeared to blur.

He hadn't bargained with them, which might have been a mistake. They wouldn't allow him to leave, not until they solved the mystery or gave up and demanded the answer. At least, though, he had given himself time.

He was dizzy still, but less than before. His head throbbed.

She spoke true...

The implications of the demon's first words finally reached through his pain and disorientation. Had the crazed Lenna sent them? Had she tried to kill him?

Could he blame her if she had?

She believed he meant to kill her, and in a sense she was right. He couldn't imagine any solution to this mess that allowed her to continue her own life. He would have preferred not to hurt Lenna in any form, but he wouldn't risk the sanity of the woman he loved for this... this accident of history. The sooner his Lenna Walked back in time and ended this nightmare, the better for all of them. The confusion caused by the arrival of the third Lenna couldn't go on.

On the thought, he forced himself up, braced himself against the nearest boulder. The Tirribin glanced his way, before resuming their deliberations.

He swallowed against a tide of nausea, and squeezed his eyes shut. Damn her. It was a long way back to the castle. He had his sextant with him, but he couldn't endure even a short journey through the gap in his present condition.

Voices from the south made the Tirribin straighten and blur to his side.

"Tell us what it is," the girl said, her voice high and taut.

"You'll let me live?"

"The riddle instead of years." The words rushed out of her. "A fair bargain. Please, the answer! Before they arrive!"

He was tempted to deny them, but knew he would pay a cost for such a betrayal.

"It's a spider."

The Tirribin sighed as one.

"A fine riddle," the boy said, eyes closed in relish. "Our thanks."

They left before he could respond. He tracked their blurred forms for some distance, but soon lost them amid the boulders and shadows.

He straightened, turned toward the voices. Sheraigh soldiers. He raised a hand in greeting and staggered forward to join them.

They escorted him back to Castle Hayncalde and then to the healer, who used her magick to ease the pounding of his head and the dizziness. Within a bell of his arrival, the healer had completed her ministrations and ordered him to bed. Instead, he went to Lenna's chamber.

At her word, he entered and closed the door behind him.

Lenna stood at the sight of him, laying aside the book she read. Candlelight gleamed in her dark eyes; fire glow warmed the blue of her gown.

"Are you–" She broke off. "Did you find her?"

"I did," he said, joining her by the hearth. "She fought me off and fled. She sent Tirribin for me. I'm lucky to be alive."

"How did you escape them?"

He smirked. "A riddle. The one you used when we were children."

"That was clever."

"Have you heard anything from the guards?"

"No. I think she must have left the city."

"Or this time. Have you tried your chronofor again?"

"Tried my… Yes, not long ago. It doesn't work. She must still be in this time."

He narrowed his gaze. She seemed… odd, and she wouldn't look him in the eye. "Are you all right?"

"I'm fine."

"Lenna–"

"I'm tired," she said, and sounded it. "This day has… It's unsettled me."

"I'm sure. It's unsettled me, too." He gripped her shoulders gently and kissed her brow. She smelled of woodsmoke and honeysuckle. "You should sleep. She can't hide from us forever. I'll speak with the captain of the guard tonight and have them extend their search beyond the city walls. We'll find her, and then we'll send you back to repair what's been broken."

She responded with a faltering nod. No doubt she still blamed him for all that had happened. Maybe she had cause.

"And… and after that," he went on, "I'll send you back to your own time. As soon as I can. I promise."

"Thank you," she said, her voice low. Still she wouldn't look at him.

He released her and stepped back to the door. "Sleep," he said. "You'll feel better come morning."

She nodded, thinned a smile. He left her.

The memory came to her the moment he pressed his lips to her forehead. It shouldn't have surprised her. From the instant the other Lenna left, everything had grown clearer. Of course this would follow.

The reason she had Walked back these twelve days. The cause of all that had happened since her arrival.

The time to share this with him had passed. She couldn't tell him without revealing who she was and where the other Lenna had gone. And after all he had done and said, she wasn't sure she wanted to.

Still, she heard the words in her head, shouted in her own voice. *He escapes! The Walker escapes from your dungeon!*

He didn't deserve the warning, and so she wouldn't give it. Time would reveal the truth of it soon enough.

CHAPTER 19

23rd Day of Kheraya's Waking, Year 634

After Maeli commanded her to leave Hayncalde, Droë considered calling for Tresz. He would bear her again; he had told her as much. She had no idea where to go, and no means of reaching another isle. Under the circumstances, the Shonla would gladly help her.

She spotted the Shonla's mist on the bay, drifting toward a ship. She needed only to sing. Lyrics danced on her tongue; a melody repeated itself in her mind. She kept it locked there.

Pride.

He would want to know what had happened, and she wouldn't be able to tell the story without weeping. The cruelty of the other Tirribin, the condescension of the Arrokad – she didn't wish to think about either. She wouldn't speak of them.

For centuries, she had lived alone, hunted alone, provided for herself in every way. She could do so again. Yes, she was hundreds of leagues from the isle she knew best. What did that matter? She was Tirribin, an Ancient. She needed no one.

She crept back to the Daerjen wharves and stole onto a ship, hiding herself in the hold among sleeping men and women, the foul smells of humans surrounding her. None saw her or heard her. Her own smell was masked by those of the sailors. Humans were so often oblivious of the world around them, foolishly secure.

She didn't know where the ship would sail, and she didn't care.

Away from Hayncalde. Nothing else mattered to her. As long as they departed come the morning. She didn't wish to be on these waters at night, in case the captain wasn't wise enough to light torches on his deck. It would have been humiliating had Treszlish attacked the vessel with her aboard.

The crew stirred at dawn and soon bustled above, readying the ship for the sea. She remained below, hidden, hungry. She didn't like the slip and roll of voyaging. She would have traded the warmth of the hold for the cold of Tresz's mists if it meant she could end this disorienting up and down and experience again the joy of flying with the Shonla.

For all that day and two more, they sailed. Droë's need for years consumed her. Time and again, she started to crawl from her hiding place, intending to feed on the nearest of the crew. On each occasion, fear of discovery stopped her. She could fight off the strongest humans. She might best three or five in a fight to the death. Against all of them, though, many armed with pistols and blades, she couldn't hope to survive.

But neither could she live long without feeding. Her gut ached. She struggled to keep her thoughts clear, to maintain her restraint. It was worst at night, her natural hunting time. She slept poorly when she slept at all. The aroma of so many years insinuated itself into every thought, every dream, every breath. She feared she might go mad with desire.

Ironically, her one consolation also came at night, when couples retreated into the hold to take pleasure in one another. Love, the act and the emotion. Her fascination. Her obsession. It was here in abundance. Men and women, men and men, women and women. She had never seen or heard so much. It surrounded her, permeating the air much as the years did. Her kind saw well in the dark, and here, with humans writhing and panting all around her, every one of her senses was heightened. So, too, was her determination. For arousal did not follow fascination. It seemed it couldn't, wasn't part of her. She resolved anew to change that, and so was doubly eager to leave this vessel.

Late on the third day, with daylight waning, the ship's motion changed. Shouts from above. Sounds she didn't understand. When she realized that the crew had furled their sails and taken up oars, she nearly cried out.

Her relief didn't last long. She listened, and even left her nook to determine where they were.

Still not at a wharf. They had anchored the ship near a port, but, she gathered, would not approach the dock until the next morning.

Men and women neared the hatch. She scrambled back to her hiding spot. Waited, watched, listened, dreamed, her desire for desire as keen as her hunger.

Later, when all the humans in the hold had fallen asleep, Droë left her hiding place again and climbed onto the deck, making not a sound. Above, a few humans still prowled the ship. She kept out of sight, peered over the rail at the torches burning on the nearby wharves. The distance wasn't great. Her kind didn't like water, but she could swim if she had to. After she fed.

A young woman stood near the ship's prow, gazing toward the city. Easy prey, even for one as famished as Droë.

She stalked, rushed the woman when she was near enough, clambered onto her back, clamped a hand over her mouth to muffle her screams. She rode the woman down to the deck, mouth at the sailor's throat, sweet years on her tongue. She fed until the woman had nothing left to give. A man approached, wary, a blade in his hand.

"Winn? That you?"

Hungry still, Droë waited until he was close and then took his years as well. His struggles alerted others. She was sated now, and eager to get away. She climbed over the rail and down the side of the ship, and slipped into the water without a splash. Sailors on the deck of the vessel lit torches, cried out at the sight of their dead shipmates. Droë glided away in the inky waters, her strength restored. More torches burned. They would scour the hold and then the deck and then the hold again. No one on the ship would sleep this night.

She swam silently, chilled by the brine, but pleased to be away. Her one fear was that she would find Tirribin in this city as well, wherever she was.

She reached a stone-strewn strand some time later and dragged herself out of the cold surf, weary from swimming so far. As she scanned the shoreline and the city beyond, she saw much that struck her as familiar. The arc of the rocky coast, the soaring spire of the city's sanctuary. She had been here, recently.

"Rooktown," she whispered. She was back on the isle of Rencyr, in the royal city, where she had been with Tresz not so long ago. She didn't know whether to be frustrated or amused. In the end, she decided she was neither. It was a place, like any other, filled with prey and largely unknown to her.

She made her way to the city gate, passed through at Tirribin speed, unnoticed by the guards, and set out through the lanes, searching for others of her kind. Since she had fed on the ship, she didn't have to risk hunting in another's territory. It took her a bell or two to pass at speed through most of the city's streets. By the time she finished, she was hungry again, but also convinced that no Tirribin dwelt here. She could prey at will.

She fed, found a lair in which to pass the day, hunted that next night and during the ones that followed. No other Tirribin appeared to disrupt the rhythm of her new life. For the first time since beginning her wanderings with Tresz, she had found contentment. She had abundant prey, a city to call her own. What more could one of her kind want?

A great deal, she learned. For while she had found the ingredients necessary for contentment, true peace eluded her.

She wanted to find Ujie again, to convince the Arrokad that she had been wrong about Droë's desire to change. Or perhaps to be convinced that she was the one who was wrong. She tried not to think of Tobias, or of her nights in the hold of that ship. Love was for humans. Companionship was something she had eschewed for much of her existence. The purpose that had driven her from

Trevynisle – the transformation of her very being – terrified her.
But it tantalized as well. Ujie's words and admonitions implied
that she could change, if she chose to do so.

Arrokad were wise and knowledgeable, the acknowledged
leaders of all the Ancients. Droë would have been foolish to
dismiss Ujie's cautions. And she hadn't. Rather, the warnings had
come too late and from too great a distance to stop her. Fearful
though she was, she was also set on her course. This, she came to
understand, was the source of her restlessness. She had made her
choice, but apprehension stayed her.

Diagnosis did not bring a cure. Not at first. Her fear proved
stubborn, and she resented her own weakness. She was a
predator, a Tirribin. She should have been immune to fear.
An oversimplification, she knew, but true enough to make her
ashamed.

She continued to exist – to prowl and hunt and sleep and want.
Until finally want overcame all.

On the night she made up her mind to act, a hot wind blew out
of the west, carrying the whisper of distant thunder and the smell
of rain. She had hunted and fed. Now she wandered the lanes near
the waterfront, restive as always. After a time, she realized that she
wasn't wandering so much as searching. She sought that young
woman, the one she had seen give away love for a bit of coin, the
one who had warned her off the streets.

Have you ever loved any of them?

Nah. If I had, I woulda held on with both hands.

She thought of Tresz, of Ujie, even of Maeli and Teelo. She
thought of the other woman, the Walker, who had spoken to
her of Tobias and awakened within her this yearning. Though
she preferred always to be alone, on this night she would have
welcomed a conversation with any of them.

"Enough." She said it aloud, startling a stray cat at the mouth of
an alley.

You have been Tirribin for your entire existence, Ujie told her.

Perhaps that had been true, but Droë wasn't certain she was

Tirribin anymore. She wasn't even the "girl-thing." She had become something she didn't recognize: part-Tirribin, part-human, part-child, part-coward, part-exile, alone, confused, sad. Whatever she was, she hated it. Change carried with it uncertainty, perhaps peril. But at least she wouldn't be *this* anymore.

Droë angled toward the waterfront, followed a narrow strip of pebbly shore to a broader strand. This she traversed, her feet cushioned in cool sand, starlight and the gibbous moon lighting her way. Her heart beat very fast, like the wings of a hovering falcon. Her hands shook.

Apprehension had given way to anticipation, even excitement. She had started down this path some time ago, and after delays of her own making, she was glad to tread it again.

At the far end of the strand, she scrambled over a jumble of huge rocks to yet another sandy beach. Here, alone, she halted to stare out over the Inward Sea toward distant Ensydar. Lightning flickered across a bank of clouds. Thunder mumbled a response. The rain would reach Rencyr before long. For now, the world seemed balanced: storm and clarity, lightning and starglow. She stood on a knife's edge.

She took a step toward the water.

"I would speak with one of the Most Ancient," she cried, her voice swallowed by the pounding surf.

Droë wondered if any would answer. Her resolve to act meant little if no Arrokad swam in these waters.

She shouted her summons a second time, and after waiting, once more. She would not call again. Thrice made it a true supplication. More would be rude.

Wind whipped her hair. Lightning brightened the foamy swells and the boulders around her. Thunder rumbled in the sand beneath her feet.

Something broke the water's surface, tiny and distant.

Droë fought the impulse to flee.

Whatever it was vanished, only to rise again, closer now and recognizable. A face, framed by dark hair.

It dove, surfaced nearer still, swam in her direction. As it neared the shore, it stopped swimming and advanced on foot.

It – he – emerged from the sea like an animate statue. His skin was alabaster, his shoulders wide, his body tapered to a narrow waist. His legs were darker, and Droë realized that he had covered himself with scales, rather than appearing naked. A kindness and a relief, unexpected.

His face was as sculpted and perfect as that of a Tirribin. His eyes were pale and serpentine, much like Ujie's. Indeed, he could have been her brother.

Water ran down his body as he stepped from the surf and halted in front of her.

"There is a price to be paid for summoning my kind, even for one such as you, cousin."

"I know. What price?"

"We shall decide, you and I. Why have you summoned me?"

She opened her mouth to answer, but no words came. Instead, to her shame, she burst into tears. For some time, too long, she could not speak for her sobbing. The Arrokad regarded her, unmoving and apparently unmoved.

When at last she found her voice, she apologized.

"What is your name, cousin?"

"I am Droënalka. Most call me Droë." She would have expected a human or another Tirribin to reciprocate, but such conventions did not apply to the Most Ancient Ones. Either he would tell her his name or he wouldn't. His to choose.

"Do you seek a boon, Droë of the Tirribin? Is this why you summoned me?"

She hesitated before nodding.

"I see. That, too, carries a cost."

"I know that," she said, wearying of being spoken to as if she knew nothing. "I'm Tirribin. I understand the commerce of summons and boon."

A canny smile revealed gleaming sharp teeth. "Better. That is the spirit I expect when treating with Tirribin. I had begun to think you simple."

"That's rude." But his teasing made her feel better, more like herself.

"Yes, I suppose it is. I am Qiyed. You showed great restraint in not asking. I know how much your kind care about etiquette."

Her cheeks warmed.

"Tell me more of this boon you seek."

"I- I don't know how."

"That is intriguing, but I do not wish to remain on this strand for long." Lightning flashed, and thunder followed, sooner than she had expected. "A storm comes, and I long to swim with it." Another sly grin. "Have you ever done this?"

"No."

"Would you care to?"

She reflected with distaste on her swim from the ship. "I don't think so, no."

"Very well. Quickly then."

Where to begin?

"There is a Walker. I'm told I knew him when he trained in the palace at Trevynisle."

"You have come from the northern isles?" he asked, surprise in the question.

"Yes."

"And what does that mean: 'I'm told I knew him'?"

"He traveled back in time, and created this misfuture we're in now. The humans have fought over Hayncalde in Daerjen. One supremacy has given way to another."

"I knew nothing of this."

She canted her head. "Payment for my summons?"

He bared his teeth again. "Clever, cousin." He considered this. "Done. That part of your debt to me is paid in full. Go on."

"This boy – a man now, no doubt – I'm told we were friends, and I've come to suspect that… that perhaps I cared for him even more than that."

His eyebrows rose. "This is unusual for Tirribin, is it not?"

"More than you could know," she said, the words tumbling out of her. "I am… I have always been fascinated by love, by passion. The act, the emotion. Everything about it."

His brow creased, but his grin remained. "You would have me teach you of such things?"

"No. I would have you…" She broke off, swallowing. Her gaze slid to the clouds behind him, to the flicker of light in their depths. "I tire of being Tirribin, of being a child, of being denied the… the fruits enjoyed by other sorts of creatures. I wonder if you might change me."

He gaped. Cunning as he might have been, as all his kind were, he clearly hadn't expected this.

"I don't know if your power runs that deep," she said, filling a yawning silence. "I have spoken of this with another Arrokad, and…" Her words came haltingly; Ujie might not wish for others to know of their conversation. "And this Most Ancient One suggested it might be possible, though inadvisable."

"Allow me to understand," Qiyed said. "You wish to be brought to mature form."

"That's right."

"I assume you also wish to remain Tirribin, to retain your time sense, your abilities."

She hadn't given this much thought, but didn't wish to admit as much. "I do," she said, hoping she sounded certain.

"Well, cousin, I will confess to being astonished, almost beyond words." His forehead furrowed again. "You are set on this course? You have considered it from all perspectives?"

"I… I have thought about it a great deal."

"You could never go back to being Tirribin in the way you are now. You would be unique, but also alone. You would be a creature unto yourself. That strikes me as a lonely existence."

"I'm lonely already." She regretted the words as soon as they passed her lips.

Qiyed studied her, not with sympathy as she imagined Ujie might, but with cool appraisal. The wind rose and a bolt of lightning stabbed the sea. For the moment at least, the Arrokad had forgotten the storm and his desire to swim in it.

"I might be able to do this thing. It has never crossed my mind to try and so I do not know. It could be a risk allowing me to try. Do you understand?"

His response frightened and thrilled her.

"I do. What price such a boon?"

"No price. Not for now. In time, if we do this, and if you are pleased with the result, perhaps we can revisit the matter. In the interim, we would… become friends. And perhaps you would tell me more about this misfuture. Access to your time sense would be payment enough. Is this agreeable to you?"

"Would I have to come into the sea with you?"

He laughed at that. "You might enjoy it, Droë of the Tirribin." He shook his head. "You would not have to do anything you are not prepared to do. In time, you may wish to experience the surf as I do. Until then, you can live on land as you have, and I will swim the sea as I have. You may summon me at will, without cost."

For the first time since reaching the shoreline, Droë allowed herself a smile. "Thank you. That would be… Those terms are acceptable."

"An arrangement then, freely entered and fairly sworn."

"An arrangement, freely entered and fairly sworn."

He nodded. "Good then." Lightning illuminated the strand and sky. Thunder boomed. "I take my leave, cousin. Until next we speak."

"When?" she asked before he could turn from her. She sounded too eager. Fortunately they had completed their negotiation.

His grin, fleeting though it was, raised bumps on her skin.

"Tomorrow night would be fine. Or the next. I will leave it to you to decide." He pivoted and waded back into the surf. When the water reached his chest, he dove, the scales on his legs catching the gleam of lightning like a fish tail. Droë watched him swim away, envious of his comfort in the swells, the memory of his beauty, of his powerful chest and narrow hips, like the aftertaste of the sweetest years.

A few raindrops pelted down on the sand and on her. In mere moments, the skies had opened, soaking her hair and her shift. Droë didn't mind. She remained by the shore. The storm roiled the water and she lost track of the Arrokad. After a time, she started back to the city. She was hungry again. Few humans would be abroad in such weather, but those who were would be careless, in a hurry. Easy prey.

Droë didn't return to the shore the following night. She didn't wish Qiyed to think her too eager. She couldn't say why. She had revealed much in their encounter, and she would have to share far more in days to come. Before long, the Arrokad would know her better than any creature ever had. This made her uneasy, which might have been why she kept away. She didn't go the next night, either.

By the third night, she could wait no longer. They had an arrangement. Reneging on a bargain struck with one of the Most Ancient would be as perilous as any change in her form.

Besides, she had made her decision.

The night was warm and still. A thin haze obscured most stars and smeared the moonlight. The surf at the strand was much calmer than it had been several nights before. Droë walked to the water's edge, allowing low waves to lap at her toes.

"Qiyed! I would speak with you!"

She called only one time, assuming she wouldn't have to repeat her summons.

Within a spirecount or two, he broke the surface of the water far out to sea, and swam toward shore, his body undulating like that of a porpoise. She marked his approach, noting as he drew near that he had changed somehow. She wasn't certain what was different until he reached the shallows, stood, and walked in her direction.

Her face heated. No scales this time. He was naked, unashamed, glorious.

"I sense your discomfort, cousin," he said, halting several paces short of where she stood, seawater eddying around his knees.

She had seen naked humans many times, male and female. She had thought nothing of speaking with Ujie. Why should this bother her so? Was it because he was so beautiful? Was it because of what they intended to do?

"Shall I change my form? Cover myself as I did when last we spoke?"

Droë stared at the seafoam gathering around her ankles. "Yes, please."

From the corner of her eye, she saw him making a sweeping motion with his pale hand. Magick whispered against her skin.

"Better?"

She looked up. He was scaled again from his waist down.

"Thank you."

"I have spent little time with Tirribin in all my centuries. Your kind are most peculiar."

She scowled. "That's rude."

"I merely meant that you are children in more than just appearance."

He stepped closer to her. He smelled of brine and seaweed and rain. She breathed him in and looked off to the side.

"I am told that your kind do not breed as we do," he said. "Is this true?"

"Yes. We simply are. We spend our years, but then we replenish them. We don't age, we don't die unless we kill each other, and we don't reproduce as humans and other Ancients do."

"Is this why you wish to change? Do you wish to have a child?"

She shook her head, still avoiding his gaze.

"So it truly is love that you crave."

Droë made herself face him. "Do Arrokad love?" Before he could answer, she added, "I mean, do you experience the emotion? I know that the act itself is integral to what you are."

"Is that a judgment, cousin?" Amusement shaded his tone.

"It's an observation."

"A valid one, I suppose." A drop of water wound a crooked course over the muscles of his arm. "Yes, we love. And anticipating your next question, I have loved and been loved."

"Who?" she asked. She was being rude, but she couldn't help herself. And wasn't this part of what they had agreed to begin together?

"Many. I have lived a long time. I have loved many of my own kind, male as well as female."

"You don't love them anymore?"

His slitted eyes surveyed the shoreline. "I remain fond of many, but love is impermanent."

"Not for humans. Not always."

"True. Humans live for a breath and are gone. We – your kind and mine – we live long lives. Too long, I believe, to confine ourselves to a single love. It is something you should consider. This human you love will be here for but an instant. Your change will last forever."

"Do you have offspring?"

"I do," he said. "That is different as well. My sons and daughters have lived for centuries, as I have. They have not been my children in any meaningful way in a very long time."

"Do you love them?"

"As a human parent loves his offspring, you mean?" He shook his head. "I do not believe so. It is pleasant when I see them. Most of them. I have a son who I do not like at all. The rest..." Another shrug. "The rest are no more or less to me than other Arrokad I have known."

Droë pondered this, frowned again.

"My responses have troubled you. Are you reconsidering our arrangement?"

"No," she said, thinking her voice sounded odd.

"It is all right if you are. To be honest, I am still uncertain as to whether I can do what you have asked of me. The power required might well prove beyond my capabilities. I would not consider it a breach of our arrangement if you were to withdraw from it now."

She faltered, unsure of herself. Again. She had thought she might become something akin to an Arrokad, but with time sense. Now she wasn't so sure. In preying on humans, she had come to know them: their habits, their customs, the many flavors of their love. She wanted to love one being for a long time. If she were to have offspring, she would want to love them as a human mother did. But an immortal human? With time sense? Frozen in time once more, but at a more advanced stage? As Qiyed had told her when last they spoke, she would be alone and unique.

"You have doubts," he said.

"Yes, but I don't want to end our arrangement. Not yet."

"At some point it may be too late to do so. Thus far, I have done nothing for you. That will not always be the case."

"I understand."

"Very well. You summoned me again. Why? What did you think would happen tonight?"

"I don't know," she said. "If you were to try right now to begin to change me, what would you do?"

Qiyed stared at her, eyes narrowed. "I would begin slowly. An undertaking such as this should be approached with care." He took another step, closing the distance between them. He started to reach a hand to her brow, but stopped, a question in the quirk of an eyebrow. "May I?"

She nodded, not trusting herself to speak.

His touch was as cool as a forest rill, light and gentle, yet insistent. Awareness of his presence flooded her. His scent, the chill and damp radiating from his body. He held three fingers to her forehead for a tencount, and more. The cold spread through her, calming, pleasant. It eased her mind.

When he pulled his hand away, she sighed and opened her eyes.

"To answer your question, I would begin with a soft push. It would barely be noticeable. You appear now as a child of perhaps eight or nine, as do all Tirribin. With this push, you might seem more like nine or ten. Few would notice. You might not notice either. One of your kind could read in your years more than are really there. You are young for your kind, yes?"

"I suppose."

"This might be less apparent to other Tirribin after I attempt this. In most respects, though, it would not change you in any significant way. That said, in another two or three days, when next I touch you as I just did, I might sense the change. And having done so, I might then have a better sense of what to try next."

"Could we stop after you do this? If I don't like it?"

He didn't answer right away. "Yes. This time. And perhaps two or three times more. But after that, we will reach a point beyond which asking me to stop would be a violation of our arrangement. And beyond which halting the process may become impossible."

She shuddered and folded her arms over her chest. She raised her chin, though, and said, "Then do it."

CHAPTER 20

20th Day of Kheraya's Ascent, Year 634

Qiyed didn't ask if she was sure. He didn't ask her permission to reach for her brow again, or make any attempt to change her mind. He lifted his fingers to her forehead, somehow finding the exact spots he had touched before.

Coolness returned, but only for a heartbeat. Then warmth passed through her skin and into her head. It traveled downward, spreading like flame across parchment. Her cheeks flushed, as did her neck. It reached her body and dispersed in all directions. Her limbs prickled with it, her stomach crawled with it. The sensation was neither unpleasant nor pleasurable. It simply was.

Droë didn't realize that the Arrokad had removed his hand from her head until he asked, "How do you feel?"

She opened her eyes, regarded him, and then looked past him at the sea, the sand, the boulders.

"Fine."

"Different?"

"I don't know yet. It was… I felt your power go through me, so I suppose it must have done something. Yes?"

"That remains to be seen. You do not feel ill, or uncomfortable in any way?"

She shook her head. A half-truth. She felt odd. Not sick or wrong, but… *different*. She couldn't say how, and until she could she wasn't ready to confide in him. Was that sense of caution new to her, the product of his magick? Or was she searching for difference where none existed?

"It may take a few days before you notice any change, and before I am able to judge the success or failure of this first attempt. I would suggest we not speak again for several nights. If you must summon me, you may, but only do so if something feels... wrong."

"All right," she said.

"Goodnight, Droë of the Tirribin."

He didn't wait for her reply, but strode into the surf and dove, only emerging again some time later, far out in the moonlit water. Droë sped back to the city. She had fed earlier in the evening, before she called for the Arrokad, but she was famished now and eager to hunt.

She took one man near the wharves. He was drunk and had too few years left to sate her hunger. So she fed on a second man, this one younger. A sailor, perhaps. Even after this second kill, she remained hungry. As she prowled the lanes for prey, she considered every sensation, each motion and thought. Did she feel changed?

Before long she grew impatient with this constant self-examination. Qiyed said it would take days to know; she had given herself a half-bell.

She went back to her lair and tried to sleep, ignoring her lingering hunger. She feared she would be too restless, but she dropped into a deep slumber that carried her all through the following day. Whatever Qiyed had done not only stimulated her appetite, but also exhausted her.

Over the days that followed, she continued to sleep deeply and feed more than usual. By the fifth evening, she had grown certain of other differences as well. She didn't fear her next encounter with the Arrokad quite so much. The recollection of her confrontation with Maeli and Teelo stung less. She missed Tresz still, but not the way she had. Her emotions had smoothed over.

In all respects except one.

Her longing for love remained as it had been. It might have been stronger. When she thought of Tobias, and of the woman – Mara – jealousy flared in her breast like oil poured over flame.

Time and again, she imagined draining the woman of her years, reveling in her screams, her cries for help.

That night, Droë returned to the same stretch of shoreline and summoned Qiyed again. She didn't bother to raise her voice.

He surfaced some moments later and glided through the surf to the sand before her, emerging from the water in his scaled form. He halted a short distance from her, his gaze keen, starlight in his eyes.

"You are changed," he said.

His observation both thrilled and frightened her.

"What do you see?"

"What do you feel?" he answered.

"I asked first."

"A human evasion."

She twitched a shoulder, unwilling to say more until he responded. After a brief silence, he made a small, sharp circular motion with a delicate hand. A gesture of annoyance and surrender.

"I sense... patience, calm, but also willfulness, and the illusion of maturity not yet earned."

The words stung. No doubt they were meant to. Droë kept her expression mild. "Is that all?"

The Arrokad laughed. "Very good, cousin. Perhaps there is less illusion than I implied. Now, tell me what you feel."

"My feelings reflect your observations. My emotions feel more controlled than they did." She kept to herself her dark thoughts of the woman who sought Tobias. "I believe I am more observant, more thoughtful."

"Perhaps. It will not last, not if we continue with this."

Droë frowned in surprised. "But–"

"Have you not observed humans in their adolescence?"

She had, and she didn't wish to experience what she had witnessed. "I will be like them?"

"Possibly. I have never done this before."

She considered this and shrugged again. "So be it."

"Then you intend to continue with our arrangement?"

"I do."

Emotion she could not read rippled across his face and was gone.

"Do you disapprove?"

"I make no judgement. We forged a bargain, you and I. Freely entered and fairly sworn. I will do as I promised."

She sensed that he held something back, that despite his denials, he had misgivings about going forward.

"Do you fear for me, cousin?"

"You spoke of changes of the mind," Qiyed said. "What of changes of the body?"

"I sleep more, and I feed more. Other than that, I feel much the same."

"Very well. You summoned me. I assume because you wish to have me push you further."

Fear made her falter, but not for long. "That's right. It's been five days. I'm ready."

His lips quirked. "That must be the newfound patience you mentioned."

She bristled at the irony in his tone. "That was rude. You said to wait several days. I have, and more."

"This is true. Forgive me." She heard no contrition in his words. Before she could say so, he went on. "I said previously that I wish to learn about the misfuture you mentioned. Tell me more of what you know."

"And in return?"

"Another push before we part."

"Agreed."

Qiyed lowered himself to the wet sand and she did the same a few paces away, where the sand was drier. When he gestured again, encouraging her to speak, Droë told him some of what Mara had told her, and shared a bit of what she knew about events in Daerjen. She didn't reveal all, of course. This was commerce, and he had given her but a tiny fraction of what she sought. She was only so forthcoming, and, she knew, he understood her reticence.

Qiyed did question her, but when she deflected his attempts to draw more from her, he acquiesced, addressing more general matters of time, of future and past, of the extent to which any one Walker might change the course of human history. It was, she had to admit, a pleasant conversation. Not often did a Tirribin, or any creature for that matter, earn the undivided attention of one of the Most Ancient. She enjoyed having one so lovely to look upon devote so much time to her.

They spoke late into the night, until a slivered moon rose behind her, casting long, silvery shadows across the strand.

Qiyed eyed it and stood. "I have lingered longer than I intended. Thank you, Droë of the Tirribin, for a most illuminating exchange."

She climbed to her feet and brushed sand from her tattered shift. "I enjoyed it, too."

"I am glad." He stepped closer to her, raised his hand, fingers splayed. "You are ready for another push?"

"I am."

He reached out and touched her forehead, his fingers somehow finding those same spots on her brow. Cool power flowed into her, warmed, spread as before. It felt stronger this time. She staggered, dropped to one knee. Somehow, Qiyed kept his fingers in place. He did raise an eyebrow.

"You are all right?"

She remained on one knee. "Fine."

Her stomach churned, and the muscles in her legs cramped, making her cry out. Still the Arrokad did not relinquish his magickal grip on her. On it went, Ancient power, as hot and viscous as magma, spreading through her.

When Qiyed removed his hand. Droë gasped at the release and dropped forward onto her hands and knees.

"This was more extreme than the first time." He offered it as a statement.

"Much."

"I pushed you the equivalent of two human years. You will notice greater changes this time. Perhaps more discomfort. And it will take you longer to assess these changes. I do not expect to hear from you for many days. As long as a human ha'turn. Do you understand?"

She nodded.

"Good. I take my leave." Yet, he stood over her, waiting for… something. After a tencount, she raised her gaze to his. He didn't say more, but he scrutinized her. Could he already see the effect of his magick?

After another breath, he turned from her, waded into the sea, and swam away.

Droë remained as she was until she could no longer see him. Then she pushed herself up and struggled back toward the city. She was even more famished than she had been after the first push, but her gut writhed like a living thing. Tirribin didn't get ill as humans did. Years could not be vomited. Still, her need for nourishment warred with the lingering queasiness brought on by the Arrokad's magick.

She found walking difficult. At first she blamed illness, weariness, the uneven sand and strewn rocks of the shoreline.

After some time, she realized it was more than that. She *had* changed. Qiyed had seen it, and now she felt it. Her limbs were too long, her joints oddly placed. She had *grown*.

Droë halted, swayed. Looking down at the ground she reeled with vertigo. Too great a distance to her feet. This new body was alien to her. Apprehension and excitement again. This was what she wanted, what she had sought since leaving Trevynisle. Yet the Arrokad had spoken of her having time to change her mind, of it taking three or four pushes before she could no longer stray from this path. They had arrived at that point in half the time. She wondered if she could still move at Tirribin speed, if she could still clamber onto the back of prey. What if she couldn't hunt anymore? What if she starved during the respite the Most Ancient One had demanded? An entire ha'turn. Could she last so long?

She wanted to try to move at speed, but she was too weak. If she used that power now, she might not have it when it came time to feed.

It didn't escape her notice that somehow her tatters still fit. She had worn them for as long as she could recall. Were they part of her, then? Did they grow as she did? Or had Qiyed done that with his magick?

She resumed walking, judging each step, trying to adjust to her new form. Had her face changed as well? On the thought, she paused again, raised her hands tentatively to her chest. It remained as flat as before. Relief flooded her. A surprise. She had thought she was ready to be womanly.

Upon reaching the city wharf, she slowed, scented the air. Whatever else the Arrokad had done to her, he hadn't diminished her ability to sense years for the taking. If anything, she felt more attuned to the city. She crept around corners, scanned lanes for prey. It was late and few were abroad. Few, but not none.

As she prowled, her mind eased fractionally. In hunting, she rediscovered her truest self. Relief again; she retained the essence of who and what she was.

A man slumbered in an alley, stinking of whiskey and his own urine. Not the most attractive prey, but a good start, someone on whom she could test her body. She attacked at speed, aware of the way her form blurred. Her legs, longer now, coltish, carried her to him in no time. She didn't have to leap, and wasn't sure she could. But when he woke and struggled against her, she overpowered him with ease. As fast as ever. Perhaps a shade less nimble, but far stronger, which was more than fair compensation for whatever she might have lost.

Droë's stomach settled after this first meal, leaving her ravenous still. She resumed her hunt, more confident now that she had taken prey. Indeed, she experienced a surge of recklessness that was alien to her. The old Droë – the smaller, weaker Droë – would have resigned herself to the possibility that she might not find suitable prey so late.

Now she asked herself why she should have to confine her predation to the streets. She needed only to press her hand to the wood of the nearest house to perceive the sweet, young years that dwelt within. They were hers for the taking if only she was willing to step inside. Why shouldn't she enter?

The answer came to her on the heels of the question: for this night she might be safe, but it would ruin the town for her. Before long, humans would hunt for her in numbers, armed, united, and therefore dangerous.

Reluctantly, she walked on. Her hunger deepened, and with it her frustration. What was the use of her new strength if she was forced to hunt the same old way?

The eastern sky began to brighten, which usually signaled the end to her wanderings. Not this night.

She remained in the lanes, eager for the first humans to leave the safety of their homes. She didn't have to wait long. As dawn's silver spread across the sky, a young man emerged from a small structure and started toward the wharf. He walked without urgency, emboldened, no doubt, by the burgeoning daylight. Droë followed at a distance, keeping to shadows, awaiting her opportunity.

When he turned down a narrow byway, a shortcut to the shoreline, she followed at speed. He heard her at the last moment, whirled, and raised his arms to ward off a blow. She did leap this time, and crashed into him. He toppled to the dirty stone, and she locked her hands on him, her mouth latching to his neck. He fought her, but to no avail. Her power was a thing of wonder. Never had she imagined that taking a human male in the prime of his life could be so easy. There was no stink of whiskey, no sweat from a day spent laboring. He was clean, sober, awake, alive, and his years were hers.

She took them all, and when she'd finished, she sauntered out of the byway in plain view of others who had emerged from their homes. They barely glanced at her. A child still, in tatters, taller than she had been, perhaps ungainly now, but no one of consequence. Why would the humans take notice of her?

She could have walked around the city all day. She wasn't afraid to do so, as once she had been. Having conquered her hunger, however, she fell prey to her weariness. Qiyed's touch and the growth it spurred had drained her. She retreated to the deserted stretch of alleyway where she had her lair: a pile of old wood and stone, hidden and hollowed out so that she could come and go without being seen.

On this morning, though, she barely fit inside. The space had been snug for as long as she had been here. Now it was too small. She tried to hollow it out, but as she removed more rock and wood, what remained began to sag until she feared it would collapse entirely. She crawled inside, folded herself into a tight, uncomfortable ball, and attempted to sleep.

She woke many bells later, her limbs cramped and sore, and barely managed to extricate herself from the pile. After hunting for the evening's meal – again, she fed twice – she searched for a new lair, settling on a space behind a tavern. It was rank and open to the sky, not nearly as comfortable as her old home. But it would have to do, at least until the coldest turns arrived.

The next several days passed in a haze of hunger and fatigue. Droë fed and slept, and did little else. The boldness imparted to her by Qiyed's latest push remained, but she didn't know what to do with it.

On the fifth night, she emerged from her new lair to uncommon noise. Music floated on the city air from every direction, disparate melodies mixing sourly. The lanes hummed with conversation and laughter. Smells of human food were nearly strong enough to blot out the scent of years. Droë crept from the byway, wary and intrigued. It didn't take her long to recognize the celebration. Kheraya Ascendant – the solstice.

Hunting would be easy this night. Rooktown would be filled with its usual residents, as well as with men and women from a hundred ships. Yet this once, she cared nothing for years. On this night, humans gave their love more freely even than usual for an animal species.

It was a celebration of the sensual – food and drink, music and love. She walked among the humans, not worrying that someone might notice the paleness of her eyes, and she searched for lovers, desperate to observe, to learn, to imagine. They weren't difficult to find.

She followed one pair to an alleyway, peered out from a hiding place as they kissed and touched and peeled off clothes in the warm night air. They both appeared to derive equal pleasure from the coupling; there was no exchange of coin at the end.

Two women lay together in a house along a small lane, their windows open, their voices twined in desire and satisfaction. Droë watched them avidly as well. Most of the time when she thought of love, she imagined being with a man – with Tobias. What if she found a woman to love instead?

She observed other couples, of every combination of women and men. With each encounter she witnessed, her longing to know what it meant to love grew, until her heart ached with it. She wondered if this new body of hers was capable of desire. For though she wished desperately to feel love, she could not understand the physical need that seemed to drive all that humans did. When did that begin in their species?

Later certainly than the stage at which Qiyed's push had left her. Was that his intention? Had he pushed her this far and no further on purpose?

Droë did not tire of observing the lovers. She didn't believe that could ever happen. In time, though, her hunger grew more desperate than her need to observe and learn. On the strand nearest the docks, she found a fluid crowd of men and women. They sang and danced and shared food cooked over open fires. No one noticed when a lone woman wandered from the throng and waded out into the shallow surf. Nor did anyone hear her struggle against the overgrown Tirribin who took her years and left her floating in the brine.

Over the next few nights, Droë continued to hunt with abandon. Four evenings into Kheraya's Descent, she paid the price for her carelessness. She stepped from her new lair into streets that looked unnaturally bright. Following the alley to a larger thoroughfare, she spotted a group of men standing together in a tight cluster. Some held torches. Many others carried muskets or pistols.

Droë ducked back into her byway and followed it to the other end. The lane that abutted it was empty, but another band of men waited at the next corner.

Instinct told her they were searching for her; a moment's consideration told her why. There was a reason Tirribin like Maeli and Teelo drove others of their kind from their towns and cities. There was a reason they took care to prey upon sailors from docked ships at least as often as they hunted residents of their villages.

Droë had taken too many of Rooktown's people, and now the humans wished to fight back. She didn't fear them, but neither could she ignore the danger posed by their weapons. Mostly, she didn't wish to spend every night avoiding hunters while hunting herself. She had used up Rooktown. She felt no particular attachment to the city, and so no true grief at having to leave. This was the price of her recklessness. She deserved no better.

She departed the city at speed, blurring past the armed men, and the guards at the town gate. She followed a dirt road eastward along the north coast of the isle, knowing she would find a town eventually. Along the way she encountered a peddler. Her evening's meal.

She passed one village that she judged to be too small, but soon came to a more substantial town. It had a small waterfront and a wharf. Several ships were tied there. Sea trade would provide sailors, allowing her to feed without using up this town as well.

Before long, she had even located a lair on the outskirts of the town: a shallow cave, one she wouldn't outgrow. She went to sleep hungry, woke several times during the day, but managed always to slip back into her slumber.

At dusk, she rose and crept into the town, passing through a gate guarded by one grizzled man. She left him alone, not wishing to invite attention.

By the time it occurred to her to search for other Tirribin, it was too late. They found her.

"What is it?" she heard from behind her.

She turned, pulled herself up to her full height.

Two male Tirribin stood before her, both shorter by a full head than she was. They were lovely to look at. Golden brown hair framed perfect oval faces. One had eyes of palest blue. The other had gray eyes, like Droë's. The two resembled each other enough to be brothers, but she sensed that they weren't. Too many centuries separated their ages. Gray-eyes was the elder.

"It's homely," said the one with blue eyes. "But I sense its years. I believe it's one of us."

"It's powerful enough to kill both of you without effort," she said. "So stop being rude and tell me your names."

The two males eyed each other, a question passing between them. Perhaps they thought she exaggerated her strength. After a fivecount they seemed to decide not to test her, at least not yet.

Gray-eyes opened his hands. "Forgive us, cousin. I am Strie. This is my friend, Kreeva." He lifted an eyebrow, expectant.

"I'm Droë." She surveyed the lane. "What town is this?"

"It is our town."

A bit too pointed, that. She narrowed her eyes. "What do the humans call it?"

"Humans have no imagination," said the one named Kreeva. His voice was higher than Strie's, more akin to a child's. "They call it Barleyton. Can you guess why?" He smiled as he asked this, perhaps to mock, perhaps to soften.

"Not your best riddle," Strie said, a rebuke in the words.

"It wasn't meant to be."

"They grow barley nearby," she said, drawing their gazes. "That's what they trade? That's what ships seek when they come to the wharf?"

"Mostly," Strie said. "The grain. Ale made from the grain. Bread made from the grain. Animals fattened on the grain."

"Do many ships come here?"

"Enough for two of us. Not enough for three."

She stared down at Strie. He endured her scrutiny for a tencount before looking away.

"That's the second time you've suggested that I'm not welcome here," she said. "Do you intend to chance a third, cousin?"

"What are you?" he asked, risking a quick glance at her. "You smell like Tirribin, but you don't look like any I've ever seen. And your years... they're confused, hard to read."

"I'm Tirribin," she said. "Just like you are, and yet nothing like you at all."

She allowed that to hang between them. After some time, Kreeva said, "Well, that's a much better riddle."

Droë laughed. Strie cast a withering look at his friend.

"This is too small a town for three," he said. "I don't mean that as a threat, and I'm not saying that you have to leave. If... if we must, we'll go, and you can remain. Three of us will draw attention from the humans here. We've been here a long time. It's our home."

She heard a plea in his tone, but no menace. She thought he might weep. They were afraid of her. She should have rejoiced in that. Not long ago, she would have given nearly anything to inspire fear in Maeli and Teelo. Instead, she felt a tightness in her chest. She wanted them to like her. If she could have remained here and been their friend, she would have, which was strange for her. Was Qiyed's power responsible for this, as well?

You would be a creature unto yourself, the Arrokad told her that first night. *That strikes me as a lonely existence.*

She complained then of being lonely already. She sensed now that the isolation she'd known was nothing compared to what lay in her future.

Fine. If all she could have was fear, then fear she would have.

"It *was* your home," she said. "It's mine now. Leave or stay – I don't really care. If you challenge me, I'll kill you both."

CHAPTER 21

4th Day of Kheraya's Descent, Year 634

"How do you know you can?" Strie asked after a pause. "We're two to your one. You might be bigger, but that doesn't mean—"

Droë gave him time for no more. With a single stride at Tirribin speed she closed the distance between them, grabbed him with both hands, and threw him against the nearest wall. He dropped to the ground, twisting as he fell. He snarled, launched himself at her.

Kreeva flew at her as well. They clamped themselves to her shoulders. Both bit at her neck and tried to overbalance her.

She should have been scared. Fighting two Tirribin carried perils for even the most fearsome of Ancients. But it was rage and not panic that exploded inside her. She pried Strie off her and threw him again. Before he struck the wall, she grabbed Kreeva as well. She flung him away in time to meet Strie's next assault.

As he reached her, she grabbed him by both arms and held him fast, raising his exposed throat to her mouth.

Kreeva had gathered himself for another attack, but she pinned him where he was with her glare.

"I'll take all his years," she said, a rasp in the threat.

Strie writhed in her grasp. She pounded him into the nearest wall, stunning him into stillness. Then she held him again within easy reach of her mouth.

"Shall I show you that I'm willing to kill, or do you believe me?"

Kreeva faltered, needle teeth bared, his gaze darting from her eyes to those of his friend.

"Attack!" Strie growled.

The other Tirribin eased his stance and shook his head. "No. She means what she says." To Droë he said, "What are you?" as Strie had before.

"I'm Tirribin. Can't you tell?"

"You're different, and I wish to know why."

She tossed Strie to the ground. Like a cat dropped from a window, he contorted himself, landing again on feet and hands, coiling to renew their battle. He bled from a jagged gash on his brow.

"I won't tell you that." She eyed Strie, expecting him to attack.

She had handled this poorly, allowing herself to be guided by loneliness and petulance rather than sense. She didn't want to kill them, and she didn't want them as enemies.

"But," she went on, "I'll do my best to keep your town safe for all three of us."

Kreeva glanced at Strie, who still stared up at her.

Strie canted his head. "How would you do that?"

"I would be willing to hunt on the road some nights, outside of town. Perhaps the two of you could do the same. Other nights, we can go to the little village between here and Rooktown."

"That's a long way."

"Not at speed."

"You would do this? After threatening us as you did?"

Droë winced. "That was rude of me. I apologize."

Strie straightened, surprise registering on his beautiful, blood-streaked face. "That was... unexpected."

"I know. I shouldn't have said the things I did. I would rather have you as friends than as foes."

The boys shared a look.

"You have to stop asking me what I am," she said. "I'm Tirribin. I have time sense, I feed on years as you do. The rest – the way I look – it's not something I can explain to you."

"If you're Tirribin, you understand the power of curiosity. Not asking such questions is harder than you make it sound."

The power of curiosity. Who understood it more than she?

"You're right. And when I can tell you, I will. I give you my word." She took a breath. "In the meantime, I offer my friendship." She raised her hand, palm out. "Freely offered, fairly sworn."

Kreeva and Strie exchanged glances again. Sworn friendships were common among Ancients of different races, but rare within any one sept. With all that had already passed between them, however, Droë thought it a wise precaution. Betraying a sworn friendship was punishable by death.

The two males eyed each other for the span of a breath, then nodded in unison. Strie pressed his hand to Droë's.

"I give my friendship," he said. "Freely offered, fairly sworn."

Kreeva followed. "Freely offered, fairly sworn."

Droë lowered her hand, smiled. "I'm hungry. Shall we walk the road together?"

They did, and in time they happened upon a group of four traders. Three they fed on. The oldest they might have let live, but he produced a flintlock and fired at Kreeva, who was closest to him. The man's hand shook and he missed, but he tried to reload and Droë didn't wish to risk a second attempt.

"He's yours, cousin," she said. "Meager though his years might be. He aimed at you."

Strie echoed, "He's yours."

Kreeva shrugged and fed.

They walked back to the city at human speed. Droë asked them about Barleyton, and then about other nearby villages. They described several places where they might hunt. They offered to find a lair for her near their own, but Droë declined, preferring the solitude of her cave.

Over the days that followed, their friendship deepened. For the first time in her life, Droë was part of a larger group, a band of Tirribin friends. This both pleased and frightened her. In mere days, she would call for Qiyed again. He would touch his hand to her brow and push her further down this lonely path. How would Kreeva and Strie receive her when she returned to them appearing older still?

The night of the ha'turn had come and gone, but she did not go to the shoreline. She didn't wish to remain in this form for the rest of her existence. She was between now – no longer just Tirribin, but not yet anything else. She found this unpleasant. Then again, this was the form her friends knew, and they had accepted her.

To her astonishment, and her chagrin, it was Qiyed who called to her. His summons came at dusk a ha'turn after her arrival in Barleyton. It reverberated in her mind like the crash of breakers in a rocky cove, waking her from her day's sleep and leaving her pulse pounding.

She heard only a single word: her name. That was enough to convey his impatience, his irritation. She left her lair and started toward the shoreline. Before she had gone far, Strie and Kreeva found her.

They were eager to hunt, and assumed she would be as well. When she told them she wouldn't be hunting with them that night, they took offense. When she explained that she needed to leave the town and would see them the next day, they grew leery.

"You swore friendship," Strie said.

"And I meant it. This, though, is part of who and what I am. You can't ask me more about it."

They didn't appear satisfied, and yet...

"There's more," she said. "When you see me next... I'll be changed. I won't look quite like this anymore. I'll be... older." A part of her quailed at the changes she knew would come from this next encounter with the Arrokad. A part of her thrilled.

"Where are you going, Droë?" Strie asked, concern for her shading his words.

She couldn't remember anyone sounding worried about her, ever. She nearly told them all.

"To meet someone," she said.

"Another friend?"

Was Qiyed her friend? She wanted to believe he was, but she knew better. "Someone with whom I have an arrangement, a bargain freely entered and fairly sworn."

Even that revealed much. They might guess she was meeting an Ancient. But she owed them candor.

"I can't tell you more, and I must go." She edged away from them. "I'm sorry. I'll see you tomorrow."

She blurred from the town. She knew they stared after her, and she resisted the impulse to peek back at them.

Once in the countryside, she sped directly to the coast. She was hungry, but didn't hunt. No doubt she would be both sickened and famished by the time Qiyed finished with her. Best then not to feed before their encounter.

She soon reached a promontory overlooking the Sea of the Labyrinth. A narrow path led down the cliff face to the shoreline. She called Qiyed's name and began her descent.

As she stepped onto the wet sand and rocks below, he emerged from the waves, water running down his torso and naked legs. Not scaled. She steeled herself, certain he wouldn't cover himself for her. He knew her preference in this regard and had chosen to ignore it. She would not embarrass herself by asking him to change. That, she intuited, was what he wanted of her.

Another friend?

Far from it.

"I expected you to call for me sooner."

She kept her eyes locked on his. Wind twisted golden hair around her face. "The last time we spoke you chastised me for summoning you too soon. Make up your mind, Qiyed."

He grinned. "Bravely said. You wear your new years well." He surveyed the strand. "You have left Rooktown?"

She raised a shoulder. "These changes leave me hungry. I over-hunted the city and had to leave."

"A pity."

"A trifle."

His grin this time was more brittle. "I sense mistrust on your part, or perhaps a change of heart."

"My wishes haven't changed. As for trusting you or not..." She shrugged again. "Which would you choose?"

He laughed. "Yes, you are more mature than you were. You sound more and more like an Arrokad each time we meet."

Her heart stuttered. "Is that what I'm becoming?"

"I do not know what you are, or what you will be. Not Arrokad, but perhaps not Tirribin either." He took a step in her direction. "Shall we proceed, and find out?"

She didn't back away, but neither did she approach him. "You would complete the process tonight?"

He answered with a decisive shake of his head. "No. A few more years. That is all."

Qiyed took another step.

"If I wanted to stop now, it would be too late, wouldn't it?" The question came in a jumble. She regretted asking as soon as the words crossed her lips.

He didn't mock her, as she feared, nor did he respond right away. "There is no going back," he said, speaking slowly. "We could stop now, if you wanted to, but already you are much changed. I thought you would want to go on, if for no other reason than to pass through this phase you are in now, which is neither child nor adult."

"Yes, of course. I was… curious. Nothing more."

She wasn't sure he believed her, but he kept his doubts to himself. He beckoned her closer, a question in his silvery eyes. She walked to where he stood, her breathing quick, her heart racing.

"My shift," she said, aware of how abrupt the words sounded.

His smile was indulgent. "What about it?"

"Did you change it, make it bigger?"

"No. Such clothes are a part of you, essential to the Tirribin form. Have you not noticed that all of your kind dress much the same way?"

He was right, they did. She knew this somehow, though until now she had given it no thought.

"I see. Thank you."

"Of course." A pause and then, "This night's push will be even more powerful than the last," he said. "I cannot tell you what you will feel afterward, but I imagine the effects will be the most severe yet."

She cringed at this, but did her best to keep her expression neutral. "Thank you for the warning."

He raised a pale hand to her brow, his middle three fingers finding those spots on her forehead.

A hint of cold passed through her skin, followed by heat that stole her breath. She cried out, tried to jerk away. His touch held her fast. Fire spread through her body, her arms and legs, her gut. It blazed behind her eyes, scorched her throat and lungs, seared her chest.

Droë whimpered, desperate for the torment to end, willing to forego her quest for love if that meant release from Qiyed's magick. She heard popping noises, understood after a moment that they came from her knees, her elbows, her back, her wrists and ankles.

"What are you doing to me?" she rasped.

"You are growing, becoming what you have sought."

"It hurts."

"I know."

He didn't remove his hand. Droë didn't try again to pull away. His power burned on, searing every fingerbreadth of her from the inside out, until she thought her flesh must be blackened like roasted meat. She swooned, losing her sense of time. The surge and retreat of the surf faded. The wind remained, lashing at her tender skin, fanning the flames he had conjured.

Droë didn't know he had removed his fingers from her brow until she collapsed to the sand. The blaze inside her lingered, but died down, the pain fading gradually. She couldn't tell if the Arrokad remained or had left her. She didn't care. The wind, the sand, the threadbare shift she wore – all of it chafed her. She couldn't imagine ever knowing comfort again.

In time, she sat up and brushed the sand off her face. Qiyed stood over her, as still as stone, silhouetted in moonlight. Droë gasped at the aching in her chest. She started to reach a hand there, but stopped herself, gripped by... Fear? Hope? Excitement? She looked down, stared at the gentle curve in the shift she wore.

She climbed to her feet, muscles protesting, movements awkward. This latest push had made her even taller, but that was nothing compared to the rest. She had breasts. Her hips felt odd. Running a hand down her side, she realized that they had widened.

Womanly.

A word she had uttered with distaste in speaking about others. She had never thought it would describe her own appearance.

"Am I an adult, then?"

Her eyes widened at the sound of her own voice. It was deeper, somewhat gravelly. She liked the sound of it.

Qiyed shook his head. "Not yet. You are more woman than girl, but you have a few years of human development left before this process will be complete." He paused. "How do you feel?"

"Terrible. I hurt all over. I'm sickened, and…" She trailed off. She felt odd below her stomach. Something heavy and hot weighed on her there, as if she had swallowed molten lead. "I just feel bad," she went on, aware that the Arrokad watched her.

"This will pass."

"I know that. It did last time, too. That doesn't help me much now, does it?"

"I do not suppose so."

She hadn't meant to speak to him that way, but she couldn't bring herself to apologize. This was his fault. Or was it hers? Too hard a question. She shied from it.

"What do I look like?" she asked, running her hands over the contours of her face. Even that pained her.

"You look like a human girl of perhaps fourteen years, with the pale eyes of—"

"That isn't what I mean. Am I beautiful still? I was. All Tirribin are. Or have these changes stolen my beauty?"

He considered her, eyes narrowed. "The process has not altered your countenance much. I believe it will take another push for you to grow into your features completely."

Droë scowled. "I don't know what that means. Am I beautiful or not?"

"With this, as with everything else, you are in between. Patience, Droë of the Tirribin. One more push and you will have much of what you want."

She said nothing, but glowered at him. *I'm tired of being patient*, she wanted to say, though this process had been faster than she expected. She didn't want him calling her "Droë of the Tirribin," but she didn't know why this bothered her. She was angry and in pain and had no desire to treat with the Arrokad anymore.

"I think I should take my leave," he said, perhaps reading her thoughts. "We should wait another ha'turn, I believe."

"Why so long?"

"Because I fear that trying this again sooner might harm you. And because I sense that you need time to grow accustomed to the changes we have wrought this night."

She looked down at her body again. She couldn't argue.

"Very well," she said.

He waded out to sea, his skin as pale as bone under the moon.

She lingered on the strand. Regret at having been so rude gnawed at her. He would have heard her had she apologized, but again something stopped her. Pride, perhaps.

Once he was gone, she glanced about, making certain she was alone. Then she touched a hand to each breast. The skin felt tight, sensitive, but even through her tatters she sensed their shape, their fullness. She touched her hips again and then allowed her hands to settle on her abdomen, which still felt heavy and cramped. She tried to stretch, though that brought new discomfort to her back and shoulders. This new skin didn't fit right. It needed to expand, to grow. Maybe that was what Qiyed meant.

She didn't want to feed, but neither did she wish to remain here alone. Mostly, she wanted to find Strie and Kreeva, but she feared what they might say, the way they would ogle her. After this night, they wouldn't accept her evasions. They would know that she was drawing upon magick to change herself.

She started back to Barleyton. Halfway there, she tried to move at Tirribin speed. She stopped after only a few steps. She could do it – that was reassuring. But it hurt, everywhere. She would try again another night.

By the time she reached the town, she was too weary to search for her friends. She returned to her lair, and soon fell into a dreamless slumber.

"Droë? Are you there?"

She opened her eyes to a dark, cloud-covered sky, and whispers outside her cave. The male Tirribin. Droë sat up, winced at the pain in her legs and chest. Hunger pulled at her belly, a welcome change from the night before.

Somehow she had slept past dusk, which she rarely did.

"Droë?"

She opened her mouth to reply, but stopped herself. They would hear the difference in her voice.

They're going to see the difference in how you look.

She didn't want that.

"I smell your years, Droë." Strie's voice. "They're changed, but I recognize them anyway. What's happened to you?"

Droë sighed. Unless she intended to leave Barleyton, this was not a conversation she could avoid forever. Best to get it done.

When she emerged from her lair, they gaped. She towered over them. They peered up at her face, but then studied the rest of her, their interest lingering on her chest and her middle.

She tolerated their stares for a tencount before saying, "You're being very rude."

"Sorry," Kreeva said, but his expression didn't change, and he didn't stop gawking at her.

Neither did Strie. "What happened to you? You're... you're big."

In spite of everything, this made her grin. "Yes, I know."

"How?"

"Magick," Kreeva said before she could answer. "That's the only explanation."

"I can't tell you much."

"Tirribin can't do this," Strie said to his friend. "Neither can

Shonla or Hanev."

"Arrokad, then."

Droë's cheeks warmed. She didn't deny it. "I can't talk about it. The… the Most Ancient One wouldn't be pleased."

"Why did it do this to you?"

She hesitated. "I wanted him to. I told you, remember? A bargain freely entered and fairly sworn."

"You don't want to be Tirribin anymore?" Strie asked. He sounded offended and sad.

"I'm still Tirribin. I sense your years. I'll feed tonight on years. But I… there are other things I wish to experience as well."

Kreeva gazed up at her, appearing lost. "Like what?"

Not so long ago, she had been this innocent. All of their kind were. Maybe she wasn't Tirribin anymore.

"It doesn't matter. I'm still your friend, and I would still hunt with you, if you'll allow it."

"Do you need more years than you used to?"

"I don't know. I haven't hunted since this latest change."

"Latest change?" Strie repeated.

Heat crept up her neck again. "This wasn't the first time."

The two Tirribin glanced at each other.

"I'm hungry," she said. "I didn't feed last night."

They nodded, but waited for her to start toward the wharf before falling in behind her.

This push left Droë even stronger and faster. She sped after her first prey – a man of some years – and, without thinking, leapt at him when she was still several paces away. She slammed into him and followed him to the ground. When she finished feeding, she rose to find Strie and Kreeva ogling her again.

"What?"

"You were…" Strie trailed off.

"That was magnificent," Kreeva said, pale eyes wide. "You were like a Belvora!"

"Kreeva!"

Droë wrinkled her nose.

"Without the smell, I mean. And the thick-headedness."

They all laughed.

"What I meant was, you seemed to fly."

"Well… thank you." Droë tried to mask her pleasure. She wasn't sure she succeeded.

Her chest was still tender, and she needed more time to grow used to her new form. Still, she felt far better than she had the previous night, and she was more eager than ever to complete her bargain with Qiyed.

The ha'turn that followed stretched on for an eternity. Droë hunted with her friends each night, but soon tired of their company. They were kind to her, and treated her with deference. But she longed for companions with whom she might speak of something other than trifles. She would have welcomed conversations with Arrokad or Shonla. Perhaps even grown humans. She wondered where Tobias had gone, and whether Mara was with him. At times, jealousy was an acid in her blood, eating away at her insides. On other nights, she simply longed to speak with them, even if they were together as a couple in love.

Her pain abated. She grew accustomed to this new body. One rainy night, as she and the Tirribin crept through the town, she passed a trough filled with water and caught a glimpse of her reflection. She slowed, then halted and scrutinized her face. Her jawline was longer than she recalled, her eyes more widely spaced. She had lost the childlike perfection of her kind. Yet what she saw pleased her. She was as attractive as any of the novitiates she remembered from the Travelers' Palace.

After a few moments, Strie and Kreeva urged her on, and they resumed their hunt. That glimpse of herself, though, took root in her memory.

She kept a careful count of the nights, and when a ha'turn had passed, she told the Tirribin that she would be gone the following evening. She didn't have to explain why.

"Magick again," Strie said.

"That's right."

"What will you look like when you come back?"

She shivered in the mild night air. "I don't know."

The three of them stood in silence until Strie hiked a shoulder and said, "All right."

The next evening, Droë woke at dusk and followed the same path to the shoreline. She called for Qiyed, and after a short wait spotted him far out to sea, swimming toward the shore.

She waited in the fog and wind, bumps raised on her skin. Once more, Qiyed refused to cover himself with scales. She didn't care. This night would complete her transformation. Nothing else mattered to her.

"You are ready?" he asked as he sloshed from the water.

"I am."

"These past days – have they brought doubt?"

She shook her head. "The doubt came earlier. I want to be grown. I tire of this process, and I grow bored with my kind. Whatever I am to be, I wish to become it. We have a bargain, Qiyed of the Arrokad. Fulfill your part of it."

His smile was cold. "So be it." He beckoned her closer with a waggle of his fingers.

She approached him, conscious of his scent and of the cold brine swirling around her feet.

"One last time," he said, and touched his fingers to her brow.

CHAPTER 22

3rd Day of Kheraya's Fading, Year 634

His magick coursed into her, cold then hot, rampant. It stole her breath, buckled her knees. Pain flared everywhere, as if he had filled her with boiling water. She couldn't help but give voice to the anguish, and though she resisted the urge to pull away, she writhed against what he was doing to her.

It ended abruptly, sooner than she expected. She dropped to her knees.

She opened her eyes to a world that tilted and spun, but this, too, passed quickly.

"That's all?"

"You had been through the worst of it. It would have been too much to take you all the way forward during our last encounter. But you did not have far to go."

"And I'm there, now?"

He raised an eyebrow, saying nothing.

Droë stood and studied herself. These latest changes were far less dramatic than the previous ones. Her body was more womanly, but that appeared to be all: changes of degree rather than kind.

Already the pain had abated. She felt much as she had before he touched her.

"Are we finished then, you and I?"

"Not at all," the Arrokad said. "You still owe me a boon. That is, if you are pleased with the result. And I believe you will still have use for me in the days to come."

She frowned. "Explain that. Please."

"I think I will not for now. Suffice it to say that while your transformation is complete, elements of what you seek require further attention."

Her frown deepened. "That's even less clear than what you said earlier."

He offered no response.

"Very well. Do you wish to hear more about the misfuture? Or is there some other matter of time you care to discuss?"

"No, not this night. We will speak again soon. You need not wait any particular interval. Your questions will come soon enough. And if I have need of you, I will reach for you. I ask only that you remain within a league of the sea."

"Yes, all right." Questions filled her mind already, surfacing one after another like a school of fish. Arrokad were known among the Ancients as ruthless negotiators and impatient partners in any sort of commerce. She had thought that the moment Qiyed completed her transformation he would demand payment from her.

Of course, she had no idea what that payment might entail, and perhaps that was the point. Maybe he had yet to decide.

Still, his indifference with respect to compensation alarmed her.

"Goodnight, Droënalka. I predict we will see each other again soon."

She raised a hand in farewell and waited as he returned to the sea, her doubts redoubled by his parting words. Not just their cryptic nature, but also the simple fact that for the first time since they met, he had called her "Droënalka" rather than "Droë of the Tirribin." Was she so changed?

Droë walked back to the town at human speed. Though hungry, she was in no hurry to see – or be seen by – Strie and Kreeva.

She hadn't been back in Barleyton for more than two spirecounts when the Tirribin found her. They blurred into view and halted before her. Even after taking in her new appearance, neither of them spoke.

"You're staring," Droë finally said, exasperated and frightened.

What had the Arrokad done to her? "You're being rude."

"You're all grown," Strie said, his tone hushed. "Your years are more difficult to read. It's like you've aged beyond my ability to sense them."

He glanced at Kreeva, who shook his head.

"I can't read them either."

A shudder went through her. She crossed her arms over her chest, found it more ample than it had been after the last push. "Am I still Tirribin?"

"I don't know," Kreeva said. Droë saw her own fear mirrored in his eyes. "Can you sense our years?"

"Yes. How different do I look?"

"Very," Strie said. "You're all grown. And you're... well, you're beautiful."

She blinked. "I am?"

Both Tirribin laughed.

"Of course you are. You look like an Arrokad, but your hair's the wrong color."

"And your eyes are still Tirribin," Kreeva added.

"So I'm not... I'm beautiful?"

She didn't wait for a reply, but strode toward the waterfront. Before reaching it, she halted and headed in a new direction. The wind would roughen the water's surface, but that trough of water in which she'd seen herself previously might work.

She blurred to Tirribin speed, relieved that she still could. A fivecount later, she stood at the trough. Strie and Kreeva arrived an instant after she did. She took a long, steadying breath, and stared down into the mucky water.

A gasp escaped her.

Golden hair, oval face, high cheek bones, full lips, eyes as pale as a frost moon save for a tinge of gray. Her body was that of a grown human woman, but it remained lithe, the way men and women seemed to prefer. The Tirribin were right. She was a beauty.

Thank you, Qiyed.

The thought brought a smile to her lips. She didn't know that she reached out for the Most Ancient One until he answered in her mind.

You are welcome. I am glad that you are pleased.

She didn't reply, and she made a point of closing her mind to his.

"Droë, are you all right?"

She started, tore her eyes from her reflection. "Yes, I'm sorry. I was… It's odd to see myself this way."

"You wanted this," Strie said. "You said so yourself."

"That's true, I did. Still, it feels strange."

Kreeva glanced up and down the lane, distracted, clearly uninterested in their conversation. "Can we hunt now? I'm hungry."

A younger Droë would have accused him of being rude, but more than ever she felt the difference in their years. Young Droë might also have asked the same question.

"I'm hungry, too," she said. If Kreeva noticed the indulgence in her voice, he showed no sign of it. "Let's hunt."

They turned back in the direction of the waterfront, intending to hunt for sailors from one of the docked ships. Before long, Kreeva and Strie caught the scent of years nearby and stalked them. Droë walked on, pursuing prey of her own. A man of some thirty years, heading toward a vessel.

She tried to keep to shadows, as she always had. But as she followed the man onto the wharf, she stepped on a loose board, drawing a creak from the wood.

The man spun. "Who's that?"

Droë was used to prey commenting on her size, her youth. *What's a wee thing like you doing in the city so late?* She'd heard the question, or some version of it, more times than she could remember.

This man didn't say that.

"Well, good evening," he said, the words slurred. "What's such a lovely lass doing on the wharves at night?"

She had observed enough over the centuries to sense the

meaning behind his question.

"I'm… I'm looking for someone."

"I was hoping so," he said with a leer.

She didn't fully understand, not until he dug into his pocket and produced a handful of coins.

"This enough to buy a bit of warmth for a bell or two?"

Droë didn't think he noticed her hesitation. "I don't know. Let me see."

She sauntered closer, marking the way his gaze raked over her body, her face, her hair.

"You's a beauty, and no doubt," he said, his voice dropping.

She didn't answer. Reaching him, she glanced at the coins. "Yes, that's enough."

"Well, good. Why don't we—"

Droë grabbed hold of him with both hands, lifted him off his feet and clapped her mouth over his throat. He fought her, the coins falling to the wood with a clatter and roll, but he was helpless in her grasp. She shifted a hand to cover his mouth, and went on feeding. He could no more break free than he could fly up into the moonlight.

When she had taken all his years, she lowered him into the water that lapped at the dock, and let him slip under. She nearly laughed aloud. Never had a hunt been easier. Now that she was grown, she might never again need to pursue prey at speed. Human men were so eager to mate, like beasts in rut, that she could simply lure them to her by standing in the street.

With the thought, came an echo of Qiyed's last words on the strand. Something about this encounter related to what he'd said to her. She couldn't yet make the connection.

Still hungry, she resumed her prowl of the wharf. She found a woman next, and approached her as boldly as she had the man.

"What are you doing here?" the sailor asked, her tone as hard as her words. "You with a ship?"

The woman held a small blade in one hand. She could overpower the sailor, but not without risking injury, and probably not without drawing the attention of others.

She opened both hands to show that she held no weapon. "No, I'm just... I'm walking. That's all."

"Walking. I'm sure. Why don't you walk somewhere else?"

There was implication here as well, Droë knew. Clearly the woman felt differently about her presence than had the man. In this case, she would have been better served by her child form. A lesson – about the realities of these changes, about the way she would have to hunt from this night forward. Some women, she knew, would be drawn to her as the man had been. Not all, though. Not even most, if her past observations of humans could be trusted.

Again, that echo. This was something Qiyed wished to discuss with her. Or anticipated she would wish to discuss.

She retreated from the wharf, watched closely by the woman, and made her way along the waterfront to a strand where the town's poor often congregated. Those without comfortable homes, without jobs, some of them.

Strie and Kreeva would not want her hunting in this place, but she was too weary to hunt the road or another village.

This time, she kept herself out of sight until she singled out her prey. Even then she rushed the man at speed, unwilling to be seen. Sated, and convinced that these final changes had not diminished her ability to hunt, she returned to the lanes.

Kreeva and Strie rejoined her within moments.

"Where were you?" Strie asked, a rebuke in his expression.

"The strand, west of town."

"I thought we were hunting sailors tonight."

"My first human was a sailor. The second..." She shrugged. "I had to leave the wharves. A woman saw me, and she had a weapon."

Strie's frown remained.

"One night doesn't matter," Kreeva said. "But maybe we should go to another village tomorrow night."

"That's a fine idea," Droë said, her voice falsely bright.

She knew she couldn't stay here much longer. She tried to tell herself that this was inevitable. She couldn't have remained forever, even if she hadn't submitted to the Arrokad's magick. The time had come to resume her search for Tobias.

The truth was more complicated. She had no idea where Tobias might be, and she wasn't sure she was ready to find him.

That echo reached her again – Qiyed's words, his hints.

She'd made up her mind to leave soon because she no longer wished to hunt with the Tirribin. She was too mature for them; as Qiyed had warned, she didn't belong with those who had been her kind.

For the following several nights, Droë, Strie, and Kreeva hunted the road, the farming village west of Barleyton, the wharves, and then the road again. Strie contrived to keep Droë from taking prey within the town. She hardly cared. She fed and she tolerated their company. Mostly, she pondered Qiyed's words. She was on the cusp of understanding what he wished to discuss with her.

More than once, she used her beauty to lure a young male human to her so she could take his years. On one occasion – their final night along the road – Strie and Kreeva saw her do this. They found it greatly amusing, and spoke of it as they walked back to Barleyton at human speed.

"They're such fools," Strie said. "They can't think of anything other than their need to couple."

Droë nearly stumbled at this. She righted herself, and the Tirribin took no notice of her. But at long last she understood what Qiyed had meant.

Elements of what you seek require further attention.

Indeed.

"I have to go," she said.

They halted and faced her.

"Go where?" Kreeva asked.

"To the strand. I need… I'm supposed to speak with the Most Ancient One."

"Tonight?"

"Yes. I only just remembered. I… I'm late as it is."

Kreeva and Strie exchanged glances and shrugged at the same time.

"All right. We'll see you back in Barleyton."

When they were beyond her seeing, Droë blurred to speed. She cut through copse and lea. Before she came to the shore, she spoke the Arrokad's name aloud. "I would speak with you."

She thought she heard laughter.

She reached the water's edge before he did, and paced as he swam to land. Even after he emerged from the waves, she did not stop.

"You summoned me," he said, amusement curving his lips. "I expected you would do so sooner. Did it truly take you this long to grasp the truth of what you lack?"

She paused to eye him, her cheeks flushing. "That's rude."

She resumed her pacing. He didn't apologize.

"Is this something you can give to me?" she asked after some time.

"Is what?"

Droë halted again. "You know what you withheld, and so do I."

"I would hear you speak of it. If you cannot, you are not ready to possess it."

She opened her mouth, closed it again. Her cheeks burned. Her scalp tingled with embarrassment.

"I see."

She stared past him at the breakers and the reflection of starlight on swells.

"Would you like to know what it is I see?"

"Not really, no."

"I see a creature, brought magickally to maturity, but still mired in the puerile limitations of her kind."

"That's—"

"Rude. Yes, I know. It is also true. Now, tell me what I withheld from you."

Droë wet her lips, her gaze on the sea again. "You did not give me desire," she whispered.

Qiyed's smile was knowing and cruel. "No, I did not."

"Why would you deny me that, of all things?"

"Because I brought you to maturity in a matter of a turn or so. Had I changed you – an Ancient – so thoroughly and also given you desire, you might have gone mad."

Something in the way he said this bothered her.

"I don't believe you."

"Do you accuse me of lying?"

"Not of lying," she said, contemplating what she had heard in his explanation. "Of using one truth to obscure another. You may have given thought to my well-being, but you have other motives."

"Perhaps I do. The question is, do you want me to impart this last element of your transformation? I can, of course. It is a rather simple act of magick, at least when compared with what I have accomplished already. Do you want it?"

As before, the Arrokad's manner gave her pause. Since their first encounter, her trust in him had been fragile. She had long wondered about his motivation for helping her. Now, she understood. They had come to the crux of his machinations. She wanted to refuse him, to walk away and never call for him again. Much of what she wanted she had. She was grown, a creature capable of loving and being loved as humans did.

Yet even she, ignorant of such matters, understood that without desire she might as well have reverted to her old form. Fascination with love – the act and the emotion – was not enough. To grasp it fully, she needed to understand what drove humans to pursue lovers, to sacrifice all for them, to pledge their lives to them, to betray them for new ones, to kill for them as their kind were known to do, to pay coin for them in the absence of other choices, to build their lives around this single quest. Some love, she understood, could be separated from desire: love between siblings, and friends; a parent's love for her child – although, of course, desire was integral to the origins of such love.

Those loves didn't matter to her. She wanted to love a mate.

She wanted to love Tobias. For that, she required what Qiyed had withheld.

"Yes," she said, exhaling the word. "I want you to impart desire to me."

"A wise choice," he said. "It would have been a pity to waste all that magick, and all you endured to become what you are now."

"And what is that?"

"Right now? Something incomplete." He lifted his hand. "Allow me to correct that."

She took a step toward him, and then another. Water cooled her toes. She inhaled his scent.

"Will this hurt?"

The Arrokad laughed. "No. At least not tonight. There may come a time when you seek pain as part of it. I envy you, Droënalka. You are about to step into a new world that will make this one you have known seem dull and colorless."

He didn't wait for a reply, nor did he ask her permission again. He touched his fingers to her brow.

Magick swept into her, cold and then blazing. This fire, however, was nothing like what she had experienced with his previous pushes. It tickled her lips, danced along the skin of her breasts, feathered over her belly and hips, insinuated itself into the cleft between her legs. A moan escaped her. Her knees weakened and she collapsed to the wet sand.

Qiyed kept his fingers on her brow.

Fire swept over her again, more insistent and yet as gentle as a planting turn breeze. She laughed, throaty and unrestrained. Never had she heard herself make such a sound. Her skin was ablaze and yet there was no pain. Seawater lapped at her legs, and that too turned to fire. Every sensation was transformed into pleasure, and every instant of pleasure left her desperate for more.

Another wave moved through her. Liquid, flame, sensation – they were all one, filling her blood, her mind, her most private places. A molten alloy akin to quicksilver. Wave followed upon wave, building a rhythm, obliterating all other thought. Heat was everywhere, but it settled most forcefully deep down inside her. She laughed again, heard the laughter tip over into an ecstatic groan. And still it grew. Nothing in her life had ever been so exquisite. Not the sweetest years of a child. Not flying with the Shonla. Nothing.

She felt herself rocking to a pulse that emanated from the sea and the earth and the stars. Faster and faster. Her toes curled, she tipped her head back, her breathing ragged. At last she spasmed, pleasure lifting her bodily off the sand and dropping her back down. She gave voice to a cry that was torn from her chest.

Some time later – a spirecount, a bell, a day; she couldn't possibly have said which – she became aware again of surf and strand. Gentle waves of brine. The cushion of cool sand. Qiyed no longer touched her brow. Her breathing had slowed.

She forced her eyes open. The Arrokad loomed before her, impassive, seemingly chiseled from stone. She dragged her gaze over the length of his body, something she had never allowed herself to do before. He was stunning. Arrokad were said to be dangerous lovers, sensual, but rough, even violent at times. What would that be like?

"That is desire," she said. Did her voice sound deeper than it had after the last transformation?

"That is one flavor of desire. There are others."

She took a long, deep breath, eyes on his. "Do it again."

"No."

Droë hadn't expected him to refuse. "Why not?"

"Because you are new to passion. It can be as perilous as it is wondrous. You must learn control."

"And I will. But… but first I want to experience it again."

He stared down at her, unmoved.

She forced herself to her feet, straightened her damp shift. The memory of what he had given her receded, replaced by embarrassment that he should have seen her so, helpless in the throes of her arousal. How did humans treat with each other after coupling? How did they reconcile love for each other with that loss of composure?

"I can find it elsewhere," she said. "I don't need your magick."

"No, you do not. Are you prepared to share what you just experienced with another? Are you ready to subject yourself to the passion of a human male? Someone who is a stranger to you?"

She wanted to tell him that she was, but the words wouldn't come.

"That is an element of the peril. In time it will be an element of the wonder, as well."

Droë wasn't sure she understood. She guessed that Qiyed sought to use her uncertainty and innocence to bind her to him.

"I will not share it with you," she said. "I will not couple with you. Not ever. I won't touch you. That wasn't part of our bargain."

He didn't reach for her brow again. He didn't so much as gesture in her direction. Only a twitch in the corners of his mouth warned her.

A frisson of pleasure shot through her, rekindling the fire. She drew a sharp breath, her legs nearly giving out again. She waited, anticipating more, needing more. Nothing.

She opened her eyes, her face hot with shame and want.

"I do not need to lie with you to give you pleasure." He paused. Agony flared in her breasts, as if something had taken hold of her nipples and given them a vicious twist. She shrieked, folded in on herself.

A heartbeat later, the pain vanished.

"Nor do I need to touch you to cause torment."

"Why would you want to?"

Before he could answer, she heard a footfall on the dry sand behind her.

"Droë, are you all right?"

Gods, no.

Qiyed's glare snapped up. Too late, Droë caught the scent of Tirribin years.

She pivoted. Both of them had come, tiny shadows in the darkness. "I'm fine," she said. "You shouldn't have followed me."

"We were curious," Strie said.

Kreeva gave a small shake of his head. "We were worried about you."

"This creature is not your concern," Qiyed said.

This creature?

"She's our friend," Kreeva answered, a rasp in his voice.

Droë wanted to warn him against speaking to the Arrokad so. Not that she needed to. He was Tirribin. He had lived for centuries. He knew the risks.

"You should come back to town with us, Droë," he said. "It's time we were hunting again."

"She will remain here. You will go."

"I believe that is her choice to make." Strie's voice had taken on a rasp as well. "Powerful as you may be, there are three of us. You are but one, Most Ancient or not."

"Numbers mean nothing to me," Qiyed said. "I can destroy all of you. I prefer not to, but you are interfering in a matter of commerce, a bargain freely entered and fairly sworn. The Guild might frown on the bloodshed, but they would never sanction me. You know this as well as I." His smile could have frozen Kheraya's Ocean. "Leave us, cousins, and all of this will be forgotten. And do so at speed. My patience thins."

Both Tirribin looked to Droë.

"It's as he says, and as I have explained to you before: he and I have a bargain. Freely entered. Fairly sworn."

"He hurt you."

"He demonstrated an ability, one I did not fully grasp."

"And before that? He's been hurting you a lot."

Her face burned hotter than it had at any time that night. "That was part of our bargain," she said, gaze averted. "You should go."

Kreeva frowned. "There's no need to be rude."

"I didn't... I'm sorry, but you shouldn't have come."

"Fine," Strie said, turning from her and starting back across the sand.

Kreeva lingered. "Will we see you tomorrow?"

"I don't know. If not... I've enjoyed hunting with you. I'm grateful to you both for welcoming me to your town. It was a kindness, one I would like to repay someday."

If anything, this further darkened the Tirribin's expression. He wheeled and followed his friend.

Droë wanted to call them back, but wouldn't have known what to say. She stared after them, her heart tight.

"You did well to send them away."

She rounded on the Arrokad. "You threatened their lives."

"Yours as well."

"You have no right. Plus, you lied. The Guild would indeed find fault with your actions."

He shrugged, his calm infuriating. "I wanted them gone."

"And what do you want of me? Tell me now, or I'll consider our commerce complete."

"That would be unwise on your part."

"Why? Our bargain was vague. You stipulated no price for the boon I requested. I remember your exact words. 'In time, if we do this, and if you are pleased with the result, perhaps we can revisit the matter.'"

"Yes, Droënalka, I remember the words as well. Tell me, are you pleased with the result? Did I not please you just a short time ago?"

She colored again.

"As I thought. And so I choose to revisit the matter, as we agreed at the time I could."

"That's not… we agreed that we both could. Or rather, that together we could agree to do so."

"Is that what we stipulated? You admit yourself that the wording was vague. Carelessness on your part. We also said that 'access to your time sense would be payment enough.' We placed no constraint on how long I might maintain that access. Again, carelessness. It could be days. It could be centuries." He thinned another smile. "You should know better than to bargain in desperation with one of my kind."

It seemed to Droë that someone knelt on her chest, that she couldn't possibly draw enough air.

"You need not look so frightened. I have no intention of

binding you to service for centuries. But neither will I allow you to end our agreement now. No, we have much to do, you and I."

"You deceived me."

"I took advantage of you. There is a difference, and I make no apology."

She saw little point in arguing the matter. Qiyed was right: she should have known better than to bargain in haste with an Arrokad. She had been too eager, and he had used this against her. If she could have done the same to a Shonla or Belvora, she would have. It was the way of the Ancient races.

"All right," she said. "You choose to revisit our arrangement. In what way? Tell me your terms."

"Better," he said, sounding smug. "You need not despair. We can work together, you and I, and we can both profit. I will have the benefit of your time sense and your strength. You will have access to my knowledge, my awareness of this world between the oceans. We will find your Walker. Perhaps we will rid him of the woman with whom he journeys, so that he can be yours."

She gaped. "I never told you of the woman," she whispered.

"No, you did not. An interesting choice on your part. Understandable, perhaps, but telling as well."

"You've found them?"

"I have made inquiries, during the intervals between our encounters."

"Inquiries."

"With other Arrokad, other Ancients. Knowledge of the misfuture has been most helpful in this regard. You see? You gave me that as payment for my summons and this boon, yet it benefits you as much as it does me."

"The Walker," she prompted, unable to keep the urgency from her voice.

"Yes, of course. Rare as they are, Walkers are not difficult to find once an Ancient knows to search for them. As it happens, two voyage together even as we speak."

"That must be them." She couldn't mask her excitement.

"Indeed. In time, we will go to them. Until then, we have other matters that require our attention. Agreed?"

"What other matters? Where?"

"Patience. I am asking you first: is this agreeable to you? You will help me with these matters, and then I will lead you to your Walker."

"Yes," she said. Too quickly, she knew, but he had caught her unawares. *Two Walkers...*

"Freely entered and fairly sworn?"

"Freely entered and fairly sworn."

"Very good. Now, before we go on, it is time you learned what it is to swim with an Arrokad."

It was a measure of her eagerness to find Tobias that she didn't balk at this. In her quest for the Walker, she had already soared with a Shonla. Maybe it was inevitable that she should take to the sea as well. She was past the point of caring about such trifles.

"Very well."

"You will have to touch me, despite your determination not to. You will climb onto my back and ride me across the waves, as did the porpoise riders of old."

Another capitulation. She had bargained poorly, a mistake for which she would pay a cost.

She had much yet to learn about desire, about the Arrokad, about herself in this newest incarnation. Still, she was not without resources of her own. She was stronger than she had ever been, stronger than he knew. She retained her time sense, her ability to move at speed, the cunning she had honed over centuries as a predator.

Qiyed thought his power over her complete.

She knew better. In time, he would as well.

CHAPTER 23

18th Day of Kheraya's Descent, Year 634

Rain, wind, and, finally, fog as thick as molasses kept the *Sea Dove* in Kantaad's Blackrock Bay for several days after Tobias and Mara revealed the truth of their plight to the ship's crew.

Tobias begrudged every bell. He imagined Orzili and his assassins closing in on the ship from all sides. It was all he could do not to disembark with Mara and Sofya, and hide with them in the highlands above Kantaad's royal city. He still wondered if they should have remained in Chayde when they had the chance.

When the weather allowed, he and Mara let Sofya totter around above decks, where she could chatter at the men and women working the ship. To their credit, the crew of the *Dove* did not treat them any differently. They went about their work, they laughed at the princess's antics, and they traded good-natured gibes with Tobias and Mara.

Tobias had worried that sailors on nearby ships might see or hear Sofya and grow suspicious. Captain Larr's warning about the rarity of children on merchant ships remained fresh in his memory. But with the wind keening like a wild cat and, later, that dense mist muffling every sound, he could barely hear the princess himself. He wanted to believe he had allowed fear of Orzili to overcome his judgment. Yet, he didn't dare let down his guard.

More than anything, Tobias wanted to lead a normal life – whatever that meant. Years from now, Sofya would reclaim her family's legacy, and she would need his help, and Mara's. Until then, was it too much to ask that the three of them live as a family in peace and safety?

Strangely, the answer came to him in the voice of Mearlan, the lost sovereign. *Yes*, he said in Tobias's mind. *That is too much. You serve Hayncalde, even now. And you serve this child by keeping her alive. Nothing else – not your life, and certainly not your comfort or happiness – matters as much.*

The truth was, he didn't need Mearlan's voice to tell him anything. He adored the child. He didn't think he could have loved her more if she was his daughter. He would die to keep her alive. Not for history. Not for the royal court. For her.

He would do the same for Mara, who emerged from the hold, bundled in a woolen overshirt, her hair tied in a loose plait.

"Mama!"

Sofya charged her, barreling headlong into her arms, and squealing with delight when Mara swung her high into the heavy air.

He had left Mara sleeping and he greeted her now with a kiss. Sofya puckered her lips, made a kissing noise, and laughed again.

"Did you sleep at all?" Mara asked.

"A little, yes." A lie. Thoughts of Orzili and frustration at their inability to leave this place had plagued him through the night.

"I don't believe him, Nava. Do you?"

Sofya shoved her thumb in her mouth and shook her head.

"Sorry, Papa, but we think you're saying that to keep us from worrying about you."

"Is it working?"

"Not at all."

Captain Larr approached them. Damp hair clung to her brow and drops of water rolled down her angular face like rain on a cliffside. She smiled a greeting, unperturbed by the fog.

"I wanted to let you know that I've made inquiries," she said. "Quietly, of course, and as lacking in specifics as possible. Bound devices are scarce here, as they are everywhere. I can ask in a few more places, perhaps sail us to another of Kantaad's ports, but I assume you'd prefer I erred on the side of caution rather than persistence. This is but one isle, and not nearly the most prosperous in the Inward Sea."

Tobias wasn't certain what the captain was talking about. She seemed to be continuing a conversation of which he had no memory.

"Thank you, captain," Mara said, before he could ask Larr to explain. "As you say, we're better off being cautious for now. That may change in time, but we're not there yet."

Larr gave a decisive nod. "My thinking precisely." She peered up into the unrelenting gray. "I hope to have us under way soon. I prefer not to chance the mouth of the bay in this fog, but I don't wish to remain here another night. I'll make my decision by midday."

She eyed them both, flashed a quick smile at Sofya, and strode away.

Tobias rounded on Mara, whose cheeks had darkened. "Would you care to explain that?"

"I've meant to tell you, but there hasn't been time."

He lifted an eyebrow. "We've been here for days, Mara. We've had nothing but time." He smiled to soften this, but he was keenly curious.

"A few days ago, I asked her to find us a chronofor."

"Why?"

"Isn't it obvious? Hasn't it been since the slavers took this one?" She gave Sofya a little jiggle. The princess grinned around her thumb. "We need to have access to our abilities. We're Walkers. And I'm a Spanner. Those are more than just skills coveted by the courts. Our talents make us strong. If we'd had a chronofor the night she was taken, we would have had other ways of getting her back."

He considered this.

"When we were in the Notch, before we sailed on the *Dove*, you and the Seer talked about running or hiding. We're running now, Tobias. And I know we have to. In time, though, we'll need to fight. I was looking for a way—"

He raised a hand, stopping her. "You did the right thing. It's a good idea."

Mara exhaled, relief written on her lovely features.

"You could have told me."

"Could I? What would you have said?"

She knew him so well.

"That it's too dangerous. That it risks drawing the notice of any number of people."

"Yes, and you would have been right. But we have to do it anyway. So I spoke in private with the captain, and she had an idea."

She described the generous arrangement Captain Larr had suggested. They had been more fortunate in finding her, and this crew, than he'd known. That stroke of luck, along with the very fact of his survival and Sofya's, were enough to convince him that the Two smiled upon them.

"She spoke of searching for Bound devices – not only a chronofor."

"I asked her to find me a sextant as well."

"Also a risk."

"Also a potential tool. And looking for Bound devices in general, rather than just a chronofor, will make her search less conspicuous, diminishing the risk."

He couldn't argue. She had always been intelligent, the smartest of their cohort in Windhome. It was part of what had attracted him to her when they were novitiates. In a future he had lost and she had never known.

"You're seeing all of this more clearly than I am."

She brushed a lock of hair off his forehead. "You're afraid, and you're consumed with protecting Nava, as you should be. You concentrate on that. I'll take care of the rest."

As the morning progressed, the sky brightened. Soon the fog lifted, allowing Tobias to see the shoreline and the ships around them. Several vessels departed from Fanquir's wharf on sweeps, passing the anchored ships and heading for open sea.

Some of the vessels near the *Dove* lifted anchor and rowed

to the open berths at the docks. Others, the *Dove* among them, readied to leave Blackrock Bay. Sailors on an adjacent ship sang a sea song Tobias didn't know. Men and women on the *Dove* joined in. Everyone took pleasure in this turn in the weather.

Mara and Tobias helped ready the ship for their voyage while Sofya roamed the deck. Prior to the storm, the captain had spoken of sailing to the isles of the Knot. Tobias knew little about them save that they were remote from Daerjen and the rest of the Inward Sea islands. For now, that was enough.

In time, the crew rowed them clear of the bay. Fingers of mist still hung over the glasslike water, and even after they reached the open sea, the air was too calm for sails. Captain Larr didn't appear to mind. She ordered those below to keep rowing, but didn't push them to maintain any particular pace. She steered the ship eastward.

As the sky continued to lighten, she beckoned to Tobias. He joined her on the aft deck.

"We make for the Knot," she said over the rhythmic splash of the oars.

"I remember."

"Do you approve?"

He smiled. "Would you care if I didn't?"

She shrugged, eyes scanning the sea. "I'd entertain other suggestions if you have concerns."

When do I not have concerns? "The Knot seems a fine choice." He followed the line of her gaze, spotted a pod of dolphins breaching the sea's surface ahead of them. "I've never been there, but I've read about it. I'm eager to see her isles."

"It's pretty enough. Not as lovely as parts of the Labyrinth, but what it lacks in beauty, it makes up for in other ways." She glanced at him. "Beware the drink they call Graywater. It's lethal."

He grinned. "I will. Thank you, captain. For your consideration, and also for your efforts to locate a chronofor."

"I take it you're amenable to the arrangement I proposed."

"It's more than fair."

She adjusted their heading. "I doubt we'll find any devices in the Knot. The unfortunate truth is that the farther we stray from crowded waters, the less likely we are to locate a chronofor. In the same way, as we increase our odds of finding one, we also increase the danger to you and your family."

"I understand."

"Good. Then I'd suggest that you and Mara take time while we're in the Knot to decide where you're willing to go next."

He pushed back against the panic rising in his chest. "We will. Again, my thanks."

Tobias walked away. He would heed her advice eventually, but he wasn't ready yet to confront that particular question.

A wind rose late that first day, allowing the crew to ship their oars and unfurl the sails.

Still, the voyage from Fanquir to the Knot promised to take days.

Fortunately, the wind brought clear skies, allowing Tobias, Mara, and the rest of the crew to slip back into the comfortable routine they had established before the storm. Sofya had the run of the ship, climbing into the hold and back onto the deck as she pleased.

Three days out, they passed the isles known as the Lost Children, and several days after that, they spotted Islecliff, the first of the Knot islands. By then, the weather had turned again, bringing clouds and rain.

Islecliff might not have been a center of commerce, but it was a sight to behold. The towering rock walls for which it was named dwarfed the ship. Sea eagles, resplendent in white and bay, wheeled before the crags, their high cries carrying over the pelting rain and the crash of surf. Narrow fissures in the rock faces retreated into shadow, the waters within them frothy and rough. Dark forests topped the cliffs.

As the captain piloted them past this first isle, she had one of her crew exchange the Aiyanthan flag on their mast for a flag of Zersa, the second isle on their route. Zersa's seawalls were lower than those of Islecliff, its farmland rolling and verdant. Once they cleared its shores, they turned toward the busiest port in the cluster: Piisen on the central island of Grayisle, which loomed ahead of them, distant and pale in the rain.

They sailed for several bells more, past sunset, before finally going to sweeps as they neared a broad harbor. Captain Larr always had her crew light torches on deck at night, but here she had them mount more than usual.

"These waters are filled with Shonla," she said. In response to Tobias's look of puzzlement, she added, "Mist demons. Ships in the Knot are beleaguered by them. We have nothing to fear so long as we keep these lit, but woe to the vessel that has only a torch or two, or worse, none at all."

After hearing this, Tobias scanned the water continuously, searching for clouds of mist hanging low over the ebon swells. He thought he spotted a few, but couldn't be certain. In response to a question from Mara, the captain said that other sorts of demons were no more common here than elsewhere in Islevale.

They neared Piisen's wharves close to midnight and lowered their anchor some distance offshore. At other ports, they might have continued to the docks; there was room for them. Captain Larr explained, though, that Piisen's authorities had to approve a docking, and collect wharfages, before allowing sailors and merchants access to the city.

"The Knot is different from other parts of Islevale," Larr said. "In many respects it's safer. You just have to do things their way." Tobias was sobered by the warning, as he had been by word of the mist demons. A part of him wished Larr had mentioned these things before they set their course for the Knot.

She is aware of them before she sees the ship or hears its humans. The scent of magick riding the seawind is strong and unmistakable. Two Travelers, and a third of indeterminate power. Prey.

Under different circumstances she might attack now, claim one as her own. But rewards await her if she delays her feeding and alerts others to their presence.

She prefers not to treat with humans; she refuses to submit to their authority. She is also canny enough to understand that they can be useful, and that patience might profit her. Her kind are not known for their forbearance, nor are they supposed to be in these waters. Humans again. They have asserted themselves in recent centuries. Before, they shied from the Ancient races. Now they have grown bold. She is not convinced this is a good thing, but that is a matter for discussion within the Guild. Another time, another place.

She takes to the air, her first wingbeats labored. Soon, she catches a cool wind and circles higher, wings still now, silent. They will not hear her, nor will they see her against the dark sky. Another of the Ancients might, but not humans.

A quick stoop and she could feast. However, her instructions in this regard have been quite clear. If she can identify them as those the humans seek, and if she can ensure that all three are taken at once, her payment – in additional prey, of course – will be extravagant. Locating and identifying all three will yield a reward as well. Take only one, or even two, and she forfeits what the humans offer.

Among the other Ancient races, her kind are considered dull-witted. Perhaps they are, at least when compared with Arrokad. Who among the Ancients aren't? But Shonla? Tirribin? They are no more intelligent than Belvora. Indeed, they have been slow to recognize the growing aggression of humans, and slower still to forge bonds with the young ones. Foolish, and short-sighted.

She glides near to the ship. They have lowered their sails and gone to oars. She could flap her wings directly above them, and none aboard the vessel would hear. She doesn't. She tastes the air, seeking the nuance of magick. Travelers, yes. One is a Walker. Of that she is certain. The second is something else. Not quite Walker, not quite Spanner. And the third: even this close, she can tell nothing of this one.

She circles for a time, trying in vain to learn more. Her frustration builds, until she is ready to eschew caution and her reward and simply feed.

This would be foolhardy. There are other meals to be had, even in these southern waters. And the ship's pilot is clearly intent on docking in the city. They will be there on the morrow. *Patience*, she reminds herself again.

She makes one last pass over the ship, then wheels away, back toward her perch above the harbor. Daylight and clearer skies may allow her to discern more. She has allies as well, others who might help her and with whom she can, reluctantly, share her bounty. She will not kill in haste.

One way or another, these creatures of magick will be hers. Regardless of reward, they are prey. And no creatures in all this world are more skilled on the hunt than she and her kind.

Mara awoke to a persistent tug on her fingers. She opened one eye. Sofya stood by the pallet, one hand pulling on Mara's, the other thumb in her mouth.

"I'm hungwy."

Mara put a finger to her lips and pointed back at Tobias, with whom she had shared another late night, and who slept still. Sofya blinked, solemn and silent.

Mara could have slept for another bell or two as well, but in fairness, Sofya woke him early at least as often as she woke Mara. She sat up, pulled on her shift, and carried the princess onto the deck.

The air was crisp, and smelled of fish and tar. Sunlight glowed golden on the rooftops of Piisen. Captain Larr stood at her usual spot on the aft deck, presiding over a frenzy of activity. Sailors prepared for docking, two pulling the anchor from the water, others already below, with oars in hand, ready to row the ship to port.

She and Tobias should have been among them.

Even after so many turns aboard the *Dove*, the two of them occupied an odd niche in the life of the ship. They did plenty of work, and the captain treated them as she did all her sailors. But they weren't crew, and everyone knew it. After Tobias revealed who they were and why they had come aboard the *Dove*, the crew had grown easier around them, accepting them in ways they hadn't before. Yet his confession also set them further apart, eliminating any remaining pretense.

At a shouted order from below, the oars splashed into the sea, and the ship pitched forward. Not long after, Tobias emerged from the hold, crooked a smile in her direction, and joined those who were rowing.

It didn't take them long to make port. Mara helped lash the ship to bollards on the wharf and set in place a plank that led from the ship to the pier.

Sofya returned to her side. "I'm hungwy," she said again.

Mara lifted her again. "I know you are, love. Let's get you something to eat."

They found the ship's cook, who gave them three pieces of fried honeybread – one for Tobias – and then ordered them out of the kitchen. They climbed back to the deck and perched themselves on barrels near the ship's prow.

Sofya was soon a sticky mess, but she was happy and Mara was content to let her eat in peace. They would wash off later.

As they ate, Mara eyed Piisen. No gated wall stood between the wharf and the city, so she could see some distance into the lanes. It resembled other cities and towns they had visited. The homes and shops lit by morning sunlight far up the slope were cleaner and larger than the squalid buildings nearest the waterfront.

The captain left the aft deck and descended the plank to the dock, where she spoke with a woman wearing a uniform of beige and blue. The official was solidly built, but a full head shorter than the captain. She had red hair and a round, flushed face. She nodded at something the captain said, but her expression remained dour.

Larr handed her a small coin purse. The woman pocketed it, presented the captain with a slip of parchment, and marched off. Larr watched her go, amusement in her mien and stance.

A moment later, she spotted Mara and raised a hand in greeting. She climbed the plank to the *Dove's* deck.

"Is everything all right?" Mara asked as Larr halted in front of her.

"Yes. That was the harbormaster, an even more disagreeable woman than her predecessor. I've paid the wharfages, and we're free to stay and trade and wander the city." She held up the scrip. "This is proof of our payment. If you go into the city, and you have any trouble, bring the authorities back here. We'll vouch for you."

Mara frowned. "Do you expect we'll have trouble?"

"Not really. Invariably, the authorities are the most difficult people we encounter here. Most people of the Knot are welcoming."

Late in the morning, Mara and Tobias took Sofya into the city, and they found the people to be much as the captain described. To a point.

Everyone they met was courteous and unfailingly polite, but Mara wouldn't have called them warm. Several times she caught men and women staring at the three of them, their expressions tight. It didn't take her long to figure out why. Aside from Tobias, Sofya, and herself, she saw no one in the lanes, or in the Piisen marketplace, with dark skin. The three of them stood out more than they had anywhere else.

Most of the people they encountered were pale, red-haired, compact. The men had their heads shaved save for long, thin plaits of scarlet hair. No one spoke rudely, or treated them badly, but they knew the three of them for Northislers. Mara sensed their mistrust.

After only a bell or so in the city, Tobias suggested they go back to the ship.

Mara didn't argue. They reboarded the *Dove*, and remained on the ship for the rest of the day. Captain Larr had released the crew from their duties so that they might explore the city, leaving the three of them with the run of the vessel.

As evening approached, Tobias left Sofya with Mara and wandered the city lanes in search of food for the evening meal.

By this time, a few of the crew had returned, and Sofya flitted from one to the next, chattering and playing. Mara stood at her usual spot near the ship's prow.

As she eyed the city, movement near the wharf caught her eye.

A small figure skulked in a shadowed lane, keeping close to the structures there, but making its way toward the wharf.

Mara stared, trying to pick out details. Something about the figure struck her as familiar. It appeared to be a child, but its behavior was wrong. It moved with the stealth of a hunting cat, graceful, disciplined.

Within moments, she realized she was watching a Tirribin.

When the creature crossed an open area between two buildings Mara gasped. Golden hair hung to the creature's shoulders in wild ringlets.

Droë?

She stood and crossed to the princess, her gaze repeatedly finding that small form in the streets.

"Nava, I need to leave the ship for a very short while. Can you wait for me here?"

"I wanna come."

Mara frowned, and cast a glance at Ermond, who sat nearby.

"Nava, can I teach you a new song?" he asked without hesitation.

The princess spun, wide-eyed and eager.

"Thank you," Mara mouthed. She retrieved a pistol and ammunition, then eased to the plank and descended to the wharf, searching in vain for the Tirribin, loading the weapon as she walked. Reaching the buildings that the Ancient had used to conceal herself, Mara slowed and surveyed the lane.

"I know you can hear me," she said, raising her voice only slightly. "I know you can sense my years and so recognize me as a Walker. Come out. Let me see you. Let me talk to you."

She waited. No footsteps. Not a word. After a fivecount, awareness raised the hairs on her scalp and the back of her neck. She pivoted.

The Tirribin stood perhaps twenty paces from her, at the mouth of another alley. The last rays of sunlight shone in her bright hair, and her pale eyes were locked on Mara. It wasn't Droë, though the resemblance was strong. With her nut brown skin, Droë resembled the children of Trevynisle. This Tirribin was paler, like the people of the Knot.

It would behoove a predator to fit in with her surroundings. Mara shuddered at the thought.

A faint smile curved the Tirribin's lips. Then she blurred to the entrance of the next byway, glanced back in Mara's direction, and vanished from view.

Mara walked after her; after a few strides, she broke into a run, still gripping the pistol.

At the mouth of that next alley, she caught sight of the demon again, at the far end of the lane, where it crossed another street.

The creature laughed and blurred away a second time.

"Stop doing that," Mara muttered. She ran on, cursing under her breath, aware that she was being reckless. Droë had accepted her as a friend, and Tirribin didn't usually take years from Walkers. But this was no harmless child she pursued. Tirribin were as sly and dangerous as any of the Ancients. She might well have been charging into a trap.

At the next corner, she slowed, then stopped. For a breath, she saw no sign of the creature.

Yellow hair flashed through another shaft of sunlight, farther ahead, nearly two lanes away. The Tirribin glanced back, mischief in her grin. Mara expected her to blur away once more.

So she crossed her arms over her chest, planted her feet, and shook her head.

The Tirribin's smile slipped.

"I'm done playing this game," Mara said, not bothering to raise her voice. "If you wish to speak with me, you'll come here. If not, I'll go back to my ship. Either way, I won't follow you another step."

The demon stared, genuine dismay on her perfect face. They stood thus for a full spirecount, Mara rooted where she was, the

Tirribin twisting her hands, brow furrowed, as if she pondered the most vexing of riddles.

Convinced that the Tirribin wouldn't let her go without speaking to her, Mara canted her head in casual dismissal and turned away. She had taken but three steps when the Tirribin flashed past her and halted in her path.

"You can't go!" the girl said. "That would be rude."

Mara had spent enough time with Droë to know the correct response.

"I believe you're the one who's been rude. Running from me? Taunting me at every corner? Leading me deeper and deeper into a city you know is unfamiliar to me? That's hardly courteous behavior."

The Tirribin's eyes went wide, and she covered her mouth with a slender hand. "I didn't mean to be rude. I was… I was playing."

"Is that what you were doing? Or were you luring me somewhere, perhaps on instructions from someone else?"

Mara hoped this would further unsettle the girl. It didn't. Rather, she turned coy.

"Why would I do that? And for who? Are you important in some way?"

Abruptly, Mara found herself on the defensive, afraid she might reveal too much about Sofya and Tobias. "You've led me away from my ship. I want to know why."

They considered each other, like combatants about to duel.

"My name is Mara."

The Tirribin's expression curdled. As Mara knew, it would be rude not to reciprocate with her name.

"I'm Aiwi," she said.

"Why did you come to the dock?"

"Why should I answer?"

"To make up for how rude you were."

Aiwi glared, but she didn't refuse. "I smelled your years," she said, the words wrung from her. "And those of the little one. Hers are sweet and ripe. Both of you are altered. Time around you is…"

323

She made a sharp circular motion with both hands. "It's confused. Wrong somehow."

Mara nodded but said nothing about the misfuture in which all of them lived. If the Tirribin knew of it, there would be no point in mentioning it. If she didn't, it was too soon for Mara to give her the gift of that knowledge.

They stood without speaking for a tencount, until Mara grew uncomfortable. She thought she could find her way back to the ship, but she wasn't certain. More, she didn't like being alone with the demon. Tobias and the rest of the *Dove*'s crew knew nothing of her whereabouts, and she had only the pistol to defend herself.

"I should return to my ship," she said, taking a step back. "If you wish to speak with me, you know where to find me. I'll be glad to talk any time."

"You can't leave yet!" Aiwi said, the words too rushed.

Mara's pulse accelerated. "Why not?"

"Because," came a deeper voice from above her, "I am not yet through with you."

CHAPTER 24

25th Day of Kheraya's Descent, Year 634

Tobias wandered the marketplace until he found a husband and wife who roasted red oysters over an open fire. They sold him two dozen. He also bought a small loaf of brown bread and some fruit – a kind he'd never seen before. It smelled floral and sweet and delicious.

He made his way to the ship, wondering if he and Mara had been too quick to retreat from the city earlier in the day. The people he spoke to as he orbited the market had been kind, even jovial.

As he neared the wharf, he slowed, instinct making him wary. He scanned the lanes ahead and behind. Thinking of Trevynisle, he even checked the sky, though he knew Belvora almost never ventured so far south.

A few people lingered in the street, and a flock of gulls circled high above him. That was all. He walked on, alert still, but willing to believe his instincts had misled him.

He reached the ship and ascended the plank to the deck, only to be set upon by Sofya, who ran to him, arms raised, a broad smile exposing her milk teeth.

"Ermon' taught me a song," she said. "He taught me a song!"

Tobias set down the food and picked her up. "Well, let's hear it, then."

Ermond's face reddened.

Tobias carried her to where the sailor sat, while Sofya sang for him. Some of the words came out scrambled, but he understood enough to frown at the lyrics, which spoke of ale and women and gambling.

"Sorry, lad," Ermond said. "Her mum asked me to watch her, and it was all I could think to keep her occupied."

Tobias went cold. "Where's Mara?"

The sailor shook his head, pale eyes flicking in the direction of the city. "I'm not certain. She left the ship not that long ago. She hasn't come back."

"Why did she leave?"

"I'm not sure of that, either. She seemed in a hurry, though. Like she'd remembered something and had to take care of it right away. I'd wager she'll be back before you know it."

Tobias was less sure. All his fears had returned. He eyed the city, glanced up at the sky again.

This last saved his life.

A huge winged creature dropped toward him, talons extended, razor teeth bared. Ermond shouted a warning. So did someone else. Already Tobias was moving. Clutching Sofya to his chest, he dove to the side. Tucked his shoulder. Rolled. Crashed into the side of the hull below the rail.

Sofya screeched, her voice mingling dissonantly with the outraged snarl of the demon overhead.

What is a Belvora doing here?

The creature swooped up, wheeled on tucked wings, and dove again. All in the time it took Tobias to set the princess against the curved wood span. He reached for his pistol, knowing he hadn't time to load it, knowing he had to try.

A shot boomed from nearby. The Belvora banked again. Its wail spiraled into the gloaming. Dark blood stained the demon's body beneath its left wing.

Tobias tracked the creature, loading and priming his pistol with shaking hands. A second report exploded from even closer. Sofya's screams redoubled. The Belvora swerved again, one wing beating spasmodically. It fell, missed the ship, and splashed in the brine.

Tobias released a breath and started to crawl toward the princess.

"Tobias!"

He twisted, looked up. A second Belvora was almost on him. He wrenched himself, raised the pistol, and fired, all in one desperate motion.

The demon shrieked and crashed into him, slamming him to the deck. His head cracked against wood. White pain erupted in his shoulder, his ribs, his gut. He howled. A miasma of demon-stench enveloped him: rot, noisome blood, rank breath. He bit back bile and hammered the side of his pistol into the Belvora's face. It growled. Two more pistol shots made the demon buck. A moment later, it collapsed onto Tobias, its full weight stealing his breath.

A sailor cried his name again.

"I'm all right," he answered. "Just get it off me."

Sailors heaved the creature away and dropped it onto the deck. Tobias scrambled to the screaming Sofya and held her close. His shoulder ached, as did his side. He might have broken a rib. Not that he cared.

Ermond scanned the sky for more Belvora and reloaded his pistol.

Bramm, dark-eyed, grim, pulled a sword from his belt, strode to the Belvora, and hacked off its head.

Tobias remembered Saffern doing the same his final morning in Windhome, the last time a Belvora tried to kill him.

"Why did you do that?"

Bramm stared at the dead demon. "Only way to be sure an Ancient is dead, isn't it? Take off its head."

Tobias hadn't known this. "What about the other?"

"Moth and Starra have already climbed down to get it. Don't worry. We'll take care of it."

He blew a breath, kissed Sofya's forehead. She cried and clung to him, her tears dampening his shirt.

Ermond prodded the dead Belvora with a toe. "Magick demons shouldn't be here," he said. "Never heard of them coming so far south."

"They're after us. One attacked me in Windhome the day I sailed from there."

He spoke without thinking, then clamped his mouth shut. That had been in a different time, a lost future. But neither man asked for details. Ermond merely nodded, not even questioning why demons should be after the three of them...

"Mara," Tobias said. He lurched to his feet.

Ermond's eyes widened. "Blood and bone."

Tobias retrieved his pistol and started toward the plank. After only two steps he realized that he still held the princess.

Ermond was already on his feet. "I'll come with you."

Bramm said, "We both will."

"No. One of you needs to stay with Nava. Take her below. Don't let anyone or anything near her."

Bramm and Ermond exchanged glances.

"I'm no good with wee ones," Bramm said. "She likes you."

"All right. Give her here, lad."

Tobias handed Sofya to the sailor. She screamed in protest, writhing and kicking. Ermond held her and sang to her. She didn't calm down, but Tobias didn't dare waste a moment trying to soothe her.

He descended the plank, loading his weapon. Bramm followed, a pistol in one hand, his bloodied sword in the other. Together, they raced into the city. Tobias didn't know in what direction she had gone, or how far she had ventured. He had to hope she would find some way to signal him. Or that the Two would lead him to her.

At the sound of the voice, Mara spun, then shrank back, though she raised her weapon. A Belvora crouched on the low rooftop of the building before her. She was huge, her skin pale and leathery. She had round eyes, thick features, and a mane of silver hair that flowed to her muscular shoulders.

The creature straightened to her full height and jumped to the street, her membranous wings fluttering briefly to slow her drop. Mara retreated another step, bumped up against the wooden wall of another building.

"I see you are familiar with my kind."

"What do you want from me?" Mara threw a quick glare at Aiwi. "Why are you helping her?" she asked the Tirribin.

"We are cousins," the Belvora said, her smile revealing fearsome teeth. "As are all the Ancient races. You should know that."

Aiwi said nothing, but she watched the Belvora the way a child might an unfamiliar dog.

"Now, you will answer questions, and then you will die."

Mara's pistol hand shook violently. Belvora fed on creatures of magick, including humans. Especially humans. Her abilities as a Walker made her less attractive prey to the Tirribin, but they were the very reason the Belvora would want her.

"If I'm going to die, why should I tell you anything?"

"Because I can feed on the dead, and I can feed on the living. I prefer the latter, but it is far more unpleasant for my prey."

Belvora were supposed to be mindless predators. This one seemed intelligent enough. Mara tried to aim with her trembling hand. She would have only one shot, and even if she managed to kill the Belvora, she would be at the mercy of the Tirribin.

The Belvora eyed the shaking weapon, but appeared more amused than alarmed. An instant later, she lashed out – a flick of a talon. The pistol flew from Mara's grip and clacked on the cobblestone. Blood ran from a wound on the back of Mara's hand.

The winged demon laughed. "You humans are too reliant on your firearms."

Before any of them could say more, the flat report of weapons fire echoed among the lanes and structures. An animal scream rose and fell.

The Belvora sobered. "We have not much time. I sense your magick, but cannot discern its flavor. You are a Walker, yes? And yet you smell of–"

A second distant gunshot stopped her. A third followed, and with it came another screech. The Belvora stared toward the wharves, clawed hands opening and closing. Two more reports sounded in quick succession.

"I should go, cousin," Aiwi said. "The humans will be wary

now, and ever more protective of the prey you have promised me."

The Belvora kept her gaze fixed to the north.

The prey you have promised me…

The meaning of this penetrated Mara's fear.

"No!" she said. "You can't have her! She's–" She broke off. She'd meant to say, *She's important,* but she sensed that both demons knew this. What else would bring a Belvora to the Knot? Why else would these two cooperate in this way?

The Belvora rounded on Mara. She flinched, but remained trapped by the wall at her back.

"She is what? What is the child? And what are you?"

"Cousin?" Aiwi said again, eager now.

"Yes, go. You have done as I asked. The babe is yours. My debt to you is paid in full, yes?"

The Tirribin bared needle teeth. "It is. In full."

With a quick glance at Mara, she blurred away.

Mara could barely breathe for her panic. *Sofya!* She had to warn Tobias. If he was even alive. Who fired those shots? And at what?

"Tell me about the babe. And about yourself."

"Tobias!" she screamed as loudly as she could. Desperation. She was too far. And yet… "Tobias, there's a Tirri–"

A blow from the Belvora knocked her off her feet, left her sprawled on the filthy cobblestones, her cheek throbbing, her vision clouded. But she fell near the pistol. She grabbed for it.

"You will answer me!" the Belvora said, covering the distance between them with a single leap. "Or I will feed now!"

Mara tried to aim, but the Ancient crushed her arm beneath a leathery foot. Still, Mara managed to squeeze the trigger. The boom reverberated. Maybe Tobias would hear that.

"The child!" the creature demanded.

"She's only a baby." Mara cowered. A sob thickened her words. "That's what I was going to say."

"You are lying. But no matter. She is something of value. That is what matters, and it answers one of my questions. Now tell me of yourself. Quickly!"

"I'm a Traveler."

"I know that!" The demon's voice blared in the closed space.

Mara drew her knees to her chest and covered her head with both arms. Her hand brushed something as she did this. She groped for it, grasped it just as the demon seized a fistful of her hair and yanked her off the ground. A stone. A broken piece of cobble.

The Belvora held her up so that her eyes and the demon's were barely a hand's width apart. With her other taloned hand, the Belvora raked a finger across Mara's cheek. Her claw came away bloody. She grinned, licked the finger clean.

She opened her mouth, to speak or to feed. Mara didn't give her the chance. Her scalp aching, blood dribbling over her jawline, she pounded the stone into the side of the demon's head with all the strength she could muster.

The Belvora reeled and bellowed, dropping Mara to the street.

Mara landed awkwardly, but scrabbled away. The demon roared again and pursued. She kicked out with a clawed foot, catching Mara's shoulder. The force of the kick tore Mara's flesh and flipped her over as if she were a child's doll.

The demon bent over her. Though dazed and in pain, Mara managed to throw the stone. It hit the Belvora in the chest and bounced away. She might as well have thrown it at a rock wall.

"Enough," the demon said, as much to herself as to Mara.

She dropped to her knees over Mara – a feeding position. She raised her hand, talons extended to rip open Mara's gut. Mara sobbed.

Another weapon boomed in the alley, much closer than the others. The demon twisted and screamed. Mara covered her ears.

A second shot. The demon fell against the nearest wall, but righted itself. Dark blood flowed from wounds to its back and side.

Tobias and Bramm sprinted at them. Tobias reloaded his pistol as he ran. Bramm bore a sword.

The Belvora glanced at Mara, considered the approaching men, and spread her wings. She leapt into the air, her wingbeats uneven and weak.

Bramm leapt, slashed at the Belvora with his sword, slicing through part of a wing. The demon crashed onto the nearest roof, writhing, keening. It fell off the building and landed beside Mara. Before it could stand or even crawl, Bramm struck at it again.

Mara dragged herself to the far side of the alley. When the creature's severed head rolled free, she closed her eyes.

Tobias rushed to her, gathered her in his arms. At her gasp of pain, he examined her shoulder.

"This doesn't look good," he said. "We need to get her back to the ship."

"Sofya," Mara said.

"She's safe. She's with Ermond."

Mara shook her head, addled still, desperate to make him understand. "There's a Tirribin. Working with the Belvora. She's headed to the ship. Probably there already."

"Blood and bone!"

"Go, Tobias. Save her."

"Bramm?"

"Go! We'll get there as fast as we can."

Tobias kissed Mara's brow and eased her down to the stone. Then he was running, his steps receding into the night.

In a blur of Tirribin speed, she slipped by sailors and wharfmen, peddlers and laborers. She passed several children, all of them filled with sweet years. There was no shortage of suitable prey in the city this night. Any of them might have satisfied her hunger.

Still, Aiwi didn't stop. She didn't even slow.

It would never have occurred to her to bargain with a Belvora. She disliked the winged ones. They were dim, and crass, and they smelled awful. This female, though – there was more to her than most. And she offered the most tantalizing of treats.

For Tirribin, nothing used up a city faster than taking children. Grown humans grew vengeful, inconveniently vigilant. So Aiwi had long contented herself with sailors, merchants, wharfmen.

The Belvora, however, had offered a true child. Not ten. Not even eight. A tiny one, barely more than an infant. The sweetest years imaginable, filled with promise, unsoured by disappointment or loss or grief.

And so she entered the bargain. Freely, and fairly.

Only after sealing their bargain, on pain of Distraint, did Aiwi learn she had been cheated. Oh, there was a child, young as the Belvora said.

But its years were already tainted by misfuture, bittered by profound changes in the trajectory of her life. Aiwi would feed on them anyway. They would be sweeter than most. But the perfect innocence of an infant's years, which she had thought were hers for the taking, had long since been lost.

As she neared the wharf, she slowed to human speed.

Weapons fire crackled behind her. She wondered if the Belvora was dead. If so, she was free to abandon this hunt. The Distraint was only binding so long as all parties involved lived.

She couldn't be certain though, and the promise of those years compelled her toward the ship. She crept along the pier, clinging to shadow.

The smell reached her while she was still well short of the vessel: sharp, foul. Belvora blood. A good deal of it.

The ship's deck teemed with men and women, all of them bearing firearms and blades, all of them alert to the possibility of further danger. Another disservice done her by the winged ones.

Never again would she submit to any bargain with their kind.

She caught the scent of the babe as well. Not perfect, but lovely just the same.

Aiwi slid into the water, giving the ship and its humans a wide berth. She hated swimming, but she wouldn't allow that to keep her from this feeding, particularly with the punishments of the Distraint possibly looming over her.

She moved in silence through the harbor, barely disturbing its surface, always keeping to shadow, even here. She approached from the open water west of the wharf and soon reached the ship's stern. She climbed the hull, clinging to the wood like a spider on stone, and followed the contour of the ship around the side of the vessel to the oar holes. Once inside, she sensed that the child was in a hold above and behind this one.

She crept to the stairs, climbed them until she could peer out over the deck. Sailors crowded the rails, looking toward the city. A few scanned the sky.

She spotted the other hatch. At Tirribin speed, she crossed the deck to that stairway and blurred out of sight down into the hold.

The aroma of the babe's years was almost overwhelming here. It was intoxicating.

"Don't move."

A sailor stood between her and the child, who slept on a small pallet. He was thick, powerful looking for a human. His brown hair was straight and salted with silver. Humans might have thought his eyes pale.

He held a sword in one hand and aimed the barrel of a flintlock at her chest with the other.

"I know what you are," the man said. "Even with your powers, a bullet can kill you."

"Yes." She moved slowly, stepping away from the stairs, giving herself a clear path to the man and the child beyond him. "And I know about that weapon in your hand. You have one bullet. If you miss me, you'll die."

He adjusted his grip on the pistol. She sensed his unease.

"One shot, and every man and woman on deck will be down here. You can't kill all of them."

A fair point, but for her surety that she was faster and stronger than he could imagine.

"Perhaps we can reach some accommodation," she said.

He shook his head and started to respond, but already she had blurred to speed. She was on him before he could say anything, before he could fire the pistol.

She slapped it from his hand, still moving at Tirribin speed. It hit the floor, bounced away. By then she had scrambled up to his neck and latched on. She took several of his years.

Something bit at her shoulder. Hot, painful. She released him, retreated a quick step. Blood poured down her arm, dripped to the floor from her elbow.

The man gaped at her, his breathing labored, his features sunken, the skin around his eyes and mouth wrinkled. He appeared ten years older than he had.

Her blood glistened on his sword. He was better with a blade than she had credited.

"You should not have done that," she said, her voice coarse with rage and pain.

He cried for help. Footsteps scraped overhead, and then on the stairs.

Aiwi dashed past him, snapping her needle teeth at his face and delivering a sharp punch to his gut. He shied from her, grunted at the blow. All the time she needed to grab the child.

It started to squall the moment she touched it. It twisted and fought her, kicking its tiny feet and swinging its arms.

The man dove for the pistol and aimed it at her once more.

Men and women streamed into the hold, more weapons pointing at her. Only the babe kept them from shooting. Aiwi held it before her, a screaming shield. For the first time she could remember, she feared for her life. And because of humans. It was intolerable.

A tall woman stepped to the fore. She, too, carried a pistol, and she projected an air of unflappable strength.

"Put down the child and we'll let you leave here alive," she said. "If you take her years, or harm her in any way, we'll open fire. With all the flintlocks in this hold, one of us is bound to hit you."

Another human pushed his way down the stairs. She sensed his years and knew him for the other Walker. The throng parted for him, and he came forward, halting when he stood shoulder to shoulder with the woman.

"Your Belvora friends are dead," he said.

Aiwi glanced around, making certain that none of the other humans tried to attack her. She doubted the man understood the significance of his words.

When she didn't respond, he raised his pistol. "They will have offered you your life in exchange for the child's. They're afraid to fire because you're holding her. I'm not. I'm good enough with a flintlock to kill you where you stand."

"Then why don't you?" she asked.

"I know several Tirribin, and I count them all as friends. I prefer to let you live."

Not what she had expected him to say.

"I also know an Arrokad, one who has promised me a boon. Shall I call for her? Shall I let her see you as you are now, surrounded by humans, trapped like an animal, a child in your hands? What would she say? What would she think if she knew you had allied yourself with Belvora?"

Clever.

"The question, human, is whether you are prepared to trade my life for this child's. I don't believe you are."

She raised the screaming babe and put her mouth to its neck. It was all she could do to keep from feeding right there. She didn't, because she didn't wish to die this night.

"No!" The man lowered his pistol.

"Make them put down their weapons."

Indecision clouded his expression. Aiwi darted out her tongue and licked the side of the child's neck.

"Make them do it now!" she said, the rasp deepening her voice again.

"Do as she says," the human said, a plea in his words.

Slowly, reluctantly, the others lowered their pistols and set them on the floor. It seemed Aiwi might get away after all, and with the babe.

"Ujie," the man said.

Aiwi frowned. "What did you say?"

As she spoke, the answer dawned on her. It had been a summons. Already, she sensed a power approaching at speed. The Arrokad he'd mentioned.

She didn't wish to be on this ship when the Most Ancient One arrived. Even this child wasn't worth such humiliation.

Aiwi threw the babe. As she expected, the man lunged to catch the girl before she fell. She darted past them all, up the stairs, and onto the deck.

"Hold, cousin!"

Aiwi halted, body swaying. She pivoted, the motion feeling excruciatingly slow after the blur of her escape from below.

An Arrokad stood on the ship's deck, a female, her body still glistening with seawater, her argent eyes fixed on Aiwi.

"I was summoned by a human," she said, in a voice like crashing waves. "Are you the reason?"

"She is," the man said, emerging from the hold, his pistol reclaimed, the babe in his arms.

Aiwi wished she had killed him and the child when she had the chance.

CHAPTER 25

25th Day of Kheraya's Descent, Year 634

The Arrokad appeared just as Tobias remembered her: beautiful, alluring, terrifying. Her skin was pale aqua and as smooth as a sea-tumbled stone. Blue-black hair hung to the small of her back, and shining, slitted eyes raked over the deck of the *Dove*. As Captain Larr and her sailors joined Tobias on the deck, he heard gasps and exclamations of alarm from those behind him. He heard sighs as well, from several of the men and a number of the women.

"You called an Arrokad to my ship?" Larr asked from behind him. "You thought this wise?"

"I thought it necessary." His eyes didn't stray from Ujie. "No harm will come to your ship. I promise. Ujie and I have... engaged in commerce before. She has reasons to want me alive."

"Walker," Ujie said. "You summoned me to settle a dispute with this Tirribin?"

"I summoned you to save us from her, which you've already done. She tried to take the years of this child."

Ujie regarded the Tirribin, and then Sofya, appraisal in the gaze. "The one you told me of before."

"That's right."

"I was simply hunting, Most Ancient One," the Tirribin said, wringing her hands. "I didn't realize that the human was your friend. I would never have–"

"Hunting on a ship filled with other humans? This early in the night?"

The Tirribin didn't answer, but glanced at Tobias, a plea in her pale eyes.

"Why do I smell Belvora blood?" Ujie asked. She glanced around. "The city is rank with it."

"We killed two here," Larr said.

Tobias tucked his chin. "And another in the lanes."

"Allies of yours?" Ujie asked the Tirribin.

The Tirribin stared, mouth open in a small "o."

Footsteps on the wharf below drew Tobias's attention. Bramm guided Mara toward the ship, one hand holding the elbow of her wounded arm, the other on her good shoulder. They reached the plank. Sailors from the ship headed down to help them.

"Tell me why, cousin?" Ujie said.

Tobias faced the demons again.

The Tirribin peered at her feet, her lips pressed thin.

"Tell me!" Ujie's words crashed like breakers in a storm, making the Tirribin jump.

The Tirribin pointed at Sofya. "You have to ask? Look at her!"

Tobias gripped the princess more tightly. Sofya gave a small cry and tried to break free of his grasp.

"Her years are... Even marred by a misfuture, they're so sweet. I can smell them from here."

Mara gained the deck. Tobias went to her, but she steered him back to the demons, intent on the Tirribin. Blood glistened on her shoulder and seeped from a ragged gash on her cheek. She was bruised, limping. She didn't seem to care.

"Who sent you?" she demanded, halting in front of the time demon. She glanced at Ujie. An instant later, her gaze snapped back to the Arrokad.

Ujie smirked. "You will answer her, cousin."

"The Belvora," the Tirribin said, pale eyes flicking between Mara and the Arrokad. "I entered a bargain with them. Freely and fairly. They promised me the child. In return I was to deliver the Walkers."

Ujie considered Mara again, eyes narrowing. "You *are* a Walker, and yet your magicks are confused. I sense more in you."

"I Span as well." To the Tirribin, Mara said, "Who sent the Belvora? Why did they want us?"

"That I don't know."

"I don't believe you."

The Tirribin bared her needle teeth. "Careful, human." A rasp coarsened her voice. "I will not be called liar by one such as you."

"They told you nothing?" Tobias asked.

"That's right. And I didn't ask. They promised me her years." She dropped a covetous glance to Sofya. "I cared for nothing else."

"Well, it can't be just happenstance that three Belvora would attack us here, so far from northern waters."

"I agree," the Tirribin said. The corners of her mouth twitched. "Perhaps you shouldn't have been so quick to kill them."

"Did they say what drew them here?"

"No."

Tobias wasn't sure he believed her.

"She tells the truth," Ujie said, perhaps sensing his mistrust.

He thought it unwise to ask how she could be certain.

"The Tirribin bleeds from a wound to her shoulder. Did she take any years?"

"Mine."

A man came forward, his steps stiff. It took Tobias a moment to recognize Ermond. He winced at what he saw. The man had aged years this one night, all because Tobias had entrusted him with Sofya's safety.

"How many, cousin?" Ujie asked.

The Tirribin shrugged with infuriating equanimity. "Ten years, perhaps. Maybe a few more."

Captain Larr took a single stride in the Tirribin's direction, her hand falling to the hilt of her sword.

Ujie stepped in front of the time demon. "Do not!"

"This is a valued member of my crew. And your friend took years off his life."

"My 'friend' is a hunter. You are prey. It is as simple as that."

"Are prey never allowed to fight back?"

Ujie's smile was even more frightening than the Tirribin's. "Do you honestly believe you can prevail in a fight with a Tirribin? Even wounded, she will kill you with ease."

"Then why do you protect her?"

"Because I will not allow a mob of humans to harm her." To Tobias, Ujie said, "You summoned me, which, as you know, carries a cost. We bargained in good faith some turns ago – boons promised at some future date. I have fulfilled my side of our bargain. You will fulfill yours."

Apprehension shaded Mara's hazel eyes. "What is she talking about?"

"I speak of an arrangement the Walker and I made some time back," Ujie said, before Tobias could answer. "You were not there and are not a part of this conversation."

"She's my wife," Tobias said. "So she is part of it."

The Arrokad made a sharp, dismissive gesture, one Tobias had seen from her before. "I care nothing for human unions. We have a bargain, freely entered and fairly sworn. I will take you now to the sea. If you survive our encounter, you may return to her." She bared her teeth again. "I assure you, though, after being with me, she will not satisfy you. No human female will."

"Wait," Captain Larr said, slanting a glance at Tobias. "Are you telling me that you're going to take him for... for..."

"For sport, yes. Do not be concerned. He will enjoy the experience as much as I will. More perhaps."

"Isn't there some other boon–"

Ujie cut Tobias off with that same hand motion. "We have spoken of this before, you and I. I require no wealth as humans count it. I have more knowledge than you ever will. But I do find your kind most... entertaining." She regarded Mara. "Perhaps you would offer your mate in your stead?"

"No," Mara and Tobias said in unison. They shared a glance.

"I'll go."

All of them looked at Ermond.

Ujie considered him. "You are too old, I think."

He pointed at the Tirribin. "Only because of her."

The Arrokad answered with a slow nod. "You speak true. I might reverse what she has done. That power lies within my grasp. You would come with me to the sea freely?"

His cheeks colored. "I would."

Her smile this time was hungrier, less menacing. As devoted as Tobias was to Mara, he couldn't deny that her expression stirred him in ways that made him blush.

"A new bargain, then," Ujie said. "I will restore your years, and you will entertain me for a time. Yes?"

Ermond straightened. "All right, then."

"Freely entered and fairly sworn?"

"Ermond—"

"It's all right, captain. I know what I'm doing. Freely entered and fairly sworn," the sailor repeated.

Ujie eyed Tobias. "You still owe me a boon, Walker. And rest assured: I will collect."

Tobias could only nod his agreement. "Thank you," he said to Ermond.

"If she gives me back the years I lost, I'll count myself fortunate."

"What about the Tirribin?" Mara asked.

Ujie appeared to ponder the question. "She will leave here, whole, unpunished beyond the wound she already bears. And she will swear not to hunt you again. Agreed?"

"All of us," Tobias said, knowing from his experiences with Droë, and also Teelo and Maeli, that he needed to be as specific as possible. "Mara, Sofya, and me, and everyone else on this ship."

"Just so."

"She's to stay away from us, as well. And she shouldn't speak of us to anyone."

The Tirribin didn't hesitate for long. "Agreed," she said.

"Go then, cousin. I trust I will have no further cause to treat with you."

"Yes, cousin." The demon blurred to the plank, descended at

Tirribin speed, and sped into the city.

Ujie sauntered to where Ermond stood, passing within two hands of Tobias. He caught her scent – rain, sweet lightning, brine, seaweed. It made his head spin, like the finest Brenthian wine. She walked a slow circle around Ermond. The sailor's face shaded bright red, and his breathing deepened. Some among his fellow sailors regarded the Arrokad with fear, but as many eyed the demon with desire, and their friend with envy.

Ujie took his hand and led him to the larboard rail.

"We'll wait for you here," Captain Larr said.

"There is no need. I do not wish to rush our time together." She lifted her tapered chin in Tobias's direction. "I am linked to the Walker. I can bring him to you no matter where you are."

She didn't wait for a reply, but lifted Ermond into her arms like he was a mere child, and leapt over the rail. The rest of the crew, as well as Tobias and Mara, rushed to that side of the ship. Aside from a slight ripple in the moonlit surface of the harbor, Tobias saw no sign of them.

"Do you believe we'll see him again?" Larr asked.

"I do. Arrokad may not think much of humans, but they do care about commerce and bargains, and they keep their promises."

"Very well. I'd suggest then that we leave these waters with first light. It's too dangerous to remain."

"I agree. Must we wait for morning?"

She took a breath and scanned the ship. "No."

She pivoted away from him and barked orders at the rest of her crew. Sailors readied the ship for departure.

Tobias took Mara below with old Yadreg, who was as near to a healer as the *Dove* had. Together, they cleaned her injuries. Yadreg prepared a poultice for her shoulder, and Tobias tore strips of cloth for a bandage. Mara held Sofya on her lap. The princess chattered happily, oblivious to all they had been through this night. She did point to the gash on Mara's cheek, but even that seemed to amuse her.

After helping Tobias wrap her wound, Yadreg left them. Tobias led Mara to their pallet and had her lie down. Sofya remained wide awake; he sensed she was hungry. Mara, in contrast, could barely keep her eyes open.

"You survived a fight with a Belvora," he whispered. "Is there anything you can't do?"

"Apparently I can't please you the way an Arrokad would."

He laughed, his cheeks warming. "I'm not sure I believe that." He kissed her brow. "How are you feeling?"

"I hurt everywhere." She exhaled the words, her eyes closing.

"Sleep. You'll feel better come morning."

"I'll feel terrible in the morning and you know it."

Tobias kissed her again. "I didn't say which morning."

By the time he took Sofya above, the *Dove's* crew were rowing the vessel into the harbor. Tobias joined the captain on the quarterdeck.

"I'm sorry," he said. "I know you didn't wish to leave the Knot so soon."

She shook her head, her expression grim. "You didn't wish to leave the waters near Chayde. And since sailing southward, we've encountered storms and demons. I should have listened to you."

He wondered if she intended to pilot them back to the northern islands.

"I have in mind to sail to the Ring Isles," she went on after a brief silence, dashing his hopes. "You and Mara have spoken again and again of finding Bound devices. I believe it's time we did that."

"Despite the dangers" he said.

"Yes. You have talents – both of you. The ship will profit if you can use them. And you'll feel safer if you can go back in time or if Mara can Span."

He heard the logic in what she said. But he saw no good choices before them, no safe harbors. If Orzili knew enough to send Belvora to the Knot, they weren't safe anywhere. Either the assassin was bearing down on them already, or he had dispatched the winged demons to every corner of Islevale. Either way, tonight's events were likely harbingers of greater perils to come.

"You have another idea?"

"I wish to return to Chayde," he said, unable to stop himself. "Maybe Mara and I can make a life for ourselves somewhere on the isle. The people who are after us might not think to look there."

The captain studied him, her lips pursed. "We can take you there, but I thought that you intend eventually to place Nava on the Daerjen throne."

"We do."

"Forgive me for saying so, but that's not something you can do on a whim, when you decide she's ready. It will take planning, foresight. You'll need allies, not just in Hayncalde, but also in Daerjen's other cities. You might need help from Aiyanth and other kingdoms. You can't arrange all of that from a place of hiding. Yes, you can spirit her away to some remote village. That may well be your safest course. Or you can prepare to install her as the ruler of Daerjen, which would be more perilous. I don't believe you can do both."

Tobias held the princess to him, as if beset by Belvora, and he stared at reflections on the water from the ship's torches. He feared he might weep at the truths he heard in what the captain said. In many respects, he and Mara were children still themselves. The masters and mistresses of Windhome had taught them well to be diplomats, ministers to royal courts. But planning and executing an insurgency was beyond them, or at least beyond him.

"I'm sorry," the captain said. "We've all had a difficult enough day without…"

He shook his head, and she trailed off.

"You've done nothing wrong, captain. I needed to hear that."

Sofya struggled in his arms. He set her on the deck and stared after her as she walked away, her steps sure despite the motion of the vessel.

"How old are you, Tobias?"

He went still, afraid to reveal anything with a change in his expression. Others had asked this of him, and he had put them off with evasions, lies, even pleas that they not press him. Captain Larr was different. He and Mara owed her everything. More, after sailing with the woman for so many turns, he trusted her completely.

This, though – he and Mara had held to this secret even as others had been stripped away.

"I know a bit about Walking," she said. "I know the cost it exacts. You've come back very far, haven't you?"

"Very," he said in a whisper.

"I've suspected as much. You don't have to tell me. I ask mostly because I want to assure you that no matter how daunting your task, my crew and I won't allow you to do it alone." She stared after Sofya. "I didn't want her on the ship. I didn't want any of you. You know that." She faced him, ferocity in her dark eyes. "Now, I'd kill for all of you. And I'd die for you as well."

Tobias could think of no worthy reply, except one.

"I'm nearly sixteen," he said, his voice still low. "Mara is a bit older – nearly seventeen."

Larr stared, shock and sympathy in her gaze.

"Most of the time, I don't think of us as being that young." He gestured at himself. "I don't think of us as being this old, either. We're caught in between."

"I would think. Why did you Walk so far?"

This secret had long since been robbed of its value. The future from which he had come was lost, and so too was the new history he and Mearlan had hoped to create.

"I came back at the request of Daerjen's sovereign. We hoped to prevent a war. Instead I precipitated his assassination."

"Mara came back with you?"

"She came back later, for me, to help rebuild the future we'd lost." He thought of her sleeping in the hold, shuddered at how close he'd come to losing her this night. "I gave up all those years because the sovereign asked me to, and I believe I was right to do so. Mara – she came back out of love, or rather her belief in the possibility of love."

Larr frowned, turning the ship's wheel a few degrees. "I don't understand."

"It's… complicated." He exhaled, heard Sofya give a whoop of laughter. "That first night, when you granted us passage on your ship, you mentioned a Binder in Aiyanth, and a peddler who traffics in Bound devices."

"I remember. She can be found on Aiyanth as well. In Belsan."

"Then that's where we should head next."

"You're certain?"

"No," he said. They both smiled. "I'm tired of running. Of hiding and being afraid. Even if we retreat to the hills of Chayde, Orzili will find us." He indicated the princess with a lift of his chin. "He won't give up his search for her, and his reach is long. He tried to have me killed in my own time, and somehow he followed me into this past. If he can do that, he can track us anywhere. So maybe our choice isn't between hiding in safety on the one hand, and planning for the restoration of the Hayncalde line on the other. Maybe our choice is between being killed while standing still and dying while fighting back. In which case, it's an easy decision to make."

Her grin conveyed many things. "Well said. With a favorable wind and clear weather, we should be there within a turn, perhaps sooner."

"Thank you, captain."

He walked forward, to where Sofya entertained several members of the crew. His fear lingered, but he felt lighter.

Yes, Orzili might find them, but on some level he'd known since escaping Hayncalde's dungeon that he would face the assassin again before this was over.

So be it.

Aiwi watched the ship from a crag high above the city, her limbs trembling. Rage, shame, frustration: she couldn't have said which afflicted her most. They boiled inside her, searing her heart, robbing her of her ability to hunt, to move, to think. She stared, and she fumed, and she railed at herself for her own helplessness.

Her shoulder throbbed. The injury would heal quickly; injuries to her kind always did. In the meantime, the mortification of having been dealt a wound by a human rankled, further darkening her mood.

She was Tirribin. She was a hunter. She couldn't recall ever feeling this weak.

She knew the Most Ancient One was to blame as well. She had prevented Aiwi's escape, presided over her humiliation, meted out her punishment. It was a dangerous thing, though, to bear a grudge against an Arrokad. They were canny, inscrutable. They possessed magicks Aiwi scarcely understood. Safer then to direct her wrath at the humans. The Most Ancient One had prohibited her from striking back at the Walkers and the child, but she could avenge herself on others of their kind. She would take some small satisfaction in that. Soon. Tonight she brooded, too consumed by her emotions to do more.

In time, she tired of sitting and returned to the city, to the lanes near the wharves, to the hunt. She fed without enthusiasm, and wandered along the waterfront, always keeping that ship within sight. She couldn't have said why. She didn't dare strike at them, but neither could she bring herself to ignore the vessel.

"I smell blood. We lost kin this night, did we not, cousin?"

Aiwi whirled, hands raised, fingers clawed, a snarl on her lips.

Another Arrokad stood in the moonlight, harbor water pooling around his feet and running down his body.

"Do you intend to fight me?" he asked, amusement in his flawless features.

"Do you intend to be rude?"

He canted his head, acknowledging the riposte. "Forgive me. I did not mean to startle you, nor do I wish to be rude. My name is Qiyed."

She lowered her hands, straightened out of her crouch. "I'm Aiwi."

"A pleasure to make your acquaintance."

Why couldn't the Most Ancient Ones leave her alone? "And yours."

He laughed. "I do not believe you."

That coaxed a smile from her. They began to walk together along the water's edge.

"Now I'm being rude. I'm sorry. How can I be of service to you, Most Ancient One?"

"I would know who spilled Belvora blood this night."

Her face colored with the realization that she would have to revisit her shame. One did not keep information from Arrokad.

"Humans," she said. She pointed. "On that ship."

He considered the vessel. Then they resumed walking. "Why?"

"The winged ones attacked."

"Again, I ask: why?"

Her cheeks flamed.

"I sense your unease," Qiyed said. "I assure you, I ask out of curiosity and nothing more. I have no ties to the humans, and no affection for Belvora. When Ancient blood is spilled, we among the Most Ancient must learn the truth of what happened."

"One of your kind already knows."

Aiwi regretted the words the moment she gave them voice. Qiyed halted, forcing her to do the same. She didn't know if she could have gotten through this encounter without revealing Ujie's role in events, but she sensed that she should have tried.

"There was an Arrokad here tonight?"

"Yes."

"Did he or she give her name?"

She reflected on their confrontation aboard the vessel, hearing good fortune in the phrasing of his question. The human spoke Ujie's name in his summons, but the Arrokad never did. Some of her humiliation might remain hidden from this creature and thus others.

"No, Most Ancient One. She did not."

"A female then."

"Yes."

"Intriguing." He started walking again. She followed. "Belvora

would only attack a ship bearing humans if they sensed magick."
He tossed an expectant glance her way.

"A Walker, Most Ancient One." Aiwi wasn't sure why she played
this game with the Arrokad. Something in his manner made her
cautious, mistrustful. She feared revealing too much; she didn't
know why.

"A Walker," he repeated, clearly interested. "The one responsible
for the current misfuture?"

She couldn't mask her surprise. Even Arrokad, as powerful as
they were, could not sense the threads of time the way Tirribin
did. "How do you know of this?"

He answered with only a smile.

Rude. She didn't dare say so.

"You did not answer my question. Is he the one responsible?"

"I believe so."

"Is he alone? Or are there other Travelers with him?"

She should have known he would think to ask this, too. "He's
not alone. He voyages with a second Walker."

"Two Walkers. A man and a woman?"

Aiwi nodded.

"Which of them injured you?"

She muttered a human oath within her mind. For all their
flaws, humans did know some rather satisfying profanities.

"A sailor aboard the vessel. I attacked him. He cut me."

"That is unusual, is it not? A human managing to wound a
Tirribin?"

"You're being rude again," she said, sounding petulant, unable
to stop herself.

"Nevertheless."

"I was distracted." Her tone remained hard. "He was protecting a
child."

"Ah, yes. Young years: a weakness of your kind."

She didn't reply.

"Why did the other Arrokad not heal your wound? I would have."

Enough. She couldn't hope to keep anything from this Most

Ancient One. Better she should tell all and end this encounter. "She was punishing me. For helping the Belvora, and for attacking the Walker, who had entered a bargain with her some turns back. Freely and fairly."

"And why were you helping the Belvora?"

"They promised me the child, who belongs to the Walkers. They wanted all three of them dead, and so we chose to work together. They would take the Travelers and I would have the babe. The humans proved more capable than we anticipated."

"Most interesting," Qiyed muttered. "Most interesting, indeed." After a few steps, he asked, "Do you know why the Belvora wanted these particular Walkers?"

"I don't. They didn't tell me and I didn't ask."

"It does not matter," he said, his voice still low. "With what you have told me, I should have no trouble learning the rest." He favored her with a smile seemingly free of irony. "You have been most helpful, Aiwi of the Tirribin. I am grateful to you."

A thrill of magick danced over the wound. The throbbing ceased. She looked down at her shoulder. The slice in her shift had mended. She pulled up the sleeve. Her skin had healed.

"Thank you."

"You earned such consideration. Go in peace, cousin. Do not speak of our conversation with anyone else." He bared his teeth. "You have my word that I will be equally discreet."

"Again, my thanks, Most Ancient One."

He turned from her and waded out into the calm waters of the harbor. Aiwi started back toward the city. Before she had gone far, the Most Ancient One spoke her name. She halted and faced him.

"What was the name of the other Arrokad, Aiwi?"

Her shoulders dropped fractionally. "Ujie, Most Ancient One."

"Thank you," he said and left her.

CHAPTER 26

17th day of Sipar's Fading, Year 618

For more than a ha'turn after Cresten's encounter with the smugglers, Quinn kept his distance. He often eyed Cresten from across the tavern, but he said not a word to him. Despite Cresten's desire to take on more jobs, the innkeeper seemed unwilling to place his life at risk again.

Cresten didn't push the matter. For now Quinn's guilt outweighed his need, but that wouldn't last. He liked having a Spanner in his employ; he wanted to "play with the big boys." Before long, his misgivings would fade.

In the meantime, Cresten continued to cut gaaz and practice his Spanning and sword work. Several times, Droë joined him on the strand. Neither of them mentioned the smugglers, or what she had done to help him. Cresten noticed no change in their interaction. He felt safer with her, though, and he no longer worried about her spying on him as he Spanned.

With what he had earned from Quinn and Poelu, and what remained of the coin Chancellor Samorij had given him, he had more money than he could spend. He hid his purse in the straw of his pallet, where he hoped Lam wouldn't think to look. He hadn't yet decided what he would do with his treys and quads, but he knew they were the key to whatever future he chose to pursue. He had reconciled himself to never seeing Lenna again; he wouldn't remain in Trevynisle for her. But where should he go?

The question kept him awake some nights, the thrill of possibility holding sleep at bay. He wasn't so foolish as to think himself rich. In time, though, if he was smart…

Quinn finally approached him on a stormy night in Sipar's Fading, as Cresten ate roasted fowl and stewed greens in the tavern. He was bone weary after another long day in the shallows, and he didn't realize the innkeeper had walked to his table until the man asked to join him.

At Cresten's gesture, Quinn sat. He narrowed his eyes, staring at Cresten's healing wound.

"Can't hardly see a mark. I don't think you'll even have a scar."

"Guess that means girls won't think I'm handsome."

Quinn hesitated, then smiled, as if just remembering their exchange with Claya. "You'll do all right, I think." He glanced at Cresten's platter. "You want more?"

"No, thank you."

The old man nodded, his gaze roaming the common room. Cresten sipped his watered wine.

"I was wonderin'," Quinn said, "if you meant what you told me that night. That you was still willin' to work for me."

"I'm willing, under the right circumstances."

Quinn frowned. "What's that mean?"

"I want seven treys, five quads next time, and every time after."

"You said before you were satisfied with five."

Cresten shrugged. "I changed my mind. There seems to be plenty of gold about. I'm guessing you can afford an extra two and five."

"That so?"

He lifted his shoulder again. "If I'm wrong, you don't have to hire me. I'm sure there are plenty of other Spanners out there, willing to risk their lives with smugglers."

Quinn's brow bunched. "How'd you know they was smugglers?"

Too late, he remembered that the white-haired woman at the shop had said this in confidence.

"It wasn't hard to figure," he said, after the briefest of pauses. "You never told me what was in the parcel, and those men on the ship weren't like any sailors I've known."

Quinn's look soured, but he didn't argue. He eyed Cresten, then let out a sigh. "Seven and five is fair. No more, though. I might have raised your pay after a time. You're gettin' that raise now, you catch?"

"All right." He leaned forward, bracing his arms on the table. "What's the job this time?"

The innkeeper grinned. "You enjoy it, don't you? The danger, I mean."

Why deny it? He would have worked for Quinn even without more pay. "I do."

"Well, don't take chances you don't have to. It's your life, but it's my coin. And Paegar's."

"I understand."

"Good. Meet me in the back courtyard when you're done eating. I'll tell you more there."

He stood and walked away, not bothering to wait for Cresten's reply. Cresten bolted down the rest of his meal, drained his cup, and left the table. He stopped in his chamber to make certain his sextant and purse were safe, and then made his way to the courtyard. Quinn joined him there.

This newest job, planned for the following night, was similar to the last one. Cresten would act as courier for Paegar, some smugglers, and another merchant.

The next morning, when Cresten walked to the gaaz beds, he carried with him a change of clothes and a knife given to him by Quinn. He hid these in the same place he had used the previous time, cut bricks under a bright sun for the entire day, and plodded back to the inn, exhausted beyond words. More storms darkened the sky as he walked. By the time he reached the tavern, a torrent had soaked him.

After his evening meal, he retrieved his sextant and left the inn for the rise. Quinn offered to accompany him, but Cresten demurred.

"I know what I'm doing," he said.

Droë appeared mere moments after he reached the strand. His vision still swam from his passage through the gap, and he barely had time to pull on his breeches.

"You Spanned here," she said.

"I have work to do tonight."

She regarded him, grave as a ghost. "The same as last time? With those men?"

"Different men, but yes, the same."

"I'll come with you."

"You don't have to." He spoke with surety, but hoped she would anyway. He didn't want Quinn watching his every move, but he welcomed the Tirribin's protection.

"I don't mind." She bared needle teeth. A hint of rot sharpened the air around them. "I might even get another meal out of it." She laughed, high and crystalline.

Cresten tried not to shudder.

She accompanied him to the wharf, remaining hidden while he treated with the smugglers. Then she walked with him into the heart of the city, where he delivered his parcel.

They returned to the waterfront, and Droë held Quinn's gold while Cresten paid the smugglers. From there, they walked back to the strand so he could Span back to the rise, Moar's five rounds held under his tongue. The entire transaction took less than a full bell. No one threatened him, or tried to harm him. Quinn paid him and let him know more jobs would be coming.

The innkeeper proved true to his word. Three days later, he met with different smugglers and bore their goods to yet another merchant, this one not far from the wharves. All went as it should, but as Droë walked with him back to the strand and his hidden sextant, she broke their customary silence.

"I saw your friend last night."

"My friend?"

"Lenna."

He stumbled, nearly fell.

"Is she all right? Did she mention me?"

"She's healthy, for a human. Her years are more confused than I remember. She's been Walking a good deal, honing her craft. She's leaving."

Cresten halted in the middle of a narrow lane. "Leaving?"

"That's why she called for me. I didn't want to enter the palace, and I think she was afraid to ask me to come, but she wanted to speak with me once more."

Leaving. Lenna is leaving.

He had resigned himself to not seeing her or speaking with her. But to know she would no longer be at the palace...

"Where is she going?"

"Herjes."

At first he thought the Tirribin must be mistaken. Windhome's lone Walker – its first Walker in years – and they were sending her to Herjes? Not Milnos or Vleros? Not Aiyanth or Daerjen or Oaqamar?

Thinking about it more, however, he saw logic in the assignment. Herjes wasn't a great power, nor was it prone to frequent wars, like the Bow and Shield. But trade in spices, firearms, and wines had brought the isle considerable wealth, it was strategically located near Aiyanth, Milnos, and Westisle, and its young leader was said to be ambitious. What better way to raise his isle's status than to outbid other powers for the services of a Windhome Walker?

"Is she excited?" he asked, his voice flat.

"I think she's frightened, but yes, excited, too."

They resumed walking, neither of them speaking. He couldn't bring himself to meet Droë's gaze.

"I told her I had seen you."

He eyed her sidelong. "And?"

"She wanted to know how you are and what you've been doing."

"You didn't–"

"I told her you cut gaaz and make money working for a tavern keeper. That was all I said."

Cresten couldn't say if he was relieved or disappointed. His existence, described that way, sounded boring, pathetic even. If the Tirribin had said, *He treats with smugglers,* Lenna might have feared for him, and disapproved. She might also have been impressed.

"She told me to tell you that she's sorry for all that happened, and that she misses you."

"Truly? She said that?"

Droë nodded, still studying him. "Do you think that means she loves you?"

More than anything, he wanted to say yes. It would have been a lie, though, to her, and to himself. "No. It means she's sorry and she misses me. Nothing more."

They covered the remaining distance to the shoreline in silence. Cresten's stomach had soured, and he feared the Span to the rise would sicken him.

She's leaving. She's going to Herjes. You'll never see her again. She'll find someone, marry, have a family, a life. You won't be a part of it.

More than ever, he wanted to leave Trevynisle. Not to follow her, but simply to be gone, to forget her.

Seven treys, five quads. It will take years to earn the coin you need.

"I've made you sad," Droë said, halting near the spot where he had left his clothes.

"Leaving the palace made me sad. This is…" He shrugged, made a small, meaningless gesture. "I'm glad you told me. Thank you."

Droë smiled at that and blurred away.

Cresten undressed slowly, folding his clothes with undue care, and set the rounds under his tongue. He aimed his sextant, thumbed the release, and hurtled into the gap, his senses so dulled that this once he didn't mind the journey or think it overly long.

When he returned to the tavern, the innkeeper regarded him, concerned and suspicious.

"What happened?" he asked.

"Nothing. It all went as it was supposed to."

"Then why do you look like you saw a ghost?"

Cresten shook his head. "I'm tired. That's all." He held out his hand.

Quinn gave him his treys and quads. "No trouble with the smugglers? Or in the city?"

"It was all fine. I swear. When will you send me out again?"

"Soon, lad. Very soon."

Cresten nodded and retreated to his room, wishing he could sleep for a turn or two, knowing he would be up with the dawn and back under Poelu's critical eye. His last thought before falling asleep was that at least one of them was getting out of Trevynisle.

Quinn gave him a fourth job a few days later, and a fifth soon after. Cresten completed both without incident.

Two nights later, Quinn sent him out again. This time his instructions were slightly different.

"Paegar wants to see you," the innkeeper said. He didn't seem happy about this. "He wants you to come to his door. Says he wants to make sure you're following instructions."

"You don't believe him?"

Quinn didn't answer right away, and Cresten wondered if he should have swallowed the question. But the innkeeper surprised him. "I think he wants to hire you direct, instead of through me. He could probably pay you more and still save some coin that way." Quinn eyed him, awaiting a response.

"I work for you," Cresten said. "And even if he pays me more, I'd have to start paying for my room again, wouldn't I?"

Quinn smiled. "You're a smart lad."

As it happened, the merchant this night was the same white-haired woman he met the night the smugglers tried to kill him. He had yet to deal with any merchant or smuggler a second time. He wondered if this further increased the danger.

Quinn insisted on accompanying him to the rise, and as Cresten prepared to Span he said, "Have a care tonight, lad. This is a more... sensitive item than the others you've delivered. Make sure you're not followed."

Cresten assured him that he would.

Droë joined him at the strand, as always arriving with uncanny precision, just after he slipped on his breeches. They walked together to the waterfront, where Cresten searched for a ship called the *Kelp Runner*. She was the last boat on the longest of the three piers, and he thought her deserted. He approached the vessel warily, scanning the wharf, expecting to be waylaid. Droë, he knew, watched from a distance, ready to blur to his rescue should any threat arise. Still, he felt vulnerable. Quinn's warning had set him on edge.

"Ahoy, the *Kelp Runner*," he called from below her rails.

Silence.

He glanced back at Droë before trying again.

After a fivecount, he heard motion within the vessel and then footsteps.

"Ahoy," came the response, the voice deep but thin, like distant thunder.

A shadowed form appeared above him, framed against a darker sky.

"Who's that?" A man's voice, the words thickened by an accent Cresten couldn't place.

"I was sent by Quinn."

"Who is Quinn?"

Cresten stared up at the silhouette. This had never happened before. "Quinnel Orzili."

"Never heard of him."

"He's… You should have a parcel. Something I'm supposed to deliver. And then bring you gold."

The man didn't answer.

Instinct drove him to say, "He works with Paegar."

The man might have nodded. "Wait there."

He stepped away from the rail, vanishing from view. A short time later, Cresten heard more footsteps, closer this time. A plank at the ship's stern. A man – perhaps the same one – emerged from the darkness, stopped a couple of paces short of Cresten, and held out a small, pale parcel.

Cresten reached for it, only to have the man snatch his wrist with his other hand.

"What's your name?" he asked in that elusive accent.

Cresten should have lied, but in his fear could only manage the truth. "Cr- Cresten Padkar."

"Padkar. Easy to remember. That thing in your hand – not much you can do with it, but to us, very valuable. Muck this up, or try to steal, and we spend the rest of our days hunting you. Catch?"

He dipped his chin.

The man squeezed his wrist, grinding bone on bone. "I say, you catch?"

"Yes, I understand."

The man released him. "Go. Bring us our gold."

Cresten took two steps backward, then pivoted and hurried away, his wrist aching. The parcel was small but heavy, the cloth around it rough against his fingers.

Droë fell in step with him as he reached her.

"You're frightened," she said, the hint of a rasp in the words. "What happened?"

"It's nothing. I'm fine."

"I thought I heard him threaten you."

"It's all right, Droë. These are rough men. Sometimes they threaten. He didn't hurt me." *Much.*

He wondered if she could tell he was lying. They didn't speak as they navigated the lanes to the merchant's shop.

"Ah, Quinn's friend," the white-haired woman said as he closed the door behind him. She favored him with a smile.

"What do you have for me tonight?"

He crossed to the wooden counter and handed her the parcel. She hefted it, her smile slipping. She glanced up, meeting his gaze, then turned and pushed through the dark curtains to the back of her establishment. When she returned, she carried three purses. She lifted them one at a time. "Moar's, the... the sailors'." She raised the third. "And this is for Quinn. Payment for something else."

"All right." Cresten placed one purse in each pocket and tied Quinn's to his belt. "Thank you."

By the time he emerged from the shop, the moon had risen, red and hazed. Dim shadows stretched across the lanes. The city looked like it had been dipped in blood.

At the wharves, Cresten approached the ship once more and called a greeting.

"Padkar," came the reply, immediate and unaccented. "Leave it on the plank."

"The plank–"

"At the stern. Leave it and go."

A shiver went through Cresten, and his legs shook. He set the purse on the plank, and strode back to the lane as quickly as he could without running.

"It was all right this time?" Droë asked as he joined her.

They started back toward the strand.

"I think so. I hope so." He peered back at the ship. Even with the moon higher in the ebon sky, he couldn't see the plank, much less the purse he had left there.

Once at the strand, he asked the Tirribin to hold Quinn's gold, and to give him a few moments of privacy. He stripped off his clothes, put Paegar's gold in his mouth, and Spanned across the city to the man's house. He dressed, approached the door, and knocked.

The door opened, revealing the young woman he had seen last time. She didn't give him time to speak. Disdain curled her lip, and she shouted for her father.

Moar came to the entry a tencount later.

"The Spanner," he said. "I've been waiting for you."

"Yes, sir."

Cresten held out the rounds, and Moar plucked them from his palm.

"Everything went as it should?"

"So far."

Moar frowned. "So far?"

Cresten feared he had said too much. "Yes, it's all been fine."

Moar stepped closer, looming over him.

"You have more to do? Have you been to the ship yet?"

"Yes! I was only– Quinn said you wanted me to come here." The words tumbled out of him. "I need to retrieve something for him and go to the tavern."

"Well, you'd better be moving on, then. You should be finished by now." He gestured at the bulge under Cresten's shirt: his sextant. "Everywhere you go with that bloody thing, you draw attention to yourself, and to our affairs. You catch?"

"Yes, sir."

"Get out of here."

Cresten spun and left, heart pounding. He searched for anyone who might be watching him, but saw no one. As he removed this set of clothes he decided that Moar's fears were unfounded. Paegar and Quinn both – they had convinced themselves that all the world cared about their business.

He thumbed the release on his sextant and sped back through the gap to the strand. There, he pulled on his breeches, not bothering with his shirt. He called for Droë. She blurred into view and stopped beside him, the purse held out before her.

"You're not as frightened now," she said. "I'm glad."

"Thank you, Droë. I'm grateful for all your help."

She canted her head and smiled up at him. "So you want me to go with you next time, as well?"

"If you don't mind."

"I don't mind at all," she said before leaving him. "I like it. I'm glad we're friends."

At the rise, Cresten stumbled out of the gap, his head aching, the world around him spinning. Too many Spans this night. When he could manage it, he pulled on his clothes one last time and staggered down the hill to the tavern. He walked in a weary daze, only taking notice of his surroundings as he neared the *Brazen Hound*.

He halted. Something was wrong.

The quiet. Aside from a dog's distant barking, he heard nothing. No voices. No laughter. He surveyed the building. The windows had been shuttered, though it was a mild night. No light leaked out around their edges or seeped from the door.

The door, which stood ajar.

Cresten drew his blade and crept forward, hand shaking. He almost called for Droë, but wasn't certain she would come. His breathing sounded loud, his every footstep echoed like cannonfire.

He pushed the door. It swung open a short distance before catching on something. He couldn't tell what.

But the stench knocked him back a step. The iron smell of blood, overlaid with the stink of human feces and piss.

Cresten eased inside, his eyes adjusting to the gloom. Bodies littered the floor. Claya and the other serving girls lay in a cluster near the bar, their throats slit, blood pooling around their bodies.

Lam's corpse had stopped the door, his body cleaved from neck to groin. The smell of shit came from him.

And from Quinn, sprawled on the floor of the common room, gutted as well, his throat carved open for good measure.

Cresten walked to him, breathing through his mouth, fighting not to be ill. He would miss Quinn. The innkeeper had been good to him, had given him work and taught him a few things. But theirs had been a partnership born of opportunity and mutual need, and this was no time to grieve.

A creak from the door made him whirl and tighten his grip on the knife. The hinges squeaked a second time. The wind.

Time to go.

He ran to his chamber and reclaimed his belongings, including the hidden purse from within his pallet. He strapped to his belt the short sword he had taken from the palace armory, and swung his carry sack onto his shoulders. Quinn's gold hung from his belt.

I have money now. I can go anywhere.

He returned to the great room, scanned the carnage again, and eased out into the moonlight, taking care to leave the door as he had found it.

"Spanner."

He stiffened, hand still on the doorknob.

"You would have been better off not coming back."

CHAPTER 27

28th day of Kheraya's Fading, Year 619

Cresten wheeled, his blade hand slick with sweat. Paegar Moar stood in the street, flanked by two men. All of them held swords. Moar's blade gleamed with moonlight. Dried blood darkened the weapons of his toughs.

They hadn't come to talk or scare him. For reasons Cresten didn't understand, they wanted him dead, as they had Quinn, Claya, and the rest. He darted back into the tavern. Slammed the door shut and dropped to his knees. Heedless of the blood, he shoved Lam's body. The stink made his eyes water, and at first the corpse wouldn't budge. At last it gave, with a wet, sucking sound that made his stomach squirm. He pushed it flush against the wood, just as Moar and his men reached the door and threw their weight against it.

He lurched to his feet and backed away, eyes wide in the darkness. His foot caught and he nearly tripped.

Quinn's body.

Turning again, he hopped over the innkeeper and ran to Quinn's chamber. Moar and his men hammered at the door and at the shutters of a window.

Cresten rifled through the drawers of Quinn's desk until he found what he sought: a flintlock, ammunition, powder, and paper. Another blow to the door shook the building.

Cresten left Quinn's chamber and tiptoed through the kitchen to the dark passage beyond. It led to the entrance he and the innkeeper used whenever Cresten Spanned. As he walked, unable to see a thing, he loaded the pistol. Albon had insisted that he and the other novitiates learn to prime a flintlock blind. Now he understood why.

The building rocked again. Cresten thought he heard wood splinter.

At the end of the corridor, he unlocked the door, the click of the bolt loud enough to catapult his heart into his throat. He prayed to the Two that Moar and his men hadn't heard. He eased the door open and stepped into the alley behind the inn. Before he could close the door, leather scraped on stone.

He whirled.

A bulky form. Reflected moon glow. The whistle of steel slicing cool air.

Cresten dropped to the cobbles. A sword swept over his head. Prone on his back, Cresten aimed and fired.

A blaze of fire lit the byway. The report blared. A man stumbled back against a wall, dropped a sword, toppled to the street. Dogs barked nearby. Acrid smoke clouded the lane.

Men shouted within the tavern and from the next lane over. Scrambling to his feet, Cresten fled, loading his weapon again, spilling as much powder as he managed to put in the barrel.

Footsteps sounded behind him. His carry sack bounced on his back, and the sword strapped to his belt slapped his leg, slowing him. He ducked down a narrow lane, cut toward the center of the city, hoping to lose them in the confusion of Trevynisle's oldest streets.

After a series of turns, he found himself near the shop of the white-haired woman. He heard no pursuit, and allowed himself to hope he had lost them. Knowing he took a risk, he headed to the shop. The woman might have been working with Moar. Or she might take pity on Cresten and protect him. A chance worth taking; he could fight her off if he needed to.

He found the shop dark, and assumed she had left for the night. He tried the door. It swung open, the bell above the frame ringing like a fanfare. Cresten spat a curse, listened for footsteps. Hearing none, he entered the shop but left the door open, lest he stir the bells again. He saw no sign of a struggle, no blood-soaked corpse in the middle of the shop floor.

This eased his mind. He stepped around the counter, intending to search the back room where the white-haired woman stowed the items he brought her.

A mistake.

She lay in a puddle of blood behind the counter. Her throat had been slit, too. Her eyes were open, fixed on the ceiling, and she clutched something in her right hand. His heart labored, his breath came in gasps, but he squatted and pried her fingers open.

A door key. Probably she had been about to lock the shop when she died.

Whispers from outside chilled his blood. He raised his head slowly and peered over the counter toward the front window. Moar and his toughs stood in the lane. Moar spoke to the men, pointing at the shop, and both ways down the street.

Cresten snaked his arm up over the edge of the counter and took aim, steadying his trembling hand on the wood. He would have to shoot through glass, so he aimed for the center of Moar's torso.

He pulled the trigger. The pistol bucked, boomed. Glass shattered. Moar fell, clutching at his thigh. His men dove to the cobbles.

Moar roared at them to give chase. Cresten crawled over the woman's body and through the curtains. Then he stood and searched frantically for a second door to the shop, aware of the toughs closing in on him. He tried to load again, but dropped the first bullet. He had time for no more than that.

Moar's men pushed through the curtains. Cresten dropped his pistol, drew his short sword.

They separated, coming at him from different angles.

"Should've kept running, boy," one of them said. "Now you're a corpse."

Cresten still held the powder purse for the flintlock in his off hand. He leapt at the man who had spoken, feinted with his blade. The tough raised his sword to block the blow. Cresten flung the contents of the purse at the man's face.

Albon would have called it a waste of Aiyanthan powder.

The tough screamed and clawed at his eyes, his sword clattering to the floor.

Cresten hacked at him, striking him at the base of the neck once, twice. The man fell, blood spewing from the wounds. Cresten reeled in time to parry an attack from the second man. The force of the blow drove him to his knees. A second forced him onto his back. The man hewed at him again. He blocked this strike as well, but the tough's blade skipped off his own and bit into his forearm. He grunted at the pain. The tough leered.

Cresten rolled to evade another attack and kicked out with both feet. One missed. The other slammed into the tough's knee. The man staggered, growled an oath.

Cresten rolled again, putting distance between himself and Moar's man. He clambered to his feet. The tough stalked him, limping now.

The man lurched at him, swung his blade. Cresten ducked away, tripped into the wall, righted himself before he fell. The man came after him. He was slow, strong but predictable. He jumped at Cresten again. Cresten spun away from the blurring sword and countered with a slash of his own. Blood blossomed from a gash on the man's side. He grabbed at it with his other hand. Cresten danced forward as the weapons master had taught him and chopped at the man again, opening a second wound on his sword arm.

You fight to live, to win. It doesn't have to be pretty.

Albon's words, whispered in his mind in the master's voice.

Moar's man slashed at him, but this strike was slower, less powerful. Cresten stood his ground, parried. His counter nearly severed the man's head from his neck. The tough collapsed in a heap of blood and flesh and forgotten steel. He didn't move again.

Still gripping his sword, Cresten reclaimed his pistol and

stepped between the curtains. Moar was still on the street, resting on one knee, his bloodied leg stretched out to the side. Cresten spotted the pistol, dove as a tongue of flame brightened what remained of the shop's window. The report thundered an instant later. The bullet struck the wall above him.

Moar bellowed his frustration. Fighting through fear, Cresten forced himself up. He dodged around the counter, flung open the door, and charged the man. He pounded at Moar with his sword. Moar blocked the strike, but had to drop his pistol and powder to do so. Cresten kicked the flintlock away. Moar waved his blade at Cresten, the attack weak and ineffective. Blood glistened on his breeches and on the cobbles beneath him.

"Why did you kill them?" Cresten asked.

Moar laughed. "Why should I tell you?"

Cresten hammered at him. Moar blocked the first blow, but couldn't fight off the second. Cresten's blade bit into his shoulder. Moar dropped his sword, and Cresten snatched it up before he could recover it.

"Because if you don't, I'll kill you. Like I killed your men. All three of them."

I've killed three men tonight.

His stomach knotted at this. He would pay a price for spilling blood, for the things he had seen. Quinn, Claya, the white-haired woman… Not yet, though. Not until he was away.

Moar eyed the shop and then Cresten, calculation and pain in his gaze.

"You killed the two in there?"

"That's right. Palace boy, remember?"

"There's gold enough to go around, you know. Mine." Moar tipped his head toward the shattered window. "Hers. Quinn's and the smugglers'."

"I have Quinn's, and I'll take yours when you're dead."

Moar flinched. "There's no need for that. I need new men. Quinn trusted you. And I've use of a Spanner."

"At the first opportunity, you'll put a knife in my back."

"I think you're right," said another voice.

They both turned. Moar looked more puzzled than frightened. He didn't understand how much more perilous his situation had grown.

Droë sauntered to them, hair shining, moonlight in her milky eyes.

"You shouldn't trust him," she said, glancing up at Cresten. "You should let me have him."

"Maybe I will. First, I need information."

Her smile could have rimed the cobblestones and storefronts. "I can help with that." She played with a strand of hair. "I heard the shots. Others did, too. I'm faster, of course, but they'll come before long."

"What is she talking about? Who is this?"

Droë considered him. "He's rude. So many of the men you deal with are rude."

"He's worse than rude. He tried to kill me. He killed the man I worked for, and the serving girls in the tavern, and the woman who owned this shop."

"Why?" she demanded in a rasp.

"He hasn't told me."

She stepped closer to Moar, baring her teeth. Moar recoiled. Fear distorted his features.

"What are you?"

"I can take his years," she said. "One at a time, until he tells you what you want to know. I'd be glad to do it."

"A time demon. You're friends with this... thing?"

"Very rude indeed." Her rasp had deepened, slurring her words.

"That's right," Cresten said. "Now, why did you kill them? Why did you want me dead?"

Moar didn't answer.

"Help yourself, Droë."

She grinned, then blurred to Moar and attached herself to his throat. That same shifting, oily glow surrounded them. Moar cried out, flailing at her. Then the light was gone and Droë stood off a few paces. Moar held his hands to his neck. His chest heaved. His face might have appeared leaner, more deeply lined.

"That was one year," Cresten said. He looked to Droë for confirmation. "You should have enough left to make this a very long night."

Moar cast a desperate look at the Tirribin. "It was a stone, a gem. Very valuable."

"That doesn't explain why you would kill for it." He thought of the men he encountered on the wharf, the first with that odd accent, the second without it. "You even killed the smugglers, didn't you?"

Again, Moar faltered.

Droë flew at the man, latched on to his throat again. Moar wailed. Droë retreated, hunger in her wide, pale eyes. Moar sagged and let out a choked sob.

"It was stolen from Milnos," he said. "A royal gem, revered for centuries. I was to send it on to a man in Vleros."

Of course. The accent of the man on the *Kelp Runner*. He hailed from the Bone Sea – probably Vleros.

"Why?" Cresten asked him.

Moar gazed up at him. This time, he didn't have to say a word.

Droë coiled to attack again, but Cresten stopped her with a raised hand.

"It's all right. He doesn't have to answer. I understand."

"You do?" she asked.

"He means to start a war. That's all it would take, isn't it? The alleged theft of a priceless heirloom."

Moar nodded.

"Who wants this war? Who hired you?"

"I don't know."

Cresten flicked a glance toward the Tirribin. He might as well have pressed the barrel of his flintlock to Moar's brow.

"I swear to you! I was paid, told what to do. That's all. I don't know who it was."

"How did they pay you?"

"Courier. A lad from a ship."

"Dead now?"

Moar didn't reply.

"You can have his years, Droë."

"No! I have gold. Heaps! You can have it all!"

"Your gold is meaningless as long as you're alive and this scheme of yours goes on. You've killed to preserve the secret. We both know you'd kill me, too." He nodded once to the demon, and turned away.

A strangled cry, the frenzied scrape of cloth and flesh on stone, and Cresten's faint shadow cast onto the shop wall by shifting, colored light. In the short time it took Droë to feed, the first inkling of a plan came to him: a place to go, someone who might be glad to see him.

"I should leave you," Droë said when she was finished, her voice still husky with need. "That wasn't enough to sate me."

Cresten faced her, unafraid, certain she wouldn't harm him. "I understand. You should know, though, that I have to leave Trevynisle. Others may be hunting for me. And I have no place to stay, no humans left here who know me or care about me."

Her brow creased, the expression of a hurt child. "You have me."

"You'll always be my friend," he said. "But I can't stay here. I want… I want more of a life than Trevynisle can give me."

"Very well." She sounded distressed. "Farewell then. I really must go."

She didn't wait for his reply, but blurred away toward the waterfront. At the same time, men appeared at the other end of the lane. Cresten bent over Moar's body, trying not to look at the dead man's face. And failing. Cresten could see every contour of his skull, the desiccated lips pulled away from his teeth in a permanent grin.

He searched the man's pockets, found a ring of keys, several rounds of gold, a few treys and quads, and a small blade. The parcel wasn't here. Cresten took the keys and money, and also took Moar's powder purse to replace the one he had emptied. Then he fled.

The men shouted for him to stop. A few briefly gave chase, but all of them halted in front of the shop.

Cresten didn't stop running until he reached Moar's house. The windows were dark, making him wonder if Moar had killed his own family. He considered trying a key, but first he pounded on the door with a closed fist.

Someone stirred within the house. Candlelight illuminated the edges of the shuttered windows flanking the door.

"Don't you have your bloody key?" a woman's voice demanded from within. The door flew open. "I was—"

Seeing Cresten, she clamped her mouth shut. It was the same dark-eyed woman he'd seen earlier. Belatedly, Cresten realized that he had an open wound on his arm, blood on his breeches and who knew where else.

"He's not here."

Cresten met her glare. "I know."

They stared at each other, his reply hanging between them. Understanding smoothed her scowl, deadened the anger in her eyes. A tear ran over one cheek. She swiped at it and looked away.

"Damn," she whispered. "You were there?"

"Yes."

Too long a hesitation.

She regarded him again, features hardening. "You killed him." Before he could answer, she added, "I'd wager he gave you no choice."

Cresten dug into his pocket and produced the coins he had taken from Moar.

"This was—"

She gave a hard shake of her head. Tears flew. "I don't want it. There's blood all over it."

"You'll need it. You and the child."

That gave her pause. Cresten held the coins out to her. After a moment, she took them.

"You're young," she said.

Not after tonight.

"I suppose."

"Don't grow up to be like him," she said. She withdrew into the house and started to close the door.

"Wait!"

She stopped.

"I need to come in, to search for something. I think he left it here tonight. It's... it's important. If others learn that you have it, they'll come here."

The woman smirked. "You fear for our safety?"

"No. I'm thinking of myself. I want it." He pulled Moar's keys from his pocket, and held them up for her to see. "I could wait and steal it from you. I'd rather not."

She stared at the keys and then at him. Finally, she stepped out of his path and motioned him into the house.

"His study is this way."

Cresten followed her along a narrow hallway to a door at the back of the house. She tried to open it, but it wouldn't give. She glanced back at him and held out her hand. Cresten gave her the keys. After unlocking the door, she moved aside and allowed him to enter the room. It was small, cluttered. The parcel sat in the open, atop a sheaf of papers on a standing desk.

Cresten took it and turned.

"That's all?" the woman asked.

"That's all."

"You work for Quinn, don't you?"

"I did. Quinn's dead. Your father killed him, along with everyone else who worked in the *Brazen Hound*."

She showed no surprise, but glanced at the wound on his arm. "Did he do that?"

Cresten shook his head. "One of his men." He exhaled. "I'm sorry that–"

She cut him off with a sharp gesture. "Just go."

He stared, and she suffered his gaze. At length, he tucked his chin and left her. As he exited the house, he slipped the parcel into his carry sack. Then he loaded his flintlock.

Cresten crept through the city, wary of every shadow, alert to every sound. He had given his name to the men on the ship, and the man who spoke to him upon his return to the vessel knew it as well. He would have to leave that name here. Trying to secure passage on a ship from Windhome's wharves might cost him his life. He veered at the next corner. Instead of walking to the waterfront, he made his way to the city gate. Along the way, he paused in a deserted alley to change out of his bloodied clothes. He left them in a pile on the stone.

The gate guards asked him a few questions. Where was he going? Why was he leaving so late in the evening? What did he have in his carry sack? The lies came easily. He'd had a fight with his father, the last in a long sequence. He was going to live with his uncle on a farm near the southern shore. His sack held all his belongings. This last, of course, was true. The guards let him pass.

Only when he had covered some distance along the track to Ghell, the next port town along Trevynisle's western coast, did it occur to him that this was the first time he'd been away from Windhome since his parents sent him to the palace all those years ago.

Cresten walked through the night, reaching Ghell the following morning a bell or two past dawn. He had coin enough to buy himself breakfast at an inn. From there, he went to the waterfront and secured passage on a Kant headed to Belsan, on Aiyanth, by way of isles in Sipar's Labyrinth. Belsan wasn't his final destination, but this ship, the *Isle Strider*, out of Bellisi, was leaving soonest, which mattered to him most.

"What's waitin' for you in Belsan?" asked the *Strider*'s first mate, as he made a careful count of Cresten's payment.

"Nothing. In time I'll be going to Caszuvaar."

The man, narrow-shouldered and lean, looked up at that. "Caszuvaar? We're not headin' there."

"I know. I'll find passage there once we reach Belsan."

"You could sail out of Windhome, and get there direct."

"Probably," Cresten said. "I hear Windhome is a long walk."

The sailor shrugged. "Suit yourself. It's your coin. One of the crew will show you where to stow your things, and where you'll be sleeping. You know anything about crewing a ship?"

"No, but I'm willing to learn."

The man grinned. "Good on you, lad. You oughta fit in fine." He started to turn, but stopped himself. "What's your name?"

Cresten had pondered this as he walked. Chances were no one would think to hunt for him here, or in Belsan, or Caszuvaar. But he couldn't be certain, and he wouldn't risk his life by clinging to a name his father had poisoned for him years ago. Cresten Padkar, he'd decided, ceased to exist the moment he left Windhome.

The men who might be after him would know that Quinn was dead. They had no reason to ask after him. And Cresten now realized that for all the man's faults, Quinn *had* been a friend. Other than Albon, he'd been the closest thing to a father Cresten ever had.

"My name is Quinnel," he said. He liked the sound of it, and couldn't help but smile as he tried on his new identity. "Quinnel Orzili."

He voyaged through waters and visited lands he had only known from books and Windhome lessons. He swabbed decks, cleaned holds, mended sailcloth, and learned all he could about sailing ships. He ate fish he had never heard of, sampled fruits that were unlike anything he had ever tasted, and taught himself the difference between the wines of Miejis and Brenth.

He worked on two more ships after the *Isle Strider*, and at last came to the Bone Sea and Milnos, a land of arid mountains, sprawling vineyards, and dark green groves of blacknut trees.

Life on ships had been to his liking, save for three days of stormy waters in the Oaqamaran Sea. That, though, had been enough to convince him that his future lay on dry land. He left this last vessel with no regrets, and followed a broad stone lane from the wharf, through the city of Caszuvaar, to the royal palace, perched on a gentle rise above the lanes and buildings. Palace guards, in smart uniforms of green and blue, stopped him at the gate. They appeared more amused than alarmed by his presence – a lone boy in worn clothes, his hair long and wild, his Northisler's skin darkened further by sun and wind. Perhaps they thought he had approached on a dare from unseen friends.

"My name is Quinnel Orzili," he told them, respectful but uncowed. "I would like to speak with your King's Spanner, Fesha Wenikai."

The woman to whom he directed his request glanced at the older soldier beside her.

This man asked, "Does she know to expect you?"

"No. But if you tell her that a certain beetle she knows has come to speak with her, she'll see me."

"'A certain beetle.'"

"That's right." He hoped she would remember him, that she would consent to see him. He tried to conceal his doubts.

The man nodded to the younger soldier, who strode into the palace. The guards who remained watched Cresten but said nothing to him. Before long, the young woman returned and whispered briefly with her superior. They searched his pack, made him leave his flintlock and sword at the gate. To Cresten's relief, they ignored the parcel he had taken from Paegar's home.

The young soldier escorted him into the palace, across courtyards of red stone and past fountains and sculptures and elaborate gardens.

Milnos had long been allied with Oaqamar, and so Cresten had viewed the isle as an enemy, a kingdom in which he hoped never to serve. It hadn't occurred to him that the palace of Caszuvaar could be so magnificent.

They entered a tower through an arched portal, climbed a broad marble stairway, and followed a corridor past paintings and busts to a door made of pale, veined wood. At a knock from the soldier, someone within the chamber called, "Enter."

The guard opened the door for Cresten and waved him inside.

Wink stood in the middle of the room, looking much as he remembered, save for the robe she wore, which was green satin, trimmed in silver.

"Spanner Wenikai," he said, bowing to her.

"It really is you." She walked closer, scrutinizing him. "You've grown. You're not a kid anymore."

"You're one to talk."

Wink grinned, glanced down at her robe. But she sobered quickly. "What are you doing here, Cresten? Why aren't you in Windhome? You're not old enough to be a court Spanner."

"No, I'm not. And it's not Cresten anymore."

For a half-bell and more, as they sat near an open window, he shared with her nearly all that had befallen him since her departure from the Travelers' Palace. A few times she interrupted him with questions, but mostly she listened in silence, staring out the window toward the Bone Sea.

Even after he finished, she didn't stir, until at last she turned his way. "I'm sorry. Sorry for all you've been through, but also because I don't think I can help you. You're a friend, but I'm afraid that won't mean a lot to my king."

"I thought as much," he said. "But I left out one detail: the smugglers I killed had something that was stolen from Milnos." He opened his travel sack, lifted out Moar's parcel, and handed it to her.

Wink regarded him, and then the bundle. She peeled away the stained cloth and gaped at the object it had covered.

Cresten sat forward to get a better look. He had been too rushed that first night to examine the gem, and too leery of revealing what he carried to look at it later.

It was a polished orb of crystal about the size of his fist, swirled in blues and greens, translucent, iridescent, flecked with gold. It gleamed in the late day sun, entrancing.

"It's called Drayla's Jewel," Wink whispered. "It's... There isn't enough gold in all of Milnos... For turns now, its disappearance has consumed the entire court. There's been talk of war."

"That was the idea," Cresten said. "Someone intended to smuggle it into Vleros. I don't know who or why."

Wink straightened, met his gaze. "It doesn't matter. You're about to be a hero. The king will let you stay as long as you like. He'll probably make you rich."

The way she said this…

"I'll share what he gives me. Honestly, Wink–"

"It's all right. I have all the gold I need. And it sounds like you earned this." She stood. "Come along. We need to request an audience with His Majesty."

Cresten stood as well, abruptly feeling nervous.

"It'll be all right. He can actually be quite kind." She grinned. "And he doesn't know that you're just a shit-beetle."

Cresten smiled at this, and followed her from the chamber.

CHAPTER 28

30th day of Kheraya's Descent, Year 634

After her conversation with Lord Orzili in Hayncalde Castle, Gillian convinced herself she wouldn't have to endure too many more days with Bexler. Orzili spoke confidently of contacting her again, of sending her somewhere, of supplying her with coin. How could she not hear in their exchange a promise of adventure to come?

She returned to the flat that first night, escorted by a soldier, elated at how well the encounter had gone. Bexler seemed happy enough with the payment she brought from Orzili. They celebrated with a sumptuous meal and a flask of Miejan red. She allowed the Binder to take her to bed, and even managed to enjoy herself.

A qua'turn at most. So she told herself that night, as Bexler snored beside her. Surely, Orzili wouldn't make her wait longer than that. Another qua'turn, or perhaps a bit more, to prepare for her departure and arrange passage aboard a ship. She would be on her way before the end of Kheraya's Stirring. Anticipation brought a smile in the darkness.

They would send her to Aiyanth. Or maybe Ensydar, or Milnos, or somewhere in the Labyrinth. That night, the possibilities struck her as limitless and magickal.

But word didn't come within a qua'turn, or a ha'turn, and her elation withered. She spent much of each day listening for messengers at their door, her spirit darkening with every bell. Bexler waited for the materials required to build the tri-sextants, his mood nearly as foul as hers. They stalked about the flat, avoiding each other, saying next to nothing. He was so absorbed in his own misery that he never stopped to question what caused hers. Probably he didn't notice; he wasn't exactly blessed with empathy for others.

Gillian blamed the woman, the one who entered Orzili's chamber the day she visited the castle. Something about Gillian's presence had disturbed her. And Orzili had made a point of saying he would consult with her about Gillian's desire to work on their behalf. No doubt the woman convinced him to search elsewhere for his spies. Well, damn her. Damn them both.

Still, she held out hope. Orzili had sounded so certain.

Another qua'turn crawled by. A shipment of gold arcs arrived, allowing Bexler to resume his work. If anything, this made matters worse. His mood improved. He grew more attentive to her emotions, at least when he wasn't Binding. She knew why, of course. He was as predictable as he was self-absorbed. He wasn't a fool, though. He soon grasped that she awaited word from someone. The questions that followed infuriated her, even as they filled her with guilt.

"Who would send you a message? And why? Who did you see when you went to the palace? What did you talk about?"

She told him as little as possible, but she couldn't ignore him entirely. Invariably her cryptic answers begot more questions, until every conversation became a joust.

"What kind of work would you do for them? Why would they need spies here? Where would you go? How long would you be gone? When did you intend to tell me all of this?"

This last proved hardest of all.

Never.

That would have been the most honest answer, and a part of her longed to speak the word. The longer she waited for Orzili's message, however, the more she doubted that one was forthcoming. Once again – still – she had no choice but to rely on him, his magick, his ability to earn gold.

She held her tongue, smiled when he spoke to her. She meted out her affection, being as miserly as she could without alienating him completely.

All the while she continued to wait and hope, though the latter required more and more effort.

It rained the day a fold of parchment finally slipped under their door. Bexler had left the flat for the market, Sipar be praised. She didn't know or care what he sought. All that mattered was the message.

"Prepared to engage services. Come tonight."

She read the message three times, its meaning sinking in by degrees. Relief, excitement, the revival of her early elation. All of it overlaid with panic. How was she to prepare without drawing Bexler's suspicion?

Gillian scrawled "Received" on a tiny roll of parchment, tied it to the leg of one of their remaining pigeons, and sent the bird on its way. She packed her things, her pulse racing, sweat souring her gown. She decided to leave before he returned. She would pass the day at an inn or tavern, or in the market if she could avoid him. She would wander the lanes if she had to. Because if she didn't flee the flat now, she never would.

She considered leaving a note, but that would only alert him to her intentions. He might search for her, or worse, go to the palace and ruin everything for both of them. She wasn't sure he loved anything or anyone other than himself, but if he did, he loved her. Best then to let him think she had run an errand. By the time he realized she wasn't coming back, she would be beyond his reach.

As she emerged from their building onto the street, she saw him coming. She ducked out of sight, hid in shadows as he climbed the stairs to their flat, and slipped into the lane once their door closed. She heard him call her name as she rounded the corner onto the larger street, but she didn't slow.

She found a small tavern and for several bells sat in a dark corner at the back of the great room, sipping a passable Fairisle white. When night fell, she made her way through the lanes toward the castle. A fine rain misted the city; puddles shone among the cobblestones. The streets were largely empty; each time she heard footsteps, she thought it must be Bexler. She pulled her cloak tight about her shoulders and watched the cobblestones ahead of her. She passed several patrols of soldiers, and a few men and women hurrying through the rain to their homes. She didn't see the Binder.

Recalling her last visit to the palace, she readied herself for a confrontation with the gate guards. It seemed, though, that Orzili had sent word that she would be coming. The soldiers at the outer gate let her pass. At the inner gate, a woman in uniform greeted her by name. She escorted Gillian to Orzili's chamber, knocked, and, at a word from within, waved her through the doorway.

Orzili stood at his desk, the side of his handsome face lit by hearth fire, his bronze hair pulled back in a loose plait. He glanced her way, then looked again, taking in the bag she held.

"I didn't intend for you to leave tonight."

She swayed, cheeks aflame, unsure of what to say. She felt like an overeager child. How could she possibly go back to the flat?

Silence stretched between them. He set aside the parchment he'd been studying.

"It's all right," he said. "I hope to have passage arranged for you by tomorrow. I'm sure we can find a chamber for you tonight."

"Thank you," she said, barely managing a whisper.

"How go the sextants? Do you even know?"

She nodded. "Th- the second is nearly done. He went to the market today seeking materials for the third. I don't know if he found them."

"Does he hurt you?"

She straightened, mortification battling with outrage. And losing.

"No. If he did, he'd be dead by now. I don't love him. I'm not sure I ever have. Do you know what it's like to be trapped with someone you're supposed to love but don't?"

His expression turned brittle, and he pivoted back to his desk. "I don't. I suppose I've been fortunate." He reached into a drawer and withdrew a leather purse. "The coin I promised," he said. "Enough to cover expenses for a time. You'll need to find employment once you arrive, but that was always going to be the case. People need to believe you belong there."

"Of course." She crossed to him, took the purse. This close, she could smell him. Sweat, bay, a hint of spirit on his breath. She wondered if the woman she saw last time was his wife, or his mistress. "Where will I be going?"

"I'm sorry, I thought you knew. We're sending you to Aiyanth. Are you familiar with Belsan?"

"Somewhat, yes."

"Good. We think he might need a chronofor."

"He does. His was broken the night of Mearlan's assassination." Orzili's gaze sharpened. "How do you know?"

"He asked Bexler to fix it. Before he realized we were working for the Sheraighs, of course."

"Why didn't you tell me when last we spoke?"

"I didn't think of it. That day was… confused. So much happened."

Disapproval creased his brow. "I'll expect your reports from Aiyanth to be more thorough."

"Of course, my lord."

He huffed a breath. "As I was saying, you're to go to Aiyanth. There are few places one can hope to find a Bound device. The Belsan marketplace is one. You're to listen for word of inquiries about chronofors. Report any to me."

"By bird?"

"Yes. You'll take three of mine with you. I'll have them brought to you in the morning."

"Thank you."

"Is there anything else, minister?"

The dismissal felt abrupt, but she fixed a smile on her lips. "No, my lord."

"Fine. Let's find you quarters for the night."

She followed him to the door, waited as he summoned a steward.

Soon an older man arrived and relieved her of her bag. She should have followed, but instead had the steward wait in the corridor. She crossed back to Orzili, who had returned to his desk.

He eyed her.

"Yes, minister?"

"Forgive me, my lord. The last time we spoke, you asked if I could kill. I'm wondering if I should prepare myself–"

"No," he said, his tone flat. "That won't be necessary. When the time comes I intend to kill the Walker myself."

Belsan in the growing turns was as fine a city as Gillian could imagine. Its bay sparkled under clear skies, and ships carved to the wharves on warm westerly breezes. The city's homes and shops, built of white stone and roofed with blue-gray tile, glowed under the hot sun. Storms blew through the city, bringing wind and lashing rain, but they soon moved on, leaving Belsan clean and smelling of lightning and brine.

Foods and wines from every land between the oceans flooded the marketplace, all of it fresh and cheap.

Gillian rented a flat on a cozy lane two corners from the market square. It was close enough to the waterfront to be inexpensive and to bring little notice to its lone occupant. Yet it was far enough into the city to keep her clear of the worst smells from the low lanes.

She found work as a shopkeeper for an old merchant. He was white-haired, but hale and ruddy. As a younger man, he might have been handsome. Gillian thought him the perfect employer. He fancied her, doted on her unabashedly, and paid her a good deal more than she would have expected for such work. But he was too proper to make advances, or even speak of his attraction. She greeted every kindness as she would a father's attentions. If this frustrated him, he gave no indication of it.

When she wasn't at his shop, she was in the marketplace, chatting amiably with men and women selling their wares, seeking out those who might traffic in Bound devices. At first, it seemed a different set of peddlers descended on the square each day. Soon, she came to understand the rhythm of the place. Ships came to the Axle, unloaded their goods, and moved on. For a time.

Aiyanth was called the Axle because it lay at the center of Islevale, accessible from Oaqamar and the Bone Sea, the Inner and Outer

Rings, the Labyrinth and the Sisters. It was the hub of commerce between the oceans. Oaqamar might have been Islevale's preeminent naval power, and the Ring Isles were wealthy beyond measure, but Aiyanth was the heart of all.

Belsan's marketplace teemed with people and gold. Peddlers came and went, but the most successful among them always returned. Once Gillian realized this, she befriended those she recognized. Slowly, unobtrusively, she began to ask questions, and to mete out information about herself – some real, some invented – that would make her questions sound innocent.

"Do you ever get out to the Knot?" she asked one merchant, an Oaqamaran captain named Xhevenol, who preferred to sell his own goods rather than treat with the city's peddlers.

"On occasion. You thinking of going there?"

"No, that's where I came from."

Gray eyes narrowed. "The accent, the look? I would have guessed you was from the north Ring. Ensydar, or maybe Daerjen."

She smiled, inwardly cursing his shrewdness. "Very good. I was born in Trohsden, but I came here from one of the Knot isles. A royal city. I probably shouldn't say which."

That caught his interest. "Noble?"

"Hardly. I was married to a Binder in one of the courts."

"That right?"

"I'm afraid so."

"He no longer to your liking?"

"You could say that. He drinks too much, and he's a mean drunk."

This prompted a silence that she allowed to stretch uncomfortably before asking, "You get many Bound devices coming through here?"

"Belsan, you mean?" Xhevenol couldn't have been happier to change the subject. "Sure. Lots of 'em. There's only a few who want 'em, and fewer still who can afford 'em, but when you find the right buyer, it means some gold, doesn't it?"

"I would think so. I gather quality can vary quite a bit. From Binder to Binder."

"Sure it can," he said, speculation in his glance. "Does your…

your husband do good work?"

"His master thinks so. I've heard others say – when they thought I wasn't listening – that his pieces are less refined than those of others."

"I see."

She knew she had him. She could have answered his next question before he asked it. Instead she wished him good day and turned to move on.

"Wait a moment there," he called. He stepped out from his booth, gently steered her back to it. "Would you know your husband's work on sight?"

"I might," she said, trying to sound guarded. "I'm not interested in stirring up trouble. I had enough with him."

"No trouble." He kept his voice low. "Just a little information now and again. I don't get a lot of Bound devices, but when I do, I want to be sure they're quality, catch? You could maybe look at 'em for me. Tell me if you recognize the workmanship. Do you know anything about 'em, other than what's your husband's and what's not?"

She twitched a shoulder. "A little. You live with a Binder for ten years and you learn a bit."

He smiled. "I'd think so."

Before long, Xhevenol had spoken to other merchants about his friend who could tell them which Bound devices were of quality and which weren't. Once cloaked in that reputation, she had no trouble learning all she needed about who was selling the pieces and who expressed interest in buying them.

Xhevenol offered to pay her ten treys for every sale in which she assisted him. Other merchants promised the same. Over the turns that followed, she examined only three devices: two sextants and an aperture. To her surprise, and to the delight of the merchants, Gillian did point out subtle flaws in craft that had escaped their notice. She had learned more from Bexler than she ever imagined. The thought brought a twinge of regret.

No one asked her to look at a chronofor, or mentioned buyers who sought such a device. Orzili, though, had sent her here for a reason; she trusted that eventually word of such an inquiry would reach her.

She was right.

The first rumor of a merchant captain seeking a Bound chronofor came early in Kheraya's Fading, by way of Kantaad, too far for her to do more than send a message to Orzili relating what she had heard.

That night, while lying in bed unable to sleep, an idea came to her, in the form of a question that repeated itself in her mind. Why wait for Tobias to seek a chronofor in Belsan or somewhere else? Why not use the merchants she had befriended to steer him wherever Orzili wanted him to go?

She didn't know what Orzili would think of this. He might dismiss the notion as foolish or heavy-handed. He might tell her he hadn't hired her to do anything more than spy.

Nevertheless, she swung out of bed, drafted a longer missive in tiny letters, and tied it to the leg of a second dove.

Even after she sent this bird, slumber eluded her. Her thoughts raced, not because she had more she wanted to tell Orzili, but because she knew her idea would work and wanted to set it in motion. She hoped Orzili would give her permission to do just that.

The dove arrived late, scratching at the shuttered window with quiet insistence until Orzili fetched it from the sill. He had agents throughout Islevale, and, of course, Pemin might send word to him at any moment, demanding information or an audience.

This message, scrawled in a flowing, slanted hand, was so cryptic, the signature so unfamiliar, that for a spirecount he couldn't make sense of it.

"Inquiry in Kantaad. – GA."

When it dawned on him who this was from, and what it meant, he dropped into the nearest chair. At last.

Of course, there were other Walkers between the oceans. This could be anyone. Orzili chose to believe it was Tobias. He could almost hear Pemin mocking him.

Wishful thinking, Orzili?

"Instinct," he whispered, alone in his chamber.

He considered going to Lenna and telling her that finally he had received word of the Walker. That would only remind her, though, of how long she had been here, in his time. More, he wasn't sure how he would respond if she asked who had sent these tidings. Something about Gillian Ainfor bothered her. The other Lenna, the madwoman who still existed somewhere in this time, had been obsessed with Mearlan's former minister. As it was, his rapport with this Lenna had grown ever more strained and distant. He barely knew how to speak with her.

Better to keep this information from her.

He eyed the missive again. Kantaad. Where young Lenna still lived, waiting for him, no doubt wondering when he would return and resume their life together.

He considered Spanning to her, telling her that the Walker was on her isle. She could find him, kill him, and end all of this. Except these tidings were probably days old, or more. Chances were, Tobias found no chronofor in Kantaad and moved on. Was he back in the Ring, sailing the Inward Sea? Had he gone elsewhere? The Knot perhaps, or the Labyrinth? Where might he find the device he sought?

Long ago, Lenna told him that she would go to Aiyanth. But was that too obvious? Were chronofors more common in the northern isles, near Trevynisle and Sholiss?

He pushed himself out of the chair and crossed to the door, only to stop himself with a hand on the lever. He turned away, turned back, muttered a curse.

Let her be angry. Let her ask who had sent word. Pemin wouldn't remain patient forever. The time for such trifles had passed.

He flung open the door and strode to Lenna's chamber. He knocked twice before she responded. She opened the door a crack, barely enough for him to see her. She wore a diaphanous sleeping gown, and her hair was tousled. Even after all this time, his heart staggered at the sight of her.

"What do you want?"

"I'm sorry I woke you," he said. "I've received a missive. One I've been waiting for. I want to discuss it with you."

"Now? Tonight?"

He nodded. Her lips thinned.

"Very well. I'll come to your chamber." She closed the door without waiting for his response.

Orzili stalked back to his room and poured himself a cup of Miejan red. At her knock he called for her to enter.

She had put on a gown, purple and flowing. More than was necessary. A simple robe would have done. Whatever trust and affection had existed between them had died since their encounter with the crazed Lenna. One more regret among many.

"Wine?" he asked, holding up his own cup.

"No, thank you. What message did you receive?"

Fine. "Word of someone seeking a chronofor. In Kantaad."

"You believe this is the Walker. The boy you're after."

"Tobias. Yes, I do."

"Tobias. That's right."

Her eyes took on a distant look that he had noticed repeatedly in recent turns. Not for the first time, he wondered if the madness of the other Lenna had infected this one in some small way. Naturally, he didn't give voice to his suspicions.

"You once mentioned to me," he said instead, "that Aiyanth would be the best place to find a Bound device. I have an agent there. I need to know where else he might go."

"Any large city. There's always gold to be made from Bound devices."

"Of course. But is he more likely to find something in the north? Or maybe the Knot?"

"The north," she said. "You mean the Sisters? Or the Labyrinth?"

"Yes."

"It's possible. The Ring is best."

"I expect he'd choose to avoid the Ring."

"Out of fear of you."

He frowned. Was she mocking him, or still addled with sleep? "Right. I don't think he'd come anywhere near Daerjen."

Before she could answer, Orzili heard more scratching at his window. Another bird?

He opened the shutters again. A second dove flew to his desk. Orzili crossed to the creature, gripped it gently, and untied this newest missive from its leg.

The message was longer this time, the letters cramped on the tiny parchment. Still, he recognized this hand from the last note. Gillian Ainfor again. He read the message twice, a smile tugging at his lips.

He'd known she was clever, but this was brilliant, a way to lead Tobias exactly where Orzili wanted him.

"Who is it from?" Lenna asked.

He tensed, kept his gaze on the parchment, his expression neutral. "Another of my spies," he said lightly.

"Can I see it?"

He closed his fist around the missive. "It's written in cyphers. I can tell you what it says. This agent suggests that we steer the Walker toward certain parts of Islevale with well-placed rumors of Bound chronofors."

"Your spy – he would talk to merchants?"

Orzili didn't correct her. "Yes, he would."

"A crude deception. Won't the Walker guess that he's being led into a trap?"

"Probably. He's clever enough. So is this spy, however. And… he suggests a way to use Tobias's suspicions to our advantage."

She raised an eyebrow. "Interesting. How?"

"I'm happy to explain, but first a question for you: do Westisle's pirates ever traffic in Bound devices?"

Her eyes widened, the question seeming to come as a revelation. "Yes," she said. "Whenever they can."

CHAPTER 29

2nd Day of Kheraya's Fading, Year 634

The *Sea Dove* seemed a different vessel as it tacked north and west toward the Ring Isles and the Inward Sea. Tobias had never sailed aboard a ship of war, but he imagined the experience would be similar to this latest leg of their voyage.

Every sailor who ventured out of the *Dove's* hold carried a loaded firearm. Those who spent any time on deck held muskets, or wore weapons strapped across their backs. Any who climbed into the rigging carried pistols on their belts. At all times two members of the crew were assigned to watch for Belvora, one at the prow and one at the stern. Others kept vigil on the sea, searching for Shonla mists or any sign of Arrokad. At night, at least six torches burned in sconces mounted to the masts and rails. Captain's orders.

Tobias didn't believe the crew could defend the ship from Arrokad if the Most Ancient Ones chose to attack, but he drew comfort from the precautions Larr had taken.

He would have preferred to keep Sofya below, but he could no more insist on that than he could deny her food. The princess needed sunshine and cool air and the freedom to roam the vessel. She noticed the weapons and regarded them with apprehension. In her short life, she had heard and seen enough firearms discharged to connect them with frightening noises and foul smells. Still, she teetered from one end of the ship to the other, as if it was her demesne, and those aboard her subjects.

Clouds darkened the sky over the Sea of Wraiths, and a stiff wind keened out of the west, roughening the waters and forcing the *Dove* to follow a jagged course toward the Rings.

The joviality of their earlier voyaging had given way to a grim, wary quiet. Tobias felt responsible for this, and regretted it. Others on the ship gave no indication that they blamed him and Mara. Events in Piisen might have dampened the crew's spirit, but they had also drawn those on the ship closer to one another, and closer to Tobias, Mara, and Sofya.

Before they left the Knot, Captain Larr told Tobias that she would fight, and if necessary die, to keep them safe. Her crew embraced that promise. The ferocity of their friendship humbled him.

Seven days after they sailed from Piisen, Ermond returned to the *Dove*. No one could say when, precisely, he boarded the vessel. One moment he wasn't there, and the next he stood at the rear of the ship, appearing dazed, his gaze roaming the deck. His clothes were disheveled and torn, but somehow they were bone dry. He looked to have regained the years taken from him by the Tirribin, and several more besides. He bore no injuries that Tobias could see.

Captain Larr and others peppered him with questions. Had the Arrokad hurt him? Where had she taken him? Had he been below the sea's surface?

He offered no replies, and regarded his inquisitors the way he might strangers speaking in a tongue he didn't know.

Larr ordered Bramm and Gwinda to shepherd him below and put him to bed. There he remained for more than a day. When he emerged onto the deck again he seemed no more inclined to discuss his ordeal. He did resume his duties, apparently as at home on the vessel as he had been before the Knot.

With the wind howling against them and the sea high and rough, their progress came grudgingly. The morning Ermond resumed his duties, they were still within sight of Islecliff, leagues shy of the Lost Children. At this rate, it would take them more than a turn to reach the Inward Sea.

Late that day, as the sky darkened, Mara shouted the words all of them had dreaded since leaving Piisen.

"I see Belvora!"

She stood by the prow, a musket slung over her shoulders. She pointed ahead of them, but peered over her shoulder, searching the deck for Tobias.

He strode to her side, pistol in hand.

There were three of them, distant still. Shadowed forms against a smoke gray sky, circling like enormous buzzards.

Other members of the crew joined Tobias and Mara. Sofya toddled to them and tugged on Tobias's breeches. He stooped, lifted her into his arms.

"What you see, Papa?"

He and Mara shared a bleak look.

"Birds," he said, pointing. "Big ones."

"I see 'em!"

Larr was last to come forward. "I want everyone below come nightfall," she said. "We'll light the torches, furl the sails until morning, and take shifts guarding the hatches. Two muskets in each, and sailors to reload. Maybe they haven't spotted us yet. Maybe they'll come close enough tomorrow for us to get clear shots at them. Until then, I want every member of this crew sheltered."

No one challenged her.

Tobias assumed the Belvora were already aware of the vessel, and knew Walkers were on board. They were hunters, keen of sight, smell, and hearing, and attuned to magick. Darkness wouldn't dissuade them. He feared armed sailors wouldn't either.

They had their evening meal below, eating little, saying less, darting glances toward the hatch. Tobias and Mara put Sofya to bed, and sang with her until she fell asleep. Then they lay together on their pallet, tense, ears tuned to the ship, sifting through gale and swell and the usual creaks and groans of worn wood, for sounds of invasion. Tobias dozed off and was roused some time later by Bramm, whom he was to replace at the forward hatch.

The sailor handed him his musket and shuffled to his hammock, clearly exhausted.

Tobias climbed the stairs and crossed to the hatch that led to the ship's sweeps. Ermond had already taken position there.

He nodded to Tobias, but didn't say anything. For a time they searched the sky.

"It a good idea for you to be doing this?" Ermond asked, after perhaps a half-bell. "You having magick and all."

"I insisted. They're after us. At least one of us should share in the risk. And the lack of sleep."

The sailor chuffed a dry laugh. They lapsed back into a lengthy silence. Tobias eyed Ermond nearly as much as he did the sky. Like everyone else on the ship, he was curious about the man's time with Ujie. His interest wasn't prurient, at least not entirely. Few humans spent so much time with any Ancient, much less an Arrokad, and lived to describe the experience.

"I can't talk about it, lad," Ermond said at last, leaving Tobias abashed at having been so obvious in his interest.

"She swore you to silence?"

"No, nothing like that. It was… We went everywhere. She swam with me all over the isles and through every sea between the oceans. We were… together, as you'd expect. She gave me years back, but she might have robbed them of meaning. I'm not sure I'll ever be as alive as I was for those seven days. So, talking about it is… All I've got now is the memory of it, and I want that for myself. Is that wrong of me?"

Tobias shook his head. "Not at all. Forgive me."

Ermond smiled. "It's nothing the others haven't done, or that I wouldn't be doing if you'd been the one to go." He leaned closer, sobering. "She mentioned a boon that you owe her. That night on the ship, when she saved the wee one."

"Yes. She and I struck a bargain, before I came aboard the *Dove*."

Ermond shook his head, solemn as a cleric. "Whatever you do, don't give yourself to her the way I did. It'll ruin you for your woman, and her for you. Promise me, lad: you'll find some other way to repay her."

"I'll do my best."

Wind shook the vessel and rustled the furled sailcloth. Tobias surveyed the sky, and thought he glimpsed a pale form overhead.

At the same time, one of the sailors at the rear hatch said, "Did you see that?"

Ermond shifted on the top step and raised the butt of his musket to his shoulder. "They're here."

Tobias took position opposite him, scanning the sky in the other direction.

"They'll come for me first," he said, his voice low. "Probably from behind."

Ermond stared. "Is that why you insisted on keeping watch?"

"That's why I'll insist every night."

Another shape swooped over the ship. Both of them ducked, though the demon was already past, and hadn't flown very low.

"They're too fast for us to get off a shot," Ermond said.

"Maybe." Tobias raised his musket. "Maybe not. If both of us fire – you, then me – we might have a chance."

The sailor answered with a slow nod. "We might at that. But only if you don't flinch."

Tobias flashed a grin.

A moment later, Ermond's eyes went wide. He sighted, aimed, and pulled the trigger. The barrel of his weapon was so close to Tobias that flaming powder burned the side of Tobias's face, and the report left his ears ringing.

Still Tobias kept his composure. As the Belvora veered overhead, its pale body illuminated by torchfire, he aimed and loosed a shot of his own.

The beast shrieked, sprawled out of view. Tobias heard a splash.

Sofya cried below, the sound mingling with shouts and footsteps.

Tobias and Ermond shouldered loaded muskets as others joined them on the deck.

A wail from another demon to starboard drew their gazes. Tobias could see nothing of the creature.

"Did either of you hit it?" Larr asked, stepping onto the deck.

Ermond still peered up into the darkness. "Tobias did."

"Where's Mara?" Tobias asked.

"Below, with Nava."

One of the Belvora screamed again, and was answered by a second. Both had put some distance between themselves and the ship.

"Where is the one you shot?" Larr asked.

Tobias and Ermond pointed at the same time.

Bramm moved to the rail. "Someone should row out and take off its head."

Gwinda joined him on that side of the ship. "I'll go with you."

Yadreg took one of the torches from a sconce. "So will I."

Captain Larr gave them leave, and soon they were oaring away from the *Dove* in the direction of the fallen Belvora. All three of them carried pistols and swords.

Before long, another pistol shot told those on the *Dove* that they had found the demon. A second shot sounded an instant later. Larr stared into the darkness, worry etched in her lean face. No third shot came. Tobias thought the demon must be dead.

"You did well to kill one of them," the captain said. "Maybe the other two will think twice about coming back."

Tobias wasn't sure he believed this. "I should keep watch for a few bells more."

"Usin' himself as bait, he is," Ermond said.

Tobias cast a scowl his way.

"Sorry, lad. The captain needs to know. It's her ship."

Larr walked to where they stood. "What's this?"

Ermond and Tobias exchanged glances.

"If I'm on deck, they're most likely to attack me," Tobias admitted.

"So you're putting my ship at risk."

"Your ship is at risk no matter what. By putting me in plain view, we're making the Belvora more predictable. They're predators, dangerous to be sure, but not as canny as other Ancients. They can't resist magick."

Larr glared. "I should put you in chains and keep you below."

"I'm too good a shot."

"And how would you feel if your wife put herself at risk the way you have? I seem to recall that she's as good with a flintlock as you are."

Better, actually. Tobias looked away rather than admit this. The corners of his mouth twitched.

"I thought as much."

The pinnace glided back into view, Bramm rowing, the other two positioned at either end of the boat, both with pistols at the ready.

Larr glowered at Tobias for another moment before turning her attention to her sailors.

"The demon is dead?"

"Yes, captain."

"Good. We'll–"

Another shriek cut her off. This one came from far closer than had the others.

Larr ducked and pressed herself to the nearest rail. "Get down! All of you! And get those sailors back on board!"

Several of the crew scrambled to the side of the ship and threw ropes to Bramm, Gwinda, and Yadreg. While they climbed, others knelt at the rails, muskets at shoulder height.

Tobias and Ermond stared into the darkness. Fearing he might endanger the crew, Tobias tried to separate himself from the rest. Larr hissed an order he couldn't hear. There could be no mistaking her frantic gestures toward the hatch.

Reluctantly, he hurried to the nearest opening. He kept low, watched the sky. He refused to descend into the hold. Orders be damned.

A demon soared overhead. A shot boomed, but the Belvora wheeled out of sight before another sailor could fire. A second pale form appeared and vanished to port, as elusive as a wraith. An unnatural stillness settled over the ship, broken only by the slap of swells, and Sofya's soft crying from below. Tobias stared into the blackness, afraid of inviting attack on those around him.

Again, a pale form loomed over the ship. And another. Then four more. Where had they all come from?

"There are more of them," Tobias called. "Six at least."

"I count seven," came another voice.

Larr muttered a curse. "Either is too many. Suggestions?" She eyed Tobias as she asked this.

He didn't know what to do. In the waters around the Knot they had sources of cover. They might enter a narrow cove or position themselves close to one of the cliffs. Anything to limit the directions from which the Belvora might attack. Here, in the middle of nowhere, they were defenseless. He wouldn't have thought it possible, but he wished for foul weather.

He tripped on the notion, hearing in it an echo of words spoken to him recently. He raised himself enough to peek over the rails at the frothing waters, only to duck down again at another glimpse of pale wings in the torchlight.

Tobias regarded the captain. The memory crystalized. He scurried to her in a crouch.

"You told me when we reached the Knot that the waters around the isles were thick with mist demons."

"Shonla. I remember. What of it?"

"Are they out here as well? On open sea?"

"Not as many, but Shonla plague ships everywhere. That's why we burn torches after dark. What does this—"

"Might a Shonla mist hide us from Belvora?"

Larr tucked her chin, her eyes widening a little. "Possibly. But Shonla are no friends to humans. And Ancients, even those of different septs, are usually reluctant to anger one another."

"From what I've seen, all Ancients are creatures of commerce. The Belvora are attacking us because they've been promised… something if they kill Mara, Nava, and me. What can we offer Shonla that would make them want to help us?"

"Screams," Larr said with a frown. "They're terrifying. They might not kill as some demons do, but there's a reason ship captains on every isle try to keep them at bay."

"They like songs."

Larr and Tobias turned toward Yadreg, who knelt nearby.

"Songs?" Tobias asked.

"That's right. They can be put off with singing, just like time demons can with a riddle. They can be summoned that way, too. If ever you wanted to summon one." The old sailor glanced around. "I'm just about sure all that's true."

Larr faced Tobias again. "You want to summon a Shonla to my ship…"

"You said it yourself: they don't kill; Belvora do."

A musket shot boomed from the rear of the vessel, and one of the sailors let out a string of oaths.

"We can't keep them away forever," Tobias said. "We only have so much ammunition and powder. And more may be coming."

"So we would call for a Shonla, allow it to envelop us in its mist, and then… row to safety?"

"I know a Shonla can't protect us forever. I'm trying to survive this night. We can plan beyond that come morning. Before long, one of those demons is going to kill someone, and I don't want more blood on my conscience."

As if to prove his point, a Belvora swooped low over the prow, clawed feet extended. One of the crew tried to fire, but the demon raked a talon across her shoulder and neck before speeding away. Musket fire chased the creature into the gloom. Tobias heard nothing to indicate that either shot hit its mark.

Sailors rushed to the wounded woman. Her injuries bled profusely, but didn't appear to be lethal.

"You say they can be summoned?" the captain asked Yadreg.

"So I've heard. If you can sing something that draws them."

The captain frowned. "I'm not much for music."

Yadreg sat motionless for a tencount, mouthing something Tobias couldn't hear. Then he gave a single nod, turned his face skyward, and started to sing in a strong baritone.

Is there a Shonla on the sea who hears my song?

Is there a mist to be borrowed all night long?
We seek a cloud to keep out of sight,
And will pay in songs throughout the night."

When he finished, he glanced at Tobias and the captain, then lifted a shoulder.

"Best I could do on a moment's notice."

"It was better than I would have done," Tobias told him. "Sing it again."

Yadreg sang it several times more, with no response. Tobias crawled to one rail and then the other, searching for an approaching cloud. One would have been easier to spot on a clear night, under the glow of the moon. But with the sky blanketed, he couldn't see beyond the reach of the torches.

Of course.

"We should extinguish the torches," Tobias said. "At least, most of them."

Larr's lip curled at the suggestion. "Won't that make us easier prey for the Belvora?"

"Not if most of us go below."

"You included."

He shook his head.

"This isn't a negotiation. You're a member of my crew and will follow my orders. You've had an idea, a good one. And we'll see it through. Now, go below and stay there until I call you back on deck. Do you understand?"

Everyone around them heard their exchange. Tobias couldn't defy the captain and hope to keep the respect of the crew.

"I understand, captain. Forgive me."

She gave a brusque nod. "I want everyone below," she said in a raised voice, "except Yadreg, Ermond, Bramm, Gwinda – you'll remain with me."

Sailors scrambled to the hatches, some descending to the oar locks. Tobias and others joined Mara and Sofya in the rear. The princess's cheeks were damp with tears. Seeing Tobias, she reached for him, opening and closing her tiny hands. Tobias took her from

Mara and kissed her brow.

"It's all right," he whispered.

She grabbed his shirt with one hand and stuck her other thumb in her mouth, something she did less often now, almost exclusively when frightened.

At Mara's prompting, Tobias described what had happened above, and what they had decided to do.

As he spoke, the torch glow leaking into the hold diminished, until only a weak, flickering shaft of yellow light angled down the stairs.

"I've never met a Shonla," Mara said, "but I learned a lot about them in the palace, from other trainees mostly. Do you know much about them?"

"Almost nothing."

"That was a bold suggestion to make in ignorance." She softened this with a grin.

He didn't argue.

They waited in the dim light, no one saying a word, all with their gazes fixed on the hatch. The report of a musket clapped above, reverberating in the closed space and drawing fresh cries from Sofya. Not far off, a demon screamed. But they heard no more shots, leaving Tobias to wonder if the creature had been killed or merely wounded.

Time crawled by, measured in the slow rocking of the ship and the rise and fall of Yadreg's voice as he sang his summons again and again.

Eventually, his singing halted. Tobias and Mara eyed each other. Sofya had long since fallen asleep, lulled by the call to mist demons. As Yadreg's silence stretched on, some in the hold whispered to one another.

Only when cold air crept into the hold, did Tobias realize that the song had worked.

"Do you feel that?" Mara asked, rubbing the pebbled skin on her arms.

"Yes."

"Mister Lijar, would you come up here please?" The captain's voice, taut.

He handed Sofya to Mara. The princess woke and began to fuss. He left them that way, feeling guilty, knowing Mara understood.

He crossed through the hold, past curious sailors, and ascended into a cold, shifting mist, tinged yellow and orange by the lone torch still burning by the mast.

An indistinct shape hovered near the prow, as far from the flame as possible. Larr, Yadreg, and the others stood in a tight arc, facing the creature. They held weapons. Tobias joined them, but left his pistol on his belt.

As he neared that shadowy figure, its form and features came into relief. It was about Tobias's height, but gray in color, with skin that shone as if wet. It had large feet and hands, a lean body, and a round, hairless head. Its features were flat and broad, and the pearly glow of its eyes carved through its mists like the beacon on a lighthouse.

The creature floated a hand or two above the deck, the fog around it thickening and thinning as if wind blown, though the chill air felt still.

"Have you come to treat with me?" the Shonla asked, in a voice as dense and slow as molasses.

Tobias looked to Larr. She nodded.

"Yes," he said to the demon. "My name is Tobias."

"My kind know me as…"

The sound he made then – a series of hisses and clicks and swishing noises – was as meaningless to Tobias as the whistles and trills of a sparrow. Seeing Tobias's expression, the creature frowned. "Other Ancients call me Shafizch. Or Shaf. You may as well."

"Thank you. You honor us."

"Hardly. Why did your friend summon me?" The glowing eyes shifted to Yadreg. "It was an acceptable melody. The rhyme was… pedestrian."

"We summoned you because we need your help," Tobias said, demanding the Shonla's attention.

"The Belvora."

"That's right. We wish to remain within your mists until daybreak. In return we'll sing for you. We'll provide you with song for the entire night."

The Shonla canted his head, seeming to peer through the mist toward the Belvora.

"It is considered inappropriate for members of one sept to interfere with the commerce of another. I have no wish to make enemies of these Belvora. Witless they might be, but they are dangerous creatures, prone to tantrums, and possessed of long memories and almost human levels of vindictiveness. I must refuse."

"We're not engaged in commerce with the Belvora."

Tobias and the other humans turned. Mara stepped through the mist, leaving swirling tendrils of vapor in her wake. She didn't have Sofya with her.

"Your point?" Shaf asked, as Mara halted beside Tobias.

"You're not interfering in anything. We summoned you. We proposed an arrangement, a bargain. One you can enter with us, freely and fairly."

"But the winged ones—"

"The Belvora might have an arrangement with others, but not with us. For all we know they're simply on the hunt. Tobias and I possess magick. That would be enough to draw them here, wouldn't it? Or do you know of some bargain that drew the Belvora to our ship?"

The Shonla drifted closer. "I have no such knowledge."

Mara opened her hands. "Then the only bargain here is the one we're offering. Surely you're free to enter into such an agreement."

"It is not as easy as that," Shaf said, "although I admire the cogency of your argument, human. For Belvora, as for Tirribin, and even Shonla, the hunt *is* commerce. Ancient definitions are not as… fussy as those used by your kind. I interrupt their hunt at my own peril. That said, if you survive this night, and summon me at tomorrow's dusk, before the Belvora beset your vessel again, I will be free to help you. Your offer of music is most attractive."

The creature floated backward, away from them, a hand raised in farewell.

"Wait!" Tobias said.

Shaf halted, eased toward them again.

"Can you at least tell us how many Belvora there are?"

Shaf's frown returned. "That would be interference as well. A different sort, to be sure, but a violation just the same. I believe I would be wise to refuse."

As the Shonla spoke, Tobias leaned closer to Yadreg. "Sing," he said, breathing the word.

"What?"

"Sing something. Now. It doesn't matter what."

Yadreg stammered a line or two, before settling into a song, something bawdy that Tobias had heard on the ship many times.

"When you finish this, start another," he whispered to the old sailor. "Don't pause at all. I'll get others to follow you."

The man nodded without interrupting his song.

Shaf hovered above the deck, glowing eyes fixed on Yadreg. A slight frown still pulled at the corners of his mouth. Tobias hoped that like a Tirribin ensnared by a riddle, the Shonla would be rendered helpless by the crew's music.

"Yadreg will sing another song after this one," he whispered to Bramm and Gwinda. "When he finishes the second, one of you has to start another immediately. There can be no gap, no opportunity for the demon to leave us."

"I know more songs than I do recipes," Gwinda said, her voice low.

Bramm gave a sly glance. "I hope they're better than your recipes."

She punched his shoulder, but then both of them sobered.

"Don't worry," Gwinda told Tobias. "We won't let it leave."

Mara and Tobias descended into the holds to inform the others of what they had done, and what they needed the rest to do now. Before long, sailors crowded the deck around Gwinda and Yadreg, all donning overshirts against the cold of the Shonla's mist, all with a song at the ready.

Ermond brought Yadreg his lute, and soon the sailor was playing as others sang. Ermond produced a mouth harp, and played as well. Another sailor tapped on a lap drum.

Through it all, the Shonla remained as he had been, suspended a few hands above the ship, clearly eager to be away, but unable to leave.

Captain Larr stood near the mast and the torch there, a musket in hand, gaze raised, though Shaf's mist enveloped them still.

"I don't think you need to worry," Mara said, as she and Tobias joined her.

"The Belvora are still out there."

"Yes, but they can't find us now."

"This mist—"

"It's not just the mist," Mara told her. "Shonla are magickal creatures, and their mists are controlled by that magick. I don't think the Belvora can discern Tobias and me from the cloud around us. For now, we're safe."

The captain appeared reassured by this. Not enough to put down her weapon and sing with the rest. But her stance eased. In time, she ordered some of the crew below and had them take up oars. While the singing continued, she steered the ship northward.

Tobias wandered to the ship's stern and listened. He thought he heard shrieks of rage from the Belvora around them. Larr was right. The winged demons followed them. For this night, the mists shielded the *Dove*. He expected that ship and crew would pay a price for their gambit come morning.

CHAPTER 30

3rd Day of Kheraya's Fading, Year 634

When at last dawn's glow penetrated the Shonla's mist, turning the cloud around the ship a sullen pewter, every member of the *Dove's* crew was hoarse and exhausted.

Yadreg sang yet another song, picking notes on his lute. Mara thought he must know every song ever sung or hummed on an Islevale ship. Neither Mara nor Tobias knew if singing a song twice might break the spell that held Shaf rapt above their ship. They needn't have worried. Under the old sailor's direction, the crew made it through the night without repeating a single tune.

With daylight's arrival, Mara suggested to Tobias and Captain Larr that they allow the demon to leave.

"Shonla are creatures of night," she said. "I don't know what will happen if he lingers here too long."

They agreed, and the captain signaled to Yadreg. The old sailor ended his song, and shook his fretting hand. The Shonla hovered in place for a fivecount more before giving a small shudder and rousing itself. Its brilliant eyes scanned the deck and then the brightening mist around them. The homely face resolved into a scowl.

"You have entrapped me."

"Yes," Tobias said. "We were in danger, and we did what was necessary to protect ourselves."

"You kept me here against my will."

"Hardly. We sang, and you stayed."

The Shonla made a low rumbling noise that might have been intended as a growl.

"You're right: you were trapped here," Mara said. "You're blameless in this. The Belvora can't fault you for staying. You may resent what we did, but you have no cause for complaint. You enjoyed a night of music, and it cost you nothing to remain here. Wouldn't you call that good commerce?"

Shaf considered her, some of the anger draining from his expression. "That is clever, for humans."

"We have our moments."

"We would be willing to sing for you again," Tobias said. "Tonight, if you wish."

"For your protection."

"We don't know what the day will bring. It may be that the danger posed by the Belvora will have passed by then. But yes, possibly for our protection."

"There is more sustenance in scream than in song, and I do not usually choose to eschew the former for more than a night." The Shonla glanced at Yadreg and smiled. "Still, I will think on it."

Shaf floated higher above the ship, clearing its masts and lines, and then drifted off. His cloud lifted and followed. Once the Shonla was gone, the air around the ship warmed. Mara wasn't sure she would ever be truly warm again, but she was grateful for the change.

As soon as they could see beyond the deck, every person on the *Sea Dove* looked skyward.

Ermond spotted them first: six distant, large shapes, circling over the sea on broad wings, muscular legs stretched out behind them.

A soft cry sounded from below. Sofya was awake.

"I'll go to her," Tobias said. As he passed Mara, his hand brushed hers. They shared the most fleeting of smiles.

The Belvora glided well beyond the range of the crew's muskets and pistols. Mara guessed that they would track the vessel through the day, but wait for nightfall before attacking.

"I'm not sure how many nights we can remain awake with a mist demon," Captain Larr said from behind Mara. "Eventually, we have to fight them."

Mara turned. "If they sense my magick from that distance, and if

I remain on deck, we might lure them here before sunset."

The captain narrowed her gaze. "You and your husband are far too alike."

"It's us they want," Mara said. "The least we can do is act as bait–"

"Yes, yes. He said as much last night. I still don't like the idea."

"Do you have a better one?"

Larr glared at the circling demons. "No."

"I know Belvora," Mara said, dropping her voice. "Better than Tobias does, and better than I know Shonla. In my future, they were everywhere in Windhome Palace, watching over us like guards in a prison. They don't tire, and they don't surrender, but they also don't rely on cunning or deep thinking. If we can trick them into flying closer, we can kill them."

"And by trick them–"

"They don't want the rest of you. They feed on magickal beings. That means Tobias and me."

The captain continued to track the Belvora. In time, she sighed. "What do you have in mind?" she asked, surrender in her voice.

"The pinnace."

Larr rounded on her. "No. Absolutely not."

Mara merely stared back at her.

The captain blew out another breath. "What would you do?"

Her plan wasn't complicated. Half a dozen of them, each armed with two muskets and two pistols, would row some distance from the ship and wait for the Belvora to attack. The *Dove* would remain near enough to come to their aid if the battle went poorly, though Mara knew a vessel the size of Larr's ship couldn't respond swiftly enough to save them.

Larr balked at the idea; the crew didn't. The captain had nine volunteers before she even agreed to Mara's suggestion. Within a half-bell, they had lowered the pinnace to the water. Tobias and Mara climbed the rat lines down to the boat and were joined by Bramm, Ermond, Larr herself, and Jacq, one of the younger crewmen, who was said to be a fine marksman.

Bramm and Ermond rowed the pinnace some distance from the

Sea Dove, and shipped the oars. The Belvora continued to circle, their bodies dark against pale gray clouds.

"What if they don't come?" Ermond asked after the boat had bobbed on the swells for some time.

Tobias didn't look away from the demons. "They'll come."

"But if they don't—"

"We could fire at them," Jacq said. "Draw their notice."

Mara and Tobias shared a glance.

"It's not a bad idea," she said. "We have enough ammunition, and they're far enough away that we'd have time to reload."

They turned to Larr.

She shrugged. "I don't like any of this, but if we're going to see it through, let's get on with it." She swiveled to face Jacq. "You may fire, Mister Sarrage."

Jacq grinned and brushed back a shock of wheaten hair. He stood in the boat, setting his feet without upsetting its balance. He lifted his musket, aimed, and pulled the trigger. The open sea seemed to swallow the musket's report.

The sailor didn't hit any of the demons. But after gliding one last circle, the Belvora reeled toward the boat.

Jacq reloaded.

"Well," Larr said, "we've got a fight on our hands now."

The others didn't speak, but marked the demons' advance, each with a musket in hand, and another, also loaded, at the ready.

The Belvora flew swiftly, closing on the pinnace. As they neared the vessel, and came within range of the firearms, they divided, tucked their wings, and dove. In an instant, what had been an orderly formation burst into a whirling storm of wings and talons and teeth.

Mara, Tobias, and the others twisted and turned in place, trying to track the creatures with the sights of their weapons. Their movements increased the pitch and roll of the boat, complicating their task. All of them missed with their first shots.

Mara grabbed for her other musket, knowing that if they missed again they would be in grave peril from the demons.

"Don't fire at once," Larr said, aiming herself. "Each of you pick out a target. I'll go first."

She tracked one of the demons for nearly a fivecount and then squeezed off a shot.

The Belvora screeched, veered, and climbed higher on labored wing-beats. Tobias fired next and also struck one of the Belvora. It fell and thrashed in the water. Mara's shot struck a demon in the chest. It flipped over in flight and plunged to the swells. She didn't see it move again.

"Nice shot," Ermond said, tracking one of the demons.

Pale smoke hung over the pinnace, stinging Mara's nose.

Ermond's musket boomed, but he missed his target. So did Bramm. Jacq's second volley struck a demon in the forehead. Mara thought it must have died before it hit the sea.

Two of the demons remained uninjured. All the muskets needed reloading. Pistol fire probably wouldn't reach the Belvora until they were too close for safety.

Mara and the others scrambled to reload, glancing at the sky repeatedly. It didn't take the demons long to understand that for the moment they were safe. The two that remained unhurt wheeled toward the pinnace, attacking it from opposite sides, soaring at startling speed.

Someone cursed. A bullet bounced on the bottom of the boat and rolled. Ermond started to crawl after it.

"Leave it!" Larr said. "We have more."

The captain was first to reload and aim again. Tobias raised his weapon as well. The two Belvora twisted their wings and swooped up and out of range.

Ermond finished loading. Stood.

Only then did Mara notice the faint shadow that fell across the boat.

"Ermond!"

The sailor spun, threw up an arm. A pale shape crashed into him and carried him overboard, nearly tipping the boat.

The wounded Belvora, the one the captain hit with her second shot. Mara had forgotten it. All of them had.

The demon and Ermond struggled in the brine. The Belvora fought with only one arm. Still Ermond couldn't escape it. They flailed and splashed. Blood stained the water. Mara finished reloading and tried for a clear shot at the creature. But she feared hitting Ermond instead. Tobias had a pistol in hand, but he didn't dare shoot either.

Jacq shouted a warning. Larr jerked herself away from Ermond's battle and fired at an attacking Belvora. It sprawled into the sea, skipped once across the water's surface and went still in the swells.

The last unhurt demon hovered above the pinnace, then banked away.

"Mister Sarrage!" Larr called.

Two muskets thundered in quick succession. The last Belvora spasmed and dropped to the sea. Jacq and Tobias shared a glance.

Mara turned back to Ermond's battle with the Belvora. Ermond bled from gashes on his neck and face and back. The demon pounded at him with its good fist. It was all the sailor could do to protect himself.

"Row me closer!" Mara said, aiming her musket again. There had to be a way to get off one shot.

Before Bramm and Larr could do as she commanded, something flashed in Ermond's hand. A blade. Seeing this, Mara knew a moment of hope. He plunged his knife into the demon's chest. At the same time, the Belvora slashed at his neck with a clawed hand. Blood thickened the brine. Both of them ceased their struggles.

"No!" Tobias gripped the side of the pinnace. "No! Get us closer!"

Bramm and the captain rowed the pinnace to where the bodies floated, but by the time they reached them, there was nothing to be done. Mara and Tobias pulled Ermond's body into the pinnace. The wound at his neck gaped, more horrible for having been washed clean of blood.

Jacq beheaded the demon with his sword and left it floating in the sea. Bramm and the captain oared the pinnace in a grim circle from one Belvora to the next. Jacq took off all their heads. They had to shoot one of them first. When all the demons were dead, Bramm and Jacq rowed them back toward the *Sea Dove*.

Mara and Tobias sat opposite the captain. Larr stared at Ermond's corpse, lips pressed thin.

"They shouldn't have gone for him," Tobias said, his voice leeched of emotion. "They were supposed to come after us."

"Belvora are hunters, Mister Lijar. They don't discriminate."

"They hunt magick."

"Ermond had magick," Mara said, the realization coming as an epiphany.

Larr scowled. "What are you talking about?"

"Ujie. The Arrokad. She made him younger, gave him back the years he'd lost. It's possible that Arrokad magick lingered in him, and the Belvora sensed it."

Larr paled. "Blood and bone. I never thought of that. If I had—"

"None of us knew," Mara said. "How could we?"

When they reached the ship, members of the crew brought Ermond's body aboard and prepared it for burial at sea. Larr locked herself in her quarters. Tobias and Mara took Sofya to the prow of the vessel and spent the day singing to her, telling her stories, pointing out seabirds as they glided past.

Near sunset, Larr emerged from her quarters to preside over a simple, brief ceremony. She spoke of Ermond's bravery, his solid competence, his wit. As Bramm and Jacq slipped his body into the sea, Yadreg led them in a sailor's paean.

Salt in the sweat of my sisters and brothers;
Salt in the blood that calls us to sail and roam;
Salt in the sea of Kheraya, the Mother;
Salty our tears as we commit you to swell and foam.

Night fell, and the crew lit the usual number of torches to mount on the deck. Not long after, a roiling mass of vapor floated into view just above the sea's surface. It remained off the port rail as the *Sea Dove* tacked north and west.

Captain Larr had returned to the wheel. She beckoned to Tobias and Mara and pointed at the Shonla mist. "Your friend is back."

"Surely he can tell that the Belvora are gone," Tobias said.

Mara scanned the sky as he spoke. Doing so had become habit. "Probably," she said. "But we promised him song again tonight."

Larr nodded, and adjusted the ship's course. "Then shall we douse the torches?"

Tobias glanced at Mara, eyed the captain. "I know how you feel about Shonla. I assumed that with the danger past, we'd sail on and keep the torches burning."

"We can do that, but as your wife says, we promised the creature song. And I've sailed between the oceans long enough to see the wisdom in pleasing an Ancient." Her gaze roamed the ship, the lines around her mouth tightening. "I think another night of song might do all of us some good," she said, her voice lower.

Tobias didn't answer.

Mara took his hand. "Of course, captain. We'll tell the others." They started away.

"No one blames you," Larr said, forcing them to face her again. "I know I don't. We agreed long ago to take you on, and once you became crew..." She opened one hand, a gesture of surrender and acceptance. "We protect one another against any enemy. You would have fought for him, just as he fought for you."

"Yes," Mara said. "We would have."

"Then stop blaming yourselves." Larr stared hard at Tobias. "You in particular, Mister Lijar. By assuming guilt, you dishonor his sacrifice. Let it go."

The muscles in Tobias's jaw tightened, but he nodded.

They extinguished all the torches but the one on the center mast and marked Shaf's cloud as it drifted closer and enveloped the vessel.

The air chilled. Mara knelt to tighten the too-large overshirt draped around Sofya's shoulders. As she did, Sofya pointed past her and asked, "Who that, Mama?"

Mara picked her up and approached the demon, who again hovered near the prow. "His name is Shaf," she said, eyeing the Shonla. "He's our friend."

Shaf glided closer. "You name me a friend, human?" he asked, the words viscous.

The tone of the creature's question gave Mara pause. No doubt there was significance to declaring oneself the friend of an Ancient. Certainly Droë thought so. "What would it mean if I had?"

"Do not fear. It is not a bargain and carries no cost. It implies few obligations beyond the obvious: a promise not to harm, an invitation to keep company, an openness to commerce in the future."

"You wouldn't prey on my ship?" Captain Larr asked.

"I would accept song in place of screams. And as your friend, I would offer the opportunity to give one before attempting to take the other." He didn't wait for a reply. "The Belvora are gone. Did you drive them off? Did they leave you?"

"They're dead," Larr said. "As is a member of my crew."

Shaf nodded, seeming unmoved by the crew's loss. "You are resourceful. I do not normally treat with humans. But a... a friendship with this vessel and those on it might serve my interests as well as yours." He turned back to Mara. "I would accept you as friends and name you such in return, if the offer was genuine."

"May we discuss it among ourselves?" Larr asked.

"Of course."

"Good. In the meantime, we would sing for you again."

Another smile. "That would please me."

Yadreg produced his lute and tuned the instrument. Other members of the crew gathered around him. Soon they were playing and singing. The Shonla looked on in a sort of contented trance.

The captain, Tobias, and Mara retreated to the middle of the ship. Tobias kept an eye on Sofya, who bobbed and danced from one person to the next.

"For all we know, there are more Belvora waiting for us between here and the Ring," Larr said. "And being in the good graces of an Ancient might help us in ways we can't even imagine right now. First, though, I need to know, what are the potential perils?"

Mara shrugged. "The obvious. Befriending an Ancient might imply more than we can anticipate, or ensnare us in obligations we don't yet understand."

"Have you ever claimed friendship of an Ancient?"

"We both have," Mara said before Tobias could answer. His brow creased. "Droë," she said. To the captain, she added, "A Tirribin in Windhome. Tobias knew her in his time, and I in mine. I believe she accepted both of us as friends."

"And?"

"Ancients are unpredictable and difficult," Tobias said. "Their customs and traditions go back to a time when the world belonged solely to them. That said, there might also be consequences to refusing an offer of friendship."

"I spoke rashly," Mara said. "I was trying to reassure Nava. I'm sorry."

The captain waved off the apology, and they joined the singing. The crew entertained the Shonla for several bells, until even Yadreg started to tire. He finished one last song, and the captain came forward to bid Shaf farewell.

"Perhaps we will meet again," the Shonla said. "I do enjoy the music on this vessel."

"You're welcome any time," Larr told the demon. "We would like you to consider us your friends."

"So I shall, and you shall be mine." The Shonla sketched a small bow. Moments later, the cloud moved on, leaving the ship in warm breezes under a star-filled sky.

Larr followed the cloud with her gaze and ordered the crew to relight the torches. Sofya had fallen asleep in Tobias's arms. He carried her into the hold.

"You did well to name it a friend," the captain said, so only Mara would hear. "We may never see the creature again, or we might need its protection tomorrow. Either way, I'll sleep better tonight knowing we can call on it for help." She flashed a smile and started back toward her quarters.

Mara followed Tobias below.

Over the next ha'turn and more, the *Sea Dove* continued its slow, crooked course toward the Inward Sea. The winds continued to blow against them, though not with the force of those first days out from the Knot.

They encountered no more Belvora, and for several days after Shaf left them, didn't even spot another ship. Still, Mara sensed that Tobias's apprehension grew with every league they covered. He said little and spent much of his time with Sofya, playing with her, talking to her, singing her favorite songs.

In contrast, Mara welcomed a return to more crowded waters. Where Tobias saw risk, she saw the safety of numbers. Alone on the swells, they were an obvious target. On the Inward Sea, they would be one ship among many.

First, though, they needed to gain entry to the Ring.

As they neared Kantaad again, after passing the Lost Children, they spotted warships.

The captain couldn't determine from this distance whether they were Daerjeni war eagles or Aiyanthan frigates. They weren't large enough to be Oaqamaran marauders, but that hardly mattered. Tobias, Sofya, and she had as much to fear from the Daerjeni navy as from the autarchy. Perhaps more.

Larr angled them northward, toward Rencyr, a course they followed throughout that day and the next. To no avail. Warships patrolled every gap that allowed access to the Inward Sea, and likely the entry to the Sea of the Labyrinth as well.

Tobias might have preferred to continue northward to Chayde and Flynse, but Captain Larr was determined to reach Aiyanth and begin their search for Bound devices. Mara was trapped between.

"If we can avoid the Daerjenis and deal with the Aiyanthans, we should be fine," Larr told them that night. "The Aiyanthans have no love for either the Sheraighs or the Oaqamarans." She grinned. "And they're notoriously easy to bribe."

Tobias remained doubtful. He didn't argue with the captain in front of the crew, but when he and Mara retired to their pallet he admitted to fearing encounters with any navy.

"The Aiyanthans might not be looking for us, but they're sure to notice Sofya. It's only a matter of time before word reaches the wrong ears."

The following morning, they spoke of hiding the family while authorities searched the ship. Much of Captain Larr's trade was perfectly legal, but on occasion, she conducted business with smugglers and privateers. The *Sea Dove* had several concealed compartments, and even a false wall along the inner hull of the forward hold. They had no shortage of hiding places.

The problem was, Sofya couldn't be counted on to remain silent. If they were discovered in hiding, they would forfeit any chance they had to claim she was simply the child of a union between crew members.

Larr finally convinced Tobias that they were best off sailing toward an Aiyanthan vessel and hoping that whoever searched the ship wouldn't think too much of finding a child aboard. They agreed that they would attempt to time the encounter to coincide with Sofya's nap. Best that she be below, asleep in the dim recesses of the hold.

They maintained a northerly heading as the sun climbed higher and Sofya had her midday meal. After, Mara took her below. She lay down with her and whispered a nonsense story until the princess fell asleep. She remained with Sofya and soon heard the warship pull alongside their vessel. Voices, footsteps above deck, and finally the scrape of wooden hulls as the ships were lashed together. Sofya woke briefly, but Mara sang her back to sleep before returning to the deck.

A frigate flying the gold and blue of Aiyanth floated hull to hull with Larr's ship, which now flew an identical flag from her highest mast. As Mara watched, men and women in Aiyanthan uniforms streamed onto the *Sea Dove*, polite but clear in their intent to search the vessel.

"May I ask what you're looking for?" Larr asked the Aiyanthan commander.

"The usual," the woman answered. "Westisle pirates, Westisle blades and pistols, and, of course, wines and other spirits. We'll search both your holds."

"Of course."

The captain darted a glance Mara's way.

"My daughter is asleep in the aft hold," Mara said, her tone mild. "I only just got her to lie down. If your sailors can take care to be quiet, I'd be most grateful."

The commander considered her before turning back to Larr. "You have a child on the ship?"

"Yes. Unusual I know, but—"

"Only the one?"

"That's right."

"How old?"

"One year and four turns," Mara said.

The commander's shoulders dropped a bit, and some of the tension drained from her face.

"We're not slavers," Larr said, "if that's what you were thinking."

"You said it yourself: it's unusual finding children on a merchant ship. But one that young…"

"She's not in chains," Mara said, her tone flinty.

"They're not always on slaver ships, either."

"She's not—"

"It's all right," Larr said, laying her hand on Mara's arm. "Search our ship, commander. Try not to wake the little one. You'll see that we are exactly what we claim to be. A merchant ship seeking gold in the Ring."

The commander gave a stiff nod, eyed Mara, and walked away.

"She was saying—"

"I know what she was saying. When they go below, it will be obvious to them that we're not a slave ship. There are no cages in the holds, no chains."

Mara glared after the Aiyanthan.

"Their search won't take long, and then we can be on our way."

Mara looked Tobias's way. He already stared at her, appearing every bit as scared as she felt. They had decided before the boarding not to identify Sofya's "father" if they didn't have to. Tobias's scars might raise additional questions. Mara could tell he didn't like feigning indifference.

As Larr predicted, the search of the *Dove* took little time. Nothing aboard the ship drew undo notice. Except Sofya.

"You're free to sail on, captain," the commander told Larr, after the rest of her sailors had crossed back to the frigate.

"Thank you."

"The girl is a curiosity, though. I might have heard something about a child on a ship. I can't remember what I was told. My memory comes and goes."

"Does it?" the captain said, her tone light. "And the memories of your crew?"

"They remember nothing I don't, and everything I do."

Mara didn't see Captain Larr pull the coins from her purse or pocket. They weren't there, and then they were: golden, winking in the sunlight. Mara had no chance to count them. Larr cupped the coins in her palm and the commander gripped the captain's hand in both of hers. She gave it a vigorous shake, as if to bid Larr a fond farewell, and released her. Mara didn't see the coins again.

The commander boarded her vessel, and soon the two crews had unlashed the ships. They sailed on in opposite directions.

Tobias and Mara converged on the captain as she reclaimed the wheel.

She noted their approach and turned her gaze back to the sea and the isles ahead. "That went well."

"How much do we owe you?" Mara asked.

Larr shook her head. "That's not how this works. I've told you before: you're crew. All three of you."

"But–"

"Don't you have work to do? Or after all these turns do you fail to grasp that this ship doesn't sail itself?"

She said this with the faintest of smiles. Mara and Tobias left her – she for a pair of tangled lines high in the rear rigging, he for a portion of the port rail that needed repair.

CHAPTER 31

20th Day of Kheraya's Fading, Year 634

In the days that followed, the *Sea Dove* stopped at ports in Rencyr, where the captain and crew traded rope and cloth purchased in the Knot for Ijjoni kelp, wine, and jewelry. Some of what they acquired in the north they offloaded in the south or in ports in eastern Ensydar. They crossed the calm waters between the isles several times, conducting transactions on behalf of merchants in New Ijjon, Ensydar's royal city, and Murcston, a port on the west shore of Rencyr.

Tobias begrudged the leisurely pace of their voyaging. Now that they had chosen to pursue Bound devices, he was eager to find them. Captain Larr, though, cautioned him against his impatience, and assured him that they were doing precisely what anyone observing merchant ships in these warm waters would expect.

"I don't want to appear in too great a hurry to reach Aiyanth," she told him. "Trade in this corner of the Outer Ring can keep a ship occupied for turns. We'll get to Belsan soon enough." She offered one of her confident grins. "Trust me, Mister Lijar."

What choice did he have?

He and Mara worked the lines and the rigging. They cleaned the deck and mopped floors in the holds. They mended worn patches on the sails. Tobias even helped Gwinda with a few meals, discovering a hitherto unknown talent for cooking.

Sofya had the run of the ship as ever, and enjoyed these crowded waters. She stood for bells at the prow or one of the rails, pointing at ships, noting the colors of different flags, goggling at the cities dotting every shoreline. Yadreg built small shelves for her to stand on at intervals throughout the deck. They raised her enough that she could peer through the open spaces near the tops of the rails, above the curve of the hull.

Mara and Tobias didn't need to carry her as much as they had. She didn't fuss as often. On occasion, sailors aboard other vessels spotted her and waved. Always the princess waved back. To Tobias's relief, few seemed particularly surprised to see a child on a ship.

Captain Larr continued to navigate the common routes along Ensydar's eastern shore, but over the course of a qua'turn they added voyages to Qyrshen at the northern end of the Inner Ring, to the southern ports of Aiyanth, and even to Trohsden at the northernmost reaches of Daerjen.

"Only a great fool would bring the exiled princess of Daerjen back to her homeland," Larr told Tobias, again seeking to ease his concerns. "And surely the people pursuing you don't think you're a fool."

During one of their stops in southern Aiyanth, the captain left the ship for the nearest marketplace, intending to inquire about Bound devices. Tobias and Mara remained on the *Dove*. He was no more impatient than usual. Mara was. She lurked along the rails, paced the deck, and finally resorted to swabbing the hold, her least favorite duty aboard the vessel.

When the captain returned, they followed her to her quarters.

Once they were inside, and the door closed, Larr opened her hands and hiked her shoulders.

"I found nothing. I'm sorry."

"Maybe we should sail back to Rencyr," Tobias said. "Rooktown might have something."

"It might. But all three merchants I spoke to told me the same thing, in almost the same words, which is unusual to say the least: if we want Bound devices, and we don't wish to do business in the autarchy, there are only two cities worth visiting."

Tobias dragged a hand over his face. "I'm almost afraid to ask."

"One is Hayncalde."

He gave a dry, bitter laugh. "Of course."

"The other is Belsan."

Tobias eyed the captain and then Mara. "That's not so bad. We can reach Belsan in a day."

Larr nodded. "Yes, we can."

"Then what's the problem?"

The captain glanced Mara's way.

"Think about it, Tobias," she said.

He stared back at her, weighing Larr's tidings, trying to grasp what they plainly did. When it came to him, he sagged. "Damn," he whispered.

"Were the merchants lying to you?" Mara asked the captain. "Could all three be working for the Sheraighs?"

"No. I believe they're getting information from sources, who are getting their information from other sources, and so on. Somewhere along the way, people who want us in Belsan have made it known that it's the one reliable and safe place where you can buy a working chronofor."

Tobias's thoughts swirled. "Do you think it's true?" he asked. "Do you think we can find Bound devices in both cities?"

"I don't know," Larr said. "It would be dangerous to find out. They want us in Belsan. So clearly we can't go there. And they don't think you would dare return to Hayncalde."

"Those can't be the only two cities where merchants sell sextants and chronofors."

"I agree, but I don't know where to find the information we need. If we're right about this – if the information I'm getting is intended to steer us somewhere of your enemy's choosing – then we have to assume that the channels I use to learn of such things have been polluted with lies. We can sail from city to city until we find what we're after, but that could take turns. It could take a year."

"Do you know merchants in the autarchy?" Mara asked.

Tobias slanted a look her way. So did the captain.

"I do," Larr said. "Wouldn't making port there be as dangerous as going back to Hayncalde?"

"Perhaps. Did any of the merchants mention Qaifin or Sholiss or Little Plenston?"

Larr shook her head, and glanced at Tobias. "No, they didn't."

"Orzili and his friends will be watching the market in Belsan, and they might think we're daring enough to chance a visit to Hayncalde. Maybe they won't expect us to try a city in Oaqamar."

They lapsed into silence.

In time, the captain gave another shake of her head. "No. You make a compelling case. And if it was merely a matter of risking one of the cities you mentioned, I'd be willing to try. The problem would be navigating the waters between here and Oaqamar. Bribing Aiyanthan naval officers is one thing. Surviving an encounter with a marauder is quite another. The three of you would be found and all of us executed before we sailed within twenty leagues of Oaqamar's shores. We can't risk it."

"Then—"

Larr cut her off with a raised hand. "One of the men I spoke to mentioned another idea, one that keeps us far from the autarchy, and allows us to avoid snares in Hayncalde or Belsan."

She had their interest.

"What would you think of doing business with pirates?"

"Westisle?" Tobias asked.

"We wouldn't have to go that far. Pirates patrol the Sea of Gales."

"I'm not sure I want Nava anywhere near them."

"Your caution would be warranted if we weren't interested in trading with them. They can be ruthless in dealing with the navies of the Ring Isles, and they'll prey on merchant ships that trespass in their waters. Offer them the opportunity to turn a profit, though, and they become as pliant as any merchant."

Tobias didn't mask his skepticism.

"Maybe not any merchant," the captain admitted. "They can be rough. Then again, so can I. The point is, I've done business with them before. And I assure you, no one in Oaqamar or the House of Sheraigh can buy their loyalty." She grinned. "They have none except to themselves."

"That's hardly a flattering portrait."

"You don't have to like them. You only have to believe that they can supply us with what we need." After another pause, Larr said, "We don't have to decide this now. It would be a long journey, and in the meantime, we can remain in these waters, perhaps increase the frequency of our runs to Qyrshen. There's money to be made here. Talk about what we've discussed, let me know what you think."

Tobias and Mara thanked her and returned to their duties. Only later, on their pallet, did they speak in whispers of Larr's proposal. Even then, they reached no easy decision. Tobias mistrusted the pirates of Westisle, recalling that in his own time they had been another enemy of Daerjen.

Mara, determined still to find a sextant and chronofor, disputed this when he mentioned it.

"Mearlan told me about the war, Mara. He admitted he'd been mistaken to fight in two theaters."

"I understand," she said. "But in my future, there was no war. There may have been tensions between Hayncalde and Westisle, but that was all, and from all I know of this future we're living now, the Sheraighs are content to leave Westisle alone."

This eased his worries some. "So you would trust them."

"No. They're pirates. I don't trust them at all. I trust the captain. If she thinks we can find what we need in the Sea of Gales, and she's willing to put the *Sea Dove* at risk, we ought to let her. She's given us no reason to doubt her." Mara kissed him, ran a gentle finger over his cheek. "Sleep. You heard her: we don't have to decide tonight."

She soon followed her own advice. Tobias remained awake, turning over possibilities in his mind, finding promise under some and serpents under others. Having Bound devices would be a great help to them. She could span to places they needed to explore, potentially saving them days, or even turns, at sea. And if they found a chronofor, he could go back to Hayncalde and warn Mearlan of the attempt on his life and family.

Or could he? Already, Orzili or one of his allies had followed Tobias through time. Might he do so again? Wasn't it likely that Orzili would find a way to thwart any attempt Tobias made to correct this misfuture? If so, a voyage into the Sea of Gales would be an unnecessary risk, a vain pursuit of a stratagem doomed to fail. His thoughts circled in this way for a bell, and then another. The ship creaked and rocked. He heard footsteps on the wharf outside the vessel, then voices.

He tensed and felt for his flintlock, which he kept within reach.

When he heard drunken laughter he exhaled and let go of the pistol. His hand was sweaty and his heart raced.

This is no way to live.

Maybe it didn't matter that having a Bound chronofor wouldn't allow him to repair the damage done to Sofya's past. Maybe it was enough that having devices would help them fight Orzili now, in this time. Maybe it was enough that he would be less afraid.

Orzili had Spanners and all of them had sextants. By now, they had probably replaced the tri-sextants. Tobias believed the assassin had a Walker working for him as well, one with a working chronofor. They were outgunned and that was unacceptable.

He didn't wish to treat with pirates, but after all they had been through, he was ready to follow Mara's instincts and Captain Larr's. He wasn't sure he trusted his own.

CHAPTER 32

20th Day of Kheraya's Fading, Year 634

Riding Qiyed over waves of sea and bay pleased Droë more than she had imagined it would. Just as she had found joy in flying with Treszlish so many turns before, she relished the speed and grace of the Arrokad's body as he skimmed over breakers or dove through them, dousing her, leaving her laughing with such abandon she could barely breathe.

Her resentment of the Most Ancient One lingered. Curled within it, hidden, she hoped, from his perception, she nurtured her defiance, her determination not to remain forever under his thrall.

Still, she took genuine delight in their explorations. Though centuries old, she had seen precious little of Islevale. Now, with Qiyed as her guide, she visited the isles of the Bone Sea, the wild waters of the Sea of Gales, the quiet lands at the southern end of the Outer Ring. She fed on sailors, merchants, men and women of every isle, from the Knot to Westisle, from the Sisters to Liyrelle.

As they journeyed, Qiyed demanded that she tell him more of the misfuture, of all that Mara said that day on the promontory, and all that she knew of events in Daerjen. When she tried to deflect his questions, to mete out what she knew and maintain some leverage in their commerce, he grew angry and threatened to hurt her. In the end, she told him all.

He also used her as a tool in his commerce with other Ancients. One night on the southern sands of Vleros, after he had found a human woman who wished to lie with him, he instructed Droë to seek out a Shonla who owed him a boon.

"She frequents these waters," he said, eyes on the woman. "She answers to Mivszel."

The human stared back at him, smiling, taking in his naked form, their silent exchange as opaque to Droë as an unknown language, as fascinating as a thousand riddles.

"You will find her, tell her I have come to collect," Qiyed went on. "She will understand."

"I don't."

At that he looked her way. "*She* will," he said again. "Now, go."

She regarded them both, curiosity burning like a bonfire in her chest. But she left them for a nearby bay, where ships lay at anchor. Before long, she spotted what appeared to be a Shonla mist. She raised her voice in song – a ballad that Tresz had enjoyed. Her heart constricted on the thought.

The mist floated toward the strand where she waited and soon enveloped her, raising bumps on her skin. A dark figure emerged from the cloud's center.

"Greetings, cousin," Droë said. "Are you Mivszel?"

The Shonla eased closer. "Do I know you?" she asked, her voice syrupy. "You are not familiar. Even your form is strange to me, though I sense that you are an Ancient."

Droë's cheeks burned. "You don't know me," she said. "I'm Tirribin, though I don't look it. I journey with a Most Ancient One. Qiyed. He sent me to settle commerce with you. A matter of a boon."

A long pause, and then, "You are his friend?"

"I journey with him."

"Also commerce?"

"Yes."

"I am sorry for you."

A turn before, Droë would have asked what she meant. She no longer had to. "I am to collect... something."

"I do not wish to pay. Could you... could you tell him you did not find me?"

Droë didn't answer. She didn't have to; they were both Ancients.

The Shonla made a strange noise. It took Droë a moment to realize that she wept.

"What is it he wants of you?" she asked, her voice hushed.

"It does not matter," the Shonla said. "Forgive me. I should not have asked what I did." She paused, glanced over her shoulder toward the bay. "Tell him... tell him I shall do his bidding."

"But–" Droë shook her head, unsure of what to say. Sorrow for the Shonla flooded her.

"He uses me to wreak vengeance on a human who wronged him, a minor noble in the north. I am to... to linger at the wharves of this human's house for five centuries, to choke off trade in his port, denying riches to his family and heirs."

"Five centuries?" Droë whispered.

"Just so. I can no longer journey in search of fear and song."

"How can he make you do that?"

A chuff of dry laughter escaped the Ancient. "I bargained carelessly. Beware the Arrokad, cousin. He cannot be trusted."

This Droë already knew. "I'm sorry. Had I known..."

"If you journey with him, you cannot defy him. We have that in common."

She wondered if this was true, but kept the thought to herself. Instead, she raised her voice in song again, completing the ballad with which she had summoned Mivszel. When she finished she bowed to the Shonla.

"Thank you. I will hold to the memory of that song. And perhaps, if ever you are on the isle of Djaiste, you will come to the human city on its southwestern shore and sing for me again."

"I will," Droë said. "I give you my word."

The Shonla bowed in turn, before cloaking herself in her mists and floating out over the bay. Droë stared after her until she vanished from view. Then she returned to the strand where she had left Qiyed.

The Arrokad was alone when she found him, languid and far too pleased with himself. "You found the Shonla?"

"Yes," she said, resentment shadowing the word.

Qiyed considered her through narrowed eyes, but said nothing. He signaled for her to climb onto his back once more, and they returned to the water.

Days later, on a wooded cliff on Kisira, overlooking the Inward Sea, Qiyed attended a guild gathering with other Arrokad, several Tirribin and Belvora, and a pair of Shonla. Before the gathering, he asked Droë about Tirribin customs, about the nature of their time sense and their hunger for years. She answered grudgingly, reluctant to betray her sept, but Qiyed pressed her.

"I seek a bargain with the Tirribin and Shonla on this isle," he said. "I merely intend to use the needs of your sept as a cudgel against the creatures of mist. The Tirribin will benefit, as will I. If any suffer, it will be the Shonla, and even they will get most of what they want."

"I do not like betraying other Ancients. I didn't like it when you sent me to finish your commerce with the Shonla on Vleros, and I don't like this."

"I do not care," Qiyed said. "We have our own commerce, you and I. Freely entered, fairly sworn. You will do as I ask."

Fond memories of Tresz and sympathy for Mivszel thickened her throat and brought a dull ache to her chest. Still, she told him what he wished to know, hating herself as she did.

She didn't join him at the gathering, or even hide from view in the adjacent wood. The other Ancients would have sensed her, and Qiyed seemed reluctant to let his kind see what he had done to her. She tucked this information away, believing it might serve her in the future.

While he negotiated, she hunted. When he had finished and was ready to return to the sea, he summoned her and she joined him. Dutiful, meek, seething within. Less than a turn had passed since he granted her access to desire, but it felt like years. It was odd for her – a creature of time, alive for centuries – to chafe so after such a short interval.

With the maturing of her body, though, had come a deeper

understanding of herself, her needs, her mind. Time sense and feeding on years were but part of what it meant to be Tirribin. Wisdom, strength, obsession with social niceties, insatiable curiosity, childlike infatuation with nearly all that caught her interest – these were elements of her being, and qualities she recognized in others of her kind.

Not all of them had survived the changes she and Qiyed had imposed upon her form. She had grown less inquisitive, less prone to the sort of compulsions she had seen most recently in Kreeva and Strie. An irony. The very forces that compelled her to seek her transformation had abated with its completion. She cared less about rudeness in others. She did comment on Qiyed's discourtesies, but more to mask her antipathy for him than out of resentment of his poor behavior.

On the other hand, she sensed her mind expanding in ways both subtle and unexpected. Understanding desire in its purest form allowed her to see in others, and in herself, the effects of need, of want, of greed and lust and hunger in all their incarnations. She observed and listened, and was amazed by the world that opened before her. Human behavior she had found confounding in her child form now made sense to her. For all the kinship she had once felt with Arrokad, she now realized that in many respects Qiyed and his kind had less in common with most Tirribin – and Shonla – than they did with humans. The Most Ancient Ones would have been loath to admit this.

Droë also continued to wonder at her new-found physical prowess. As she grew accustomed to this new body, she discovered that she could still blur to Tirribin speed. She was larger, of course, heavier, and so perhaps not quite as nimble as she had been in her girl form. But her strength... Gods, never had she been so powerful. The largest, healthiest, most muscular humans on whom she preyed had no chance against her. She might even have been a match for Qiyed's strength, though he possessed magicks and abilities that kept her from testing this.

Qiyed still treated her as he had when she was small. His

condescension seeped into every conversation. He thought her a naif, and in some ways she remained one. Long after he and the human woman from Vleros parted, he continued to speak of their time together in the most explicit terms. Droë could do nothing about the heat that spread across her face, down her neck, over her chest as he described the intricacies of their coupling. Embarrassment warred with fascination. She bit her tongue to keep from asking questions.

She knew he sensed and enjoyed her discomfort, just as she knew that he meant to wound with the various slights he inflicted upon her throughout their days together. Arrokad were known for their arrogance and capriciousness. She believed him worse than most.

These small abuses gave her an excuse to withdraw from him, to shield her thoughts and emotions, to the extent that she could against a creature of his power. Let him believe the distance she imposed between them was born of pique and shame. Perhaps this would keep him from realizing that she searched for some way to break his hold on her and, if possible, to break him in the process.

Try as she might, Droë could not conceal her impatience to find the Walker. She often asked what he had learned about Tobias and the woman voyaging with him. On those occasions when he responded at all, his answers were vague and unsatisfying.

"Where are they?"

"I do not know."

"Where were they headed when last you heard?"

"West, I believe, though I would imagine they have changed course since then."

"West of where?"

"Kheraya's Ocean."

Sometimes, when she grew too insistent, he stopped answering at all, leaving her shaking with rage. More often she gave up, knowing he would tell her nothing of value.

One night, nearly a qua'turn removed from the gathering of the Guild, Droë's patience ran out. She pestered him, asking one question after another. Long after he stopped answering, she persisted, going so far as to repeat questions she had posed earlier.

She clung to his back as they raced over swells in the Inward Sea between Qyrshen and Aiyanth. The night was warm. Lightning flickered in the east, the answering thunder barely audible, even to her ears. She had savored such nights since commencing her journeys with the Arrokad. Wind rushed through her hair and salty spray cooled her skin. When they bounced over the higher swells, she couldn't help but laugh aloud.

Even so, thoughts of the Walker consumed her. She wouldn't have admitted this to Qiyed – though she expected he knew – but she hungered for physical contact with a human, or even an Arrokad. Not him. Never him. But someone.

She fired questions at him, undeterred by his terse responses and then his stony silence.

"Those who told you about the Walkers – where did they encounter them?" Pause. "Who was it told you of them?" Silence. "Are they on a ship? On land? Are they alone, or are they journeying with others? Have they Walked through time again? Are they trying to repair the misfuture? Were those who told you about them friends of the Walkers? Were they looking for them, too? Or was this a coincidence? How long ago did they–"

"*Enough!*"

He stopped swimming. She maintained her hold on him, her arms crooked loosely around his neck.

"I tire of your incessant questions!"

"I didn't think you were listening," she said, her tone mild. "You didn't do me the courtesy of replying."

"I have no wish to speak of these matters now, and no intention of telling you what you wish to know. My silence should have told you this. You will remain quiet for the rest of this night. Ask me nothing more. Do you understand?"

"No."

He pushed her arms off him and kicked away from her, forcing her to swim in place. Droë tried to conceal her panic. She could swim and keep herself afloat for a time, but they were leagues from the nearest shore. And Tirribin could not blur to speed in water. She would drown before she reached land.

"You defy me?"

"I do," she said, pleased by the evenness of her voice.

He dove, gave a single, mighty undulating kick. When he surfaced, he had put much distance between them.

"I can leave you here, swim on without you. I doubt you would survive. I would, on pain of Distraint, forbid any other Ancient from helping you. Is that what you want?"

"You know it isn't." Already her arms and legs had started to tire. She didn't know how long she could keep herself above the swells. She had swum in harbors and bays. Never before had she contended with the open sea.

"I sense your fear," he said.

He flashed a malevolent smile. In the next instant, a ridge of inky water concealed him from her.

"And I sense your annoyance," she called. "Who knew one of the Most Ancient would be so easy to goad?"

"Are you trying to provoke me?"

She tipped onto her back and tried floating that way. She remembered it being easier. A swell swept over her, filling her mouth and nose with water. She sputtered, righted herself, went back to treading.

"It seems I don't have to try. I need only ask a few questions."

"I *will* leave you, Droë."

"No, you won't."

She caught sight of him. He looked furious still, but remained where he was, floating in the brine, as at home in the water as a seal.

"You expended a good deal of magick to transform me, and you've made clear your intention to put me to use on your behalf. You've already done so. You have no more desire to leave me here than I have to be left. So come back here, let me hold on to you, and we'll continue our voyage."

"No more questions?"

"I want to know about the Walker. I want to find him."

"And we will," Qiyed said, ire shading his tone again. "When I decide it."

"When will that be?"

"We have been together for less than a turn." A low growl underlay the words, something akin to her own rasp. She had pushed him far.

"A turn is a long time."

"To a human, perhaps. Not to our kind. We have all the time we could want."

"The Walker *is* human. His time passes quickly. In just a short while, by our reckoning, he'll grow feeble and die."

Qiyed shrugged in the moonlight, rippling the water around him. "I do not care. Again and again you have bargained poorly, driven by haste, impatience, your lack of discipline. We will find the Walker. That is what I promised. That is all I promised."

Droë glared, unable to mask her hatred. He would know it for what it was, would be more leery of her. Perhaps he would treat her with more courtesy, but she doubted it. More likely, he would take greater pains to convince her that his control over her was absolute.

"Are you ready to continue?" he asked. "In silence?"

Her arms felt leaden. Her legs ached. She wished she had never thought to change herself. She wished she had never met this Arrokad.

The wishes of a child. Maybe you haven't matured as much as you believe.

Another swell passed, hiding him and revealing him again.

"Yes," she said. "I'm ready."

He smiled, too smug, too eager to mock her. If she could have killed him in that moment, she would have.

Qiyed kicked once. In the span of a breath he was beside her, damp, dark hair swept back from his chiseled face, starlight shining in the serpentine eyes.

"I have been kind to you," he whispered. "You think me cruel, but have I hurt you? Have I forced you to submit to me? Have I used your desire – and my access to it – to coerce you?" He didn't wait for her response. "I have not. And I can, Droënalka. Never doubt that I can. Defy me again, disobey me again, and you will discover precisely how cruel I can be."

He allowed her to climb again onto his back. She crossed her arms around his neck. It was a measure of how much she had come to hate him that she seriously considered snapping his neck, though it would mean her death as well. And perhaps it was a measure of his own surety that he didn't hesitate to turn his back on her.

A tencount later, they were gliding over the swells again. Now, though, she took no pleasure in the rise and fall, in the spray and wind.

She resolved to avoid provoking the Arrokad. And succeeded for a single day. That was how long it took her to realize that provoking him was the smartest thing she could do.

Already she had noted the similarities between Qiyed and the humans she knew. Now it occurred to her to exploit his most human tendencies. She recognized the perils of such a course. She didn't care. His hold on her was too infuriating, too humiliating. Better to be dead and free, if it came to that.

They reached a strand in the Labyrinth, where Qiyed found another lover: a young man with dark eyes and smooth skin the color of whiskey.

She left them to hunt on the town wharves. Even after she fed, however, even after she had given Qiyed ample time to complete his tryst, she lingered near the docks. She knew he would grow impatient. That was her intention. She knew as well that he would refuse to search for her. To do so would be to acknowledge in the smallest way that she had influence over him.

By the time she returned to the strand, three bells had passed. A trifle in the lives of Arrokad and Tirribin, but enough to nettle Qiyed.

"Where have you been?"

"Hunting, of course. Did you enjoy your human?"

"I finished with him nearly two bells ago. I expected you then."

She glanced around. "He did survive the encounter, I hope. He was pretty."

"Yes, he is well! Where were you?"

"I told you–"

"You were hunting. That has never taken you so long."

"Were you concerned for my wellbeing? Did you think some human had overpowered–"

A blow high on her cheek knocked her to the sand. Qiyed hadn't moved to cover the distance between them. Magick, as she'd hoped. She masked her satisfaction by focusing on the pain, which was all too real.

She glowered up at him. "Why did you do that?"

"Do not think to toy with me. You may resemble a human adult, but you are nothing more than a child next to me."

He lashed at her again with his power. Another blow, this one to the temple. She collapsed again, white points of light swimming before her.

Qiyed started toward the sea. "Get up. I am ready to leave this place."

She dragged herself to her feet, pain pulsing in her head. She wondered if she was mad to pursue this course.

Nevertheless, the following night, she angered him again. It proved all too easy. They followed the Sea of the Labyrinth westward, past isles large and small. As far as she knew, Qiyed had no destination in mind. He said nothing about Guild meetings or new human conquests. So she resorted to a proven irritant.

"Where do you think the Walker is right now? Do you have any idea where he was headed?"

She felt his muscles tense beneath her.

"What sort of ship were they on? From which isle does the vessel hail? Is the captain a merchant? A pirate?"

"Stop it."

He kept his voice low, but couldn't mask his ire.

"Stop what? You know Tirribin: we're naturally curious."

He grabbed her arms, pulled her off him, and threw her bodily across swells and troughs. She slammed into the water, the impact stealing her breath. For a fivecount she could do no more than hang below the sea's surface, too hurt and stunned to move. As salt filled her nose and mouth, she kicked up and gulped at the air.

"I will not do this again, Droënalka," he called from a distance. He had thrown her far. "I will not be pestered and provoked. Ask any more questions and you will die."

"Any questions at all? I'm not allowed to ask about your history, or where we're headed, or when I will get to feed next?"

"You know what questions I mean."

"Ah, yes. The Walker. Are you jealous, Qiyed? Or is he closer than you have admitted, and you don't want me—"

He allowed her no more than that. An invisible hand – magick again – forced her under and held her there. She thrashed, because he would expect no less, and because she was frightened. She didn't wish to die this night.

Qiyed seemed intent on killing her. Her lungs burned, pressure built behind her eyes, her struggles grew more frantic. Even so, as fear and lack of air fractured her thoughts, she tried to push back against his magick. He was powerful, and she remained weak, or, more to the point, ignorant in the use of whatever power she possessed. She couldn't overcome him now. But she sensed the limits of his strength, and had an inkling – born of instinct, or perhaps sheer hope – that she might use them to her advantage.

If he gave her that chance. He held her still, his magickal grip as uncompromising as stone. She didn't think he would end her life, but with every passing moment, every strained beat of her heart, her certainty weakened.

Unable to endure any more, she released her held breath. Nothing. No surrender on his part. She had miscalculated. Water flooded her mouth and nose, her chest. Death, then. So be it.

When he released her, she could only lift her eyes to the sea's surface, which stirred and shimmered like satin. Magick touched her again. Prodded her, to no avail. Then Qiyed himself was there, pulling her up and onto his back.

They breached and he shook her until her lungs spasmed and her stomach revolted. She vomited water back into the brine, coughed until tears ran over her cheeks.

"You are a fool," he said, scornful.

Droë was too weak to answer, but in her mind she said, *Perhaps, but you aren't willing to let me die.*

He carried her on, and for the rest of that night she spoke not a word. Nor did she provoke him the following night.

By the third night, she had recovered enough to challenge him again. She waited until they were on land. Another strand, this on one of the Bone isles. She defied him over a trifle: He gave her a bell to hunt; she insisted on two.

As they argued, he regarded her with suspicion. He might have understood that she sought to provoke him. Yet, he couldn't help himself. The more she fought, the angrier he grew. She stood within his reach, and expected that he would lash out with fists and feet.

He didn't. As before, he attacked with magick, raining blows upon her. When that failed to tame her, he squeezed her chest until she couldn't breathe, which proved every bit as horrifying as being drowned.

Droë fought to inhale. Her heart and lungs ached again. Even so, she also considered Qiyed's choices. No physical attack. Did he fear her strength? And his magick, while as powerful as ever, had grown predictable. She felt it as something akin to pressure, a hand pushing through her flesh to reach organs that were more vital. If she could shield her heart and mind with her own power, might she block his assaults? If she sheathed her entire body in magick, might she prevent his every violation?

She didn't dare try. Not so soon. If she alerted him to what she had divined, he might find some new assault. All she learned, though, made his abuse easier to endure. And knowing he wouldn't kill her, kept her worst panic at bay.

Eventually, he let her breathe again, and she agreed to hunt for a bell and one half. A compromise he accepted. Another lesson.

Over the qua'turn and more that followed, she continued to test, provoke, and retreat. More vulnerabilities revealed themselves. His magick could only reach so far. The one time she dared fight him physically, on a night at sea when she pestered him with questions, she discovered that she was indeed as strong as he, and quicker. She didn't push her resistance far; she couldn't risk having him leave her in the middle of the Aiyanthan Sea. Strong as she was, she couldn't swim like an Arrokad. Yet, before she surrendered, she convinced herself that in a fight on land, without magick, she could overpower him.

Most satisfying, she realized that her mind was stronger than his. He, and all Arrokad, knew more of this world than she ever would. He had lived thousands of years longer, had explored every league of every sea, bay, and harbor between the oceans. By comparison, she remained a child.

But he was hostage to his temper, to his capacity for rage, to his need for control. Again she thought him far more human than he would ever admit.

In contrast, she trained herself to defy her temper, to curb her hostility for the Arrokad. She came to see him as pathetic and weak, and she grew more confident in her own abilities.

On this night, after they grappled briefly, she let him force her underwater. He didn't rely on his hands to hold her there, but surrendered to his need for magick. She fought, because he would expect no less.

She didn't panic. *Panic is the enemy,* she told herself. *Hate is the enemy. Magick can only do so much. I need only myself to prevail.*

She repeated these words to herself until he let her breathe. She didn't swallow a drop. She thought she could have held her breath for an entire bell if necessary.

Panic is the enemy. Hate is the enemy. I need only myself to prevail.

Long after their fight ended, as they skimmed again over the swells, the words repeated themselves in her mind, like the invocation of a human priestess.

Panic is the enemy. Hate is the enemy. I need only myself to prevail.

The litany wrapped itself around her, a magick of her own making, armor against all Qiyed might do to her. When next she defied him – again at sea – the words strengthened her. They were proof against all he tried to do to her. She sensed his magick, recognized it, knew how she should react to it. He never realized that it didn't touch her, that she could break free any time she wished. She fought and struggled and surrendered.

And within her mind and heart, she smiled, knowing she had won, content for a little longer to let him believe he controlled her. Soon she would reveal to him her mastery. She would know the right time when it presented itself.

She didn't have to wait long.

Four nights after this last fight, Qiyed carried her past the forested isle of Tirayre, out of the Inward Sea, and into the Sea of Gales.

Throughout the day, awareness of… something lurked at the edge of her consciousness. Qiyed might have sensed it as well. He spoke less than usual, and he swam without his customary abandon.

Late in the afternoon, she realized what had been bothering her. "Belvora," she said.

He slowed and then halted, bobbing in the water, his face tilted to the sky. She searched for the winged ones as well.

He spotted them first and pointed. "Three. They always travel in threes."

"Not always," she said, drawing on a distant memory.

Qiyed didn't argue, but swam on. Droë clung to him, peering back at the creatures, fascinated and unable to say why. They were no threat to her. They would never challenge an Arrokad, or, for that matter, a being such as herself, whatever she was. What had brought them here? Why would they circle above these waters?

"We should remain close," she said after a time. "I want to

know what they're doing here."

She thought he might see this as another challenge. Instead, he slowed again.

"Yes, all right." He swam toward the Belvora, toward the southern shore of Herjes.

As night fell, they neared the isle. The winged ones soared directly above them. And now, other scents reached her as well, tantalizing, but elusive. As darkness gathered, she thought Qiyed became aware of them.

By then, she knew.

"Walkers," she said.

"No."

"I smell them. I taste their years. It's Tobias, isn't it? And the woman who travels with him?"

"It is not. We have to leave."

She released him and pushed away. They were but a league or two from land, close enough that she was willing to risk the sea. "I will go no farther," she said. "Tobias is here. I will see him."

Droë began to swim toward the isle.

Magick grabbed her, lifted her from the swells, and hurled her through the air. She struck the sea with a resounding slap and a huge splash. She sank a few hands, but pushed herself back to air. Qiyed had tossed her to within a few hands of where he floated. She cursed her carelessness.

"Shall we fight again?" he asked, overconfident.

He would think her hesitation a symptom of fear. Let him. She fought herself. She didn't wish to have this battle in water, but she would not allow him to pull her away from here. Not when she was finally so close to Tobias. Was she ready to reveal her strength and all she had learned?

Before she could decide, a new sound reached them: the dry crack of flintlocks. They stared into the night. Droë sensed Qiyed's curiosity. He might not have been ready for her to find Tobias, but he did want to know what was happening with the humans and the Belvora. Perhaps they wouldn't have to fight after all.

More weapons fire crackled. A Belvora shrieked. A death cry.

And then a sound neither had anticipated, a sound that changed everything.

She looked Qiyed's way. "We have no choice now."

"Do we not?"

"No, Qiyed, we don't. If you won't take me there, I swear to tell every Ancient I meet of your dereliction. Every one, for as long as I live."

"I could kill you now."

"You're free to try; I'll summon another Arrokad before you manage it. Or we can do this together."

The slitted eyes narrowed, but only when his mouth twitched did she know she had prevailed.

"Climb on," he said, turning his back to her.

She did.

He dove, dousing her, as if to punish. She didn't mind. As they surged through the salt waves, toward bitter smoke and the smell of Walker magick, her pounding heart threatened to burst from her chest.

CHAPTER 33

18th Day of Kheraya's Settling, Year 634

A qua'turn after Larr suggested that they seek a Bound device from pirates in the Sea of Gales, the *Sea Dove* made land in Vondehm, the royal city of Herjes, on the isle's eastern shore. As in the Knot, the crew and captain had to await permission from city authorities before leaving the ship. This was a busier port, however, and they waited several bells before being approached by a uniformed man.

He was tall, muscular, his dark hair salted with white. Elaborate etchings covered the right side of his face, centered around his eye.

Captain Larr spoke with him on the wharf, a pouch of coins tied to her belt. The official remained stoic. Larr's expression tightened through the encounter. In time, she paid him several gold rounds and ascended the plank to the dock.

Standing with Tobias, Mara gazed after the official as he followed the pier to the next ship. Men and women disembarked from the various vessels moored to the docks, but the only Herjeans she saw – the only people bearing the geometric etchings for which the isle was known – were men.

"That didn't seem to go well," Mara said, as the captain passed.

A frown lined the captain's brow. "It wasn't so bad. Their wharfages have increased."

Mara quirked an eyebrow.

"Herjean men can be… unpleasant," Larr admitted. "This is the only isle between the oceans where I'm made to feel presumptuous for captaining my own vessel." She gave a thin smile. "Well, here and Westisle. No matter. We're free to visit the city," she said, raising her voice so the rest of the crew would hear. A cheer greeted these tidings. "Back on the ship by midnight."

This earned a groan, but in moments, members of the crew were headed off the ship and into Vondehm.

"I have matters to attend to," Larr said. "Some of it is of interest to the two of you. Would you care to join me?"

Tobias glanced at Mara. "I'll stay with Nava. You should go."

Mara agreed, and soon she and the captain had disembarked, and ventured into the heart of the royal city. Mara spotted more Herjean women here, all of them marked with those same etchings. The city itself resembled others she had seen during their travels. Beyond the squalor nearest to the waterfront, Vondehm might have been cleaner than most. Soldiers, in green and silver livery, patrolled the streets in numbers. Pairs of them, swords on their belts, muskets fixed with bayonets, stood on nearly every street corner.

Captain Larr showed no alarm at their presence. She walked with confidence, surveying the shops and peddlers' carts that lined the lanes. They didn't stop at any of them, nor did they linger in the city marketplace.

"Where are we going, captain?" Mara asked.

"To a smaller marketplace on the west end of the city," Larr said, speaking as she might of the weather. "The main market caters to the city's wealthy, and merchants who come here to get rich off them. This other is for traders and farmers and craftsmen who operate beyond the city's walls."

"So there's more gold to be made in the main market."

"Yes, but one of the traders at this other is a man I've known for many years. He traded with my father. And he has friends who…" She glanced around them. The street wasn't as crowded as those nearest the wharves, but neither was it empty. "Who live west of here," she went on, her meaning clear enough. "I sent a message ahead. He may have information for us."

The back of Mara's neck tightened as the captain said this. She looked over her shoulder.

"Is something the matter?"

"Probably not. I'm just not used to… to this place." *Or to treating with pirates and smugglers.*

They walked on. Mara scanned the byways.

She expected this second marketplace to be different from others she had seen. Seedier. More menacing. It was neither. Had she not known that Vondehm had another market, she would have assumed this one served the entire city. Men and women, most marked with etchings, crowded around peddlers' tables and carts, shouting for attention, waving purses or holding up coins they squeezed between finger and thumb. Children and dogs ran underfoot. The entire plaza smelled of woodsmoke and rotting greens, fried bread and dead fish.

Larr led Mara around the perimeter of the market, dark eyes peering into shadows, searching. After circling nearly the entire space, she muttered something Mara didn't hear and angled into the crowd. After a few steps, she paused and leaned close to Mara.

"I probably don't need to say this, but let me talk. Don't say anything unless you're spoken to. These are Herjean men, many of them. A few might hail from Westisle itself. Most of them are asses. They're quick-tempered, used to getting their way, and dangerous if provoked."

"All right."

Mara followed the captain to a broad table set beneath a canvas shelter. The table was covered with a random array of items: pistols, knives, blue bottles full of wines both pale and dark, strands of dried kelp, gemstone-crusted brooches, necklaces, and bracelets, and more. Mara didn't see any chronofors or sextants, but she wasn't sure peddlers would display such items. Three men sat in chairs behind the table, all of them marked with etchings, all of them wiry and olive complected. One was sleeping. The other two had eyes of pale green. They might all have been brothers.

The middle one wore a black shirt and matching breeches. The one to his right, who carved a piece of bone with a small blade, wore a leather vest over his bare torso. The shelter stank of stale whiskey, but those pressed around the wares didn't notice or care. Larr halted behind the men and women closest to the table, and peered over their shoulders as they jostled one another and bartered with the two sensate men.

Mara stood with her, hearing more than she saw. The booth seemed a den of chaos, of argument and barely controlled violence. She sensed the peddlers were enjoying themselves.

At one point, Vest spotted Captain Larr and dipped his chin fractionally in recognition. No words passed between them. The peddler began haggling with a burly, bald man over a flask of dark liquor.

Shortly after, the man in the black shirt stood, and slipped out of the booth through a slit in the canvas. He said nothing and didn't spare Larr and Mara a glance. A spirecount later, the captain touched Mara's shoulder, gestured with a quick cant of her head, and led her away from the booth. They strolled to the next table, and the one after that.

Then they slipped between two booths to a sheltered patch of brown grass, out of sight of others in the plaza.

Black Shirt awaited them there. He was a full head shorter than the captain, and barely taller than Mara herself. A pistol hung on his belt, as did a large knife.

He flashed a dark smile at the captain, exposing crooked yellow teeth. "Seris." He barely took notice of Mara.

"Weld."

"You's looking well. Merchant life must be good."

"No," Larr said, her eyes wide in an innocent stare. "We're barely scratching by. We had a dog on board for a while, but we were forced to eat him. Would have starved otherwise."

He laughed, high and harsh. "Right, I'm sure." He nodded in Mara's direction. "This your new girl?"

"This is an associate of mine."

Black Shirt looked Mara over, his gaze brazen and hungry. Mara suffered it without squirming, and refused to avert her eyes.

"She's a pretty one," he said with a leer. "She have a name?"

"Not that you need know," Larr said.

He faced the captain again. "All right."

"You received my message?"

"Bound devices."

"Just so."

"Everyone wants 'em, you know. We get inquiries all the time. Not only merchants and traders. The Oaqamarans are after 'em. So are the Sheraighs and the Aiyanthans. Milnos, Vleros. You'd think all these places have Binders of their own, but they want devices quicker than their folk can make 'em." He considered Mara again. "Northisler, right? You the one wantin' a bound piece? A chronofor maybe?"

"I'm a Spanner," Mara said.

"Is that right?" He sounded doubtful.

"You want me to Span for you right now? Sell us a sextant and I'll do it." She smirked. "I'd even have to strip down."

The leer returned. "I like this one, Seris. She has spirit." He pivoted back to the captain. "But I've got nothin' for you. There's none to be had here."

"None at all?" Larr asked. "I don't believe it. There've been none in the Ring Isles either, or in the Knot. How can there be no Bound devices for sale anywhere between the oceans?"

"Bad luck, I guess."

"I'd rather not go on into the Sea of Gales, but I will. I'll go to Westisle if I have to. So if you're holding out, hoping I'll pay more…"

She trailed off as Weld shook his head. "You're not listenin' to me. You think I don't want the sale? You know me better. You also know that I take care of them I call friends. We've had our differences, you and I, but you're a friend. And I'm tellin' you now to think on what I said."

Larr blinked and stared. Color drained from her cheeks.

"Blood and bone."

"There's nothing for you here," he said again. "I'd be on my way if I was you. You catch?"

The captain touched Mara's shoulder, already turning to leave the patch of grass. "Come along."

Mara glanced back at the peddler, who watched her, speculation in his glance. She hurried after Larr.

"What's the matter? What did he mean by all that?"

"'The Oaqamarans are after them,'" Larr repeated in a whisper. As they entered the plaza again, she scanned the throng. She held her pistol; Mara hadn't seen her pull it from her belt. "The Sheraighs, the Aiyanthans. Vleros and Milnos."

"Some of them are after us, too."

"I fear all of them are. We need to get back to the ship, and then we need to leave these waters."

"And go where?"

"Wherever we can. The southern Ring maybe. Or the Labyrinth. Anywhere but here."

"Do you think we're in danger from the pirates?"

"He all but told us we were. I'd guess there's a bounty on your heads. Trading with pirates is one thing, but a bounty? That's free gold as far as they're concerned." Larr cast a look over her shoulder. "I'm sorry. We should have listened to Tobias."

As the sun turned a slow arc above the Vondehm waterfront, the air warmed. Small clouds scudded across the blue, but nothing that threatened rain. When Sofya woke from her midday nap, Tobias took her into the bay for a swim.

She was still too young to float on her own, but she held on to his hands and kicked her feet, squealing with delight as he pulled her in broad circles. After a bit of prodding, she put her face in the water. The first time, she came up sputtering and coughing, but Tobias showed her how to hold her breath and how to blow bubbles in the brine. Soon she was submerging her entire head and poking it up again. She laughed so hard she gave herself hiccups.

A cloud passed before the sun, plunging them into shadow. Tobias checked its size and position. The sun would peek out again before long.

Something in the broad patch of blue beside the cloud caught his eye. Sofya called to him, but he barely heard.

It had to be a seabird.

It's too big.

"Papa!"

He pulled her close and put an arm around her. "One moment, love," he said, still squinting at the sky.

Three of them, circling. Too large.

"Blood and Bone."

"Bloody bone," she echoed in a singsong. "I go under again."

"Later," he said, kicking them back toward the rope ladder on the *Dove*'s hull.

"No!" She struggled in his arms. "I go under again!"

"One time," he said. "Then we have to get back on the ship. Mama will be back soon."

She agreed to this, and dunked herself twice more. They climbed back onto the deck. The sun had cleared the clouds. Tobias had to shield his eyes to study the sky. They were still there.

Belvora. Again.

He dressed Sofya and pulled on his own clothes. Leaving the princess to wander the ship, keeping an eye on the soaring demons, he approached Bramm, who had already returned from his foray into the city.

Leaning on the rail beside the man, he said, "Quietly, calmly, look overhead and tell me what you see."

Bramm regarded Tobias, then did as he asked. He spotted them within a fivecount. His imprecation was stronger than Tobias's had been.

"What do we do?"

Before he could answer, he spotted Mara and the captain striding toward the wharf. Both of them held pistols.

"Take someone into the city," Tobias said. "Find the rest of the crew and get them back here. I think we need to leave."

The sailor had spotted Larr as well. "Right."

Bramm and Moth left the vessel. They met the captain on the wharf, spoke with her for a tencount. Larr made no effort to stop them.

She and Mara rushed up the plank. He met them at the rail.

"How did you know?" Larr asked.

"Know what?"

She shook her head. "Why are Bramm and Moth—"

He pointed at the sky, cutting her off.

Larr spotted the demons before Mara.

"Damn!"

"What happened in the city?"

Mara described their encounter with the peddler. As she talked, Sofya ran to her and pulled at her shift until Mara picked her up.

"I put my head in da water."

"Good for you, love."

Larr squinted up at the Belvora again. "What kind of enemy works with pirates and demons and merchants?"

"Orzili," Tobias said. "Back in Hayncalde, I had the sense that he was working for the autarch and the Sheraighs and even for himself. We shouldn't be surprised that his reach is this long."

Bramm and Moth had the rest of the crew back on the *Sea Dove* within a single bell, and still that felt too long to Tobias. He expected the Belvora to pelt down on them at any moment. He should have known better. By day, the demons would keep their distance. As long as they circled so high, they could track the ship in complete safety and report to their allies, whoever they might be.

"Are we safer on land or sea?" Mara asked, as the crew readied the ship for departure.

Larr stood at the wheel, overseeing preparations. At the question, she came forward.

"Neither choice is good. The demons are a threat no matter where we go."

"I'm not as worried about the Belvora as I am about Orzili and his men," Tobias said. "We're safer from them on water."

"Not if they're on a marauder, or a war eagle."

"They won't be. They'll use tri-sextants to Span directly onto the ship."

Larr frowned. "Tri-sextants?"

"Spanning devices that… It's too much to explain right now. The point is, if we're at sea, they can't surround us. We fight on equal footing."

"You're forgetting the Belvora!"

Tobias frowned in turn.

"If we stay, we might have help," Larr said, more to Mara than Tobias.

"The men we saw today?"

"They harbor no love for the autarchy, or for the Sheraighs, I would imagine."

"Can they be trusted?"

A bitter smile crossed the captain's lips. "Not even a little. But we don't have many options."

"We should at least leave the wharf," Tobias said. "If we're going to be attacked from the city, I want to see it coming."

"Agreed," Larr said. "We'll oar out to the middle of the harbor and drop anchor." She started back toward her quarters. "In the meantime, I'll get word to Weld and his brothers."

"I thought you didn't trust him," Mara called after her.

"I trust in gold," she said over her shoulder.

Seeing Mara's furrowed brow, she halted and returned to them. "He warned us today. If he and the others were working with the Sheraighs, or whoever is after you, he wouldn't have done that. He's a cutthroat, and he'd sell his mother for the right price. That said, he also named me a friend. He wouldn't do that lightly."

She left them again and closed herself in her quarters.

Tobias considered the Belvora, and then the wharf and the lanes beyond them. He could almost feel Orzili at his shoulder and smell the man's sweat, mingled with the fetor of Hayncalde's dungeon. He nearly gagged.

"Are you all right?" Mara asked, a slender hand on his arm.

"No. We're trapped. We're right where he wants us."

"I'm sorry, Tobias. I–"

He took her hand. "It's not your fault, or the captain's, or mine for that matter. If it wasn't here, he would have found us somewhere else. We knew we couldn't run forever."

Larr emerged moments later with a pouch of coins and a folded piece of parchment. She gave both to Bramm and spoke to him at length. When she finished, he nodded and left the ship. Next, the captain had Moth and Yadreg lower the pinnace to the water and tie it to a bollard.

Not long after, Tobias and Mara cast off lines, and other members of the crew rowed the *Sea Dove* away from the wharf and to the center of the harbor. Other ships lay anchored there. Not many, but enough to keep the *Dove* from being too conspicuous.

Of course, with the Belvora soaring above them, it hardly mattered if they were conspicuous or not. As long as the demons sensed his magick and Mara's, those working with them would know exactly where to find the ship.

Larr joined Tobias and Mara again.

"Bramm will deliver my message to Weld and his brothers, and he'll buy us fresh supplies of ammunition, powder, and paper. We may have run out of good fortune, but we won't run out of bullets."

Tobias didn't answer.

"We've done what we can," the captain said. "There's naught to do now but wait. The attack will come, or it won't. We'll prevail, or we won't." She flashed a wry grin. "That's probably not very reassuring, is it?"

Mara said nothing, eyes on him.

"Actually, it's more reassuring than I would have expected. I've been afraid of this fight for so long, the fear has settled in my bones. I'm sick of it. Better to have it come, one way or another."

"I couldn't have said it better." The captain moved off, shouting orders to others.

"So you're not afraid?" Mara asked, when they were alone.

"Oh, I'm terrified." A quick smile passed between them. "But if we have to face Orzili, let's get it over with."

They checked the Belvora once more, then joined others as they gathered weapons at the ship's prow. Nearly a full bell later, Bramm returned with the ammunition, powder, and paper. The powder wasn't Aiyanthan white, but Herjes produced decent yellow powder, which would be good enough, as long as the weather held.

Time crawled by. Larr watched the mouth of the bay, anxious, her lips pressed into a taut line. Occasionally Tobias heard her mutter about the other ships and how they should have arrived already. Tobias had been suspicious of the pirates, leery of this alliance of convenience. But he saw their failure to join the *Dove* as an ill omen. Just before dusk, Bramm spotted two thin plumes of dark smoke rising from beyond the bay. Tobias feared the worst. Judging from Larr's grim expression, he guessed she did, too.

The crew ate a cold dinner on the ship's deck. Tobias saw his own tension mirrored in the faces of the men and women around him. Aside from Sofya, no one said much. She chattered as usual, wandering from one cluster of sailors to the next, coaxing smiles from even the gravest of them, like a commander circulating among her warriors on the eve of battle.

After they finished eating, Tobias took the princess below and sang her to sleep.

Soon after that, the attack began.

Tobias watched the city, in case Herjean authorities took it upon themselves to commandeer the ship. As he gazed westward, a group of men appeared along the shore near the wharf, on an empty stretch of lane lit by torchfire. They didn't march onto the street, or emerge from a barrack. They simply winked into view, as if placed there by magick. As if they had Spanned. It might have been a trick of the light, but he thought he saw something golden flash with torchfire.

The men wore black. Assassins. Orzili's killers. He kept his eyes on them even as he called Mara to his side and pointed.

She didn't spot them until they struck out toward the pier. Tobias counted fifteen, maybe sixteen. He assumed they were armed, and that Orzili was with them.

His heart pounded, and his stomach knotted like wet rope.

"I'll get the captain."

Mara started away, but hadn't taken more than two steps when a piercing wail from above rent the quiet of the harbor. Tobias searched the darkness, but couldn't spot the Belvora. Turning back to the city, he saw that the men had halted. Several pointed out at the harbor.

A second demon scream came from so close that Tobias ducked. Others among the crew had armed themselves and now took positions around the ship. Tobias and Mara did the same, their muskets loaded and full-cocked, pistols on their belts.

Tobias scanned the sky, checked the city again.

He had lost sight of the Spanners.

He opened his mouth to shout a warning. Too late. Volleys of musket fire erupted from a nearby Kant. Bullets whistled past and gouged chunks of wood from the *Dove*'s rail. Flashes of fire illuminated the night. Smoke hazed the air around the other ship.

Tobias braced his weapon, aimed, and fired. A man in black dropped out of sight.

Bursts of flame, the roar of weapons fire, gouts of white smoke. He reloaded as quickly as he could. Heard musket fire around him. One of Larr's men gave an odd sigh and collapsed to the deck, blood gushing from a hole in his brow.

Another howled and dropped her musket, clutching at a bloody shoulder.

"Tobias!"

He twisted, threw himself down and to the side. A talon carved through his shirt and the flesh on his back, tearing a cry from his lips. He fell onto the wound, pain burning like a brand. The Belvora. Forgotten for just an instant. *Fool! Idiot!* A child's mistake.

The demon wheeled a tight circle, dove at him. He fumbled for his pistol, managed to pull it free. The Belvora veered again, up and out of the torchlight.

Mara rushed to his side.

"Are you—"

"I'm all right." He forced himself up to a crouch, agony between his shoulderblades. "Aim for the tri-sextants!" he called to the others. "The golden devices, and the men who hold them."

The two ships continued to exchange musket fire. Winged demons swooped over the *Dove*, menacing its crew.

Another of Larr's sailors fell, blood staining his shirt.

The captain glared as Yadreg scuttled to the wounded man. "My crew are used to fighting pirates and slavers, not trained assassins. We'll be wiped out in no time! They don't need to board us!"

Another Belvora swept over them, a clawed fist barely missing Moth. Bramm and Gwinda spun, tracking the beast with their weapons. They fired at the same time. The demon wailed.

Muskets boomed from the other ship. Gwinda collapsed and didn't move again. Blood from a wound to her back stained her shirt, pooled at her side, and coursed over the deck.

Tobias and Mara gaped. Even the captain didn't appear to know what to do. Yadreg left the wounded sailor and crawled to Gwinda. Upon reaching her, he merely hung his head, his eyes squeezed shut.

Another Belvora dove at the old sailor, only cutting away when others on the ship turned their weapons in its direction.

"I'll call them off, Tobias!"

Tobias froze, then stared across the ebon sea to the other vessel. He knew that voice. Everyone on the *Dove* watched him.

He heard crying from below. Sofya was awake. They couldn't spare Mara's musket, or he would have asked her to go below. He feared what might happen if Sofya climbed to the deck and Orzili Spanned to the ship.

"I'll call off the demons; I'll call off my men. Surrender yourself and the child, and the rest can live. Even the woman."

He looked at Mara, who shook her head.

"Keep fighting," Orzili went on, "and you'll die anyway. And you'll take the rest of them with you."

CHAPTER 34

18th Day of Kheraya's Settling, Year 634

Mara knew Tobias well. He would give his life to keep her and Sofya alive. He would never surrender the princess. And he would fight until every hope had exhausted itself.

Captain Larr misread his silence.

"The only thing worse than losing members of my crew, Mister Lijar, would be losing them for nothing."

Sofya wailed below. Mara wanted to go to her, but refused to leave the deck.

"You needn't worry, captain," Tobias said. "I'm not about to agree to his terms."

Relief smoothed her brow. "Then what do you have in mind?"

To Mara, he said, "Ujie?"

"Do you think she would answer another summons?"

"I don't know. There are Ancients involved, so she might. But she won't allow me to put off my... my boon again. She'll take me away. I don't know that I'd ever see you again."

"Then you shouldn't call for her."

His smile made her heart ache. "Sofya would be safe. And so would you."

"That's not a trade she and I are willing to make."

"If not Ujie, then what?" Larr asked, drawing their gazes.

Mara lifted her brows. "The mist demon?"

"My patience wears thin, Tobias!" Orzili called from the Kant.

Larr turned, keeping low. "Yadreg, sing! Now!"

Tears still ran from the old sailor's eyes, but he answered with

456

a jerky nod. He swallowed, tipped his face toward the night, and sang the song he had composed for the Shonla. His voice shook at first, but it strengthened as he began the verse a second time.

Mara spotted the cloud of mist racing over the sea in their direction. Simultaneously, the Belvora trumpeted a warning. She wondered if Orzili understood.

Apparently, he did.

As fog enveloped the *Dove*, shadows appeared amidships.

Tobias shouted a warning. He needn't have bothered. A salvo of musket fear greeted the invaders. Orzili and his men fired as well. Pain blazed in Mara's thigh. She screamed and fell back, clutching her leg. Blood ran hot through her fingers.

Weapons went off to her left and right. Men and women fell, some wearing black, some from Larr's crew. Burnt powder stung her nose.

She saw Orzili drop his musket and reach for his pistol. A form flew at him and knocked him back. The pistol clattered across the deck to the base of the hull, not far from where she lay.

Tobias hammered a fist to Orzili's face and another. The assassin landed a blow of his own, threw Tobias off. They locked eyes for a heartbeat. Then both scrambled toward the pistol.

Tobias reached it first, but Orzili slammed him into the hull, cracking his head against the rail. Tobias sagged onto the deck, his bulk covering the pistol. Orzili grappled with him, tried to push him away. Mara dragged herself along the wood planks, which were slick with her blood, and kicked out with her good leg. She caught Orzili in the side of the head, addling him, though not for long.

He hissed a curse, pounded his fist into her wounded leg. Mara bellowed. Tears blurred her sight. He hit her again. She sobbed.

By now, Tobias had recovered. He grabbed Orzili by the collar and threw him to the deck. Seizing the pistol, he pounced on the man and pounded the butt of the weapon across Orzili's temple. Orzili blocked a second blow, took hold of Tobias's wrist. He wrapped his other hand around Tobias's throat.

Tobias clawed at that hand, struggled to free his wrist from the assassin's grip.

Another shot from nearby made Mara flinch.

A ghostly yawl, sharp, ear-splitting, mournful, rose from the prow of the ship. Twisting to look that way, Mara saw a vague figure shudder and fall. It landed on the deck with a dull thud.

The mist and cold receded until the only cloud around the *Sea Dove* was the thin, gray residue of powder smoke. The form on the deck was gray, hairless, blunt-featured. Shaf. Thick, pinkish blood oozed from a wound to the Shonla's chest.

Every man and woman on the vessel – sailor and assassin alike – paused to gape at the creature. Even Tobias and Orzili separated. Both labored for breath. Blood oozed from a welt on the assassin's temple and from Tobias's nose and lip.

Two Belvora glided to the ship's deck, alighting on either side of the Shonla. They eyed each other and then dropped to their knees. Mara wondered if they sought to honor their fellow Ancient. It took her but a single heartbeat to understand that they intended to devour it.

Three muskets boomed in quick succession. Both Belvora spasmed. One tipped over and didn't move again. Foul blood streamed from its head. The other screeched, writhing, bleeding from its neck. One last pistol shot snapped its head back, silencing it.

After another moment of stunned calm, assassins and sailors attacked one another again. Swords clanged. Pistols spat flame and smoke. Orzili charged at Tobias, shoving him back until they crashed into the hull. Tobias dropped his pistol. His feet left the deck. Mara was certain he would flip overboard and fall into the bay.

Somehow he righted himself. He wrestled Orzili back a pace and then another. Orzili tried to draw his knife. Tobias reached for his. Mara scrabbled to where the pistol lay. She pulled the powder and ammunition from her belt, desperate to load. Trying to keep from being noticed by the men wearing black.

"Hold, humans!"

A woman's voice, deep and powerful. Yet, it was the words as much as the tone that stopped them.

Hold, humans.

Two of them stood near the prow. Near the dead Ancients. The woman might have been the most beautiful being Mara had ever seen. Even more lovely than Ujie. She had golden hair, milky gray eyes, and nut brown skin almost as dark as Mara's. Her clothes were tatters, more befitting a street urchin than one of the Ancients.

An Arrokad stood with her, naked to his waist and scaled below. He was as pale as his companion was dark, with the slitted, snakelike eyes of his kind, and hair as black as pitch.

The Arrokad stepped to Shaf's body with the grace of a dancer and knelt beside it.

The other creature stared at Mara, eyes wide with something akin to shock, or fear.

"You," she whispered. Her ghostly gaze swept the deck. When she spotted Tobias, she froze. She raised a hand, her fingers curling, except the one she pointed at his heart. "You're Tobias."

Mara stared at her, viewing her now in profile. Recognition burned through her with the sizzle of a lightning strike.

"Droë."

Tobias and Orzili both gawked in her direction before turning to the Ancient.

"You're Droë?" Orzili asked.

The Ancient seemed to notice him for the first time. Her eyes went wide yet again. "Cresten?"

Color suffused his cheeks. After the briefest of hesitations, he nodded. "That's right."

Tobias eyed him. "Cresten? It almost makes you sound human." He didn't wait for an answer. He pivoted toward Droë. "What happened to you?" he asked.

"I want to know what was done to the Shonla," a voice cut in before she could reply.

All of them faced the Arrokad.

"Come here, Droë."

She cast a furtive glance at Tobias and Orzili, but retreated to the Arrokad's side, as docile as a hound.

"Who shot him?"

The sailors and assassins eyed one another.

"Who!" the Arrokad demanded, his voice echoing with the power of a hundred breakers.

"Him," a sailor said, pointing at an assassin. Orzili's man sat propped against the hull, bleeding from a wound to his arm.

The Arrokad walked to him, silent, his mien as hard as carved marble. He made a fist of his right hand, a small gesture, barely noticeable.

The assassin gave a strangled gasp. His good hand scraped at his chest. He stared up at the Arrokad, teeth bared and clenched. After a few moments, his eyes rolled up in his head, and he fell onto his side. He kicked out a foot once, twice, and sagged.

"What about the Belvora?" Orzili asked. He pointed at Moth, Jacq, and Bramm. "Those men shot them. Will you punish them, too?"

"No," the Arrokad said. He returned to the dead Shonla. "Belvora are predators," he continued as he walked. "They prey on beings like you, who possess magick. You have every right to defend yourselves. You would be within your rights to kill Droë as well, if she attempted to feed on you. A Shonla..."

"Shonla attack ships."

The Arrokad halted mid-step, half-turned to glare back at the assassin. Even in this, his body flowed like water. After staring for two breaths, he made a small motion with his hand. Acknowledgment, acquiescence. "Yes, they do. But I like them. I do not like Belvora."

He continued to where Droë waited.

"We are leaving now," he said to her.

"No," Droë answered. "We're not."

Droë's heart thrummed. Her hands shook. All that she had done and endured – her departure from Trevynisle, her endless travels with Tresz, her confrontations with Teelo and Maeli, Strie and Kreeva, her transformation from Tirribin to whatever she was now – had brought her to this moment. The Walkers were here, with another from her past whom she had forgotten. She would not leave. She would not allow herself to be dragged away.

She wasn't certain she had learned enough to defy the Arrokad. She would know soon enough.

Hearing her words – words she could hardly believe she had dared speak – Qiyed went still. "You defy me?"

She met the serpentine gaze. No doubt he sensed her fear. She didn't care.

"I do," she said, her voice steady. "We are entered in a bargain. Freely, fairly. That doesn't make me your servant or your slave. These are the Walkers I have sought. We will remain here until I have treated with them."

A savage smile exposed the Arrokad's honed teeth.

Magick charged the air between them. His assault, she knew, was meant to cause pain, and also humiliation. Brilliant and powerful though he was, he was also predictable. He had done this to her before, the night she first tasted desire. The agony remained fresh in her memory.

Vicious. Demeaning. A violation and a reminder of what he had done to bring her to this new form. Something he would never think to do to an ordinary Tirribin. Something a female Arrokad would never think to do to her.

She stiffened, saw the Arrokad's smile broaden. The first hint of pain touched her. She forced herself to remain calm, intent. *Panic is the enemy. Hate is the enemy. I need only myself to prevail.*

Using the knowledge she had gained in recent days, she denied him access to her mind, shoving him out as if with both hands.

He stormed at her, buffeted her with magick, assailed her from all sides.

Droë fought back by not fighting at all. She surrounded herself with power, shrouded herself in abilities only recently realized.

Like a storm tide pounding at a rocky shore, like rain and wind lashing at stone, his attack came to nothing. She kept her back straight, eyes locked on his. His smile died a slow death.

He gave up, though not to surrender.

He darted a hand toward her neck, the motion a pale blur in the firelight. She blurred as well. A step, no more. Out of harm's way. He tried to shift his grasp to follow her. She slapped his hand away, the smack of flesh on flesh as flat and loud as a pistol shot.

He flung a hand at her, a backhanded blow aimed at her cheek. She caught his wrist in her hand. For a fivecount he pushed against her grip, and she pushed back. At last, she forced his hand down.

His mouth hung open, his eyes bulged like those of a human denied air. Awe, shock. One might have thought she had turned herself to gold and sprouted wings.

"I am more than Tirribin," she said. "I am more than Arrokad. I am more than you, Qiyed."

She released his hand. He didn't try again to strike her. Instead, he massaged his wrist where she had held him.

She blurred again, hooking one arm around his throat, an iron grip. She put her mouth to his neck, lips tasting salt on his skin.

"I will not take your years," she said, whispering as a lover might, "though you have many, and I imagine they are sweet and rich with the promise of centuries to be spent journeying between the oceans. You will not hurt me anymore, or threaten me, or try to cause me pain. You will not hurt or threaten or kill any Tirribin. You will not hurt or threaten or kill the Walker, or his companion, or any other Ancient or human who is dear to me. Agree to this, and I will let you keep the years you have. Are these terms acceptable?"

Qiyed struggled against her, but she held him fast.

"They are," he whispered.

"Freely entered, fairly sworn?"

"You are threatening me. Not freely entered."

She released him and blurred back a step.

"Freely entered, fairly sworn?" she asked again.

He flicked his snake eyes toward the sailors and assassins, toward Tobias and the woman and Cresten. "Freely entered," he said. "Fairly sworn."

"Under threat of Distraint."

He scowled. "Under threat of Distraint." He spat the words as he would poison.

She didn't allow herself a smile, but acknowledged his words with a nod.

"What of our arrangement?"

"You did all that I asked, and I have done all that you have demanded. Our arrangement is complete."

He glowered. "I did more for you than you have done in return."

"I disagree. And I wonder what the Guild might think of your commerce with other Ancients." She flashed a thin smile. "Think on that. Right now, I have business with these humans."

She walked back to Tobias and Cresten without waiting for his reply. Before she reached them, a sound snagged her attention. She had missed it before, had been too distracted by the Shonla's death and her conflict with Qiyed to taste the years hiding below. A child. Sweet and young, but confused by misfuture.

Only a turn before, the promise of those years might have consumed her. Not anymore. She continued to the Travelers, one a friend from a long-forgotten past, the other a friend from a still-unknown future.

"You are at war with each other," she said, halting before them. "Why?"

The one she knew as Cresten shied from her appraisal. Tobias did not.

The Walker was taller than she, with long, unruly bronze hair that fell about his shoulders, giving him a wild appearance. His nose was prominent, long, his lips full. Not a perfect human face, and even less so with the ugly scars on his cheeks, brow, temple, and jawline. So much time spent in pursuit of him, so many leagues traveled. She had altered her very being out of want of him, for the sake of a vision that had taken shape in her mind and glittered like gold next to this, the real thing. She should have been disappointed. Perhaps she was.

There was more to him, however. Some of it was physical. His eyes shone, a stunning green that would make emeralds seem dull. His shoulders were broad, his hips narrow. Strong, large hands gripped his weapons.

He stood amidst this carnage, bleeding from a wound that stank of Belvora, with his back straight, his body coiled, the ferocity of a hawk in his gaze.

Standing so close that she could have touched a finger to his lips or to the small indentation at the base of his neck, just above the powerful chest, Droë understood that he was no less than what she expected. He was simply alive, a being independent of her imagination, and therefore different.

"We're at war," he said, the voice not especially deep, but clear and strong, "because he wants me dead."

Cresten didn't deny this.

She studied him. "Why do you want him dead?"

"Forgive me for saying so, but this isn't your concern."

"Not my concern, human?" she asked, allowing a rasp to roughen the question. "Was the Shonla killed because you want him dead? Were the Belvora? It is the concern of all Ancients. And I am here. Now, answer me."

He couldn't face her for long. "You can hear the reason," he said.

She listened. "The child. What of her?"

Cresten and Tobias regarded each other with such venom, Droë thought they might resume their conflict despite her presence.

"What of her?" she demanded of them again.

"I left the Travelers' Palace for the Court of Hayncalde, in Daerjen," Tobias said. "Orzili assassinated the sovereign and his family. The child below is Mearlan's last surviving heir. I've vowed to keep her alive. He wants to kill her. And me."

"You call yourself Orzili?"

"For a long time now," Cresten said. "Since Windhome."

She turned to Mara, who sat on the deck in a pool of her own blood. Of the three of them, she had the strongest claim on Droë's friendship, if only because Droë had declared the woman her friend most recently. Yet the mere sight of her filled Droë's heart with hot envy.

"What is your role in all of this?"

Mara looked past her to Tobias. Droë followed the direction of her gaze.

Love. In his eyes and hers. Green and hazel, twined like ivy on a tree. Jealousy flared to rage.

"She's my wife," Tobias said. "Mother to the child."

Mother... "But that's not—"

"It's a ruse," Cresten said with contempt. "A deception intended to keep those they meet from asking about the girl."

She considered them again – Tobias and the woman. Clearly she wasn't the mother, anymore than Tobias was the father. Their love, though – that was no ruse. Even she, as yet not well-versed in matters of the human heart, could see as much. In that moment, more than anything in the world, she wanted to take Mara's years. Every one of them, so that nothing remained of her but husk. Or better, only most of them, so Tobias would see her shriveled and ancient, her skin lined, sunken, her body bent and ravaged by time.

She hadn't fed in bells. She would welcome a meal, nearly as much as she would welcome the woman's humiliation, the chance to see Tobias's love wither and die.

Tirribin Droë would have done it. Girl-thing Droë might have believed that with the woman gone, Tobias would turn to her for love.

Mara quailed at the touch of Droë's gaze. She might have sensed the danger she was in. She was smarter than the others, at least in this. Perhaps rivals in love recognized each other, by instinct, the way prey recognized predator. Did she read her own doom in Droë's scrutiny?

No. Droë gave the smallest shake of her head. That was enough. Mara inhaled, exhaled, reprieve in that one breath.

The changes wrought by Qiyed's magick and her own embrace of whatever she had become had brought her wisdom on top of everything else. If she killed the woman, Tobias would hate her forever. That was love, too. That was passion. It didn't jump from one creature to the next, like a Shonla seeking screams in a bay full of ships. It survived loss, death, denial. Tobias loved this woman. It didn't matter if she lived or died. Just as it didn't matter to Droë that he wasn't beautiful or perfect. Just as it didn't matter that he loved another. She loved him anyway. She couldn't help herself. And so she knew – she *knew* – he would not relinquish his love, even if she acted on her jealousy. He certainly wouldn't give his love to her.

Which left her at a loss. Should she kill out of pique? Out of envy? Should she leave Tobias and Cresten to grapple with each other, and let the strongest and canniest prevail? Truly, she didn't know.

"What happened to you, Droë?" Tobias asked, snapping her out of her musings. "How did you change so?"

Her cheeks flamed. Out of the corner of her eye, she saw Qiyed smirk.

"Does it matter?"

"Of course it matters. You're my friend. I'm curious about you."

"I have no recollection of our friendship. These two–" She gestured at Cresten and the woman. "I know them. I remember them. You and I meet years from now. You might have lived it, but I haven't. And even Tirribin can't see into the future."

"Are you still Tirribin?"

The man who was Cresten tightened his grip on the knife. "A fascinating question," he said, sounding anything but fascinated. "But not the reason I'm here. I've lost men tonight, and I've yet to finish what I came to do."

She had liked Cresten well enough. She didn't like Orzili.

"You will not kill him," she said.

He kept his eyes fixed on Tobias, who raised his blade as well. "Years ago you declared yourself my friend. That's more than you've done for him."

"Nevertheless."

"Fine. What about the child? Surely you don't care about her. I'll let you have her years. I don't need to kill her myself. If she dies, I'm willing to let him go."

Tempting. The child's years, imperfect though they were, would make a fine meal.

"Would you accept this?" she asked Tobias. "Your life and the woman's in exchange for the child?"

"No. I'd sooner die." He traced a finger over one scar and then another. "You see these? Orzili gave them to me in Hayncalde's dungeon. All of them, on my face, my back, my chest. Cuts, burns, broken bones. Torture intended to make me agree to exactly the bargain he's offering now. I refused then, and I love the child even more today. I'll trade my life to save hers. She has to live."

"What about her life?" Droë asked, pointing at Mara.

"I'd make the same trade," the woman said before Tobias could answer. "I'll die before I surrender her."

Droë regarded them, her forehead creased in concentration. With all she had learned, she still didn't know as much about love as she wanted or needed. It had more currents and eddies than the sea. Still, she understood enough.

"No," she said to Cresten. "The woman is my friend, as you are, and Tobias will be. I would honor our pledge of friendship as well, but not in this way, not at the cost of this life."

He didn't move, not even to loosen his hold on the weapon. Droë wondered if she might have to hurt him, or take some of his years. But then he appeared to think better of fighting her. He lowered his blade hand and sheathed the weapon.

"Fine." He flashed a malicious smile at Tobias. "There's always tomorrow."

An idea came to her. She took hold of Cresten's arm and steered him to where Qiyed waited.

"You can take him somewhere, yes?"

"Take me where?"

"Silence!" she said with a Tirribin rasp.

He clamped his mouth shut, sullen, his trepidation palpable.

"You ask a boon?" Qiyed said.

"I seek restitution for wrongs you have visited upon me."

"What wrongs?"

She glared. "You truly need to ask?"

After some time, he said, "This would settle matters between us? Keep you from telling others about my... my commerce?"

"It would settle matters, and I would tell none of what you've done to me. As to the rest, I promise nothing if I should learn of future transgressions."

He weighed this. "Where would you send him?"

"Far. Flynse, perhaps."

Cresten's gaze flew between them. "No!"

They ignored him.

"You would tell him nothing of what has passed between us," she said. "You would enter no bargains of any kind with him. Indeed, I would prefer that you didn't speak to him at all."

"You ask much."

"I have endured much. And witnessed more."

Qiyed made a small impatient motion with his hand. "Very well. I will take him."

"Make him leave his sextant," Tobias said. "Otherwise he'll be back here within a bell. It won't matter how far they go."

Cresten turned a glare on him that could have melted steel. Qiyed scowled as well, no doubt resenting a human's interference in their commerce. Droë held out a hand. When Cresten did nothing, she bared her teeth.

He produced a sextant from within his robe and handed it to her.

"Flynse," she said. She met the Arrokad's glare. "I hope not to see you again, Qiyed."

"I make no promises in that regard." Qiyed gripped Cresten's arm. "Come, human. If you have never voyaged with an Arrokad, you are in for a memorable journey."

As Qiyed led Cresten to the ship's rail, the human glanced back at Tobias. "This only postpones the inevitable, Walker. I will find you again."

Tobias answered with a fearsome grin. "I'll be waiting… Cresten."

Qiyed leapt from the ship, pulling Cresten with him. The last Droë saw of them on the dark sea, they were already nearing the mouth of the bay.

CHAPTER 35

18th Day of Kheraya's Settling, Year 634

Tobias stared after the demon and Orzili until he lost them amid the swells.

"What about the rest of them?" Captain Larr asked, indicating Orzili's men with a twitch of her pistol.

He turned and took in the state of ship. In addition to the dead Shonla and Belvora, three of Orzili's men lay dead. Two more were hurt. He wasn't sure how many had died or been injured on the other ship. Seven remained on their feet. The *Sea Dove* had lost six sailors, including Gwinda. As many more bled from gashes or bullet wounds, including Mara.

A sheen of sweat covered her face and dampened her shirt. Blood soaked the leg of her breeches. Sofya cried below. He couldn't help either of them. Not yet.

Droë crossed to where he stood and handed him Orzili's sextant. She stared at him as she did this, strangely diffident.

"We should take their weapons," Tobias said to the captain. "And the tri-sextants."

"And then?"

"I'm not prepared to execute them."

"I am," Larr said without hesitation. "They killed my sailors. Law of the sea. Their blood is mine."

Tobias hiked a shoulder. "Then do what you must. I won't stop you." He faced Droë again. "Will you?"

She shook her head. "Their lives mean nothing to me."

Several of the assassins crouched, prepared to renew their battle.

"Do not," Droë warned. "Losing your years to me will be worse by far than whatever death these humans have in mind for you."

Judging from the captain's expression, Tobias wasn't so sure. But the *Sea Dove*'s surviving sailors outnumbered the assassins by more than two to one. In moments Orzili's men had been disarmed.

"What about the life of our child?" Tobias asked.

"I have already agreed to spare it."

"A child's years? To a Tirribin—"

"I am more than Tirribin now. Don't push me in this. Please."

He tipped his head.

Her eyes met his again, though not for long. A memory flickered in his thoughts, as distant as silent lightning. A kiss they shared in the courtyard of Windhome Palace, her mocking laughter not quite masking her desire to understand human attraction.

"You haven't answered my question," he said. "What happened to you? How did you come to be… as you are now? Grown and beautiful."

Her gaze found his. "You think me beautiful?"

"You've always been beautiful, Droë. You were as a girl, and you are now. But I've never heard of a Tirribin growing to womanhood."

She looked away, even as a faint smile curved her lips. "No, I don't imagine. I'm the only one."

"How did you do it? And why?"

"You shouldn't push me in this, either. It is done. That's all that matters." She walked away and rested her hands on the port rail. "I think I should leave you."

He followed her a few paces, but halted well short of where she stood. "You helped us tonight. I'm grateful to you. All of us are."

She nodded, keeping her back to him.

"Will we see you again?"

She peered back. "Maybe. I hope so."

"Can we take you to shore?"

"No, I'll swim."

"I didn't know Tirr... I didn't know you swam."

"I've been at sea for some time now. I'm growing to like the water." She smiled. "Goodbye, Tobias." She shifted her gaze to Mara. "Be well."

"Thank you, Droë," Mara said.

The demon vaulted over the rail and carved into the water.

Tobias strode to the ship's side in time to see her surface some distance away. She looked back, pale eyes alight with the silver moon and the dancing gold of torches. He raised a hand. She didn't, but began to swim toward the city, her strokes strong and sure.

He clung to the Arrokad as he would to a spar of wood amid a ship's wreckage. This night could not have gone worse, yet it was far from over. The demon raced across harbor and sea and strait at a speed Orzili could scarcely comprehend. Wind whipped at his face and soaked his clothes, stinging his skin, chilling him.

"What's your name?" he asked.

No answer. Droë had told the Arrokad not to speak with him. It seemed the demon would honor her request.

"I can offer you gold, gems – anything you want. Just don't take me so far."

Silence, save for the keening gale.

He thought on all he had seen this night, in particular all that had passed between Droë and this Arrokad. Something in their interaction had shifted in the time they were on the ship. He'd seen it happen. When they boarded, the Arrokad controlled her. By the time he and the Arrokad departed, she had thrown off his authority, exerted her own.

If he couldn't negotiate with the demon, perhaps he could goad him. This carried risks, but he wasn't sure the demon could do worse to him than Pemin would upon learning of another failure.

"It must be difficult," he chanced, "to lose your hold on such a stunning creature. Humiliating, even."

He didn't know how it happened. One moment he held tight to the Arrokad. The next he soared through the night at that same astonishing speed, but unmoored, spinning, beyond control. He crashed into the surf. Who knew water could hurt so much?

Dazed, he floated for an instant, then started to sink. He tried to swim toward the moonlight, but he could barely see and his arms and legs wouldn't do what he asked of them. Fear kicked in. He thrashed, fought toward the liquid light of the moon.

A hand closed around his wrist and yanked him up and out of the water.

"She wants you alive, so you will live," the Arrokad said, the growl in his words more frightening than Droë's rasp. "But you will speak no more."

He flung Orzili roughly onto his back and set off again. Orzili wrapped his arms around the Arrokad's neck, fearing their speed would peel him away, back into the sea.

After they had gone some distance, he tried again.

"I meant no offense."

"Unless you wish to drown, you will be silent."

He held his tongue for a few spirecounts.

"I knew her as a Tirribin. Quite well, actually. We spoke almost every night for two turns or more."

A hand like cold iron closed around his arm and ripped him away from the Arrokad's back. They continued apace, but Orzili crashed through swells and white caps. Water battered him. He could barely breathe without swallowing mouthfuls of brine.

At last they slowed. Orzili gasped and sputtered. If the demon released him, he would sink.

"Why do you insist on angering me, human? Do you wish to die?"

"Hardly," he said, still struggling for breath. "I'm hoping… you won't take me… all the way to Flynse."

"She made her wishes clear."

"Would that… have mattered… yesterday?"

The demon pulled him closer, until Orzili floated only a hand or two from the slitted eyes and needle teeth. "What do you mean by that?"

"Nothing. Just… I sense that not so long ago… you would have cared less… about her wishes."

The demon's lips pulled back from his teeth. Orzili was certain the creature would kill him. After a time, though, he threw Orzili onto his back again and resumed their course.

"What do you want?" the Arrokad asked over his shoulder.

"Leave me somewhere nearer to here."

"I will not. She was specific in her wishes."

"She also didn't want you to speak with me. You're doing that now."

The Arrokad didn't argue.

"The Walker then," Orzili went on. "Let me know where he goes. If you'll do that, I can–"

"No bargains. She made that clear."

Orzili ground his teeth. Droë had been clever, and had known all too well how faithfully the Arrokad would follow her instructions.

"A favor then."

"You ask a boon of me?"

Carefully. "No. A boon would be commerce, a bargain by a different name."

"You wish the Walker dead, is that right?"

"I care nothing for the Walker." A lie. Twice now, Tobias had bested him. The first time had left scars. Now he was being dragged to the most remote isle between the oceans. Of course he wanted to kill the pup. But, as in all things, Pemin's desires came first. "The child he has with him must die. The rest is unimportant."

"A shame," the Arrokad said. "As I have my own reasons for wanting the Walker to die."

Orzili wasn't sure what to say. He knew better than to probe further, but he didn't know how to continue this negotiation, or whatever it was. Still, the Arrokad had given him an opening, a chance to turn this latest failure into… something else. With Qiyed's help, and whatever resources Gillian Ainfor had drawn upon to locate Tobias in the first place, he might still do what Pemin had demanded.

"You mentioned a favor," the demon prompted. "We have leagues to go before we reach Flynse. Tell me more."

Orzili managed a smile. Perhaps this night wouldn't prove such a disaster after all.

A strange tightness gripped Droë's chest. Not sadness, not anger or envy, not the feeling she had come to know as love. Not any emotion she could name. Closer, perhaps, to all of them. A great knot she couldn't untangle.

Once back on land, she hunted and fed because her body told her to. She took no pleasure in the years she found. Or in the ease with which she overpowered her prey. When she finished, she felt no better, no less confused.

Should she have killed the woman? Should she have allowed Cresten to take the child? She was beautiful, alluring even. Perhaps she could have won Tobias's heart. Maybe she still could.

His ship remained in the harbor. She glanced at it repeatedly, reassuring herself that he hadn't yet ventured beyond her reach.

She attempted to comprehend the emotions writhing in her chest. A knot still, but worms now. Alive. Distasteful. Burrowing deeper. What did she want? Would she feel better if she went back? Killed Mara? Claimed him as her own?

Yes, probably. For a time, at least, though only if doing so would make Tobias love her. Which, of course, it wouldn't. Quite the contrary. He would mourn his lost love, curse Droë for what she had done, despise her. Despite how she looked.

Love and desire. She had been a fool to quest for them.

They were more than double-edged. They were like the deadliest of sea urchins. Lovely as they might have been, they bore a thousand barbs, each tipped with a drop of poison.

She sat on the strand, stared at the ship, understanding what she should have grasped turns ago: Tobias had never been within her reach. Tresz – solid, kind, lovable – had tried to talk her out of pursuing Tobias when first she proposed that they journey together. She should have listened. Failing that, she should have remained with him. Cold as his mists had been, she would have preferred his company to Qiyed's. She would have preferred to remain in her Tirribin form. Something in her chest shifted painfully.

That was it then, the emotion lying at the root of all others. Regret. She had erred, a poor choice that had changed her forever. Before she knew it, tears coursed down her cheeks.

She let herself cry for a long time, until at last she grew weary of grief. She stood, wiped her tears away. Belatedly, it occurred to her that she had freed herself from Qiyed. For all she had forsaken this night, she had gained something precious: freedom. And so she thought it ironic that what she wanted most of all was to skim over waves again.

By now, she thought, Cresten must be on Flynse. Not for long, she knew. But perhaps he was far enough to give the Walkers time to get away.

Another barb.

Qiyed might already be on his way back. If he wished to find her again, to avenge his humiliation, he would begin his search here. She didn't wish to face him so soon.

A name entered her thoughts: the one creature who could bear her from this place in her grown form, the one being she knew who might share her concern for the Walkers and her antipathy for Qiyed.

She stepped to the edge of the surf, and said, "Ujie."

Yadreg treated as many of the wounded sailors as he could, but Mara's wound was beyond him. Tobias and Bramm rowed to the city and returned sometime later with a healer, a young woman, barely more than a girl.

She proved more adept than Mara would have guessed. Using a honed blade and a two-headed instrument Mara had never seen before, she removed the bullet. Mara lost consciousness during the surgery, but she assumed the healer then drew upon her magick to repair the damage and close the wound.

Mara woke late in the night, when most of the others aboard

the *Sea Dove* had retreated into the hold to sleep. Not Tobias and Sofya, though. Upon seeing Mara open her eyes, Tobias released a ragged breath, his eyes welling.

"Was it that bad, then?" she asked, her voice like sand on wood. A blanket covered her. A second, folded, cushioned her head.

"No. They said you'd be fine. I had to see it for myself."

Sofya gave a little squeal and reached for her, hands opening and closing.

"It's all right," Mara said. "Put her on my belly."

He did. Sofya clapped her hands before putting a thumb in her mouth, content to sit on Mara's stomach. Mara stroked the princess's cheek with a finger. Her leg throbbed and she was certain that beneath the bandages the skin remained a mess. She wondered if she would ever walk without a limp.

"We need to leave the ship," Tobias said, breaking a lengthy silence.

She tucked her chin. A tear slipped from one eye.

"Orzili knows to search for it. And even if the captain sells this vessel and finds another, he'll know to search for her."

"I understand." More tears fell. "Where?"

"I wouldn't decide that without you."

"I have no idea." *I don't want to leave the* Dove.

"Wherever we decide to go, it won't be the last place. This is going to happen again."

And again. And again.

"Probably."

"I love you, Mara. Sofya loves you. And I want you with us. But if you'd prefer—"

"Don't you dare!" She glared at him, tears blurring her vision. "Don't you even think of saying that to me! Look at me. Look at how old I am. Look at my leg. Do you think I'm doing this on a whim?"

His eyes had gone wide. "I didn't—"

"I love you both, apparently more than you think I do!"

"No! I never—"

"You have no right to say that to me, to make such a gesture! I'm your wife, Tobias! I have no ring. We've had no ceremony. But

I am your wife, just the same! So don't you ever speak to me of 'if I would prefer!'"

She stared daggers at him. He seemed to will himself to hold her gaze. A smile crept over his face. Still he said nothing. In time, she couldn't help but smile as well. She glanced away, a small laugh escaping her.

"It's not funny," she said. Which only made her laugh more.

"I'm not the one laughing."

"You smiled. That made me laugh."

He took her hand, raised it to his lips.

"I'm sorry," he whispered.

Her mirth subsided. "Thank you."

"I do love you. And I know how much you love both of us. I was... Seeing you get shot. It terrified me."

"I know the feeling," she said, the words pointed. "But I made my choice a long time ago, and I haven't questioned it since. You need to trust that, and trust me."

"Then I will," he said. "Forevermore. Until the Two grant us rest."

The words brought a smile, and fresh tears.

"Forevermore," she echoed. "Until the Two grant us rest."

He leaned forward and kissed her lightly on the lips. Blood rushed to her cheeks. Sofya clapped again, making them both laugh.

"All right, then," Mara said, forcing a bright tone. "Where should we go?"

Tobias laced his fingers through hers. "We'll decide in the morning. You should sleep. We all should. I can carry you down to the hold."

She shook her head. "Bring up our blankets. I'd like to sleep here."

He grinned and left her, only to return moments later with blankets and pillows. He arranged a family bed, and lay down next to her with Sofya between them. The princess put her thumb in her mouth and began to hum tunelessly. Tobias and Mara held hands, darkness all around them, and a million stars above

GLOSSARY OF TERMS

Aperture – A Bound device used by Crossers. An aperture is a golden circlet that expands and contracts according to the needs of the Crosser. When placed against a wooden or stone surface, it creates a portal that allows the Crosser to move through that surface.

Arrokad – Creatures of the sea, they are considered by humans to be demon-kind. They take human form and possess magicks that remain poorly understood. Capricious, sexual, powerful, dangerous, they can be reasoned with and bargained with, though their tolerance for human interaction is limited.

Bell – A measure of time equal to fifty spirecounts. There are twenty bells in a day.

Belvora – Also known as magick demons, they are winged predators, tall, muscular, lethal, but slow-witted. They are found mostly in northern waters, near the Labyrinth and the Sisters, the isles from which Travelers and Seers hail.

Between, The – The space traversed by Walkers as they navigate from one time to another. A place of intense sensory stimulation, totally lacking in breathable air.

Binder – A crafter, usually employed in noble courts, who shapes and imbues with power the gold devices (apertures, chronofors, and sextants) used by Travelers.

Chronofor – A Bound, golden device used by Walkers. A chronofor resembles a chainwatch, but has three dials on its face, and three corresponding stems to set those dials, which represent turns, days, and bells. A fourth stem activates the device.

Crosser – A Traveler who can move through solid matter – stone or wood – with the use of an aperture. A Crosser who encounters metal or some other material created by humans during a Crossing risks injury or death.

Fivecount – A measure of time equal to the amount of time it takes to count to five.

Gap, The – The space traversed by Spanners as they navigate from one location to another. A place of significant sensory stimulation and stinging wind.

Ha'turn – A measure of time equal to fifteen days.

Kant – A small to medium-sized merchant ship made in Kantaad.

Healers – Most similar in their magick to Binders, Healers can mend wounds and ease illness, though their powers are limited and they are not proof against death.

Kheraya – The Goddess, who represents birth, war, sexuality, water, the heat of summer.

Magi – Also known as Seers, they include those who can divine the future, perceive truth or falsehood in the words of others, and remember in perfect detail everything they see or hear. For their ability to manifest, they must constantly imbibe (through drink or vapor) tincture, a highly addictive spirit.

Marauder – A large warship made in Oaqamar and used by the Oaqamaran navy.

Press, The – The traverse experienced by Crossers as they move through matter, which can include painful compression of the body, blindness, and deafness.

Quad – A square brass coin, the least valuable of Islevale currency.

Qua'turn – A measure of time equal to approximately seven days.

Round – A round, gold coin equivalent to twenty silver treys.

Seer – Also known as Magi, they include those who can divine the future, perceive truth or falsehood in the words of others, and remember in perfect detail everything they see or hear. For their ability to manifest, they must constantly imbibe (through drink or vapor) tincture, a highly addictive spirit.

Sextant – A Bound, golden device used by Spanners to cover great distances. A sextant includes an arc for plotting distance, an eyepiece for selecting a route, and a trigger for activation.

Shonla – Also known as mist demons, they only exist with clouds of vapor, though not all mists carry Shonla. They are vaguely human in form, smell of must, and bring cold. They are linked to one another and have knowledge of events occurring all through the world. They swallow sound and can be bribed with song. They disorient those at sea and even on land, feeding on screams. But they are not truly deadly.

Sipar – The God, who represents death, peace, love, land, the cold of winter.

Spanner – A Traveler who can cover great distance in a short period of time with the use of a sextant.

Spirecount – A measure of time equal to the amount of time it takes to count to one hundred. There are fifty spirecounts in a bell.

Tencount – A measure of time equal to the amount of time it takes to count to ten.

Tincture – An addictive and narcotic spirit used by Seers (Magi) to enable their talents for divination, perception, and remembrance.

Tirribin – Also known as time demons, they appear as children, beautiful, but smelling faintly of rot and decay. They are deadly, preying on humans and consuming their years. They have an understanding of time that goes far beyond that of humans, even Walkers. But they can be distracted by riddles.

Traveler – Often a native of the Sisters or Sipar's Labyrinth, trained on Trevynisle, and assigned to a noble court, s/he can be a Crosser, Spanner, or Walker. A Traveler expresses his/her talent through the use of a Bound device (aperture for a Crosser, sextant for a Spanner, chronofor for a Walker). Travelers using these traditional devices must Travel unclothed and unburdened by any objects save the devices themselves.

Trey – A triangular silver coin equivalent to ten brass quads.

Tri-Aperture – A Bound, golden device resembling an aperture, but constructed in three circlets that intersect to form a wedge. Three Crossers, standing in a triangular formation, can move themselves and any people standing in the space defined by their positions through matter, so long as one of the people within the triangle is also a Crosser bearing a traditional aperture. Crossers Traveling by tri-aperture can be clothed and can bear objects in addition to their bound devices.

Tri-Devices – Bound, golden devices developed in the 630s and used by Travelers. They enable groups of Travelers to Span or Cross together, fully clothed and bearing objects, including weapons. There are tri-apertures and tri-sextants. There are, as of yet, no tri-chronofors.

Tri-Sextant – A Bound, golden device resembling a sextant, but constructed with three arcs. Three Spanners, standing in a triangular formation, can transport themselves and any people standing in the space defined by their positions, so long as one of the people within the triangle is also a Spanner bearing a traditional sextant. Spanners Traveling by tri-sextant can be clothed and can bear objects in addition to their bound devices.

Turn – A measure of time equal to thirty days and corresponding to the cycle of the moon.

Two, The – Kheraya and Sipar, the Goddess and God, worshipped in some isles or cities in tandem, and in others individually.

Walker – A Traveler who can move through time with the use of a chronofor. For each day a Walker moves backward or forward through time, s/he ages a corresponding day.

The Year:
Each season is equal to three turns; each turn is equal to thirty days.

Spring:
(Kheraya's Emergence – Equinox, Goddess's day, first day of the year. Powerful, sensual day and night.)

Kheraya's Stirring – Storms and wind, the first hint of life's return
Kheraya's Waking – Warm, rainy, peaceful, plantings begin in the northern isles
Kheraya's Ascent – Warmer, blooming, resplendent, plantings begin in the southern isles

Summer:
(Kheraya Ascendent – Summer Solstice, a day of feasts, celebration, gift-giving)
Kheraya's Descent – Hot, dry, northern crops begin to come in
Kheraya's Fading – Hot, stormy, southern crops begin to come in
Kheraya's Settling – Hot, languid days

Autumn:
(Sipar's Emergence – Equinox God's day, the pivot of the year. Powerful, sensual day and night.)
Sipar's Stirring – Stormy, windy, harvest begins in the southern isles
Sipar's Waking – Cool, clear, harvest begins in the northern isles
Sipar's Ascent – End of harvest, leaves changing, resplendent

Winter:
(Sipar Ascendent – Winter Solstice, a day of fasting, contemplation)
Sipar's Descent – Cold, snows begin in southern isles
Sipar's Fading – Cold, storms and snow in northern isles
Sipar's Settling – Cold, quiet, shortest days

ACKNOWLEDGMENTS

As always I am indebted to a number of people for their help with this manuscript.

They include Faith Hunter, AJ Hartley, Leanna Renee Hieber; my friends in the Rivendell Writer's Group: Laura Willis, Virginia Craighill, Megan Roberts, April Alvarez, Patrick Dean, Adam Latham, and Brooks Egerton; my dear friend and wonderful agent, Lucienne Diver; and the terrific people at Angry Robot: Marc Gascoigne, Phil Jourdan, Penny Reeve, Nick Tyler, Lottie Llewelyn-Wells, Gemma Creffield, and editor Simon Spanton-Walker.

Finally, as in all things, I am most grateful to my wife, Nancy, and our daughters, Alex and Erin. As I said in the acknowledgments of the first Islevale book, when all is said and done, this is a series – a story – about family. My family lies at the heart of all I do and all that is possible in my world. I love them more than words can say.

ABOUT THE AUTHOR

D. B. Jackson is the award-winning author of more than twenty books and as many short stories, spanning historical fiction, epic fantasy, contemporary fantasy, and the occasional media tie-in. His novels have been translated into more than a dozen languages. He has a Masters degree and a PhD in US history, and briefly considered a career in academia. He wisely thought better of it. He lives with his family in the mountains of Appalachia.

Visit him at http://www.dbjackson-author.com.

By the same author...

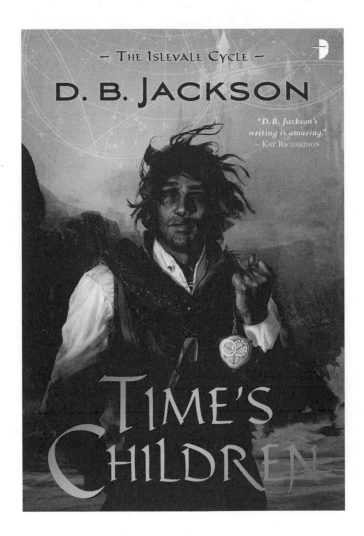

UNDER THE PENDULUM SUN BY

JEANETTE NG

PAPERBACK & EBOOK
from all good stationers and book emporia

Two Victorian missionaries travel into darkest fairyland, to deliver their uplifting message to the godless magical beings who dwell there… at the risk of losing their own mortal souls.

Winner of the Sydney J Bounds Award, the British Fantasy Award for Best Newcomer

Shortlisted for the John W Campbell Award

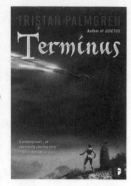
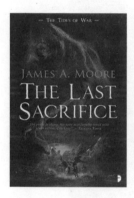
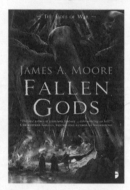
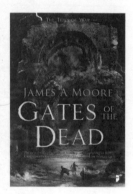

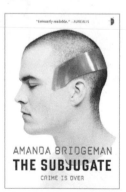